I0747651

THE GHOSTS OF NOTHING

CECILY WALTERS

COPYRIGHT

This book is a work of fiction. Names, characters, places, and incidents are the product of the author's imagination or are used fictitiously. Any resemblance to actual events, locales, or persons, living or dead, is entirely coincidental.

Copyright © 2023 by Cecily Walters

Maple seed illustrations by Carmina Kovacs (Moonflower Fairy on Facebook)

Miscellaneous illustrations licensed by Canva Pro

Cover copyright © 2023 by Cecily Walters. Cover design by Rafido Design

All rights reserved.

Scanning, uploading or distributing this book without permission is theft of the author's intellectual property. No part of this book may be reproduced in any form or by any electronic or mechanical means, including information storage and retrieval systems, nor may it be used to train artificial intelligence models, without written permission from the author, except for the use of brief quotations in a book review written by a human. If you would like permission to use material from this book for purposes other than a review, please contact gonpermissions@protonmail.com.

Thank you for supporting the author's rights.

First Edition: July 2023

Description: First edition. | Cecily Walters, 2023 | Series: The Weird and the Wicked ; 1 | Summary: Nelly Morighan, sixteen, teams up with fairies to rescue her grandmother and the town of Nothing from a terrible fate.

ISBNs: 978-1-7388524-2-0 (hardcover), 978-1-7388524-3-7 (paperback), 978-1-7388524-1-3 (ebook)

For Mom and Dad

PROLOGUE

The troubles of the Morighan family began with maple keys spinning to the ground on a summer day. The keys fell from sugar maples on the Morighan farm; big, sturdy trees that went fiery red in the fall and black and bony in the winter. On that day, at the height of summer, the trees were still a vibrant green as great gusts of wind from a coming storm knocked their seed pods from their branches, sending them fluttering to the ground like hundreds of twirling pixies.

A young woman in a pale dress walked among the maples, a basket in hand, catching the spinning keys as they fell. The woman was Mairead Morighan, though everyone in the hamlet of Nothing knew her as Madge.

Madge was a horrible name. Mairead had hated it from the moment her husband had chosen it for her as they'd boarded a boat for the Americas. It had all been part of his grand plan. No longer would they be Eóin and Máiréad Ó Muireagáin, a couple of poor Irish tenants from County Kerry. They would be John and Madge Morighan, farmers, landowners, and adventurers in a new world.

"But there's nothing here," Mairead said when John announced that they and several other families would make a life here among the maples.

John had only laughed. "That's what we'll call it, then. Nothing." And soon after, a hamlet called Nothing sprung up out of the wilderness, one felled tree at a time.

Mairead started to skip as clouds raced across the sky, enjoying the swishing sound of fluttering leaves and the creaking of branches in the breeze. She loved maple keys, the way they fell and twirled. She made a game of trying to catch them before they hit the ground. Later, when she got home, she planned to soak their seeds in water until they sprouted and then roast them as a treat for the children. She held on to these small joys.

Life in Nothing was difficult, away from her family and friends back home in Ireland, with only her children and the trees for company. Life with John was even more difficult. He was a godly man, but he had the devil in him, and it was best not to wake it.

Mairead smiled and spun around. Thistle downs were floating through the woods like balls of snow. It was like another season was trying to muscle the other one out.

She pulled her prized possession from her basket, a leather-bound diary her father had given her as a gift, and looked for a spot to sit and write. But just as she was about to settle in under a maple, she heard a woman crying.

There didn't seem to be anyone around. And yet the crying grew louder.

"Hello?" Mairead called.

The crying stopped.

A few yards away, Mairead noticed a split oak, probably the victim of a lightning strike. Its twisted parts were blackened and overgrown with mushrooms and moss. But there was something *wrong* about it: the way the bark curved into a hunched form, the way the moss dangled from it like matted hair. It looked almost alive.

And then it moved.

Mairead was so startled by this, she dropped her basket, and all the maple keys she'd been gathering spilled out on the ground.

The movement was a trick of the light, she told herself. It couldn't be what it had appeared to be, a person made of moss and bark that had turned to look at her.

She bent down to retrieve her basket.

"Will you help me?" a voice said.

The voice had come from *behind* Mairead.

She spun around.

"What?" she said involuntarily, her mind trying to catch up with what she was seeing.

A *thing* stood across from her in a patch of bluebells. Somehow this thing appeared to be a human woman, and yet could not be. Mairead knew this instinctively. It was too beautiful to be human, so beautiful Mairead thought if she looked away from it, even for an instant, she would never be happy again.

The *thing* was about Mairead's height and had black hair, glassy amber eyes, and pale skin. And it was covered in the stuff of the forest, bark and leaves and feathers and a strange, powder-like substance that shimmered whenever the sun broke through the trees.

It was crying.

Mairead's fear melted away as if by magic. "Why are you crying?" she asked the thing.

"I've lost my key," the thing said in a voice that was both hollow and delicate, like the wind through reeds. "Do you have it?" The thing pointed at Mairead's basket, and the pile of maple keys strewn about on the ground.

"These? Why, these are only maple keys," Mairead said. "They're seed pods. They can't be the sort of key you've lost, can they?"

The thing only stared. "Will you help me find my key?"

"Of course I will," Mairead said without a second thought.

It was three months later, and Mairead was running for her life through those same woods. As she ran, she wondered if things might have turned out differently for her if she had said *no* that day to the thing in the woods, if she had turned and run instead of speaking to it and allowing it to speak to her.

The leaves and maple keys that rained all around her now were a ruddy brown, dry and dead in the chilly fall weather.

She was in her nightgown. It had rained earlier and threatened to again. Everything was wet and foggy and gray. Mairead could hardly see through her own tears. Her bare feet squished into a soggy mulch of ice-cold leaves.

Voices followed her, hissing and spitting like wild geese.

"Monster!"

"Creature!"

"Thing!"

They screamed.

She was being hunted. And the men chasing after her, hurling rocks and rotten apples, were those she had once called neighbors and friends.

There was Robert Abner, whose wife Mairead had helped nurse an injured foal back to health only a month before. There was Chester Glanville, who had sat and laughed with her and her husband over dinner more than once. There was Braxton Pipes, so handsome Mairead might have fancied him if she hadn't already been married. And there was Eamon Kennedy, barely eighteen, who'd asked Mairead for advice only the week before about a girl he'd wanted to woo.

An apple hit Mairead square on the back of the head.

She fell.

As soon as she hit the ground, her hands sinking into the mud, she knew it was over.

They had her. They held her by the arms. Fingernails dug into her flesh like stinging bees. Mairead was aware of herself screaming and writhing as branches scraped at her skin. The men were forcing her through the thicket and onto the bank of the river Nought, where an old maple stretched out over the water like a contorted creature.

John, her husband, was waiting there, his face full of right-eous fury. He stood next to a wagon. On the back of the wagon was a cage covered in a dirty sheet. Mairead could see the outline of the bars under the rain-soaked linen.

Her own husband.

"Eoin!" Mairead shrieked, using his real name. "You can't do this! I'm your wife!"

"You're not my wife!" John snapped. "You're one of them." He pointed at the cage with its filthy sheet.

Robert Abner tossed a noose up over one of the maple's high branches. Underneath it was a rickety, three-legged stool.

Mairead's voice caught in her throat. Chester Glanville was binding her hands behind her back. Braxton Pipes was forcing her up onto the stool. Eamon Kennedy was putting the noose around her neck and then tightening it until she gasped. How could they? She knew these men. She had been in their homes, laughed with their wives, eaten at their tables.

"It's me, it's Mairead, I mean, Madge!" Mairead pleaded. "I swear to you, I'm not a changeling!"

John glared hatred at her. He took a step toward the wagon and pulled the sheet from the cage.

There was a ringing silence.

Mairead couldn't believe what she was seeing. There, huddled at the base of the cage, was *it*. Her. The thing in the woods. It looked younger than it had before, a girl now of perhaps fifteen. It was dressed in rags and feathers, and there were twigs and acorns and tufts of down in its hair. Its eyes were wide and innocent and flecked with gold.

It was the eyes more than anything that made Mairead think they might have a chance, the childlike purity in them, the honest fear. This girl was no monster. The men could see this, surely. It, *she*, was just a girl. A beautiful girl they'd trapped in a cage.

And yet ...

The girl's body appeared to be smoking. Thin, white tendrils rolled up from its feet and knees, the parts of it that were touching the iron cage.

Mairead's heart dropped.

How was this possible? How had they trapped the thing? It was so strong and so quick and so graceful. How had they managed to catch it, let alone lock it in that cage?

"Nothing to say for yourself?" John said.

He was holding something.

It was a book, a leather-bound book.

A cold, prickling sensation crawled over Mairead's skin. John was holding her diary. She had written everything in there; everything about her encounters with the thing in the woods, everything she had come to know about it these past months—its strengths, its weaknesses, what it hated, what it feared.

This was all her fault.

"She means you no harm," Mairead said through tears. "I swear! I swear! We'll leave. We'll never come back. Let us go and—"

"WHERE IS MY WIFE?" John shouted, facing Mairead.

"I AM YOUR WIFE!" Mairead cried.

"NO!" John said. "My wife would never betray me with … with …" He backed up, shaking his head in disbelief until he was in arm's reach of the cage.

It happened faster than any of them could comprehend. In one swift movement, the thing in the cage leaped to its feet, reached between the bars, and grabbed John from behind. It yanked him backward. His back slammed into the cage. The thing had him by the throat. The other men froze as the thing's eyes shifted between them, no longer innocent, but hard and cold as stone.

"Let her go," the thing said in strangely accented English, each word cutting like a whip crack.

There was an eerie silence. None of the men moved. The smoke billowing from the thing's body twirled and twisted like ghosts on the wind.

Robert Abner broke the silence. He moved toward Mairead, his boots crunching the leaves. He put his foot on the three-legged stool under her feet.

"Robert, what are you doing?" John asked, his voice croaking from the pressure of the thing's fingers on his larynx.

Mairead locked eyes with the thing in the cage. There was no denying what was about to happen. "I'm sorry," she said.

"It will kill me," John croaked, and repeated, "Robert, what are you doing?"

"I'm sorry, John," Robert said and then kicked away the stool.

One thing was certain, the scream that ripped from the

thing in the cage as Mairead swung was not human. It was visceral, animal-like; the screech of an owl, the cry of a hawk, the croak of a crow, the moan of a loon all together at once. It was a sound that would haunt the nightmares of everyone present for the rest of their lives.

The thing stopped screaming.

It spun John around.

It slapped him across the face.

He crumpled to the forest floor.

There was another ringing silence as the men stared at John's limp body.

"Get rid of it!" Robert Abner shouted, voice high with panic. He pointed to the cage and the thing in it. "Push it into the river!"

The men jumped to release the wagon from its horse and then they rolled the thing, wagon, cage, and all, into the black waters of the river Nought.

The wagon began to sink. Water rolled around the ankles of the thing still trapped in the cage. It stood unmoving, all except its eyes, which shifted from Abner to Kennedy to Glanville to Pipes and back again as though it was committing their faces to memory.

And Mairead Morighan saw all of this while she swung from the noose that was tied to a maple tree. Her life, minute by minute, was draining away. She could see lights on the water and in the trees, and the men, her murderers, as they felt for John's pulse and said he was dead. She heard them blame him and her for all their troubles.

"The Morighans are cursed!" Chester Glanville spat, picking up Mairead's diary and shaking it. "They brought this evil into our lives!"

In the river, as water swirled higher around the thing's waist, it scooped up a handful of the maple keys that were floating over the surface and began picking them apart one by one. After a few furious seconds, something silver flashed from between the thing's fingers.

Mairead smiled. Even as curtains of darkness swept over her eyes, even as the water swallowed up the thing, the cage, and the wagon whole, Mairead smiled. For somehow, she understood with a certainty that what had happened here today in the hamlet of Nothing would not go unpunished. One day there would be justice. One day there would be revenge. And it would be terrible.

The river bubbled and went still. Smoke rose from its surface. The last things Mairead saw were leaves and maple keys raining on the water as the world fell silent.

Two hundred years later...

CHAPTER ONE

STRANGE LITTLE GIRL

A beam of light shone in from the crack at the top of the door. Motes of dust swirled in the light and drifted down to settle on the fingers of Nelly Morighan. She held a violin in one hand and a bow in the other directly inside the thin beam. It was the only way she could see what she was doing in the otherwise dark space.

She was in a janitor's closet. As she moved, she bumped into mop and broom handles on one side and shelves of foul-smelling cleaning supplies on the other. Earlier that day, someone had shoved her in there on purpose and locked the door. But she wasn't about to kick up a fuss about it.

"We Morighans do not cry or fuss," Grandmother always said. "We bear our crosses with dignity."

Short and skinny for her sixteen years, Nelly had white-blonde hair, stormy gray eyes, and skin so pale she could be mistaken for a ghost. She stood out wherever she went, like some livid, haunted thing, and often drew stares. Though in the town of Nothing, where Nelly grew up, those stares were more about who she was than what she looked like.

Nelly hovered her bow an inch over the strings, the light illuminating her hair like spider threads and quivering over one of her pale eyes. She pretended to play, practicing her finger work, hearing the music only in her head.

She grinned, imagining what would happen if she played her violin for real, allowing the music to seep under the door and flood into the prep school's hallways. That would be one way to alert people to her predicament.

But who was she kidding? Nelly never played for an audience. Not well anyway. And even if she played poorly, as she always did when she thought people were listening, she would cause a scene. Teachers would want to know how she had come to be locked in the closet, other students would snicker and stare, and worst of all, someone might comment on her playing. Nelly could hardly imagine anything worse than that.

The school bell rang, deafeningly loud in the small closet. It was the last day of school. The last bell on the last day of school, for that matter. As the ringing stopped, the sounds of her classmates pouring into the halls, shouting and cheering, making plans for summer parties, took over.

Nelly sighed; it was time to face the music. She held up her fist to the door, about to bang on it and call out for help, but paused. This was so humiliating. Maybe she should wait a little while until there were fewer students in the corridor, fewer people to witness her shameful exit from the janitor's closet.

Nelly placed her violin in its hard case, silently cursing the girl who had locked her in here. *This is revenge,* she thought irritably as she shrugged off her school cardigan and traded it for the wrinkled hoodie she kept stuffed in her backpack.

An hour ago, Nelly had made the mistake of pausing next to this closet, which had been open wide and waiting like a bear trap. Then, as she had fished headphones out of her schoolbag, a pair of hands had shoved her from behind, forcing her in here. She had whirled around just in time to see Bianca Lim with an evil grin on her face, slamming the door shut.

Bianca Lim was Nelly's roommate. She had dark hair, an angelic face, and a less-than-angelic disposition. The pair of them lived together in an apartment Nelly's grandmother had rented a few blocks from school. Nelly knew Bianca well. They had grown up together in the town of Nothing and both hated it there, but for different reasons.

Bianca hated Nothing because it was a speck. The sort of place you couldn't find on a map unless you zoomed in. Way in. And squinted. And Bianca was a big-city girl at heart.

Nelly didn't mind the size of Nothing. It was quaint as small towns went. It had family-run shops and historical houses, topped with gables and gingerbread eaves. But there was a pervasive chill in Nothing that made you shiver no matter the time of year, a weathered dreariness that no amount of decorative trimming could hide.

It was also haunted. Famously so. Nothing consistently topped worldwide lists for "most haunted town."

And Nelly's family was the cause of it all, or so the people of Nothing agreed. The Morighan family had an unfortunate history in that town. And the townspeople had become convinced that the family was cursed and the town along with them. This was why Nelly hated the town of Nothing: because it hated her.

This had caused its fair share of problems for Nelly growing up. There was one incident in particular, an incident she didn't like to think about.

Nelly had been sitting in her fifth-grade class at Nothing Elementary. The teacher had just asked her a pointed question about her family's history, a question she hadn't wanted to answer, when the lights had gone out.

"Freak!"

"Creep!"

"Weirdo!" her classmates shouted at her later in the schoolyard.

"It's your fault," pronounced the ringleader, Orson Kennedy, a freckle-faced boy with copper hair and a cruel sneer. "All the weird stuff that happens in this town, it's because of you and your freaky family. Why don't you just leave?"

"Yeah, get out of this town!" Alexis Abner, a popular girl with an upturned nose, joined in. "We don't want you here; no one does!"

Nelly, who had been sitting on a bench at the edge of the yard, scribbling in her diary, stood up straight and faced her accusers as Grandmother had always taught her to do.

"Believe me, I'd love to," she snapped. "But I don't exactly have a choice!"

"Don't talk to us like that, you little snot!" Alexis shouted.

And then Orson stepped up close to Nelly. "You know it's true," he said. "Something isn't right about you. And you know it deep down."

This stung.

Orson slapped the diary out of Nelly's hands. It landed in a puddle. He stomped on it. He ground it into the mud.

"Orson, stop it!" Bianca Lim shouted. Bianca was the new girl at school back then. Her family had just moved into town, and for a moment Nelly had thought that Bianca, who had not been raised on Morighan family curse stories like the others, was stepping in to defend her.

No such luck.

"You got mud on my shoes, you jerk!" Bianca shouted instead.

Orson smiled wickedly and then stomped on Nelly's diary again, splashing Bianca with more mud.

Nelly lunged at him.

"FIGHT! FIGHT! FIGHT!" the crowd chanted.

Orson shoved Nelly backward and then jumped up and down on her diary like it was a trampoline, laughing all the while. And so, Nelly hit him. She slapped him right across his smug, mocking face with her open palm with everything she had.

Surprise and anger flashed across the boy's face. Nelly flinched, afraid he was about to hit her back. But the anger on his face ebbed away. He gasped with a sudden, rasping breath. The crowd went silent. Orson's eyes rolled back.

He collapsed.

Screams rang out from the other kids. They scattered, shouting for a teacher. Nelly didn't scream, nor did she run. She stepped forward and peered into Orson's pale face as he trembled and convulsed on the ground. *Had she done this to him?*

The paramedics arrived soon after and carried Orson away, his still-twitching body strapped to a stretcher. Later, the school principal said that Orson was a very sick boy and that what had happened wasn't Nelly's fault. But he suspended Nelly for three days all the same. The school had a strict anti-bullying policy and all the other kids agreed that Nelly Morighan instigated the fight.

Later that day, while the other kids were back in class, Nelly stood quietly by the school's front entrance, waiting for her grandmother to come and collect her for the start of her suspension. Her insides were twisting with the memory of Orson's eyes rolling into his head. She couldn't shake the feeling that she was somehow responsible for Orson's illness.

But it was impossible, she told herself repeatedly. She had only slapped him. A slap couldn't cause a reaction like that, could it?

Nelly didn't know how long she stood there before the sound of voices interrupted her worries. Three women in yoga pants of various colors stood next to a car in the parking lot, sipping from takeout coffee cups and chatting loudly about silly things. It wasn't long before their attention turned toward Nelly.

"Who's that little girl all by herself?" gray yoga pants asked. "Should we go over and—"

"No! Don't you know who that is?" white yoga pants hissed. "That's Nelly Morighan."

Nelly stiffened. The last thing she needed just then was to hear more rumors about the "Morighan family curse." She told herself to ignore them and stared with feigned interest at something down the road, willing Grandmother's car to appear over the horizon.

"*That's* Nelly Morighan?" gray yoga pants said. "Hmm, yes, I see it now. She is a strange little girl, isn't she?"

A crow cawed somewhere nearby.

"It's a shame about her father, though," pink yoga pants offered in a lower but still perfectly audible voice. "Merritt Morighan is one gorgeous man."

"Tell me about it," white yoga pants said in a bragging tone. "Did you know he asked me out once?"

"Really?"

"Yeah, when we were in high school."

"What did you say?"

"What could I say? I wasn't going to start dating a Morighan. Can you imagine?"

"Oh yeah, I can imagine, all right," said pink yoga pants, leaning back against the car and smiling wide. They all laughed.

Nelly frowned. She wished they wouldn't talk about her father like that with her standing right there. They must have known she could hear them.

"Did anyone ever find out who ended up with him?" the woman in gray asked. "I mean, who's that girl's mother, anyway?"

"No clue. I always figured she was from out of town."

And now they were talking about Nelly's mother. *Please, Grandmother, hurry!* Nelly thought, focusing hard on that empty road.

"Everything about the Morighans is too strange," pink pants said. "Merritt may be pretty, but I sure wouldn't want to be caught up in all that mess."

"She's probably dead," said white pants offhandedly. "The mother, the mystery woman? She's got to be. With that family's history? Mad, missing, or six feet under; happens to every Morighan eventually. I guarantee that woman is ..." White pants stomped on the ground. "And Merritt's probably the one who put her there."

Nelly's face went hot, her heart was pounding. How dare they! Right in front of her. She turned and faced the women with an enraged glare.

"My mother is not dead!" she said in a loud, clear voice.

They all fell silent. The blood drained from their faces. And at that exact moment, the woman in the white pants fainted.

There was a commotion as the other women gathered around their friend, squawking like seagulls, fussing over her as she regained herself. It was all very dramatic.

But white pants didn't seem hurt, not really. She was standing herself up again as Grandmother's black car rolled up to the curb.

Nelly climbed into the car and shut the door. The three women were staring into the passenger side window at Nelly now, their eyes full of fear, as if she, Nelly, was the reason that woman had fainted, as if she was responsible for it.

But she wasn't responsible for it. She couldn't be. She hadn't even touched the woman. But she had touched Orson. She had slapped him, and he had collapsed.

The women continued to stare as the Morighan car pulled away from the curb and a crow cawed. And Nelly wondered, not for the first time, if the townspeople were right to stare at her, if they were right to be afraid.

CHAPTER TWO

BIANCA'S REVENGE

Still locked in the janitor's closet, Nelly looked down at her hand, the one she had slapped Orson with all those years ago, and rubbed it. *Oh, pull yourself together*, she told herself.

Nelly knocked on the back of the closet door. "Hello!" she said in a loud voice. "I'm ... locked in the janitor's closet."

She would never forgive Bianca for this.

As she flicked on her cell phone, thinking she might call the school and tell the secretary where she was, its electronic light fell on a tiny mouse standing by the door. She gasped and stepped back. But it didn't run. She turned her cell phone light on it fully. Still, it didn't move.

"Uh, hi mouse," she said as it stared up at her. She imagined for a moment that it wanted to say something to her. But that was silly. Mice couldn't speak. And yet it continued to stand there, perfectly still, eyes focused on her. "I'm not supposed to notice you," she said to the mouse as if it could understand her. "Why are you letting me?" It sniffed the air but kept right on staring.

Maybe it was hungry.

Nelly searched in her backpack for a piece of leftover lunch to give it, but before she could find any, something spooked the mouse and it scurried into the shadows.

The lock on the door had moved. Nelly jumped back. The door swung open. Light flooded in, and someone yelped. It was the school janitor. He clutched his chest as if he had just seen a ghost.

"Hey! What are you doing in there?" he said.

"Sorry, gotta go!" Nelly said, swinging her backpack over her shoulder and dashing past him. "Have a good summer!"

The janitor muttered something about teenagers as Nelly bolted away down the corridor, which was by now almost empty of students. That was one humiliation dodged. She pushed open the school's double doors and raced out into the parking lot, where her bike was chained to a rack. Students were still milling around here and there, whooping and cheering that school was out for the summer. Storm clouds gathered overhead.

She scanned the parking lot for Bianca. Today was the last day Nelly would ever have to put up with Bianca Lim—or so she hoped. A month ago, Nelly had finally found the courage to ask her horrible roommate to move out. Bianca hadn't taken it well. Locking Nelly in the janitor's closet had been Bianca's revenge. Even so, Nelly wanted to get home before Bianca did, just in case her soon-to-be ex-roommate had some other bit of pettiness planned.

Nelly flipped up her hood and stuffed her too-blonde hair inside it. She had always hated the color of her hair. She thought that along with her pale skin, her hair made her look disturbingly ghostly, and in Nothing *ghostly* was not how a Morighan wanted to look. She had tried dying it brown once, but the color wouldn't stick. It was the strangest thing. She had waited a full 48 hours after having it professionally dyed to wash it, but the second her hair hit the water, the dye ran down the drain like shampoo, not a trace of color left behind. The hairdresser said she'd never seen anything like it.

Nelly strapped her violin to her back, hopped on her bike, and then peddled down a side road lined with trees. Maple seedpods spun into her hood and crunched under her tires as she rode. In Nothing, people called maple seedpods "maple keys." It was an eccentricity of the area, one of many, though most of them weren't so charming. Nelly dreaded going back there.

Three days. This was all the time she had left before her grandmother would pick her up for the long drive back to Nothing for the summer where Nelly and her family were pariahs.

For the last ten months, Nelly had been attending Mountain Wood Academy, a prestigious prep school in the city, far away from the town and its superstitions. But a little piece of Nothing had followed Nelly there. That little piece was named Bianca Lim.

"Oh my god!" Bianca had squealed, running up to Nelly on her first day at the academy. "I'm so glad somebody I know goes here! When I got into Mountain Wood, I died. I swear, I actually died. You are talking to the walking dead right now. You know Alexis, Charmaine, Pauline, that whole crowd? They're all stuck in Nothing. Losers, right? The city is so huge, though. I feel lost! Where are you staying? It's stupid they don't have dorms here. I have to stay with my aunt, and the whole place smells like cat pee. I can't. You wanna meet after school? I have to see your place. It'll be so fun! M'kay, better get to class, babes. Kisses!"

And then she was off, sauntering away in a cloud of strawberry body spray, leaving Nelly standing there utterly baffled. Back in Nothing, she and Bianca had been enemies. Bianca had been a bully. She had been Nelly's bully, one of them, anyway, and had spent most of middle school making Nelly's life a living hell. So why the sudden change of heart?

They weren't in Nothing anymore, Nelly told herself. Maybe Bianca had only bullied her out of peer pressure. Maybe Bianca didn't care that Nelly's last name was Morighan. Maybe here in the city, things would be different.

The next thing Nelly knew, Bianca was moving into the bedroom next to hers, and then they were up all night talking about the city and the school and their classes. Then they were going to the movies and thrift store shopping together, and dodging Madame Poirier, the kindly old woman who lived downstairs, whom Grandmother had hired to keep an eye on Nelly during the school year.

And then something changed. Bianca turned cold and distant and snarky again. It was like she had reverted to the bully she had been in Nothing, and Nelly couldn't do anything about it or understand why. Whatever the reason, life in their shared apartment had become increasingly unbearable for Nelly until she finally reached a breaking point.

"She'll be in the country all summer, thank gawd," Nelly heard Bianca say on the phone in her bedroom one afternoon.

Nelly had been in her own room at the time, but Bianca's obnoxious voice had been loud enough that Nelly could hear her clearly through the wall that separated their rooms.

"I'll finally have the place to myself," Bianca went on, referring to the apartment Nelly's grandmother paid for. "I let her live with me 'cause I felt sorry for her 'cause she has no friends, but trust me, I've learned my lesson." Bianca paused, then burst out laughing. "I know, right? And she's always writing in these stupid diaries. I wish I could get my hands on them. I bet everything about her and her freaky family is in those things. I wonder if I could sell them, like to one of those obsessives back home. Seriously though, how much do you think they'd pay for the diaries of Nelly Morighan?"

Nelly, who had been writing in one of those diaries when she overheard this, closed the paperback notebook and put it in her desk drawer. Then she walked the four feet to Bianca's room, anger smoldering a slow fire inside her. As she walked, the lights in the apartment flickered on and off. A storm was coming.

Bianca, who had been staring at her powder-pink phone, a confused look on her angelic face, nearly fell off her bed when she noticed Nelly in her doorway.

"Oh, it's you," Bianca said, her hand over her heart. "You almost gave me a stroke. I didn't know you were home."

"I am," Nelly said, and with a chilly calm, she informed her treacherous roommate that she had until the last day of the month to move out.

Today was the last day of the month. Nelly stood up on her pedals and pushed herself uphill toward her duplex at the end of the next block. A crow flew past her and landed on a tree up ahead. There was music in her head. When she got older, Nelly wanted to be a conductor and would often imagine herself at the head of an orchestra, drawing soaring melodies from choirs and musicians with a wave of her magic conductor's baton.

She played several musical instruments already. The violin was the one she played most often, but she could also play the tin whistle, which was the first instrument she had ever learned, as well as the piano. As Nelly rode forward, branches creaked, leaves rustled, and the crow cawed. She imagined they were instruments playing along to the music in her head, as if she were part of a great, wild orchestra.

Something wet dripped onto Nelly's cheek. It was starting to rain. She sped up her pedaling, but she wasn't fast enough.

The clouds burst and the rain came pouring down before she could make it to her apartment.

"Oh, this is just perfect," she complained out loud as she rounded the corner onto her street, bringing up a spray of water. Another crow (or maybe the same one) landed on the rooftop of her duplex and released a booming *CAW! CAW! CAW!*

For a moment, she had the feeling that the crow was trying to warn her of something. But that was silly. She rolled her eyes at her own fanciful imagination and parked her bike. Then she leaped up the steps and shouldered open the door to her duplex.

Drenched, hair drizzling down her back, Nelly took the stairs two at a time up to her top floor apartment. Inside, all was silent. There were no signs at all that Bianca was moving out today or ever. She hoped this didn't mean Bianca was going to force a confrontation.

A framed photograph of Bianca's was still sitting on the hall table, gathering dust. The photo showed Bianca, pretty and dark-haired, her parents, and her little brother at the county fair in Nothing holding candy floss, making silly faces. A happy family.

Nelly set the frame face down.

"Nelly," a voice said.

Nelly's heart missed a beat. The voice sounded like her grandmother's. But Grandmother wasn't supposed to arrive for another three days.

Nelly walked into the living room, leaving a trail of rainwater in her wake. Her stomach fluttered as her eyes fell on her grandmother, who stood stiff as a blackthorn stick, next to the fireplace, her thin lips pursed, her small eyes glaring.

To say that Nelly's grandmother was intimidating was an understatement. Moira Millicent Glanville Morighan had the presence of a disapproving school principal and could make a grown man cower with a single withering stare. An eccentric woman, she always dressed like she was on her way to a Victorian funeral. She wore black fascinators and black feathers and stringy necklaces with little bells dangling from them that all together gave her the look of a strange, jangling bird. In Nothing, she had a reputation as the Morighan you did not want to mess with. This reputation was well earned.

"Grandmother?" Nelly said cautiously. "I wasn't expecting you until—"

"Have a seat," Grandmother said.

Nelly sat, her wet clothing sticking uncomfortably to her skin.

A fire crackled in the fireplace behind the old woman, which was odd because it was June, and the air conditioning was on. Grandmother's small eyes were locked on Nelly. They were cold and hard as hailstones.

"What's going on?" Nelly asked, trying to figure out what she could have done to upset Grandmother enough to bring her into the city three days ahead of schedule.

"Some disturbing information has come to my attention," Grandmother said, her voice thin and quavery. She held something clasped behind her back, but Nelly couldn't see what it was. "Now, I am not one to invade another's privacy, but ..."

Grandmother pulled the thing she was holding from behind her back and dropped it, *them*, onto the coffee table.

Nelly felt all the blood drain from her face.

Ever since she could write, Nelly had kept a diary. Every year, Grandmother bought her a stack of thin paperback notebooks for her music classes. Every year, Nelly kept one aside to use for a diary. For years these diaries had been her only refuge from the superstitious people of Nothing, from their accusing stares and whispering voices. They were like a junk drawer or a locked cabinet where she stowed all her worries—about the town, about her family, about herself. And now there they were on the coffee table in front of her, flimsy and vulnerable, in a pile held together with an elastic band.

"–Y-You read my diaries?" Nelly said in disbelief.

Grandmother sniffed. "I did not want to read your diaries, but in light of—"

"In light of what?" Nelly said, rising to her feet.

"Do not raise your voice to me, young lady!" Grandmother shouted, her eyes flashing.

Nelly sat back down as every word, every dark thought, every confession she had written in those diaries rushed at her in a hailstorm of broken images.

And then it hit her ... Mother's visits ... Grandmother knew.

CHAPTER THREE

THE VISITS

Nelly's mother had long been the subject of speculation in the town of Nothing. She was a Morighan by marriage, not by birth. She and Nelly's father, Merritt Morighan, had married in secret, denying the gawkers their fun.

Her name was Louise. That was the rumor, anyway. No one in town knew this for certain. No one in town knew the woman. Few had even laid eyes on her. But those who had claimed there was a striking, unearthly beauty about her as if she wasn't from this world.

She disappeared when Nelly was just six with no explanation, which did nothing to slow the town's churning Morighan rumor mill. But what no one knew was that the mysterious Louise Morighan had been periodically slipping back into Nothing since her "disappearance" to visit her only child.

There was one night in particular, when Nelly was eleven. Mother appeared at the window under the moonlight. Nelly wasn't at all happy to see her. She had long ago grown resentful of her mother's infrequent presence in her life and of all the secrets she kept.

"What are you doing here?" Nelly asked.

Mother stared down at Nelly from between the billowing window curtains. She wore a lacy, old-fashioned dress with a complicated collar and what looked like dead flowers stitched into the seams. A tiny acorn made of amber glass dangled from a spiderweb-thin thread around her neck.

"I've come to check on you," she said in a voice like hollow wind. "To see if you've obeyed my rules."

Nelly frowned. The rules again. Every time Mother visited, she wanted to know if Nelly had followed her rules. They were simple enough.

Rule 1: Strike no one in anger.

Rule 2: Speak to no one but Mother in the secret language.

Rule 3: Tell no one of Mother's visits.

Rule three was easy to follow. Nelly had no desire to tell anyone in Nothing about her mother's spooky late-night visits.

Rule two Nelly couldn't break if she wanted to. The "secret language," as Mother called it, was a language that, as far as Nelly was aware, only she and her mother spoke. Nelly had once typed a few secret-language words into a search engine, but as far as the internet was concerned, she had typed a bunch of nonsense. Apparently, the secret language didn't exist for anyone else in the world, though Nelly found it as intuitive as English to speak and often missed speaking it when her mother wasn't around.

As for rule one, Nelly had broken it. In fact, she'd broken it for the first time that very same day when she slapped Orson Kennedy.

Mother was standing over Nelly now like a reproachful ghost. The guilt of what Nelly had done gnawed at her until she finally blurted out what happened in a spill of words and tears.

Mother's eyes flashed. She was holding a cup of tea. It seemed to have appeared out of nowhere, and yet Nelly wasn't at all surprised to see it.

Every time Mother visited, she had a cup of the same sort of tea with her. Nelly hated the stuff. It tasted bitter and made her feel heavy and tired. But it seemed important to Mother that she drink it, so whenever Mother asked her to, she did.

But not this time.

This time Nelly wanted comfort. She wanted her mother to tell her that what had happened to Orson wasn't her fault. She wanted a reassuring voice and a gentle hand, not a cup of bitter, lukewarm tea. She shoved the cup away just as Mother released it. The teacup fell. Nelly held her breath as it tumbled and then clattered on the boarded floor. There was a silent moment like an inhale. The bed in the next room let out a loud creak. Grandmother didn't know about Mother's visits and there would be hell to pay if she ever found out.

Mother grabbed Nelly by the arm. The shadows made her eye sockets look empty, like two black holes. She yanked Nelly off the bed and dragged her out into the narrow hallway, where the eyes of dead Morighans stared from dusty picture frames. No sound was coming from Grandmother's room now as Mother pulled Nelly down the steep farmhouse staircase. And then they were through the kitchen and out the backdoor. It all happened quickly.

"Mother, you're hurting—"

"Hush!" Mother snapped and yanked Nelly over the tangled grass of the lawn. The night was warm but windy. Clouds rushed across the moon and sent shadows shifting over the dank fields. As Mother pulled her across the farm lane, which cut across the fields like a pale scar, Nelly felt her blood go cold. There was only one place they could be going on this side of the lane.

There were two farmhouses on the Morighan family farm. Nelly grew up in the newer one, which was only thirty years old. Grandmother's third and most recent husband, Gilbert Glanville, had paid for its construction. He was extremely wealthy and indulged Grandmother in anything she wanted. The townspeople agreed that Nelly's grandmother must have cast some kind of weird spell on Gilbert Glanville. Why else would such an upstanding and respectable man marry a Morighan?

The other house, known locally as the Morighan House, was over two hundred years old. It stood abandoned and derelict on the property. This house was rumored to be haunted. Almost every Morighan who had ever died had died in that house. The townspeople said the place was cursed and so were the spirits of the dead Morighans who haunted it and the town. To enter that house was to invite evil into one's life.

This was where Mother was dragging Nelly, toward that infamous house. And though Nelly usually dismissed the townspeople's fears, she trembled as she looked up at the old place. It towered overhead, tall as the sky and black as soot, its windows boarded like crooked teeth.

Waves of decay wafted from the house. The stench became intense as they approached. Mother yanked Nelly up the low porch steps, which cracked underfoot. The backdoor dangled on its hinges and rattled in the wind like a dancing skeleton.

This was the closest Nelly had ever come to the Morighan House. She found herself agreeing with every crazy rumor she had ever heard about the place. Haunted? Yes. A mind of its own? Probably. Gobbles up little children who come too close? Most definitely.

She jerked away from her mother, who released her in that

same instant. Nelly reeled backward into the porch railing. *CRACK*. The railing splintered and Nelly fell off the porch onto the brittle stalks of a dead raspberry bush.

Mother glared down at Nelly with eyes terrible and alive inside her livid, moonlit face. She opened the back door of the Morighan house and disappeared inside.

Nelly didn't move. Caught up in the deep tangle of the raspberry patch, she shook like an injured deer. She couldn't fathom why her mother would bring her here. She couldn't fathom much of anything. Her mind wasn't working properly.

After several minutes, she managed to stand up on legs that felt like jelly. A cloud crossed the moon and there was only the dark; the smell of rot and her own shallow breaths. And then ...

Footsteps.

Mother emerged from the darkness. She walked to the edge of the porch and held out her hand. Nelly did not take it. Behind Mother, the door to the house had been left wide open.

Nelly peered into the total darkness of the house.

"Why are we here?"

No answer.

Nelly dragged her eyes from the house. "I ... I don't understand. All I want is to understand."

Mother continued to hold out her hand. The acorn-shaped necklace she wore made of what looked like amber glass bobbed from her collar. For a moment, a scene seemed to play out inside the acorn: hundreds of lights in a dark wood, and eyes that flashed from under hoods.

Nelly reached up and took her mother's hand. She was up on the porch again a second later but now there was something foreign in her hand.

She opened her palm and found a miniature glass bottle full of a thick, sticky-looking liquid, like blueberry syrup.

Nelly blinked. "–W-What is this?"

"Drink," Mother said.

Nelly was more confused than she had ever been. She pulled the cork from the bottle and sniffed the contents.

It did not smell like blueberry syrup. It smelled pungent, narcotic as if an entire stalk of some strong and bitter herb had been crushed into the tiny bottle.

"It won't taste good," Mother said, "but that can't be helped. You've spilled the last of my tea."

Nelly felt like she had been struck. She looked from her mother to the bottle and back again.

"You've been putting this stuff in my tea?"

"You must drink it," Mother said.

Nelly shook her head. "What is it?"

Mother stepped forward, raising to her full height. "Drink!"

Nelly's mind was reeling. She thought about smashing the bottle, tossing it at the Morighan House, and watching it shatter against the wall.

"You will never see me again if you dare," Mother said as if reading Nelly's mind.

Tears spilled from Nelly's eyes. Her heart felt as if it had shrunk in size. The whole world seemed to shrink. "What is it?" she asked again in a small voice.

"Drink."

There was a rushing sound in Nelly's ears.

Fine, she thought, *fine. I'll drink it if that's what she wants.*

"Drink!" Mother shrieked, her face distorting like a banshee.

Fine! Nelly screamed the word inside her head and in that same instant, Mother stumbled backward into the wall of the Morighan House as if she had been pushed.

Without stopping to wonder why Nelly held her breath and swallowed the bitter liquid. When she had finished it all, she threw the empty bottle at the porch floor where it shattered.

"Fine," she said out loud and leaped off the porch.

Nelly started back toward the farmhouse at a furious pace, but only made it part of the way there before her knees gave out. Everything went dark.

The next morning, Nelly woke up to find herself tucked into her own bed, a bitter taste on her lips.

Mother was gone.

Now, five years later, Nelly stared at her diaries lying limp on the coffee table. She had written about that last visit from her mother in one of those diaries, as well as many others. Nelly's body tingled. There was a ringing in her head. It was like she was having an out-of-body experience.

She knew vaguely that Grandmother was speaking.

"I am very disturbed by what I have read here," the old woman said, her voice strangely muffled. "The secrets you've been keeping from me. You let her in. After everything she's done. You let her in."

Nelly was back in her body now. "She ... she's my mother," she heard herself say, her face and ears burning.

"She *was* your mother. Women who abandon their children and then disappear off the face of the earth forfeit the right to be called *Mother*."

"You don't understand—"

"Don't you dare defend her to me!" Grandmother snapped, turning a fierce stare on Nelly. "Now listen very carefully. If she comes to you again, you will inform me immediately. You will scream, cry out the instant you see her. And you will never again accept any food or drink she offers you. Do you understand?"

After a long pause, Nelly nodded.

"What's that?"

"Yes, Grandmother," Nelly said, forcing back tears.

Grandmother scooped up the diaries in her bony hand. "Good. Then I will deal with her. In the meantime, Nelly, you must not write such things down. You know what they think of us. Imagine what they would say if they got their hands on these."

Grandmother was talking about the people of Nothing. But how would they ever get their hands on Nelly's diaries? Then Nelly looked from the diaries to the fire crackling in the fireplace and suddenly understood what Grandmother meant to do.

"You are very fortunate that the person who did come across these diaries, lying around for anyone to find, had no malicious intent. That that person was a friend." Grandmother said.

"A friend?" Nelly repeated, a dull thudding in her ears.

"Yes," Grandmother said. "Your roommate, Bianca."

It was like someone had hit her from behind. Nelly turned toward Bianca's bedroom door, still shut tight.

"She tells me you have been acting so erratically that she had no choice but to intervene," Grandmother went on. "That you asked her to leave without so much as an explanation?"

"That's not ... she knows very well why I—"

"No, that's enough!" Grandmother snapped. "I pay for this apartment, and I have the final say on who does and does not live here. Bianca was concerned enough about you to reach out to me for help. That's a good friend in my books."

Grandmother took a step toward the fireplace.

"Grandmother, you can't—"

Grandmother held up a hand for silence. Then she did it. She tossed Nelly's diaries onto the fire.

Bianca's door cracked open.

"Oh, Bianca dear, there you are," Grandmother said, as the pages of Nelly's diaries curled and smoked and crumbled apart in the flames. Nelly was only vaguely aware now of Grandmother and Bianca chattering back and forth. Grandmother's voice was cordial, Bianca's sickly sweet, while Nelly's diaries went up in flames.

"Nelly," Grandmother said. "Nelly, are you listening to me?"

Nelly snapped out of her horrified reverie and looked Grandmother in her stone-like eyes.

"We will be leaving for the country in an hour," the old woman said, "and I expect you to join us. You had better pack your things and clean yourself up at once. Look at you, you're drenched. While you do that, I'll have a word with Madame Poirier. It's as if you've had no supervision at all this year. A sixteen-year-old girl!"

Nelly wanted to defend Madame Poirier, who had been nothing but kind to her, but she was too stunned by what had just happened to speak.

With a sweep of her feathery shawl, Grandmother left the apartment, slamming the door smartly behind her.

In disbelief, Nelly faced Bianca, who stood in her own bedroom doorway, a smirk on her sparkly pink lips.

"You know your eyes get all weird and yellowish when you're angry?" Bianca said. "It's really not attractive." And with a flip of her dark hair, she disappeared into her room.

Alone now, shaking all over, Nelly walked slowly into her room and fell backward onto her bed.

Grandmother had read her diaries.

Bianca had read her diaries.

She had been laid bare.

She glared at the wall that separated her room from Bianca's, the word *revenge* rising unbidden from somewhere deep inside.

The apartment's lights flickered.

CHAPTER FOUR

THE PSYCH WARD

A storm rolled toward the town of Nothing. Grandmother's black car kept pace with it. It was like the Morighans were bringing the storm with them. At least, this was what the people of Nothing were likely to believe.

Nelly stared out the car window, sullen and silent, as rain drizzled across the glass and the town sign came into view.

WELCOME TO NOTHING

POPULATION 7200

WORLD'S MOST HAUNTED TOWN

She crossed her arms. The storm outside was nothing compared to the one churning inside her. The drive from the city had been excruciating.

"I'll meet you both downstairs," Grandmother had said after she'd thrown Nelly's diaries into the fire. It hadn't registered with Nelly at the time, but "both" had meant both her and Bianca. Apparently, between stealing Nelly's diaries and turning Grandmother into her confidant, Bianca had found the time to weasel herself a ride back to the country.

All cutesy and chipper, Bianca had settled herself in the

front passenger seat of Nelly's grandmother's car and then chattered the whole way about how much she loved school and volunteering at homeless shelters (lies!), and how she planned to be a famous criminal lawyer one day and stand up for the falsely accused. Oh, the irony. Meanwhile, Nelly sat scowling in the backseat, avoiding all eye contact and conversation.

By the time Grandmother pulled the car into the Lim's long driveway, Nelly was feeling murderous. She opted to stay in the car as Bianca unloaded her things and Grandmother ambled up to the house under a black umbrella to have a word with Mr. and Mrs. Lim.

Bianca's parents were a gorgeous young couple. Her father was Korean, her mother Scottish. They both looked like they could be models for some kind of hippie publication, all beads, bandanas, and flowing clothing. As far as Nelly knew, they kept bees and sold honey and other bee products on the internet, though they didn't appear to be doing well. The house was run down. The rain spilled from a broken gutter onto the hood of a rust-eaten pickup truck in the driveway.

Grandmother walked briskly back to the car. She hadn't spent much time in the Lim's house and Nelly wondered what she could possibly have had to say to them.

"Such a nice family," Grandmother said, sliding her bony frame into the driver's seat. "You are very lucky to have Bianca for a friend."

Her stone-like eyes came into frame in the rearview mirror.

"Now, Nelly, I know you are upset with me, but let's not allow today's events to spoil the entire summer. Buck up. I'll not have you pouty and belligerent like this in front of your father. And move to the front seat, please. This is not a taxicab."

Nelly scowled. Lucky to have Bianca for a friend? There was

so much wrong with that statement she didn't know where to start. She didn't start. She wasn't speaking to Grandmother. She got out of the car, moved to the front seat, and slammed the door.

Nought County General Hospital was a Queen Anne style building with crawling ivy and dingy windows divided by muntin bars. It had once been a psychiatric hospital. And being in Nothing, the entire building, but especially the remaining psych ward, was rumored to be haunted.

The staff at Nought General tried to discourage the ghost stories. They said the stories made the patients agitated and difficult to handle. And so, the staff was never happy to see the Morighans, whose visits sparked talk of curses and other spooky things, and they made sure the Morighans knew it.

When Nelly and Grandmother arrived at the hospital that evening, the murmuring and long stares started. A crotchety nurse ushered them out of public view and then down the partially lit corridors of the psych ward.

"It's been a day," the nurse complained, huffing and puffing her round body forward. "Something's got the patients all riled up." Her eyes said that this was the worst possible day for a Morighan visit.

"What does this have to do with my son?" Grandmother asked, pulling a handkerchief out of her purse and dabbing raindrops from her shawl.

"Merritt Morighan?" the nurse said. "Well, nothing. Nothing riles him. Not a thing. He never changes, that one."

She pushed open a creaky door and led them into a small, sparse room.

Nelly's breath caught in her throat as her eyes fell on her father, sitting in a chair by the window, as always. He wore pale blue slippers, pale blue pajamas, and a pale blue robe. His curly, chestnut hair had grown bushy, as had his beard. There was a table in front of him, on which sat scattered pieces of paper and several half-sized pencils.

He did not look at them. He did not acknowledge his visitors. He stared forward without expression, as Nelly and Grandmother walked over and stood by his side.

Nelly gazed at her father, hoping for some glimmer that there was a real person in there, somewhere. He'd been like this for years now. Nelly had been just six when he'd fallen sick and gone away to the hospital, where he would eventually become a permanent resident. Nelly's mother had gone missing around the same time. Grandmother believed the two events were connected, and Nelly wondered sometimes if the old woman was right, though she didn't like to think such things about her mother. The idea that Mother had abandoned them because she didn't want a sick man for a husband was more than Nelly could bear.

"He's had his supper," the nurse said, her voice sounding far off. "Of course, he never says thank you. Nope, never a word of thanks, despite all we do for him around here. But that's the trouble with people these days. No manners."

"There's a crack on his lens," Grandmother said. She turned a hard stare on the nurse. "Has no one noticed this?"

The nurse trundled over. She leaned past Nelly, crooked her own glasses, and looked directly into Nelly's father's face. "You mean that there?" she asked, pointing a chubby finger at a tiny, hairline crack in the corner of his left lens.

"Obviously," Grandmother said with haughty indignation. "It's plain as day. Why wasn't I informed? And his hair and beard are both in need of a trim. This is totally unacceptable."

"Unacceptable?" the nurse said, clearly offended, and she and Grandmother started to argue. They snapped back and forth, both competing to see who could be more huffy and irate. Though, in Nelly's opinion, Grandmother was the clear winner. Finally, Grandmother demanded to see the doctor in charge and she and the nurse both stormed out of the room.

Alone now with her silent, staring father, Nelly pulled up a chair and put her hands on the table in front of him. "Dad," she whispered, her voice strained. "It's me. It's Nelly."

He didn't move. She said these same words to him every time she visited, hoping that one day when he heard her name, the light and life would return to his eyes. And he would say, "Nelly?" and smile.

She reached for his hand. He did not react, did not flinch. There was a sheet of blank paper under his fingers. The nurses would leave him stacks of blank paper and little pencils, hoping perhaps that he would use them to communicate something, anything. But he never did.

Nelly sat there in silence for what felt like a long time. She wanted to speak to him, to tell him about everything that had happened to her over the past year—about her new life in the city, about the friends she had made, and about Bianca and the stolen diaries. But she did not. Because he wasn't really there, and it would feel silly somehow to talk to him. His eyes were so empty.

She stood up, adjusted his robe, and tidied up the papers on the table into a neat little pile. Then she noticed something odd. Written on the piece of paper under her father's thumb was what looked like a word.

But he never wrote words. He never wrote anything.

She pulled the paper from under her father's hand. And sure enough, there was a single word printed there disjointedly in pencil. The word *Revenge*.

"Revenge," a voice said. Nelly spun around. There was a boy about her age standing in the doorway. He wore pale blue like her father and had freckles, messy, copper hair, and wild eyes.

She recognized him. "Orson?" she said, almost positive that this odd-looking boy was Orson Kennedy, the boy she had slapped across the face when they were both eleven.

Nelly never found out what had happened to Orson after that day. She only knew that he had been struck by a mysterious illness and had been pulled out of school.

But Orson's illness wasn't mysterious at all, was it? He was here in the psych ward dressed in blue, which meant he must have been mentally ill. There was something perversely reassuring about this. Maybe she hadn't been responsible for what happened to him, after all? Then she felt guilty for having the thought. She wasn't supposed to be relieved about someone else being mentally ill. What did that say about her?

Orson turned around and walked away down the hallway.

"Wait!" she called out and followed him, hoping for some explanation for the word written on her father's paper.

Orson's bare feet slapped against the hallway floor. He did not acknowledge her as he turned and disappeared down an adjacent hallway. She followed, rounding the corner after him.

This hallway was deserted. There was no sign of Orson in either direction.

Then a yellow bouncy ball, the size of a golf ball, flew out of one of the rooms. It bounced around the walls and floor until Nelly caught it. The door to the room ahead remained open. No one came after the ball. Nelly walked forward slowly and stepped into the room. But the instant she crossed the threshold, she stopped cold.

"What the ..." she muttered, the yellow ball slipping from her fingers. The floor of the room, every inch of it, was covered in pieces of paper. The bed, the chair next to it, and the desk were covered as well. Sheets of paper were swirling toward the floor as if someone had tossed them up into the air just moments before. As one of these pages swept past Nelly, she saw written on it a single word: *Revenge.*

A hand grabbed Nelly by the wrist.

It was Orson.

"They took me away," he said, his eyes desperate and wild. "It's your fault. You let them in."

Before Nelly could react, a middle-aged woman hurled into the room. "What are you doing? Let go of my son!" she cried and wrenched Orson away from Nelly.

"I didn't mean to ..." Nelly started.

The woman's eyes widened with recognition. "You're Nelly Morighan!" she said under her breath. "Get out. GET OUT!"

Nelly took a surprised step back as Orson's mother shouted for security. Not knowing what else to do, Nelly turned, ran out of the room and down the hallway. She banked around a corner and ran right into Grandmother.

"Oh, Nelly, there you are," Grandmother said. "You'll be happy to know that your father will have his haircut and—what on earth is all that racket?"

Nelly had no chance to explain. Orson's mother was marching over with a security guard and the crotchety nurse from earlier. Nelly and Grandmother were both asked to leave. On top of that, the nurse banned Nelly from the psych ward for two months for "causing a disturbance."

Grandmother objected to this vociferously. Nelly was only in Nothing for the summer, after all, and had to be able to see her father before she started her next year away at school. But the crotchety nurse wouldn't hear it. She looked quite pleased to have an excuse to keep the Morighans away. Almost as an aside, the nurse banned Nelly from ever going near Orson

Kennedy again, as if she, Nelly, was some kind of stalker or harasser.

It was completely unfair.

Back at home in her bedroom on the farm, Nelly sat on the edge of her bed and stared at the word *Revenge* written in jagged pencil on the paper she still had clutched in her hand.

It had to have been Orson. He wrote this word on her father's piece of paper, just as he had written the same word on the pieces of paper he'd collected in his room.

It probably didn't mean anything, she told herself. It was just some random expression of madness. And yet, she didn't quite believe it.

"You let them in," Orson said, and at that moment Nelly hadn't felt frightened or confused. She had felt guilty.

The feeling lingered still.

She got up and stuck the piece of paper to the cheval glass mirror next to her nightstand.

There was more to this than madness, and she was going to find out what.

CHAPTER FIVE

THE EPISODE

Nelly crossed to the window and looked out. The sun had almost set, and the farm's shaggy, unkempt fields were shrinking away into shadows. Soon there would be nothing to see but the deep darkness of the country at night. This never happened in the city. There were always lights, no matter what time it was. Nelly found the city lights comforting. She felt at home there even though she had been raised in the country. She missed that light already.

Across the overgrown field, in a sea of long grasses and weeds, stood the Morighan House, its windows black and empty as the eye sockets of a skull. Thoughts of that night five years ago when her mother dragged her there intruded like unwanted houseguests.

She shivered. That house gave her the creeps, and not just because of what had happened there with her mother. There were more rumors and superstitions about that house in the town of Nothing than there were about the Morighans themselves. And that was saying something.

While the people of Nothing believed the whole town was

haunted, the Morighan farm, and especially that house, were supposed to be the worst. The townspeople would tap wood or bless themselves whenever the house was mentioned and take long detours to avoid driving past it, believing it was bad luck merely to lay eyes on it. They said that birds wouldn't sing near the house and horses refused to walk past it. When darkness fell, the ghosts of dead Morighans oozed out of the walls and gathered for ghastly tea parties, where they would plan their nightly haunts. Then, when the clock struck midnight, the dead Morighans would torment the innocent townspeople as they lay in their beds.

Grandmother said the superstitions were nonsense. She was right, of course. In all the years Nelly had lived on the farm, which had been every year except this last one, she had never seen so much as an unexplained shadow there. Not only did birds sing on the Morighan farm, a whole roost of crows was fond of congregating on the tree right outside her bedroom window and making an awful racket. And while it was true that horses wouldn't pass the farm, this was only because their superstitious owners wouldn't let them.

And yet Grandmother never went near that house either and she refused to have it torn down. When she looked at it sometimes, gazing absently out the window, Nelly could swear there was fear in the old woman's eyes.

The bedroom door creaked open. Nelly felt a chill rush over her skin. A few seconds later, Grandmother's farm cat Trouble sauntered into the room. The cat was soot gray and always looked dirty as if he spent all his time crawling around in cobweb-filled attics. He had appeared one evening on the porch of the farmhouse about five years earlier, waiting by the door.

"Looks like trouble," Grandmother had said. The name stuck.

Trouble jumped up onto Nelly's bed and stared at her as if waiting for her to say something. She gave him a pat behind the ears.

"I wish I could speak to you," she said, "in a way that you could understand. Because I don't know what to do."

Nelly sighed and leaned back against her pillow. She had no idea how she would even begin to investigate what had happened at the psych ward, especially now that she had been banned from even setting foot in the place. Normally, she would have sorted out her thoughts in a diary, but she had no diaries, *thank you very much, Bianca.*

Feeling restless, Nelly got up. Pacing next to her bed, she said what she would have written in her diary out loud to Trouble, who seemed in some sense to be listening.

When she stopped talking, the cat gave his paw a lick and then waltzed out of the room. As Nelly watched him go, she had the uncomfortable, exposed feeling you get when you've revealed too much, or told a secret you know you shouldn't have. But that was silly. There was no one better to tell a secret to, after all, than a cat.

The next day, Bianca's father arrived at the house to do some work for Grandmother. This was unusual. No one from town ever came to work on the Morighan farm no matter how much money Grandmother offered them, which was why the fields were always so wild and overgrown. But what Mr. Lim did for Grandmother around the house was downright bizarre.

Nelly sat at the top of the stairs next to a purring Trouble as Mr. Lim walked in with a strange assortment of tools and materials. He brought a bag filled with long nails and another filled with bells. And he had heavy iron horseshoes with him, dried yarrow stalks, and bulging cloth sacks. When Nelly opened one, she found that they were filled with red berries.

Nelly and Trouble followed Mr. Lim around the house at a discreet distance as he set to work with these mysterious items. He hammered a tight line of nails along the wooden sill of every window in the house. He hung a line of tinkly bells and upside-down bunches of yarrow above each window. He nailed the horseshoes over the doors and dropped a large sack of red berries at the entrance of every room.

Hoping for some explanation for all this, Nelly joined Grandmother in the kitchen, where the old woman was putting the kettle on the stove. She seemed cheerful. Too cheerful. A little bit crazed, actually.

"Er, Grandmother?" Nelly asked. "Why is Mr. Lim—"

"What's that? What? What?" Grandmother said, looking up from the kettle.

"I was just wondering ..."

"You're always wondering, Nelly. It's a bad habit. Tea?"

"No, thank you. I just want to know why ..."

"No tea, you said? Oh, of course not. You wouldn't want any tea, would you? Not after everything."

Nelly stiffened. The tea Mother had given Nelly during the secret visits. Grandmother read about it in Nelly's diaries, without permission, and was now hurling it back at her. "I'll just leave you alone then," Nelly muttered and decided it was better, safer, to remain in the dark about whatever Grandmother had going on.

But later that evening, Grandmother's husband, Gilbert, came home from his bridge club and was not so easily put off. Why, he wanted to know, did the house look like it had been "vandalized by some mad reject from a craft fair?"

"Please don't raise your voice to me, Gilbert," said Grandmother.

"Raise my voice?" Mr. Glanville said, storming around the main floor. "I go out for the afternoon and when I come back, there are horseshoes on the doors and flowers and bells and berries every which way. And what's happened to all the windowsills? It looks like they've been attacked by a drunk cobbler!"

"You're shouting, Gilbert," Grandmother said, her voice shrill. "YOU KNOW I DON'T LIKE IT WHEN YOU SHOUT!"

Mr. Glanville began patting his pockets. "Moira, I feel you are about to have an episode. I'll call the doctor."

Nelly and Trouble watched from the stairs as Mr. Glanville pulled his phone from his pocket. He was an odd-looking man with the face of an otter, a great flourish of bushy white hair, small round eyes, and an unfortunate overbite.

"Gilbert, no! Absolutely not," Grandmother said as she tucked the necklace she always wore, with its tiny wrought-iron bell, underneath her blouse. "I am not having an ... an *episode* or anything of the sort!"

Grandmother's "episodes," as Mr. Glanville called them, were hardly ever mentioned around the house or even implied. They happened rarely but were always alarming. Sometimes, for no reason at all, Grandmother would stiffen and get a far-off look in her eyes, and then she would start saying and doing things that made no sense.

These episodes terrified Nelly. She hoped they didn't mean what she thought they meant, that Grandmother was on her way to becoming a resident of the Nought County General psych ward.

"Then explain this to me please, Moira," Mr. Glanville said, jingling the bells dangling from the hall window. "Explain what's going on around here."

Grandmother lied. She said that she and Nelly had gone to a craft show with their new friends, the Lims. She said the flowers and the bells and berries and nails were just the latest thing in home decor. "Everyone's doing it! It's all over the websites and whatnot. It's chic. Crafty chic."

Mr. Glanville blinked. And then a huge smile spread across his face.

"Friends? You, Moira? Well, why didn't you say so? Crafty chic, is it? Yes, I suppose I can see the charm in it. The Lims! Will we be having them over for lunch sometime, or better yet, dinner?" Mr. Glanville went on like this excitedly for some time, much to Nelly's horror. Spending more time with Bianca Lim wasn't at the top of her to-do list.

Over the next few days, Mr. Glanville stopped noticing the nails, the bells, the flowers, and the berries. And so did Nelly. They seemed to fade into the fabric of the house. Another addition to Grandmother's already eccentric decor.

Much to Nelly's relief, the Lims did not receive an invitation to dinner, which meant she had plenty of time on her own to figure out her next move. Someway, somehow, she was going to find out who had written the word *Revenge* on her father's piece of paper and why. But to do that, she had to get back into the Nought County General psych ward.

She tried everything. She pressured Grandmother into calling the hospital to beg them to lift the ban. That didn't work. Moira Millicent Glanville Morighan did not beg. But she did get herself into a heated argument with the hospital director that ended in her being banned for the summer as well.

Nelly tried Mr. Glanville next. He came from some very old money and his family had always held a certain influence in the town of Nothing. But he wouldn't cooperate. He said he'd pulled enough strings for Nelly lately and she would have to solve her problem herself.

"What strings?" Nelly had asked.

But he wouldn't say anything more. It was frustrating. Nelly found herself up late most nights, pacing, imagining herself a spy or a detective, breaking into the psych ward with magical ingenuity. But magical solutions only happened in stories, not in real life.

The summer holidays lumbered on at an interminable pace. Nothing much happened. All of Nelly's attempts to see her father were thwarted, and the rest of the time she spent distracting herself, practicing her musical instruments, writing songs, and dreaming of the upcoming school year away from Nothing. Then, only two nights before she was supposed to drive back to the city for a new term at Mountain Wood Academy, something did happen.

Nelly was asleep, deep inside a bad dream. In the dream, she was running for her life in an autumn wood. People chased after her, hissing and spitting like wild geese.

"Monster! Wake up. Creature! Wake up. Thing! Nelly, wake up!"

Nelly opened her eyes and jerked upright.

Grandmother was standing over her bed, her silvery hair loose over her shoulders.

"Get out of bed quickly," the old woman whispered.

"Grammover?" Nelly mumbled, not fully in this world. She glanced at the clock on her bedside table. Half-past midnight.

"Yes, yes, get up. There's no time. They're here. On the farm. They're back." There was a crazed look in Grandmother's eyes as she stood there in her white nightgown, her bony hand outstretched.

After a moment's hesitation, Nelly took Grandmother's hand and allowed herself to be pulled out of bed. Grandmother led Nelly into the dark and narrow corridor. As they passed the master bedroom, Nelly peered inside, hoping to flag down Mr. Glanville. But he wasn't there, she realized quickly, remembering that he was out of town for his annual birdwatching trip with the boys.

"Quiet, quiet," Grandmother said, pausing before the top of the staircase. She pulled the tiny wrought-iron bell from around her neck and rang it three times. Nelly cringed. The bell sounded unnaturally loud in the silence and the darkness.

"Quiet, quiet," Grandmother said again and picked up one of the sacks of red berries Mr. Lim had left around the house. She was having an episode. Nelly wanted to call someone for help, but who? There weren't any 24-hour psychiatrists as far as she knew. And Mr. Glanville wouldn't be home for another couple of days.

Grandmother led Nelly down the stairs and into the kitchen. Trouble padded along behind them. The old woman paused at the backdoor window, her eyes fixed on the Morighan House, and rang her little bell again, three times.

Nelly winced. Was that bell getting louder?

Grandmother pulled Nelly toward the door to the basement. But as Nelly passed the window, she saw something—a flash of light from inside the Morighan House.

"What the ..." she started, but before she could finish her sentence, the light went dark.

Grandmother yanked her into the basement stairwell. "Lock the door behind you.".

"But—"

"Don't argue with me!"

Trouble ran ahead of them down the stairs and disappeared into the shadows. Nelly did as she was told. She clamped shut the four deadbolts Grandmother had insisted be installed into the basement door when the house was first erected. Then she took Nelly by the hand and pulled her down into the darkness, too.

"Quiet, quiet," Grandmother muttered, now sliding her thin frame onto the floor. She pulled Nelly down with her and then tossed handfuls of red berries in a wide circle all around them.

Trouble sat just outside the circle and watched them both, his cat's eyes glowing in the dark. On the cold concrete, Grandmother wrapped her arms around Nelly's shoulders and rocked back and forth.

"Quiet, quiet," she whispered every few seconds.

Nelly's heart was racing. She could feel Grandmother's heart racing as well. But Grandmother was right to be frightened. She wasn't imagining things. She wasn't having an episode. Someone *was* in the Morighan House. And there was only one person Nelly knew of who would enter that house.

"Quiet, quiet," Grandmother said again, though Nelly hadn't said a word.

CHAPTER SIX

THE MORIGHAN HOUSE

Morning light crept into the basement through windows lined with nails, bells, and flowers. Strange shadows reached across the floor to the corner where Grandmother and Nelly sat huddled.

Nelly shivered, and not just because of the cold concrete beneath her. That light in the Morighan House was all she could think about. It had to be her mother. She was in the Morighan House. No one else would enter that house. No one in town would dare, not even the ghost hunters. It *had* to be her. And yet in the past when Mother visited, she had always come to see Nelly in her bedroom. Was there a reason she couldn't this time? Was the light in the window a signal, a sign, a message to Nelly that Mother was there and needed her help?

Grandmother stood up. Without a backward glance, she walked through the circle of berries, scattering them with her slippers. At the top of the stairs, she unbolted the basement door and peered up into the kitchen, scanning the room. After a few moments frozen on the step, she mounted the final stair and was on the main floor.

Nelly stood up, too, her whole body aching from her night on the floor. Trouble yawned wide and then padded along after Nelly as she climbed the stairs, massaging her aching shoulders as she went.

In the kitchen there was no sign of Grandmother. Nelly hoped she had gone upstairs to bed.

Through the kitchen window, past the yard, and across the field, the Morighan House stood still and silent, windows dark. Nelly's stomach fluttered. She had to know if her mother was out there, but Grandmother would never allow her to go anywhere near the Morighan House. Not for any reason. Certainly not for anything having to do with Nelly's mother. But what Grandmother didn't know ...

The floor creaked above. Grandmother was still awake. Nelly went upstairs, washed her face, brushed her teeth, and got herself dressed, all the while listening for what Grand-mother was up to. If Grandmother took a nap, then Nelly could seize the opportunity to run over to the Morighan House, poke her head inside quickly, and call out to her mother. If Mother was there, she'd answer, and then, well, Nelly would cross that bridge when she came to it.

In her bedroom, Nelly sat down heavily on her bed, exhausted from her night on the basement floor. She lay back on her pillow and closed her eyes, telling herself she wasn't about to fall asleep ... she was only waiting for Grandmother to take a nap ... so she could run over to the Morighan House ... she wasn't chickening out.

"Nelly!"

Nelly opened her eyes and shot bolt upright.

"Yes?" she called down to Grandmother.

"Come down for breakfast, please, and DON'T MAKE ME HOLLER!"

Nelly sighed and got up.

Grandmother moved sluggishly around the kitchen, still in her housecoat and slippers. Her eyes were red and puffy. There was a tremor in her hand as she pulled a jar of raspberry jam out of the fridge.

"Nelly!" she gasped when she turned around. "How many times do I have to tell you not to sneak up on me like that? Walk with a surer foot. Don't prowl around and then appear in doorways. Let it be known you are in the general vicinity, for God's sake, before you startle someone to death."

"Sorry," Nelly muttered, with a weak smile.

Grandmother put the kettle on. She would not mention what had happened last night. This was always the way with Grandmother. She didn't talk about her episodes. She pretended they didn't happen. Usually, Nelly was content to go along with the show, but things were different this time. Nelly had seen the light in the Morighan House, too. She felt a nasty jolt of guilt. It wasn't fair to let Grandmother think she had been imagining things when she wasn't.

But what would Grandmother do if she knew the truth? Would she call the police? Would lights and sirens invade the still and silent farm? Would officers in their blue uniforms dare to enter the Morighan House? Would they find Nelly's mother inside? What would they do to her? What would she do to them?

The smell of toast and black tea took over the kitchen. Grandmother served Nelly but did not take any breakfast herself. Instead, she gazed out the window at the Morighan House. There was a tiny tremor in her hand as it clutched at the wrought-iron bell around her neck.

She sat down across from Nelly, her eyelids drooping. It was half an hour of awkward silences, failed attempts at small talk, and several instances in which Grandmother almost fell asleep where she sat before the old woman finally stood up.

"I didn't sleep well," she said as if this was news. "I think I'll go lie down for a nap."

A thrill of nerves went off in Nelly's stomach as the old woman shuffled out of the room. Grandmother's naps usually lasted an hour or so, rarely any longer. Nelly listened as Grandmother mounted the stairs, as her bedroom door creaked open, and as it clicked shut.

It was now or never. Heart bumping, Nelly crept into the front hall, slipped on her running shoes, and stepped out of the house without a sound.

The morning was warm but windy. A great cluster of clouds twisted and writhed across the sky. Nelly ducked behind the backyard maple and peered out from behind it at Grandmother's bedroom window above. The curtains were open. Nelly wouldn't dare run across the field if there was a chance that Grandmother might glance out the window and spot her. She waited there as the seconds ticked by, not sure if she wanted those toile curtains to close. Maybe it was better if they didn't close. Maybe the idea of going to the Morighan House by herself was crazy, even in the bright daylight. Maybe her mother wasn't even there. Maybe it was an intruder or an axe murderer or something. This was the Morighan House, after all. What about the rumors? What about the curse?

Nelly scolded herself. There was no such thing as ghosts or curses. Axe murderers on the other hand ...

Grandmother appeared in the window and pulled the

curtains shut. No more excuses. Nelly dashed out from behind the tree and flattened a path through the tangled yard toward the Morighan House, morning dew soaking her shoes and the bottoms of her jeans. She bolted across the farm lane and into the unkempt field. Only when the shadow of the house swept over her and she was sure she could no longer be seen from Grandmother's window, did she slow down to a walk.

The closer Nelly got to the house, the more anxious she became. Her legs had gone weak, and she worried they would give out with every step. But it was only a house, she kept telling herself. If someone other than her mother was inside, she could always run back to the farmhouse and lock the doors.

It was only a house.

A lump rose in her throat as she spotted the dead raspberry bush she'd crushed when she'd fallen off the porch five years before. Broken pieces of railing from that night still littered the ground like bones. The scent of damp wood and decay brought with it a flood of memories; Mother's livid, moonlit face and the bitter taste of that stuff she had forced Nelly to drink.

The house seemed to stare at her as she climbed onto the slanted porch. But it wasn't the great looming shadow with bared teeth it had been on that night. Now it seemed smaller, weaker somehow, a skeletal thing, starving and desperate. The door was hanging off its hinges. Where the doorknob should have been was a charred hole, like a cavity in a rotting tooth. This puzzled Nelly. It was like someone had taken a blowtorch to the doorknob. But why would anyone do that?

Nelly took a breath. She wasn't here to puzzle over a damaged door. But still, she hesitated. Was she really going to do this?

It's only a house.

She pushed at the door with her fingertips. It creaked open.

Stale, sickly air enveloped her, thick and heavy as if she stood before the nest of something terribly old and decaying.

"Mother?" she said in a small voice, peering inside.

No answer.

Nelly took another bolstering breath and stepped forward into the Morighan House.

She was in a kitchen. A wood stove on the far side of the room was coated in gray silt. A low sink stood under the boarded window, through which slits of dusty light were streaming. A spider web extended from faucet to drain like a stream of water frozen in time.

"Mother?" Nelly said again in their secret language. "Mother, it's me. It's Nelly."

Nelly took another cautious step forward. The room was strangely beautiful. Now and then, the sun beaming in through the broken windows sent a kaleidoscope of light shivering through the room, illuminating the old furniture, the peeling, jewel-blue walls, and the sparkling motes of dust floating in the air. Nelly imagined what this place had looked like before it had been abandoned and left to rot, and suddenly the air didn't feel as heavy as it had before.

"Mother," Nelly called again in a loud, clear voice. "If you're here, please say something. Grandmother's taking a nap. I can't stay long."

Still no answer. The house remained silent under a blanket of dust.

She raked her bangs away from her sweaty forehead. A table sat in the middle of the room, surrounded by wooden chairs, one of which was a baby's high chair. A word was carved into the back of it. Unable to resist the temptation, Nelly walked over to the high chair and touched it. A layer of grime came off on her fingers. Under the dust, the high chair was bright yellow. The word carved into the back of it wasn't a word at all but a name: MERRITT, her father's name. This had once been her father's highchair.

The door creaked behind her. Nelly spun around.

There was a gray streak.

"Trouble!" Nelly said as the cat leaped onto the table. "You scared me half to—" She put her hand on her chest and tried to calm her now thundering heart.

The cat prowled back and forth, sniffing the air.

Nelly laughed with relief. "You are not a ghost," she said. And yet the cat seemed agitated. When she reached out to pet him, he hissed at her as if trying to tell her he did not like this place and wanted to leave.

The air felt heavy and oppressive again. Nelly glanced once more around the kitchen. There was a doorway on the far side of the room. A broken door dangled there from its hinges. The thing was in pieces. Jagged splinters of wood stuck out in every direction like bashed teeth as if someone had taken a battering ram to it. Behind the broken door, a set of stairs was visible, leading down into darkness.

The basement, Nelly thought, and only then realized that the layout of this kitchen matched the one in the new farmhouse exactly. Was the farmhouse a duplicate of the Morighan House? Why would Grandmother build a second house, a duplicate, rather than simply repair this one? It seemed sturdy enough, just neglected.

Nelly took two cautious steps toward the broken door. Closer to the basement, the air felt even heavier and seemed to come in waves, like breath.

Something sharp pierced her ankle. Nelly gasped and spun around. Trouble had just bitten her. He had never bitten her before. "Trouble, what is wrong with—"

The words died on her lips.

Someone else was in the house. The someone else was not Nelly's mother. A woman was standing in the open doorway, perfectly still, a partially eaten apple in her hand.

Nelly could hardly believe what she was seeing. This woman was the most bizarre-looking person she had ever seen. She was beautiful. Too beautiful. An ethereal beauty Nelly had never come across in real life. Her face was heart-shaped, like a porcelain doll. She had big dark eyes, moon-pale skin, and ruddy cheeks under waves of wind-swept red hair. She wore an insane, raggedy hodgepodge of a dress with cream and lavender and blueberry layers, stuck in places with leaves and yarrow and rose heads as if she had been rolling around in a garden.

"How did you find me?" the woman said in a hoarse whisper as if she hadn't used her voice in a long time. But she hadn't spoken in English. *Not in English.* She had spoken in the secret language only Nelly and her mother shared.

A gust of wind flew into the room. Leaves and dust swirled like a mini tornado, tossing Nelly's hair. Trouble streaked out the door. The woman flicked something at him. She dropped her apple. She slammed the door shut.

The woman was glaring at Nelly now with a predatory focus.

It took Nelly several seconds to find her voice. "—I-I was looking for my mother," she stammered.

The woman was expressionless. Her eyes stayed locked on Nelly like a wolf stalking a deer.

"Answer the question," she said.

Nelly's mind was racing. Was this woman from town? Was she homeless? Was she squatting in the Morighan House? No one ever went inside the Morighan House!

She could speak the secret language.

Nelly broke the second of her mother's rules. She spoke the secret language to someone other than her mother. "Last night I—we—saw a light in the Morighan House. Here. And I thought, well, no one ever comes here, except this one time, my mother was here, so I thought maybe it was her. But you're not my mother, obviously, so I'll just be going ..."

The woman did not react. Her concentrated eyes did not falter.

"I won't go back," she said with a ferocity that made Nelly step back. "I'll die first. Do you understand? And I'll take you and your little friend with me. Do you hear me?" she called out as if she thought others were listening. "I won't go back!"

There was a ringing silence.

"You don't have to go anywhere," Nelly said quickly, feeling herself starting to panic. It was like she was in the presence of a wild animal, one that might leave her alone or decide to eat her depending on how threatened it felt.

"My family owns this farm. I won't tell anyone you're here. If you'll just let me leave, I'll make sure no one bothers you ever again."

The woman narrowed her eyes. "Are you playing games with me?"

"Games? No," Nelly said, shaking her head. "Absolutely not, no way."

The woman sneered. Then, as quick as a blast of wind, she rushed forward and struck Nelly. Hard. Right across the face.

It hurt, but that was expected of a slap. What Nelly couldn't have expected was the sensation that came next. It started with a tingle in her fingers and toes. Then, as fast as a whip crack, blinding pain exploded through every nerve in her body. The pain was so intense Nelly forgot where she was, who she was. The room spun. Lights popped and black spots floated in the air. A high-pitched ringing sound rang in her ears. Vaguely, she was aware that she was screaming.

The face of the red-haired woman swam into view.

And a voice, far-off and muffled, said, "What are you?"

There was an explosion of white.

And everything went black.

CHAPTER SEVEN

GRANDMOTHER'S SECRET

Nelly woke up. It took her a few seconds to realize where she was—back inside the farmhouse, lying in her bed, on top of her blankets. Something was wrong. A substance like dust or snow was on her eyelashes. She sat up. A strange white powder poured from her head onto the bed in a billowing cascade. She was completely covered in the stuff. It had the consistency of flour or fine sand and sparkled with blue and silver flecks in the sunlight.

The powder tickled her nose. She sneezed! When she blinked her eyes open again, the powder was gone. Completely gone. There was not a trace on her hair or her face or her clothing or the bed.

Nelly rubbed her eyes and opened them again. Still no trace of the powder. Had she been dreaming? She got up. Her body ached as if she had been beaten.

"Nelly," Grandmother called from downstairs. "Come down for supper."

Supper? Nelly glanced at the clock on her bedside table. Six o'clock. How long had she been sleeping?

Then everything that happened that day came back to her in a rush. The Morighan House ... the weird woman with the porcelain doll face ... the slap ... the overwhelming pain.

"Nelly!" Grandmother called again, her footfalls on the stairs.

"I'll be down in a minute!" Nelly called back.

She looked out the window. The long shadow of the Morighan House stretched across the field toward the farmhouse as the sun lowered in the sky. The house looked as dark, dreary, and undisturbed as it always did. Nelly wrung her hands. Had she been there today at all? Or had she fallen asleep this afternoon, right after she had dressed, and dreamed the whole thing?

"NELLY!" Grandmother called again.

"I'LL BE DOWN IN A MINUTE!"

Nelly found Grandmother already seated at the kitchen table. She had cooked her specialty, lemon-rosemary chicken with mixed vegetables. This was unusual. Whenever Grandmother had one of her episodes, she was usually in too sour a mood to cook.

"Have a seat," Grandmother said stiffly, unfolding a napkin and dropping it on her lap.

"You cooked," Nelly said, pulling out a chair at the table.

"Is that a thank you?" Grandmother asked, her back straight and her eyebrows arched.

"Uh, yes, thank you, Grandmother," Nelly stammered. "It looks wonderful."

Grandmother allowed a terse smile. She was dressed in a prim, embroidered black dress, and was looking as staid and stiff as she normally did, which meant she must have recovered from last night's episode.

"You slept all day. You must be rested," Grandmother said as if she hadn't slept much of the day herself.

Nelly glanced out the window toward the Morighan House. "Yeah, I think so."

"You think?" Grandmother said. "You mean you don't know whether or not you slept?"

Nelly looked up from her plate, swallowed a mouthful of broccoli. "No, I slept ... I don't know why I said that."

Again, Nelly glanced out at the Morighan House. She didn't like this feeling, this clawing uncertainty about whether she'd had a dream ... or something else. She shifted in her chair. This must have been what Grandmother felt like after every one of her episodes. Again, Nelly felt a thud of guilt. Last night's episode hadn't been an episode at all. She should tell Grandmother the truth.

It was only then that Nelly noticed Grandmother wasn't eating. Instead, she was slicing her chicken into tinier and tinier pieces. Pretty soon it would be minced.

"Uh, Grandmother, are you—"

"I think it's about time the two of us had a serious talk," Grandmother interrupted.

"Oh?" Nelly said, going rigid. The last time she and Grandmother had a serious talk, her diaries had gone up in flames.

There was a long pause.

"Well, I'll just have to come out and say it." Grandmother stopped mincing her chicken. "You will not be returning to Mountain Wood Academy for school this coming term."

Nelly blinked. This was the last thing she had expected to hear. "What?"

"I've done some thinking about your situation over the summer—"

"My situation?" Nelly said, her heart starting to pound.

"Yes, and please don't interrupt." Grandmother smoothed down her shirt and adjusted her bell necklace. "In light of the insight I was given into your life at the start of the summer ..."

My diaries, Nelly thought, and her face went hot.

"It is my belief that you don't have the maturity to live in the city unsupervised. You are only sixteen, after all. I must have been mad to even consider it. So, I have had you transferred to the Priory House School."

Nelly felt as if the floor had dropped out from under her chair. "The Priory House? In Nothing?"

"Don't raise your voice," Grandmother said, raising her voice.

"But everyone there thinks—"

"I know perfectly well what the people in this town think of us," Grandmother said and began slicing up her chicken again. "But we cannot allow our actions to be dictated by rumor and superstition. Besides, the Priory House is a big school, and a prestigious one, with students boarding from all over the county. I'm sure there will be plenty of opportunity to make friends there who aren't ..." Grandmother paused, sniffed, "from the area."

"—B-B-But ..." Nelly's mind was reeling. Alexis Abner went to the Priory House, the girl who'd been tormenting Nelly since kindergarten. And so did all of Alexis's sycophantic little cronies. Not to mention all the others, the classmates Nelly had grown up with in the town of Nothing, all of whom believed she was some sort of cursed ghost-magnet.

"But everyone here treats me like I've got the plague," Nelly said, continuing her thoughts out loud. "I'll be an outcast again. You don't understand what it's like. I haven't seen these people in over a year, and I don't want to see them ever again. I finally escaped. I can't go back."

"Oh, I understand. I went through it. Your father went through it. Challenges like these are meant to be faced and surmounted, not escaped. Builds character."

"Grandmother," Nelly said, groping around for something, anything that might convince the old woman to change her mind. "I can't go to the Priory House. I just can't."

"You can and you will. You've done enough escaping, Nelly, into your music, your books, your *diaries*." Grandmother gave Nelly a hard look with her stone-like eyes. "I know now that even in the city you had very few friends. You can't escape yourself."

Nelly sat back in her chair. Grandmother knew how to cut right to the bone.

"But not to worry. You won't be an outcast, not entirely. I have made an arrangement on your behalf with the Lim family."

Nelly had a sinking feeling. "What kind of arrangement?"

"This is between us, but the Lims have been having some financial trouble lately and can't afford to continue sending Bianca away to school. So, in exchange for some occasional work around the farm, I have agreed to pay young Bianca's school fees. The only condition was that the Lims transfer Bianca to the Priory House so the two of you can continue to room together."

"*Bianca?*" Nelly said, jumping up, her chair screeching across the floor.

Grandmother crossed her arms. "Nelly, sit down, please. I won't have this conversation with you looming over me."

"Room together? Bianca and I are supposed to room together? Do you mean I have to stay there, at the school?"

"Well, yes, I thought—"

"Why can't I stay here on the farm? I could take a bus or ... or—"

"There are no buses that will stop at the farm, Nelly, don't be silly."

"Couldn't you or Mr. Glanville drive me?"

"Five days a week? Come now, Nelly, that is not a considerate request. I taught you better than that."

There wasn't any way out of this, Nelly realized, the reality of the situation sinking into her like a stone. When Grandmother made up her mind, there wasn't anything that could change it. Nelly sat back down and slumped into her chair.

"This has got to be a nightmare," she muttered.

"Oh, don't be dramatic. You know Mr. Glanville can't have a teenager in the house year-round at his age. That's the whole reason we sent you away to school in the first place. Now you'll still be away, but you'll be close enough that you can come home on the weekends and even visit your father. After missing out on seeing him all summer, I thought you would appreciate the opportunity."

"But, but—"

"No, that's enough. This is for your own good. You need a structured and supervised environment right now. The Priory House can provide that in a way that Mountain Wood cannot." Grandmother paused for a deep, measured breath. "That being said, I am prepared to consider transferring you back to Mountain Wood next semester, provided you behave, do well in your classes, and prove to me you deserve a second chance."

An ember of hope flickered in Nelly. One semester? She could survive a semester. It was like a prison sentence, she told herself. Head down, good behavior, and in four months she would be free.

"I've arranged with the principal," Grandmother continued. "She will be sending me bi-weekly reports on your progress. You have an opportunity here, Nelly, to prove to me how responsible you can be, here in Nothing. And then we can talk about sending you back to the city. Don't squander it."

Nelly sat in silence. Whatever happened, no matter how the other students treated her, she couldn't let them provoke her, she couldn't step out of line. With Bianca as her roommate, this was going to be the longest four months of her life.

Two nights later, a heavy rainstorm lashed the farm. Thunder growled repeatedly, spitting lightning. Nelly was in her bedroom, in the dark, sitting on the edge of the bed, watching as rain whipped her windowpane. She couldn't sleep. Tomorrow morning, Grandmother would be driving her to the Priory House School where everyone who ever hated her or picked on her or made her life miserable was currently enrolled. They were going to eat her alive. A tall stack of suitcases, all packed, stood next to her closet, and cast a shadow like a scolding spirit, reminding her of her fate.

Trouble was under her bed, hiding from the thunder. Nelly could sympathize. All she wanted to do now was hide, shrink down to cat-size and hide under a bed, or in a cupboard, or at the back of a closet; some small, protected place where no one could find her and make her go to that school.

She lay back and covered her eyes with her fists. Her head was spinning with ugly scenarios of what could happen tomorrow at school and the relentless fear of what happened, or didn't happen, in the Morighan House two days earlier. She still wasn't sure if what she remembered was real or only a dream. This was unnerving. If it had been a dream, then there was still the matter of the light she had seen in the window of the Morighan House. She had never investigated it and had no idea who or what was out there. If it hadn't been a dream, then someone or something dangerous was inside that house. She couldn't just go away to school without warning Grandmother and Mr. Glanville about it.

Why had she left this to the absolute last minute to think about? Because Grandmother's announcement had broadsided her? Because there had been no other opportunities to sneak over to the Morighan House and find out if what she thought had happened had really happened? Because she was afraid ...

The memory of that woman with the porcelain doll face, the slap, the horrible pain, and that strange dust-like substance made Nelly shiver. It had all felt so real.

BOOM!

Thunder rocked the house. Nelly sat bolt upright. Her skin prickled. The clock on her bedside table flashed twelve o'clock and went dark. She switched on her lamp. Nothing happened. The power was out.

She got up to search for her phone and its light. Then she heard something—a faint scraping sound coming from inside her closet.

The closet doorknob jiggled.

Nelly gasped and jumped back. *A mouse*, she thought, standing motionless, staring at the closet door, and listening for the slightest sound.

Then it occurred to her that mice couldn't move doorknobs.

BOOM!

Thunder cracked again. There was a faint scent in the air of beeswax and burned matches. She spotted her phone on the edge of her desk. She grabbed it and pointed the phone's light at her closet door.

There was silence, and then ... voices.

Nelly's heart leaped into her throat.

"Ouch, watch out," a voice said from inside the closet.

"Are you sure this is the right place?"

"Yes. Well, I think so. Don't push."

"I should go first. I've met her. You'll probably frighten her half to death."

"Yes, yes, fine. There's the doorknob."

The closet doorknob started to turn again.

Nelly's heart was thudding. A scream perched at the back of her throat. This couldn't be real. This had to be a dream.

The closet door was opening. Something was coming out of it. It was large and green. It looked like ... an umbrella?

It was an umbrella, a green one, opened halfway and covered in water droplets. It was rising into the air.

Nelly couldn't believe what she was seeing. There was a person under the umbrella. And not just any person. It was the woman from the Morighan House, red hair, porcelain doll face and all.

CHAPTER EIGHT

THE NEIGHBORS

The memory of this woman, the slap and the pain Nelly had felt in the Morighan House, seized her like a cold claw.

"Don't," the woman said before Nelly could cry out.

In one fluid flash of movement, the woman pulled something out of her pocket. There was a *CLICK*, and a cloud of bluish powder exploded into Nelly's face. It was in her eyes and nose and mouth. Nelly sputtered and tried to spit it away. It smelled of sugar cookies but tasted like sour plums. Nelly forced her eyes open. The woman was still there, staring at her through a cloud of glittery blue.

Nelly screamed, but no sound came out of her mouth. She tried again. Still, nothing happened. No sound. Her voice was not working.

Clutching her own throat, Nelly backed into the wall. She could not speak. The woman from the Morighan House—a woman so phantasmal, Nelly thought she'd met her in a dream —was here. She was real. And she wasn't human. Nelly had never been more certain of anything in her life. Not just because the woman had moved at an impossible speed and tossed magic, voice-stealing powder at her. It was the woman's eyes. They were reflecting the light beam from Nelly's cell phone. They were glowing gold, like an animal's.

Nelly dropped the phone.

It clattered face up on the floor.

"Now look what you've done," a male voice said. "She's petrified."

A man's face poked out from behind the woman. The face was long, and thin, and wore a look of confusion. A blast of dark, curly hair crowned the face and stuck out in all directions.

A faint tinkling sound issued from the closet, as if from jingle bells on a sleigh, and several tiny white lights whizzed into the room and buzzed around the intruders like fireflies.

The man stepped out from behind the woman into the full glow of the phone's light. He was taller than the woman and gangly, with a narrow chest and spidery limbs. He looked like a parody of a Victorian gentleman, with a bunch of dried clover pinned to his waistcoat. And everything about him, his face, his weird clothing, was splattered in multi-colored powder as if he had just finished an out-of-control art project.

"This is the subject then?" he said, sapphire eyes gleaming behind wire-rimmed glasses. "A little girl, surely. An ordinary girl. Yes? Yes. And human besides."

"She's not," the woman snapped. She closed her umbrella and shook it, spraying Nelly head to toe with cold water.

"Look closer. She's no more a human than you or I."

The man's eyes flickered over Nelly. "Hmm. Sit her down, then, and I'll have a look. And hold her still, will you?"

What happened next was so quick and seamless, Nelly had no time to blink let alone defend herself. The woman seemed to vanish before Nelly's eyes. Then powerful, stone-cold hands landed on Nelly's shoulder, spun her around, and sat her down with a thump on the chair next to her desk. This all seemed to happen in less than a second. The cell phone light beamed up from the floor at Nelly's feet and the two intruders stood staring at her from behind it.

"Ah, yes," the man said, stroking his chin. "That's much better. Much better, thank you."

"I thought it might be," the woman said.

The intruders leaned forward into the shaft of the cell phone's light. It lit their faces, turning their eyes into solid glowing balls and making them look, if possible, even less human than they had a moment ago. They looked Nelly over with methodical, inquisitive expressions as if they were doctors or scientists. Nelly didn't move, hardly allowing herself to even breathe. When she was in the Morighan House with this woman, she felt like she was trapped with a wild animal. Now she was trapped with two of them.

The man tapped his chin. "She has the eyes," he muttered as the little lights still whizzing back and forth reflected in his glasses.

"The eyes, yes," the woman repeated in a whisper. Nelly blinked. Light images were now dancing in front of her eyes thanks to the glow of the cell phone.

"Let's see the teeth," the man said, and immediately the woman grabbed Nelly by the face and squeezed her cheeks together, roughly forcing her lips apart like a fish.

"Ah yes, I see. She has the teeth," the man said.

"The teeth," the woman said, nodding. "Yes. The teeth."

Next, the woman jammed her fingers in Nelly's mouth, grabbed hold of her tongue, and pulled it forward for the man to examine.

After a long silence in which Nelly, fearing the woman

might rip her tongue out of her mouth, stayed still and did not struggle, the man said solemnly, "She has the tongue."

The woman released Nelly's tongue, leaving it throbbing and tasting of cinnamon and honey and something sharp, like ginger.

"The tongue," the woman said, nodding.

The man and the woman exchanged serious looks. "She's one of us. There's no doubt," the man said, adjusting his silver glasses. "Part Wight and part Fire Sitter, I would guess."

"Nonsense," the woman said, hands on her hips. "She looks nothing like a Wight or a Fire Sitter."

"We'll see," the man said and pulled something out of his jacket pocket. It was a long, thick leather-like roll. He dropped it on Nelly's desk and unrolled it. Strapped inside the roll in neat little pouches were dozens of small satchels, vials filled with colored liquids, and several instruments that made Nelly's blood run cold.

Much to Nelly's relief, the man did not reach for the instruments. Instead, he opened a satchel and dipped his fingers inside. His fingers were now covered in a bright green powder that shimmered in the glare of the cell phone light.

He leaned in close to Nelly. She squeezed her eyes shut as he rubbed the green powder over her eyelids with cold, hard fingers. Her heart pounded. When he seemed to be finished, she blinked her eyes open.

"I see," the woman said. "She is a Wight, then." And she scrunched her nose as if being a Wight, whatever that was, was something base and undesirable.

The man took hold of Nelly's left hand. His fingers were strong and stone hard. He rubbed his thumb over Nelly's forefinger, and some of the green powder on his fingers rubbed onto hers. Then he pressed her finger down onto the surface of her wooden desk as if he was fingerprinting her. Nelly felt a pleasant, warming sensation shoot into her fingertip. To her surprise, smoke curled up from the desk beneath her finger.

"A Fire Sitter, too," the woman said, nodding as Nelly gaped at her own smoking finger. The man released Nelly, who immediately pulled her hand back as if from a hot stove. But she felt no pain. Apart from the green powder, her finger looked the same as ever.

The desk, however, did not. There was now a black burn mark on the wood, the precise shape of Nelly's fingertip. How was this possible? What was that powder? Nelly wanted to ask questions, she was desperate to, despite her fear, but she still had no voice. She was starting to fear she'd never get it back.

The intruders stepped back from her and began whispering in a heated back and forth as if weighing something of profound urgency while the little lights jingled above their heads in wide circles.

"But how is this possible?" the woman said, her voice rising.

"I don't know. It makes no sense," the man said, fiddling with a loose string on his jacket. "They would not have—"

"No. Never. Impossible," the woman said, cutting him off. "Which means they do not know."

"They can't know," the man said. "If *they* knew ..."

"If *they* knew ..." And the intruders stared at each other with wide, worried eyes.

Dread rolled over Nelly. She took this opportunity to stand up and then slide along the wall toward the door. As she reached the door and felt for the doorknob, she realized that the intruders had stopped whispering.

They were looking right at her. She grabbed the doorknob and pulled. A hand shot out over her head and slammed the door shut again. Nelly stood still, staring at the back of her closed bedroom door.

"It's not polite to sneak away," the woman whispered, leaning in very close, emanating a whiff of honey and clover.

"Fig," the man snapped, as though scolding her.

The woman spun Nelly around and stared at her with stone-hard eyes. "You have nothing to say for yourself?"

Nelly stood frozen in place. She still couldn't speak.

The man crossed his arms. "Her voice, Fig."

"Ah, yes, how silly of me," the woman said, and then tapped her own chin. "Hmm, perhaps introductions first."

She stepped back from Nelly. The intruders both straightened themselves. The man patted down his jacket and as he did so, clouds of dust and a few moths rose from the folds in the fabric. The woman cleared her throat, patted her wild hair, and smoothed her raggedy dress.

"Nelly Morighan," the woman said, leaning on her umbrella. "I call myself Fig. Fig-o'-the-Lantern, light of the fig tree. A representative, until recently, of the Fire Sitters, former member of House Rowan and House Hawthorn, and one of the Weird People of the Oak Trees.

"And this, this is my dear friend Jack the Spinner, Shadow Weaver, Night Stealer, member of House Yarrow, in good standing, and one of the Wicked People of the Holly Boughs."

The man, Jack the Spinner, clasped his hands behind his back and gave a quick, smart bow.

"There now," the woman, Fig, said, nodding. "We have exchanged names. We're friends now, for worse or better." She grinned wide and pulled what looked like an antique snuff box from her pocket, popped it open, and blew a shiny powder the color of fresh dandelions in Nelly's face. Nelly smelled cloves and tasted sour apples.

Her throat tickled, and then with a cough, she felt her voice coming back.

"How ..." she said and coughed again. "What ... you ..."

"You've messed it up, Fig," the man, Jack, said. "You've only given her half her voice, or maybe a quarter."

"I didn't mess anything up," Fig said, brushing the yellow powder from her fingers.

"What are you?" Nelly said, the words bursting from her mouth instead of a scream, though screaming was all she wanted to do. "How ... how did you get in my closet?"

"See?" Fig said to Jack.

"There's no need to be alarmed," Jack said, his eyes blinking behind his glasses.

"*Alarmed?*" Nelly said, raising her voice. Then she remembered Grandmother was asleep just down the hall. She was suddenly very sure she didn't want Grandmother to know about this.

"What are you?" Nelly said again, more quietly this time.

Fig and Jack grinned at each other as if sharing a private joke.

"We're the neighbors," Jack said. "We live next door."

"Next door?" Nelly repeated.

Fig motioned toward the closet. "Or any door, really."

"—B-But how did you get inside my closet?" asked Nelly.

"With this," Jack said, holding up what appeared to be a maple seed pod between his thumb and forefinger. "Good neighbors share keys. We have one for you and you have one for us."

"What?" Nelly's voice was coming out high-pitched and panicky. "You came out of my closet. You're not ... you ... what are you?"

The intruders glanced at each other as though confused by Nelly's confusion.

"We're the neighbors," Jack said again, more deliberately this time, as if he thought Nelly was a bit slow. "We're People."

"People?" Nelly echoed.

"That's how we refer to ourselves in polite company, but you know our real name," Jack said, winking at Nelly. "You must, yes, most certainly. It's with us wherever we are, floating on the air. Listen and you'll catch it."

Despite the absurdity of his statement, Nelly listened. All she heard was steady rain on the farmhouse roof.

But then, as if in a dream, she felt somehow that she did know what he meant. There was a word for what these two intruders were, but she couldn't quite get hold of it. It was on her tongue, but when she tried to say it, it would dissolve away like maple sugar.

"I'm not like you," Nelly said, thinking of something Jack said earlier. *She's one of us. There's no doubt.*

"Of course you are," Fig said, tossing back her red hair. "It's quite obvious. You speak Eldritch, don't you?"

"Eldritch?" Nelly repeated.

"The language we're speaking," Fig said as if it was the most obvious thing in the world.

That's when Nelly realized she had been speaking the secret language all this time. The intruders had been speaking the secret language too, ever since Nelly had first heard them on the other side of the closet door.

"There you are," Fig said, with a sweep of her hand. "Eldritch isn't a human language and if—"

"If you were human," Jack cut in, "you wouldn't be able to speak it if you tried. Humans don't have the tongue for it. Not living humans."

Suddenly very aware of her tongue, Nelly rubbed it against the roof of her mouth. Was it different from everyone else's? Was there something that wasn't human about her tongue? Wait a minute ... was she actually considering this?

"And for another thing," Jack said, threading his long fingers, "you certainly don't look human."

"Yes, I do," Nelly said indignantly. "And ... and so do both of you."

Fig crossed her arms. "That was impolite."

Jack leaned forward, his eyes sparkling blue behind his glasses. "Look closer."

This was unnecessary. The truth was Nelly knew they weren't human. She knew it as plainly as she knew the crows that flew over the fields weren't human or that Grandmother's cat wasn't human. Everything about these intruders exposed them: the way they both stood perfectly still, hardly seeming to even breathe; the way their clothing was crazy and colorful and foreign and appeared to have been sewn entirely by hand; the way their skin was a little too bright and their cheeks were a little too pink as if they'd both walked out of an enhanced photograph; the way their eyes were locked on her, Nelly, with an almost predatory focus and how those same eyes glowed gold in the light. So, they weren't human. Fine, Nelly could accept that. She was also quite sure that she was dreaming. This settled it. Jack and Fig weren't human and none of this was real. Nelly had fallen asleep while watching the storm. She was lying there on her bed right now, and all of this was a very vivid dream.

"We would very much like to get to know you, Nelly," Jack said, gazing at her over his glasses. "You see, your existence is a mystery to us. Yes, quite a mystery. That you are here where the humans are, having been raised by and among them just doesn't happen. We can't understand why your parents would do this to you."

"They didn't do anything to me," Nelly said, feeling defensive. This dream was getting personal.

The light of Nelly's cell phone was dimming. Jack and Fig were staring at her with unnerving focus. Nelly's ears were hot. Did cell phones fade in dreams? Did ears get hot?

Fig stiffened suddenly. She held a finger in the air for silence. She and Jack exchanged glances. Then the two intruders turned their heads in eerie unison toward the bed.

It took Nelly a moment to figure out what they were looking at. It was Trouble. He was under the bed, hissing softly, his cat's eyes glowing in the dark.

Then all hell broke loose.

CHAPTER NINE

THE BARGAIN

Trouble erupted from under the bed and began streaking this way and that around the room as if he was flying. Jack and Fig darted after him. They knocked over Nelly's lamp and clock and then her side table and then her desk. And then her whole bookshelf came crashing down.

Trouble, Jack, and Fig were moving with such speed, Nelly could barely track them. As they zipped around the room, Jack and Fig were flinging handfuls of multi-colored powder. They seemed to be aiming at Trouble but kept missing him. Powder whipped onto the walls, across the ceiling, and over the furniture in dozens of colorful, raining explosions. The little hovering lights that had come into the room with Jack and Fig were streaking around the room, too, creating a bizarre, flickering light show.

"This has got to be a dream," Nelly mumbled and felt behind her back for the doorknob. Just as she grabbed it, a great force threw open the door.

Nelly went flying toward her bed and landed hard on the

mattress. When she looked up, Trouble, Jack, and Fig were gone. The bedroom door was hanging on its hinges.

Nelly sat stunned as wafts of powder billowed in the air all around her like smoke. Her cell phone died, and everything went dark.

Stumbling into the blackness, Nelly made her way out of her bedroom. The hallway was a trail of destruction. Colorful powder stained the walls, the floor, and the ceiling like splatters of paint mixed with flour. There were cat paw prints and hand and footprints running up the walls and even on the ceiling!

Grandmother.

Nelly bolted down the hall and threw open the door to Grandmother's bedroom. The bed was empty. Heat rushed into Nelly's face. Had those creatures taken her, done something to her? She turned and hurtled along the hall again and then down the stairs, nearly falling as she went.

On the main floor, Nelly followed the sounds of breaking things and crashing furniture into the living room. There she found Jack, Fig, and Trouble racing around, wrecking the place. It was sheer and utter chaos.

"Where's my grandmother?" she shouted over the din. They didn't stop and did not acknowledge her.

"Where's my—"

RING! RING! RING!

A bell rang three times, so piercing, Nelly's eyes teared.

"FAIRIES!" a voice boomed, and the whole world seemed to stop.

Jack and Fig stood frozen in the middle of the destroyed room. Trouble was nowhere to be seen. Grandmother stood in the doorway in her nightgown, holding her wrought-iron bell necklace in one hand.

Nelly's mouth dropped open. *Fairies*. That was the word

she had been looking for, the one she knew but couldn't quite grasp. Fairies. Jack and Fig were fairies. Of course they were. It was so obvious; she wondered how she hadn't realized it sooner.

"Fairies," Grandmother said again forcefully and dropped a bag of red berries on the floor.

Jack and Fig were standing perfectly still, eyes locked on Grandmother like a pair of wolves.

"You know our name," Fig said in strangely accented English.

"Yes," Grandmother said. "I know your name. I know what you are, and I know what that means."

Nelly felt like her world had just flipped upside-down. Fairies. Jack and Fig were fairies. This wasn't a dream. Fairies were real. And Grandmother knew about them.

"An educated woman," Fig said and smiled at Grandmother; a sinister, intimidating smile that did not extend to her eyes.

"Always makes things interesting," Jack added, his glasses glinting.

"You have entered my home uninvited," Grandmother said. Her voice quavered, but she stood as stiff and tall as a military general. "I know your name. That gives me rights. You must answer my questions. You must tell the truth."

Fig and Jack exchanged glances again. The room was dim, and yet the eyes and skin of the intruders seemed to glimmer, faint and eerie, like moonlight on bare branches.

"All right. We'll play. Three questions for our illustrious host," Fig said with a little bow. "Better make them good."

The fairy, Fig, fell back into Mr. Glanville's favorite green armchair and crossed her legs. The other fairy, Jack, stood behind the chair, his elbows on it, and rested his chin on his hands. And they both stared at Grandmother with unnerving concentration while little lights zipped above their heads.

"Grandmother," Nelly said. "What's going on?"

"Quiet, Nelly," Grandmother snapped, not taking her eyes off the intruders. There was silence in the room, other than rain still pattering away against the roof.

"What ... what are you doing here?" Grandmother asked, not sounding nearly as confident as she had a moment ago.

Fig smirked. "I am sitting in a chair answering the questions of a very foolish human woman."

"Likewise," Jack said, steepling his long, paint-stained fingers. "Though I am standing."

Grandmother winced. It was a bad question. There was another long silence. Nelly was painfully aware of the sound of her own shaky breaths and of her heart thumping.

Grandmother asked her second question. "Why are you in my home?"

"To satisfy our curiosity," Fig said without so much as a pause. "Next question!"

Grandmother flinched under Fig's fierce gaze. There was a long pause in which Grandmother fiddled with something in her housecoat pocket and the fairies remained so still and so silent they looked like strange statues.

"What ... what do you want?" Grandmother asked finally.

Fig smiled wide. "At the moment? Your cat."

Fig leaped lightly to her feet. A split-second later, she and Jack were standing side by side with unsettling smiles on their faces.

"Our cat?" Grandmother said, her voice tinged with desperation. "Is that all you came for?"

"Ah, ah, ah," Fig said, wagging her finger. "Question time is done for you. Let's pinch her, Jack, black and blue."

Grandmother let out a low cry, grabbed Nelly by the arm,

and yanked her backward. Then she kicked over the bag on the floor. Red berries poured out between the two Morighans and the two fairies.

Jack and Fig both stared at the berries curiously.

"Rowan berries," Jack said, narrowing his eyes. "She's a kitchen witch."

Fig cocked her head. "She knows a bit, but not much, I wager."

"I know you can't cross a line of rowan berries," Grandmother said.

"Can't? Can't?" Fig laughed wickedly. "She doesn't know. Quick now and we'll have her by the hair!"

Fig grabbed at Grandmother, reaching right over the line of rowan berries, though she did not step across it. At the same time, Grandmother pulled a pair of kitchen shears out of her housecoat and swiped at Fig.

Fig caught the shears. She stiffened. Then, still holding the shears, Fig began to shake. She convulsed. Smoke rose from her hair. It was as if she was being electrocuted.

Grandmother, still holding the handle of the shears, was shaking just as hard as Fig. Her teeth chattered. Nelly didn't understand what was happening but knew she had to stop it. She reached for the shears. The moment her hand touched them, several things happened at once. An electric pain roared through Nelly's body. Fig went flying backward, slammed into the fireplace, and dropped to the ground, her entire body smoking. Grandmother gasped and dropped the shears.

Jack stepped forward, right to the edge of the line of berries.

"That was unwise," he said, eyes flashing. His shadow behind him grew and stretched up the wall.

A second later, a smoky-haired Fig was standing next to Jack again. "You should not interfere with us," she said, smoke billowing from her mouth. "Don't bother us, and we won't bother you. Those are the rules."

"It's never so simple with you fairies," Grandmother said, holding a protective but trembling hand out in front of Nelly.

The fairies glared. The eerie glow emanating from their eyes and skin intensified.

"Be careful, human. Do not insult us." Fig's tone was deadly.

Grandmother stood her ground. "Leave my house," she said in a commanding voice.

Jack sneered. "We will when we have what we came for."

"Our cat?" Grandmother said.

"Your cat is not a cat," Fig snapped, the smoke from her hair making the room appear on fire. "And we want it."

"Then let's make a bargain," Grandmother said, standing up straighter still. "You will have my permission to take the cat. In exchange, you will never again set foot in this house, nor will you take or harm anyone or anything else now inside these walls."

The fairies exchanged glances. There was a long silence. Rain clattered against the roof and streamed down the windows. The fairies seemed to have a wordless conversation. Then Jack shrugged and Fig tilted her head as if an agreement had been made.

"All right then, human," Jack said, a smirk playing on his lips. "We accept your terms. But you should know, we don't have to take what is already ours. She will seek us out when she's ready."

In perfect synchronicity, the fairies both looked at Nelly. A chill ran up her neck. Her scalp prickled. Then came a burst of white powder. It was all Nelly could see.

"Check your pocket," a voice whispered.

Everything went dark.

CHAPTER TEN

THE GRUDGE

Nelly woke up. There was sunlight on her face. She was back in her room, in her own bed, covered in white powder. She sat up and the powder spilled from her hair like sand.

Memories cascaded back. Voices in the closet ... intruders ... the cat ... the destroyed hallway ... Grandmother ... fairies ...

The powder tickled her nose. She sneezed. When she blinked her eyes open, the powder had vanished completely. *Again.* More than that, Nelly realized, her bedroom, which she had watched the fairies (*fairies!*) wreck last night, was now entirely back to normal. Her bookshelf was upright, and her books were in their proper places. Her desk, side table, and lamp were all exactly where they should be. Even her cheval glass mirror, which she thought had shattered, stood in one piece next to her nightstand. There were no colorful stains on the walls or the ceiling or on her duvet. It looked as though all that went on last night had never happened.

Could it have been a dream? Nelly rubbed her face. She was

in bed, under her covers, in her pajamas. Her room wasn't a disaster. She felt groggy. It had to have been a dream.

But what about that powder? It had been all over her only a second ago. It had felt real. Could she have imagined it? Could she have imagined it all? Could she be losing her mind?

Nelly got out of bed.

"Last night was a dream," she pronounced to herself. She must have dreamed the powder, too. She had been in that foggy place between sleep and awake where dreams feel real. That was all.

She glimpsed herself in the mirror as a shaft of sunlight from the window lit up her hair in a thousand white-gold strands. Her skin and eyes had a shimmery glow.

She's one of us, the fairies had said.

Nelly shook the memory away and turned away from the mirror. She noticed something sticking out from under the leg of her nightstand. She tipped the weighty antique back with some effort and pulled a slip of paper from under it. It was the paper she had taken from her father's room in the psych ward, the word *Revenge* written on it in jagged pencil.

She felt a chill.

How did this find its way under the leg of her very heavy nightstand? It couldn't have moved on its own. Nelly stopped herself mid-thought. She was going to drive herself crazy if she kept thinking like this. She slid the paper under her mirror frame.

Just a dream, Nelly repeated in a mantra as she got dressed and brushed her teeth, and then wandered down the hallway in search of the cat.

The hallway looked as it always did. No footprints or paw prints anywhere. Framed photos of dead Morighans hung perfectly level along the walls. *Because it was all a dream*, Nelly told herself for the hundredth time.

A man's voice echoed from the main floor. It was Mr. Glanville. He was back from his birdwatching trip, Nelly supposed, and chatting with Grandmother over breakfast.

"Yes, I know this is the Morighan farm," Mr. Glanville said, his voice rising, sharp and tense. "Are you suggesting I don't know where I am?"

Nelly paused at the top of the stairs.

"I don't care!" Mr. Glanville shouted. "I don't care how much it costs, just get an ambulance here now!"

Ambulance? Nelly bolted down the stairs.

Mr. Glanville was in the front hall, shouting expletives into his phone. Dread twisted inside her as she ran past him and into the living room.

The room showed no sign of the chaos Nelly remembered from her dream. Everything was just as it should be. Everything except Grandmother.

The old woman sat in Mr. Glanville's favorite green armchair, the same one that the fairy, Fig, had sat in last night. But something was wrong. Grandmother sat still as a corpse in her nightgown and housecoat. Her skin was waxy, and her eyes were empty, as empty as Nelly's father's eyes always looked.

"Grandmother," Nelly said under her breath as she rushed over.

Grandmother didn't react, didn't acknowledge Nelly at all. She only stared ahead in a far-off way, as if transfixed by something only she could see. Nelly waved a hand in front of Grandmother's face. No reaction. Grandmother, her spirit, her consciousness, the thing that made her *her*, did not seem to be there anymore.

She was gone.

Tears rose in Nelly's eyes. Her leg brushed up against something. A sack of red berries sat on the floor next to the armchair. The berries were in the sack, not in a messy streak across the floor, as her dream told her they had been last night. On top of the sack sat a pair of kitchen shears.

Nelly reached for the shears. OUCH! She pulled her hand back and held her fingers. Before she had even touched the shears, she'd received a static shock.

As she looked back into Grandmother's blank eyes, the truth shivered through her like a discordant note of music. *What happened last night was no dream. It was real. Fairies were real. And they had taken Grandmother.*

Nelly put her hand on Grandmother's bony wrist.

Grandmother gasped.

Her eyes went wide with terror.

She looked directly at Nelly. "Diary!"

"Grandmother," Nelly said, squeezing the old woman's hand. "It's OK. Don't try to speak."

"Did she say something?" Mr. Glanville called, dropping the phone and rushing over.

"Diary," Grandmother croaked again, seeming to struggle to get the word out. "Find Roger ... Get the diary ..."

Mr. Glanville muscled Nelly aside and put his hands on Grandmother's face. "Moira! Moira! Can you hear me?"

But Grandmother was no longer there. Her face had gone slack, empty once more.

The next few hours were a blur. There was the wail of an ambulance. There were nervous-looking EMTs in the farmhouse, and Grandmother on a stretcher. There was the waiting room of the Nought County General Hospital. There was test after test after test.

Finally, a doctor approached Mr. Glanville in the buzzing

white waiting room. He said the tests had all come up nega-
tive, which was a good thing, but that Grandmother's symptoms suggested a possible mental disturbance. He wanted to
keep her for observation in the psych ward.

That night Nelly paced her bedroom. She went over everything
that had happened, or that she thought had happened, over
the last couple of days. She decided she couldn't afford to keep
doubting herself. She had to assume that her encounters with
the fairies were real. After all, if they weren't real, she, Nelly,
was losing her mind and none of it mattered. But if they were
real, then she was the only one who knew about them. She was
Grandmother's only hope.

Find Roger. Get the diary, Grandmother had said. What did
that mean? Nelly didn't know anyone named Roger. She looked
out the window at the Morighan House, black and still. The
fairies would know. They were responsible for all of this. They
could fix it.

Nelly made a decision. First thing in the morning, she
would go back to the Morighan House and confront the fairies.
She considered going over there right now, in the dark, with
her cell phone for a flashlight. But the thought of facing the
fairies and the Morighan House alone at night was almost too
frightening to contemplate, the type of thing people did in
horror movies right before they were eaten alive. No, it was
better to wait until daylight, she told herself. But when
daylight came, things did not go as planned.

Nelly was up and dressed first thing. She made her way
quietly down the stairs and into the kitchen. But just as she
was about to slip out the back door, Mr. Glanville stopped her.

He was a kind man and meant well, though Nelly never quite knew what to say to him. They didn't have much in common. She made awkward small talk with him before he told her, in his gentle manner, that he would be driving her to school within the hour.

"—B-But what about Grandmother?" Nelly said, panic rising inside her. After everything that had happened with the fairies and Grandmother, she had completely forgotten about school. Her fears about the Priory House seemed so trivial now. She had bigger problems.

But Mr. Glanville didn't agree. He shook his otter-like head. "There's nothing you can do for your grandmother now, Nelly. She's being well taken care of at the hospital. This is the best thing for you. And as I'm sure you know, it's what Moira would want."

An hour later, Nelly stood at the gates of the Priory House School, dressed in a dismal gray uniform, surrounded by suit-cases. She had tried desperately to come up with some reason, some excuse to stay on the farm and out of school, some ratio-nale that didn't involve soul-stealing fairies. But nothing came to mind, nothing that would convince Mr. Glanville.

The Priory House loomed overhead. It was a converted 19th-century monastery with stone walls, stained-glass windows, and a bell tower dripping with ivy. It was Nought County's only prep school and a point of pride for people in the area, the kind of place students competed to get into. But to Nelly, it might as well have been a prison.

She gazed up at the eight-foot perimeter wall and its locking wrought iron fence. It was a forty-five-minute drive between here and the farm. Even if she could get past this wall, she didn't have a car or a license, for that matter. How was she going to confront the fairies now?

The groundskeeper met Nelly at the gate. He was an odd-looking man with a bush of hair under his nose and none on his head. He took her bags and gave her directions to the principal's office.

"She wants to see you," he said, his face grave.

Nelly made her way through the crowded hallways of the main school building, trying her best to follow the groundskeeper's vague directions. Several students shot her glaring looks as they whispered back and forth.

She had a pretty good idea of what they were saying. But for once, she couldn't bring herself to blame them. If nothing else, what had happened at the farm over the past few days had proven to her that something very wrong *was* going on and it was tied somehow to her and her family. The other students were right to be wary. They were right to stay away.

After several wrong turns, Nelly finally found the principal's office on the second floor of the school's west section. Men in construction boots, followed by a harried-looking secretary, were just leaving the office as Nelly arrived. The secretary told Nelly the principal was expecting her and then hurried after the men, calling for them to wait and waving a sheaf of paperwork in the air.

Nelly knocked.

"What is it?" a woman's voice snapped.

Nelly cleared her throat, suddenly nervous. "It's Nelly. Nelly Morighan," she said through the door.

There was a pause.

"Come in," the voice said finally.

Nelly entered. The room was dreary. Light struggled through the vines outside that had grown over the room's stained-glass windows. The dim light quivered over stark, corporate furniture that was out of place in a room that had probably once belonged to the monastery's abbot. There was a faded imprint of a large cross on the wall, partially covered by a generic motivational print that read *Building a Better Safer Tomorrow*.

The principal stood with her back to Nelly near an arched doorway that led to an adjacent room. She still hadn't looked at Nelly and seemed to be typing on her phone.

Nelly patted down her gray uniform, and her nerves, as she waited to be acknowledged. The second hand on the wall clock was ticking away. At this rate, Nelly would be late for her first class. The last thing she needed was to draw more attention to herself. She cleared her throat. The principal continued to tap on her phone.

Nelly folded her arms. She was starting to wonder if this woman was deliberately making her wait.

Finally, the older woman turned around.

Nelly felt the blood drain from her face.

She had met this woman before, at the start of the summer, in Nought County General's psych ward. The principal was Orson Kennedy's mother.

"Good morning, Miss Morighan," Orson's mother said, her face a solemn mask. Nelly uncrossed her arms and dropped them to her sides.

"Have a seat," the middle-aged woman added, pointing toward the single chair in front of an imposing executive desk. The name plate sitting on the desk read *Virginia Kennedy*. Nelly noticed with a sinking feeling that beside it sat a framed photo of Orson as a child, right about the age he had been when Nelly struck him.

Nelly did as she was told. After a brief pause, Orson's mother sat down across from Nelly on the other side of the desk. She looked very different here at the Priory House than she had at the psych ward. There she had been frazzled, panicked, her hair disheveled, her eyes wild. But here she was the picture of stern composure, dressed in a tidy cream blouse and black skirt, her dark hair pinned in a sleek coil.

Without ever making eye contact, she opened a laptop.

The silence was increasingly uncomfortable. Nelly wondered what she could say as the tension grew. Everything she came up with involved Orson and apologies that made her squirm. Should she apologize? She had hit him, but she was only a kid at the time, and she couldn't possibly be responsible for his current state ... could she? The fairies had done something to Grandmother that had landed *her* in the psych ward.

She's one of us, the fairies had said about Nelly. She looked down at her own hand, the one she had struck Orson with, and rubbed it. She was feeling very fuzzy about a lot of things at the moment.

Ms. Kennedy broke the silence. "We have something in common."

Nelly looked up at Ms. Kennedy and raised her eyebrows.

"We are both newcomers to this school," the principal went on, still looking at her computer screen. "Like you, this will be my first year at the Priory House."

Nelly smiled and nodded politely.

"And yet I have a suspicion we bring with us very different things," Ms. Kennedy continued.

What did that mean? Nelly wondered.

"You missed the first day of classes and yesterday's welcome assembly," Ms. Kennedy went on, her voice terse. "You are already behind. Not a good start."

"I couldn't be here yesterday," Nelly said, speaking up. "My grandmother—"

"I am not asking for excuses," Ms. Kennedy cut in. Then, for the first time, she looked Nelly in the eyes. For a fleeting moment, anger flashed there and something like contempt.

"I'm going to be frank with you, Miss Morighan," the principal began as she straightened items on her desk, "a great many strings were pulled with the board to have you admitted to this school. Had I held this position at the time, I never would have allowed it. You are not the kind of student normally accepted at the Priory House."

There was a look of disdain on Ms. Kennedy's face now as she glanced back at the laptop screen. "Grades? Unremarkable. Distinguishing abilities or accomplishments? Nothing of note. If Gilbert Glanville hadn't greased the wheels for you, so to speak, this conversation would not be happening."

Nelly felt heat surge into her cheeks. *Conversation? This wasn't a conversation. It was an attack.*

Ms. Kennedy leaned back in her chair. "The board hired me to make changes at this school, to build a safe and secure learning environment, to clear out the cobwebs and chase out the, *ahem*, ghosts. Is that understood?"

"Not really," Nelly said, too quickly.

One of Ms. Kennedy's penciled eyebrows shot up. "Whether you like it or not, you and your family represent everything wrong with the town of Nothing, with the whole county: a backward way of thinking that breeds superstition and ... disturbances. Well, at the Priory House, those old ways are done. Rest assured, Miss Morighan, if your presence here endangers the mental or emotional safety of any of my students, you will be out of here so fast, pardon the reference, it will make your head spin. Is that understood?"

Mental or emotional safety? Nelly thought, angry blood pulsing in her ears. The other students already hated her. They thought she was some sort of cursed ghost-magnet! How was she supposed to avoid threatening their mental and emotional safety?

"That's impossible," Nelly said, getting the feeling that Ms. Kennedy held a personal grudge against her. "I have no control over other people's emotions."

"Words can wound," Ms. Kennedy said, leaning forward and glaring at Nelly with almost as much intensity as the fairies had. "And so can toxic gestures or aggressions, no matter how small. Work on controlling those."

Nelly crossed her arms. *No wrong words or gestures?* It sounded like Ms. Kennedy wanted Nelly as silent and invisible as the "ghosts" she was trying to eradicate.

"Mr. Glanville informed me you play the violin," Ms. Kennedy said, changing the subject so suddenly that it almost did make Nelly's head spin.

"Uh, yeah, I do," Nelly stammered out. "I mean, I play a few instruments, but yes, the violin. I play it, sometimes."

"No one likes a bragger," Ms. Kennedy muttered, tapping at her computer, and Nelly's face went hot again. The printer revved up nearby and started shooting out pages.

"We have an audition process here for music classes," the principal continued. "The music teacher likes to separate the students into three classes based on skill: basic, intermediate, and advanced." Ms. Kennedy pulled the pages from the printer and handed them to Nelly. "There, you'll find all the information you need about the auditions and your classes. You've missed a whole day, and it looks like you'll be late for your first class today as well. I'm afraid that means detention."

Detention? This was so ridiculously unfair that Nelly wanted to shout at Ms. Kennedy. But she restrained herself. She had a request to make of the principal, and shouting was not the best way to go about it.

"Er, OK, but Ms. Kennedy?" Nelly said, rolling her agenda

into a tight tube on her lap. "I know I'm supposed to stay here full time, but I was wondering if I could go back to the farm this weekend to visit Mr. Glanville and ... and see my grandmother. She's in the hospital."

This was Nelly's only hope. It meant waiting until the weekend to look for the fairies and risking the possibility that they might be gone by then. But there was no way Ms. Kennedy or Mr. Glanville would allow Nelly to leave school in the middle of the week.

Ms. Kennedy pursed her lips. "I'll consider it if you attend detention without complaint, get to the rest of your classes on time, and keep your nose clean."

Nelly had a feeling this was going to be easier said than done but nodded anyway. "I will. Thank you."

Ms. Kennedy looked away and Nelly took this as a cue to leave. But as she crossed to the door, the principal stopped her.

"Nelly," she said and seemed to be inwardly debating. "Did ... did my son say something to you in the hospital the day you were there?"

Now it was Nelly's turn to debate. Orson had spoken to her. *It's your fault. You let them in*, he had said. But she couldn't tell Ms. Kennedy that.

Insides twisting with guilt, Nelly shook her head.

Ms. Kennedy looked at her computer again. "Be informed, the bell tower on the far end of the north range is under renovation. Students are forbidden from entering it. That is all."

Nelly wanted to say something. She wanted to say she was sorry about Orson.

Say it, she told herself, but the words wouldn't come out.

She turned and left the room.

CHAPTER ELEVEN

THE PRIORY HOUSE

The Priory House was roughly laid out like a giant cross with north, east, south, and west wings, or ranges, that branched around a central assembly space called Chapter Hall. Nelly's classes were spread out in the worst possible way. She had a class on the top floor of the north range, then one on the bottom floor, far end of the south range, then one on the top far end of the west range, then one on the bottom far end of the east range. She had to run between classes to make up the ground between them on time. And running wasn't permitted in the halls.

As Nelly sped through the corridors, slowing down whenever she spotted a teacher, she wondered if Ms. Kennedy had had a hand in orchestrating this marathon of a schedule. Ms. Kennedy was Orson's mother, and she clearly blamed Nelly in some way for her son's condition. This schedule and Nelly's immediate, unforgiving placement in detention felt like revenge.

Nelly barely spoke a word to anyone for the rest of the day. The other students avoided her as if she had a contagious disease. They cleared paths for her in the corridors, which actually helped her get to her classes on time. She heard the name *Morighan* hissed like an accusation as she dashed past packs of students chatting and laughing easily amongst themselves, like members of private clubs; clubs she could never hope to join.

The long, dimly lit corridors were an incongruous combination of arched, stained-glass windows, faded Christian iconography, and garish posters with platitudes like *Teamwork Makes the Dream Work, Today is a Chance to be Better*, and *We All Belong Here. Except if your last name is Morighan*, Nelly thought bitterly. She also noticed the sign-up forms for the Student Safety Patrol, a gang of student volunteers tasked with reporting anything "unsafe" to the principal. *Spies for Ms. Kennedy*, Nelly thought, feeling like the entire school was primed against her.

By far, Nelly's most hated class was history. It was in the north range, within spitting distance of the under-renovation bell tower. The constant sounds of hammering, drilling, buzz saws, and electric sanders made it impossible to concentrate. On top of this, Nelly's old nemesis, Alexis Abner, was in the class, along with Bianca Lim.

Bianca, looking drab and diminished in the Priory House's grays, had wasted no time in making a scene after spotting Nelly in the corridor before class. It was the first time either of them had seen each other since the drive home from the city.

"So, you finally found the guts to show your face after avoiding me all day yesterday!" Bianca spat at Nelly just outside their classroom.

"I wasn't even here yesterday," Nelly shot back.

"Too scared to face me? You got me transferred out of Mountain Wood," Bianca said. "It's your fault I'm in this stupid school!"

"We're both in this stupid school because you—" Nelly had been about to blurt out, *because you gave my diaries to my grandmother*. But she stopped herself. A crowd was forming, and she didn't want to give Bianca a reason to tell people the contents of those diaries. She turned her back on Bianca instead and marched into class.

"Because I what?" Bianca called after her and scoffed. "I've been nothing but nice to this girl and this is the thanks I get? Seriously?" she added to whoever would listen.

Seriously? Nelly thought, clenching her jaw. *Bianca had to be the least self-aware person on the planet.*

The history teacher, Mr. Haley, made a valiant effort to keep the class's attention over the construction noise, without much success. A group of girls seated at the back of the class, which included Bianca and Alexis, quickly began gossiping and snickering among themselves while several boys started a game of tossing bits of broken eraser at each other when Mr. Haley's back was turned. Nelly sat silently near the door, her mind occupied with thoughts of the fairies and how she was going to convince them to undo whatever they had done to Grandmother.

"Miss Morighan!" a voice said.

Nelly looked up from her desk.

Mr. Haley was scowling at her. Behind him, on the whiteboard, the words LOCAL HISTORY were written in blue.

"Er ... what was the question?" Nelly asked sheepishly.

Mr. Haley let out an exasperated sigh while Bianca and Alexis snickered. Nelly felt her face go hot.

"I asked about the history of the Morighan family," Mr. Haley said.

The history of the Morighan family? The curse ... the supposedly haunted farm ... mad, missing, or six feet under ... Mr. Haley didn't really expect Nelly to address these things, right here, in front of the whole class, did he?

"The Morighans were one of Nothing's first families, were they not?" Mr. Haley went on. "The Morighans, the Glanvilles, the Pipes, the Abners, and the Kennedys were Nothing's first five families. Together, they founded the town all the way back in 1815. What can you tell me about the Morighan family and how they lived back then?"

"–I-In 1815?" Nelly stammered.

Alexis Abner's hand shot up. Now that Nelly had been singled out, Alexis was suddenly paying attention. Alexis was petite and mousy looking with long brown hair, an upturned nose, and a pointed face. She had been the most popular girl in Nelly's class in middle school, where the other kids had all seemed to crave her approval (except for Bianca, who was a force on her own). Nelly could never figure out why this was. Alexis was moody and could be kind one minute and cruel the next. She seemed to be an even worse friend than she was an enemy.

Mr. Haley called on her.

"I know that at first Nothing was an agricultural settlement," Alexis said in a know-it-all voice. "One of my ancestors, Robert F. Abner, was the town's first resident and mayor."

Mr. Haley nodded approval. And then he launched into a lecture about small-town life in the 1800s, the way people dressed and spoke, their superstitions and beliefs.

Mr. Haley was a young teacher. He looked to be about thirty and was remarkably good-looking. Hangdog eyes, a mess of dark hair, a stubbly face, and the hint of a tattoo peeking out from under one of his rolled-up sleeves gave him the look of a rockstar or an actor playing a teacher in a movie. Earlier, Nelly overheard a giggly girl whisper that he was in a band. That same girl was now gazing at Mr. Haley with a dreamy smile on her face, and she wasn't the only one.

As the class wore on, Nelly noticed something else about Mr. Haley. As he spoke, delivering his lecture in a booming voice to be heard over the construction sounds, he would frequently pause to glare at her, Nelly, his eyes cold and accusing. He looked as if he completely disapproved of her and wanted her to know it.

Nelly looked down at her books and told herself she was imagining things. And even if she wasn't, yet another person at this school who had it out for her didn't merit much thought.

At the end of what felt like the longest day of her life, capped by an hour in the gloomy detention hall, she trudged across damp grass toward Maple Hall, her dormitory on the far west side of the grounds.

Maple Hall was one of several structures clustered around the main building. These dormitories had been built long after the monastery, but matched its style, with arches and stained glass and stone, each surrounded by trees. But no matter how charming the architecture, no matter how much green there was on the grounds, Nelly could only see the place as hopelessly confining, dull, and gray.

Inside Maple Hall, Nelly scaled the stairs toward her third-floor dorm room. She paused on the landing to gaze out an arched window. From this spot she could see, beyond the trees and the open grounds, the fast-moving river Nought. This river, wide in places, ran past the town of Nothing and farther along, through the old forest situated behind the Morighan farm. If only she had a boat, a canoe, anything to take her there.

Nelly walked the long corridor toward her room, recalling with a defeated sigh that Grandmother had arranged for Nelly and Bianca to share a room. *Because they were such good friends.*

Much to Nelly's relief, Bianca wasn't there, though she clearly had been and had made herself at home. One side of the room, Nelly's side, was simple and plain—white walls, a single bed, a side table, and a lamp next to Nelly's luggage pile and her violin. The other side of the room looked like a strutting social media post sprung to life. The color scheme was dusty pink trimmed with gold. A sheer pink canopy draped from the ceiling to cascade over Bianca's bed, which was bursting with patterned pillows and cozy throw blankets. On her desk, a golden lamp lit up a neat stack of books and her school supplies. And on the wall, three cream-painted open shelves had been installed. These held a collection of matching pots of ivy and mini succulents, several candles, and frames of various sizes that held photos of Bianca with her family or friends. Strings of fairy lights completed the look.

It was lovely, Nelly had to admit.

She recognized some of the photos from the apartment she and Bianca had shared in the city. Bianca looked so happy in them and loved. Nelly suppressed an urge to take them all down and hide them in a drawer.

Bianca didn't make an appearance until just before lights out. This suited Nelly just fine. They didn't speak a word to each other or even make eye contact.

Later that night, as the Priory House slept and Bianca snored under her lovely canopy, Nelly lay in bed awake. Her mind raced with thoughts of the fairies. Staring at a splash of moonlight on the ceiling, she kept replaying what had happened with them over the last couple of days, trying to remember everything, no matter how insignificant.

"You will never again set foot in this house, nor will you take or harm anything or anyone else now inside these walls," Grandmother had said. And the fairies had agreed. They had promised!

Nelly wondered bitterly if it was a good idea to accuse the fairies of being liars when she saw them again. *If* she saw them again.

Then she sat up.

She had remembered something else.

Check your pocket, the fairies said.

CHAPTER TWELVE

THE MYSTERY OF THE MAPLE KEYS

Nelly tore through her luggage, searching for the pajamas she had worn the other night. When Mr. Glanville told her he was packing her off to school, she had jammed a few extra things into one suitcase, including those pajamas.

They were green; they were plaid; they were ... there!

Nelly smoothed out the pajamas and shoved her hand into one pocket.

She pulled out ... a maple key?

A maple key. Every year, hundreds of these twirled from Nothing's maple trees like little green helicopters. But they didn't normally make their way into people's pockets.

She checked the other pocket and found three more maple keys. Was this a message?

The fairy Jack had held out a maple key in Nelly's bedroom the other night. What had he said? *Good neighbors share keys.* What was that supposed to mean?

On a hunch, Nelly shoved her hands into the pockets of the pajamas she was wearing now ... and pulled out more maple keys. She got up and checked the pockets of her school dress pants, her cardigans, her jackets, every piece of clothing she had with pockets. Maple keys, maple keys, maple keys.

Was this some sort of a joke?

The next day, Nelly was groggy from lack of sleep, her walk from class to class sluggish. She'd put the maple keys back in her pockets where she had found them only because she couldn't think what else to do with them.

She arrived late for the music class auditions. Violin in hand, she stood outside the room's double metal doors as a trumpet hooted on the other side. On tiptoe, she peered through one of the doors' high windows. The place was packed with students and their variously sized and shaped instruments. Her stomach roiled. Did she really have to audition in front of all those people? She was good at the violin. Alone, she had practiced this instrument, and a few others, hours a day every day since she turned five. But the prospect of playing in front of others paralyzed her.

The trumpeting stopped. Tepid applause followed. She seized the moment to slip into the room and avoid notice. Only a few disinterested heads sent looks her way. Then *WHAM*! The heavy door crashed shut behind her. Now the entire room looked at her. No one made a sound. An elderly man with disorganized wisps of white hair and leaky wet eyes sat at a desk at the front of the sloping, stadium-style room. He adjusted his glasses and peered up at Nelly.

"You are late," he said, his voice carrying with the room's acoustics.

"I'm so sorry, I was, um—" Nelly started, but the man, who must have been the music teacher, cut her off.

"I don't need the excuses, just your name."

Nelly's pulse pounded in her ears. "Nelly Morighan."

Heads leaned together and whispering broke out around the room.

"Fine," the music teacher said. "Since you're late, you have the honor of playing last. Better make it good. Well, don't keep us all waiting. Come down here. There's an empty seat right here in the front row."

Nelly felt like she was going to be sick. She made her way down the steps to the bottom of the room, hundreds of eyes on her, the whispering getting louder as she descended.

The music teacher frowned and clanged a pointer stick against the side of his desk. "We listen with our ears, not with our mouths," he said as Nelly slid herself into the free seat. "NEXT!"

A nervous-looking boy with a lank of dark hair made his way to the front of the room carrying a bass guitar. In a quiet voice, he said his name was Grady Pipes and he would play a jazz standard.

Nelly was grateful that Grady was now the center of attention. He was pretty good, she thought as he launched into his piece, though he messed up a few times. Nelly knew Grady from middle school. They were the same age and had been in the same class, but she didn't think they had ever actually spoken. Grady had been one of the quiet kids, tagging along unnoticed after the confident, commanding boys like Orson Kennedy. A pleasant feeling of heat rose into Nelly's cheeks as she watched Grady play. She had never noticed how cute he was. He had dark, floppy hair and slate-blue eyes. His glasses kept sliding down his nose in an awkwardly attractive way.

The music teacher raised a hand for Grady to stop. "Intermediate," he pronounced. "NEXT!" Grady looked disappointed but walked off stage without protest.

As the audition wore on, each student shuffled to the front of the room when their name was called, played a few bars of music, and waited for the teacher to announce "Basic," "Intermediate," or "Advanced," before they returned to their seats. It was almost an hour later before the teacher called out Nelly's name.

She stood up, awash in dread. Even facing down the fairies was preferable to this. She didn't think she could do it. She could hardly play for one person, let alone a room full of people who had tormented her in middle school.

She stepped to the front and stammered the name of the piece she was about to play, Dvorak's "Humoresque," a piece she knew she had mastered. It was one of the few pieces Grandmother let her practice around the farmhouse.

The music teacher looked her over with his watery eyes and told her that her choice was ambitious. She heard a smattering of giggles from the class and looked up to see Alexis Abner sitting next to Grady Pipes, her hand resting on his arm. Any confidence Nelly had drained away.

"Anytime now, Miss Morighan," the teacher said.

Her mouth was sandpaper dry. The rushing sound in her ears was back. She raised her bow to her violin, hands trembling, sweat gumming up her armpits. She started to play. But not well. Her hands would just not cooperate, and instead of the melody, all she could hear was that rushing noise in her ears, and the thumping of her heart. She was only a few bars in when the teacher shouted out, "INTERMEDIATE!"

She stopped.

She was disappointed in herself. She knew she should have been in the advanced class. But she was relieved at the same time. The audition was over.

The teacher dismissed the class, and the room started

buzzing with chatter and movement. Nelly grabbed her things for a fast exit.

As she weaved her way through the crowd of students and up the stairs to the doors, a heavy backpack flew out of nowhere and hit her full in the face.

Nelly stumbled back, dropping her violin case. Through smarting tears, she could see Alexis holding the backpack and smirking.

"Oopsie didn't see you," Alexis said, with a grin that shouted fake apology. She heaved up her backpack as if nothing had happened and sauntered out of the room. Grady Pipes followed Alexis like a fish on a hook. He didn't so much as glance at Nelly and was now looking a lot less adorable than he had a few minutes earlier.

Her cheek throbbed. Walking out into the corridor, Nelly glared after Alexis. The mousy girl's brown hair, tied up in a high ponytail, swung back and forth like a pendulum as she talked and laughed with a small entourage. Alexis had always hated Nelly with more ferocity than any of her other middle school classmates. Why? There had to be more to her particular brand of hatred than just the town's superstitions.

The rest of the day went by surprisingly fast. Nelly kept her head down and her nose clean, as Ms. Kennedy had instructed. She went to all her classes, did her homework, and spent every spare minute in the library researching fairies on the internet. She intended to be prepared when next she met the fairies. Information was power. The trouble with the internet was that there was too much information. How could she sift through it all and separate facts, if there were any, from fiction?

Some tidbits online rang true, given what she had just been through. Fairies hated iron. That was probably why Fig had reacted so violently to Grandmother's kitchen shears. Rowan berries were connected to fairies in some way she didn't yet understand. Nelly got no results when she searched the keywords "Roger," "diary," and "fairies" together. But it was a long shot.

She pulled one of the maple keys from her pocket and held it up to a library table lamp. It looked like any old maple key. She put it down on the table and tried an even longer shot: typing the words "maple keys" and "fairies" into a search engine.

No results.

She looked up from her research and took a break. The setting sun was sending splotches of color wheel lights through the library's stained-glass windows. She sat entranced by the quivering colors, her laptop and pile of fairy books forgotten for the moment. But soon, her dreamy reverie was squashed. Two girls she didn't know pulled out chairs and sat across from her, looking straight at her.

"Fairieeees?" one girl said in a not-in-a-library voice, picking up one of Nelly's books. The librarian's head swiveled toward their table and then back to her screen.

"Uh, yeah," Nelly said, shutting her laptop. "I'm ... writing an essay."

"Nelly Morighan, right?" the other girl said, only slightly less loud.

Nelly nodded. She didn't like where this was going.

The girl holding one of the fairy books dropped it on the table. "I'm Ramona. Ramona Abner. Alexis's sister."

Nelly stared at her. *Ramona Abner?* She had been a year behind Nelly in middle school. Back then the younger girl had glasses, straggly pigtails, and a mouth that seemed to sprout braces. She still had the glasses, but her hair had been cropped short and dyed lime green. The braces were gone and the only metal now showing was a nose ring.

"This is Gwen Praveen," Ramona said, indicating her companion, a pretty girl with large dark eyes and short, spiky black hair. This girl flashed Nelly a nervous smile.

"Don't worry, we hate my sister, too," Ramona said.

"I do not hate your sister," Nelly said, sitting back. "She hates me."

"Yeah," Ramona said, twirling a filament from her green bangs. "She's like that."

"So ..." Gwen said, after a dangling silence. "What do you think of the Priory House?"

"Not much," Nelly said with zero hesitation.

The two girls laughed.

Okay, this is weird, Nelly thought. She had the feeling that they were sucking up to her.

"It must be so cool coming from such a well-known family," Gwen blurted.

Ramona kicked Gwen under the table.

"Well, not like *cool*," Gwen added. "I mean strange, you know, with all the rumors and stuff. It's like, mysterious, which is kind of cool, I guess, and um ... you know ..."

Nelly wasn't sure what to make of this, but her instincts were telling her to get away from these two. She started packing up her things.

"We don't mean to offend you or anything," Ramona said, putting her cell phone on the table. "We're just curious. We wanted to ask you a few questions about your family."

Nelly stared hard at Ramona. "What about my fam—"

Ramona cut her off. "Do you think they really are cursed? I mean, a lot of strange things have happened to them. How many have ended up in mental institutions? Like, so many, right? And what about all the ones who went missing, or—"

"Wait," Nelly said, feeling her face heat up. "I don't want to talk about—"

"Is it true the Morighan farm is haunted?" Gwen chimed in. "I heard the paranormal activity there is, like, off the charts. Have you ever experienced anything, you know, supernatural?"

"Have you thought of inviting psychics or ghost hunters to your farm to do an investigation?" Ramona said. "That could answer a ton of questions."

"Have you ever been inside the Morighan House?" asked Gwen. "I heard it's like the epicenter of all the hauntings in the entire county."

"I heard it's some kind of gateway to hell," Ramona said with a tiny laugh that trailed off into seriousness.

Nelly sat back in her chair. Though she had lived in Nothing all her life and knew what the rumors were, she had never had the townspeople's superstitions shoveled at her all at once like this. It was disconcerting. Now that she had met the fairies and was wondering how superstitious any of it really was, it was even more disconcerting.

Ramona leaned toward Nelly. "You probably don't know this, but a lot of people say the Morighans themselves attract paranormal activity. Like wherever there's a Morighan, there's some kind of haunting going on."

Nelly did know this and had always thought it was ridiculous.

"That's why Nought County Hospital is supposed to be so haunted, right?" Gwen said in a hushed voice. "'Cause your dad's there."

Nelly felt a jab of irritation. "My dad's got nothing to do with—"

"And now that your grandmother's there, too, it'll probably be even worse," Ramona cut in.

A flame of anger grew inside Nelly. Grandmother was in the hospital, and this was what these girls had to say to her about it?

"How do you know my grandmother's in the hospital?"

"And now that *you're* at this school," Gwen said, ignoring Nelly's question, "weird things have already started to happen. Everyone's talking about it."

"That's because out of all the Morighans, you're supposed to be the worst," Ramona said, pushing her phone toward Nelly. "You're like paranormal catnip, they say. Seems like it might be true. Last year, when you were out of town, there was hardly any paranormal activity in Nothing at all, but now that you're back, well ..."

Nelly smacked her hand down on the table harder than she meant to. The gesture had the intended effect. The girls stopped talking.

Then the faint scent of burning wood rose in the air.

Nelly's eyes flashed down to the table, where she noticed two things at once. Tendrils of smoke were curling up between her fingers, and a tiny red light was beaming from Ramona's phone.

"Are ... are you recording this?" Nelly asked.

Ramona's neck was reddening. "Yeah, see, we're actually freshman reporters with the *Priory Herald*. That's the school newspaper. It's our first article, and we wanted to make a splash. We figured with you at the school and all the weirdness, everyone would be curious, so ..."

"We were gonna ask permission," Gwen cut in.

"Oh yeah? When exactly?" Nelly asked, her voice coming out loud enough to draw a sharper look from the librarian.

"Don't get pissed," Ramona said. "We assumed you'd say

yes. Why wouldn't you? It's not like you have anything to hide, right?"

Ramona now looked like a miniature version of Alexis. Nelly shoved herself away from the table, grabbed her laptop and backpack, and marched toward the exit.

"No wonder she hasn't got any friends," Ramona said as Nelly pushed open the library door.

Nelly left the room without looking back, hoping neither of the girls would notice the burn mark her hand had left on the library table.

CHAPTER THIRTEEN

PETTY REVENGE

A dismal wet mist covered the school grounds when Nelly awoke the next morning. She took one look at it through her dorm room window and wanted to crawl right back into bed. She felt as gloomy as the weather. She'd woken up frequently throughout the night, her mind working to convince herself that she really hadn't burned the library table with her palm. Those little coils of smoke between her fingers hadn't been smoke at all, but a swirl of dust illuminated in the late afternoon sunlight. As for the burn mark on the table, it had probably been there for years. None of these explanations did much to reassure her.

On the bright side, it was Thursday. *Two more days*, Nelly told herself. Two more days and she would be back on the farm. And then she would find the fairies, confront them, and get some answers. About everything.

Unfortunately, Thursday proved to be her most difficult yet at the Priory House.

Things started to go downhill on the way to history class. Nelly had a slow start that morning, not only because of her own reluctance to face the day but because Bianca had spent an inordinate amount of time in the bathroom styling her hair into a fishtail braid. Nelly ran full out across the foggy grounds to make it to her classroom at the top of the north range before the bell. The hammering of construction work ricocheted through the corridors as she ran, nursing a knife-like stitch in her side. Then she turned the corner to the north cloister and smacked right into Alexis.

"Ew, get off me," Alexis said and pushed Nelly backward. Immediately, heads turned, and voices whispered. Nelly heard her name and Alexis's name and the word *fight*. She glanced around. There were no teachers, but there were two students right in front of her with bright red Student Safety Patrol pins on their uniforms. One was Pauline Davis, a tall girl with long dark braids who was a loyal crony of Alexis's from middle school, and the other was Alexis herself. This wasn't a fight Nelly could win even if she had wanted to take it up. Eyes down, she took a wide circle around Alexis and Pauline.

"So pathetic," Alexis said as Nelly walked away.

Two more days, Nelly told herself. *Two more days.*

Then, during her afternoon music class, she unwittingly made the situation with Alexis worse. The music teacher, Mr. Nottingham, who the students had nicknamed "the sheriff," handed back the music theory exercises they had all submitted the day before. The sheriff did not look pleased. He either sighed or clucked his tongue as he went around the class, dropping assignments onto desks. He paused in front of Nelly's desk with her assignment still clutched in his bony fingers.

"Nelly Morighan," Mr. Nottingham said in his old and quavery voice. "You are the only member of this class to have received a satisfactory grade on this assignment."

He dropped her paper onto her desk. A large "A" was scrawled across the top. "Congratulations," he continued, his frown lifting. "If it weren't for you, I would have thought the *entire* class had been sleeping through my lectures this week. I haven't seen this kind of abysmal work in all my years of teaching. Each one of you except for Miss Morighan here will redo this assignment. In addition, you will each submit a four-hundred-word essay making solid arguments as to why music theory matters. Both are due next class."

The class groaned. A few rows behind Nelly, Alexis made a derisive sound and said, "Teacher's pet."

Big mistake. The sheriff turned his watery stare on her.

"Miss Abner, I must say I am surprised that you of all people should make light of this situation, considering your grade single-handedly tanked the class average. Perhaps if you took Miss Morighan's example and spent less time socializing and more time on your studies, you could astonish us all with a passing grade."

Ouch, Nelly thought with a twinge of satisfaction. After all, Alexis deserved it.

"Mr. Pipes," Mr. Nottingham said to Grady, who was sitting in his usual spot next to Alexis. "I think you are too much of a distraction for Miss Abner. You and Mr. Higuchi will switch seats."

Ken Higuchi was the skinny kid with a perpetually runny nose who sat next to Nelly. Alexis glared at Nelly with enough fury to wither a plant as Ken and Grady traded seats.

Nelly thought her face was probably flaming red as Grady sat down next to her. He looked at her over his glasses for an instant, a flash of baby blues, and then put his arm on the long desk they now shared. He was so close, Nelly could feel the warmth emanating from his arm next to hers. She could smell a faint scent of spruce-scented deodorant or shampoo.

In the seat behind her, a boy Nelly didn't know leaned forward and patted Grady on the shoulder. "Free at last," he muttered and darted a smirk in Alexis's direction. Alexis glared back and Nelly wondered if maybe things between Grady and Alexis weren't as sunny as they had initially appeared.

Nelly spent the rest of the class trying to come up with an excuse to speak to Grady. She could ask to borrow a pencil. But she was already holding one. She could ask him a question about music theory. But she had just received an A on her paper and he, presumably, had not. Nelly was so nervous at the thought of speaking to him that she was unconsciously jiggling her leg under the desk.

Then Grady spoke to her.

"Hey," he said, his voice a gentle tenor. Nelly looked into his eyes. They were as blue as beach glass. "Can you please stop shaking your leg? It's annoying."

Nelly felt heat surge up her neck and face. She stopped jiggling her leg. "Oh yeah, sorry," she muttered, feeling like a deflated balloon.

"Thanks," he said, smiled with grudging politeness, and looked away.

Nelly sank deeper into her seat, wishing she could disappear. Grady was friends with Alexis, she told herself, whether or not the pair were getting along, and he was from Nothing, which meant he had made his mind up about Nelly a long time ago. She should have known.

When the bell rang, Nelly got up immediately and tried for a quick exit. But Grady, in no hurry at all, blocked her way with his bulky bass guitar. *Now who's annoying?* Nelly thought.

Out in the corridor, Alexis stood with two other girls, relaxed and unhurried. Alexis's next class must have been nearby, not at the far end of the opposite range and three floors up like Nelly's was. She scowled. She recognized the other girls as Alexis's two closest friends from middle school, Pauline Davis, with her long, dark braids, and Charmaine Torres, a short, stocky girl who wore a ton of makeup. All three of them wore red Student Safety Patrol pins. This was a trio Nelly very much wanted to avoid. The only thing worse would be if Bianca was with them.

The hallway was jammed. Nelly tried to dart past the girls, but a hand grabbed her by the arm and stopped her. It was Alexis.

"We have to talk to you," Alexis said, leaning in close as if they were friends. "*In private.*"

Charmaine and Pauline appeared on the other side of Nelly. Charmaine held Nelly by her other arm. The three girls pressed in on Nelly and walked her forward at a brisk pace down the corridor.

"Why? What's this about?" Nelly asked, her mind racing through possibilities. Was she in trouble with the Student Safety Patrol? But she had done nothing wrong! At least she had done nothing a reasonable person would consider wrong. But Nelly knew these three. They weren't exactly reasonable.

"We'll tell you in a sec," Charmaine said. "In private."

Nelly didn't like the sound of this at all. She tried to pull away, but the girls had a firm grip and the momentum of their quick steps, with her squeezed between them, propelled her forward.

At the end of the corridor, the janitor's closet door stood open. They were heading right to it. The girls let go of Nelly all at once. She felt a shove. She stumbled forward into the janitor's closet. The door slammed behind her, plunging Nelly into darkness.

Nelly grabbed the door handle, twisting and pushing. It was locked. She pounded on the door with her fist. "Hey! Let me out!"

Laughter responded from outside.

Nelly stepped back from the door. Banging on it was only

going to entertain the girls outside. She sighed in exasperation. She was trapped in a janitor's closet. Again. And she knew exactly how Alexis had come up with this idea. *Thank you so very much, Bianca.*

She reached into her pocket for her cell phone. She could call the school and tell the secretary where she was. Then the secretary would page the groundskeeper over the loudspeaker, and he would come and open the door.

How humiliating.

And what would happen next? Nelly would be marched to the principal's office. Ms. Kennedy would ask how she, Nelly, had come to be locked in the janitor's closet. Nelly would tell the truth. Alexis, Pauline, and Charmaine wouldn't. And Ms. Kennedy would believe them. Because there were three of them. And they were on the Student Safety Patrol. And Ms. Kennedy had it out for Nelly.

Not a good plan.

The room reeked of ammonia. Nelly switched on her cell phone flashlight. There was nothing much in the room, shelves stacked with paint cans and assorted cleaners and in the corner, a bucket and mop. She put her violin case down and scanned the door, hoping to unlock it from the inside.

There was a lock on this side of the door, but it required a key. A few seconds later, she heard a clinking sound. For a moment she thought the groundskeeper was returning with his jangly keys. But listening intently, she heard only silence on the other side of the door. Classes would have started again by now, which meant the corridor was likely empty. She heard the jangly sound again and realized the schoolbag she still had strapped to her back was brushing up against something. She pointed her flashlight at whatever it was, and her heart leaped with hope. Rings of keys were hanging from hooks along the wall.

Nelly dropped her schoolbag and stepped toward the hooks and their keys, examining them closely. Each hook was marked with a letter, either E, W, N, or S, and the rings of keys were each marked with a number. Nelly guessed the letters meant ranges—east, west, north, and south—and the numbers must have meant floors. The only trouble was that the hook that should have held the keys to the floor she was on —floor one of the east range—was empty. She tried the other keys, anyway, hoping she was wrong about the letters and floor numbers. But not one of them fit the lock on the door.

Now what? She leaned back against the door. She could text Bianca. Nelly rolled her eyes and laughed at herself. *Yeah right.* Then she had an idea. She pulled up a browser on her phone and searched "how to pick a lock." It was worth a try. She had seen it done before, in movies, with bobby pins and other household items. She shoved her free hand into her pocket and felt around for a bobby pin, but found only maple keys. Useless maple keys. As she pulled her hand out of her pocket, one of the maple keys slipped out.

It fell to the floor and clattered there as if it were a heavy piece of metal or jewelry. That wasn't right. She picked up the maple key and examined it in the light of her cell phone. It looked like an ordinary maple key. Then, on a hunch, she put down her phone and peeled open the maple seed pod to reveal its seed and fleshy innards. But there was no seed inside the seed pod. There was something else: a tiny skeleton key made of what appeared to be silver.

She held up the key to the light of her phone. It looked like it could be a key to a charm box or a diary. How had this key gotten inside a maple seed pod? It was impossible. The seed pod had been sealed, not with glue or anything artificial, but with its own green, fleshy skin.

The key in her hand gave her a creepy feeling as if it was alive and letting her in on something dark.

The keyhole on the janitor's closet door beckoned. *Try the key in the door*, Nelly thought, a thought that felt planted in her and not from her own mind. She hesitated, fiddling with the key between her fingers. Oh, what was she afraid of? There was no way it was going to work. It was impossible.

She slid it into the keyhole.

It fit. It seemed almost to have changed in size, molding itself to the lock.

Nelly held her breath.

She turned the key. But the door did not unlock. Instead, there was a sound like someone had stepped on a balloon.

POP!

Nelly's phone flickered and went dark. As her eyes adjusted to the darkness, she realized she wasn't in the janitor's closet anymore.

CHAPTER FOURTEEN

FAIRY FOOD

Nelly was in a small space, much smaller than the janitor's closet. There was a faint scent in the air of beeswax and burned matches, and then the stench of rot and decay coiled around her like a constrictor. In a panic, she jabbed repeatedly at her cell phone, but it was no good. The phone was dead. *Calm down*, she told herself. *Figure out where you are.* She could make out shelves on either side of her lined with glass jars, and before her, a door. She groped for it, patting along its surface until she found a handle.

The door opened.

Nelly stepped out into a dimly lit room. Pencil-thin shafts of sunlight crisscrossed over scattered odds and ends, pieces of old furniture, and musty coats dangling from ceiling beams. The light was creeping in through small, dirt-encrusted windows just under the ceiling.

She was in some sort of basement. On the far side of the room, stairs led up toward a door. *Keep it together*, she told herself. Something supernatural had just happened to her. That much was clear. A few seconds ago, she had been in the janitor's closet at school. Now she was here. Wherever *here* was.

The room she'd just walked out of looked like a cold cellar. The skeleton key she had found in the maple seed pod was there, sticking out of the keyhole in the door.

Nelly walked cautiously toward the middle of the room. There was something familiar about this place. It was laid out like the basement of the farmhouse, *exactly* like the basement of the farmhouse, but older, danker, drearier. Then it hit her. This was the Morighan House.

"But that's impossible," she muttered.

She looked back toward the skeleton key still sticking out of the cellar door. For a moment, she thought she could hear the key whispering.

This couldn't be real.

She stepped back and bumped into something large and furry. She whirled around. For a split second, she thought she was looking at a hairy animal, but it was only a musty fur coat hanging from a ceiling beam. Then she spotted something beyond the fur coat that made her blood run cold all over again. In the far corner of the room, under a dirty window, stood an iron cage large enough to hold a person.

A sound sliced across the silence.

Nelly looked up. The sound had come from the floor above. A door was creaking. And then there were voices.

"They scorched the entire area all the way to the river," one voice said.

"I am not disputing the fact. I agree, what they did here was final," a second voice said.

Nelly recognized the voices immediately and the language they were speaking. It was the fairies, Jack and Fig. And they were speaking the secret language.

"And yet ..." Fig's voice said.

"But this will be impossible to investigate," Jack's voice said. "We have next to no information and if I start asking questions—"

"I know the consequences," said Fig.

"I would get out of here if I were you," a third voice whispered.

Nelly spun around. The third voice hadn't come from the floor above, but from somewhere in the room with her. It had come from the direction of the iron cage. There was what appeared to be a pile of old clothing on the floor of the cage.

It was moving. Something was crawling out from beneath the pile of clothing.

"Trouble?" Nelly whispered, recognizing Grandmother's cat.

"I see you've finally decided to join us," a voice said.

Nelly whirled around. Jack was standing only a few paces from her, sapphire eyes concentrated behind his glasses.

"I knew she'd come," another voice said.

Again, Nelly spun around. Fig was walking around Nelly in a slow circle, hands behind her back.

"What did you do to my grandmother?" Nelly said, blurting out the question she had been rehearsing all week. She was here in the Morighan House and so were the fairies. It didn't matter how she got here. Grandmother needed her.

The fairies were unfazed. Their cheeks were ruddy. Their clothing, raggedy and mismatched. They did not look human.

"Shall we bargain?" Jack said, his eerie eyes caught in a shard of light. "We'll answer your questions, truthfully, if you answer ours."

"–W-Why should I believe you?" Nelly stammered as Fig continued to circle, round and round like a wolf.

"You made a bargain with my grandmother. You promised

you wouldn't hurt her. You said you wouldn't hurt anyone inside the farmhouse."

The eyes of the two fairies bore into Nelly. She was in the presence of predators. The feeling was overwhelming.

"We didn't hurt your grandmother," Fig said, her voice as even as still water. "She's perfectly well."

"No, she is not," Nelly said. "Something's wrong with her. She's not herself."

For the briefest of seconds, the fairies took their eyes off Nelly and exchanged glances. And then the eyes were back, and for a moment Nelly wondered if stares alone could break a person apart.

"It may be that we define the word *harm* differently," Fig said, pausing next to Jack and cocking her head inhumanly. "But I assure you, your grandmother is well. We are People. We always honor our deals."

"But I'm telling you, she isn't well," Nelly said, now refusing to meet their eyes. "You need to fix her!"

There was silence. Nelly was staring at the floor. Finally, she looked up and back into the strange, beautiful, shattering eyes of the fairies.

"How about that bargain?" Jack said, raising his dark brows.

Deciding she had nothing to lose, Nelly nodded.

"Good," Fig said, clapping her hands together. "But first, let's get out of the dark and the damp. I don't like being underground."

She motioned toward the stairs. The door at the top of the steps was open, showing some daylight.

"After you," Nelly said, not wanting to lose sight of them. The fairies nodded in synchrony. And then, just like that, they were gone.

Nelly spun in a circle, looking in all directions. The door above creaked on its hinges.

"I wouldn't trust them if I were you," a voice said. It had come from the direction of the iron cage.

The cat who, according to the fairies, was not a cat, sat inside the cage, his tail swishing back and forth. There was plenty of room for Nelly inside that cage, she thought ominously.

"I have to do this," she said, half to herself and half to the cat.

"Don't say I didn't warn you," the voice said, as Nelly followed the fairies, climbing the steps.

As she neared the door, it occurred to her that the last time she had been inside the Morighan House, the door to the basement had been little more than broken splinters. But this door was one solid piece, painted white.

Then as Nelly stepped into the kitchen, her mouth fell open. When she had last been in this room, it had been decayed and abandoned, covered in a thick layer of dust. Cobwebs connected every object. Not only were the dust and the cobwebs gone, but the room looked to have been professionally restored. The once peeling walls had a fresh coat of paint; the floor tiles were clean and repaired. It was hard to accept that it was the same room. She looked out the now perfectly intact windows and there, across the field, was the farmhouse.

This *was* the Morighan House. There was no doubt about it.

Fig and Jack were sitting side by side at the kitchen table. Before them were dishes of cherries, apples, berries, nuts, and slices of butternut squash. There were several cups of tea and a jug of cider, cinnamon sticks, beeswax candles, and marbles.

The fairies stared at Nelly intently. Fig was eating cherries, her chin to her knee. Jack was rolling a marble deftly over his fingers. A chair on the opposite side of the table had been pushed out.

"Shall we begin?" Jack said, motioning toward the empty chair.

Nelly did not sit down. "What did you do to my grandmother?" she blurted again.

Jack looked at Fig, who swallowed a cherry. "I struck her," Fig said matter-of-factly. "As I struck you when we first met."

Nelly stiffened, remembering the wrenching agony she had experienced after Fig slapped her.

"You struck this girl?" Jack asked Fig.

Fig dropped her knee under the table. "I didn't know who she was. I thought she'd followed me from ours, you understand."

Nelly's heart was pounding. "So ... so my grandmother, she felt that pain—"

"She would not have felt any pain," Jack cut in. "Your grandmother is one of them, the humans. A strike affects them differently than it does our people."

"What do you mean?" Nelly asked.

Jack threaded his fingers. They were long and elegant and stained in paint. "A strike, a fairy strike, is an open-handed slap. When a fairy strikes another fairy, the result is pain, quite magnificent pain, as you are now aware. The kind of pain that leads to thoughts of revenge or demands for compensation, which is why we strike one another only rarely."

"It was a misunderstanding," Fig said with a half grin that seemed faintly apologetic.

"But when one of our people strikes a human," Jack continued, "the result is different. Humans cannot tolerate the pain and so they are thrown from their bodies, their spirits hurled back home, to our own. That is what happened to your grandmother."

"Her spirit?"

"Her consciousness," Jack said, nodding. "Her essence. That which infuses us all with life. The part of us all that endures when the body fails."

"—Y-You mean her soul?" Nelly said in disbelief.

"Yes, exactly," Fig said, tapping her own nose. "So, you see, I didn't break the bargain. I did not harm your grandmother. She and her spirit are both perfectly well, just in different places."

This was insane. "This is insane," Nelly muttered. "Can you put her back together?"

"Of course we can, don't be silly," Fig said, folding her arms.

"Well ... how?"

"We would have to return to our own, find your grandmother's spirit, and bring it back here," Jack said. "Then put her spirit and her body together again. Good as always."

"Your own? Your own what?" Nelly said, confused.

Fig's eyebrows went up as if surprised Nelly hadn't figured it out. "Our own world."

"Your own *world*?" Nelly's head was spinning. "OK ..." she said and blew out a shaky breath. "Will you do that? I mean, will you go to your world and get my grandmother's spirit and fix her?"

There was a brief silence and then the fairies, in perfect unison, shook their heads. *No.*

"But you have to!" Nelly said, her voice cracking. "You broke your promise. You harmed her, you slapped her! Whether she felt any pain is not the point. You slapped her and now she's—" Nelly stopped talking, not because of anything the fairies had done or said, but because her own words had made her realize something terrible.

The fairies were staring at Nelly with their shattering eyes.

They remained silent and still like judges awaiting a confession. They were unsettling to look at. Everything about them looked wrong: their skin, how it picked up the sunlight; their cheeks, how they glowed pink, too pink, like they'd both walked out of an enhanced photograph. And yet there was nothing artificial about them. They were as beautiful as old trees. Nelly wasn't like them. She couldn't be. And yet, on some level, she knew that she was. She hadn't even blinked when the fairies had said that she and grandmother had reacted to a strike differently, because grandmother was human and she, Nelly, was not. She had simply accepted it as self-evidently true.

"When I was younger, I hit a boy. Orson Kennedy," Nelly found herself saying. "I hit him with my open hand. And then he ... he changed. Do you think his spirit might be in your world, too?"

Fig popped another cherry in her mouth. "Most likely."

And then something even more terrible occurred to Nelly. She thought of her father sitting in the hospital, his face blank.

"Did you strike someone else?" Jack asked as if reading Nelly's thoughts.

"I don't ... I'm not sure," Nelly said. "I was only six at the time. But he has all the same symptoms as my grandmother."

"Six?" Jack repeated. "At that age, you wouldn't have been strong enough to deliver a full strike. It couldn't have been you."

This was such a relief, Nelly pulled out the chair across from the fairies and sat.

"It could have been another one of our people," Jack said, tapping a long finger against his chin. "Though it would be remarkable if true."

"Why would that be remarkable?" Nelly asked.

"That you are here, that you exist at all, Nelly, is remarkable to us. One of *our* people raised by humans ..." Jack said, and he and Fig both stared at Nelly for a moment, seemingly disturbed. "You see, our people do not come here to this Other place. It's not, strictly speaking, legal for us to do so."

Nelly raised her eyebrows. "But if it's illegal, then why are you here?"

Fig twirled a cherry stem. "My reasons for being here are complicated. If you ask me to explain, it will take some time. But to sum up, I am in hiding. And this was one of the few places in either world where I knew I would not be detected, given its history. Jack is here because I asked him to be."

"What do you mean, given its history?" Nelly asked, looking from Jack to Fig. She had a bad feeling.

The fairies exchanged glances. "Many years ago, one of our people came here and met one of the Morighans," Jack said.

"OK ..." Nelly said, waiting for him to continue.

Jack fiddled with a marble. "As I said, it is illegal for us to come here or to have any kind of contact with the humans. Even discussing humanity back home is a risk. Books about them are censored, possession of human paraphernalia is forbidden. Our people are meant to be kept strictly isolated from the human world."

"Of course, rules like those are easier to make than to enforce," Fig said, a tinge of bitterness in her voice. "Which means enforcers get heavy-handed."

"Enforcers?" Nelly said, and a chill ran over her skin.

Jack nodded grimly. "There is a multitude back home who call themselves the Broken Company, but we know them as the Fury. The Fury enforce the law."

Nelly did not like the sound of this at all. "So these enforcers found out a fairy met one of the Morighans and ... and what?" Nelly asked, not sure she wanted the answer.

"They released hunting parties to find the offending fairy,"

Jack said. "And to stop any ... *leaks* that may have occurred here in the human world."

Nelly looked from Jack to Fig and back again. "An unusually high number of my ancestors have gone missing or ... have died in mysterious circumstances."

The room dimmed as clouds passed over the sun. Crows cawed over the fields outside and cornstalks rustled in the wind.

"The Fury enforce the law," Jack said, his face darkening. "And no human may know of our existence and live."

Nelly couldn't believe what she was hearing. "Wait. You're saying that all those members of my family who - who died or went missing were murdered ... by fairies?"

The looks on the fairies' faces answered Nelly's question.

There was a long silence. Nelly had the strange sensation that her mind was both blank and racing at the same time. The people of Nothing believed the Morighan family to be cursed. Nelly always thought this was just a silly superstition; the tragedies in her family had been bad luck, but nothing more. But it wasn't bad luck. It was fairies. And she, Nelly, was herself one of them. She felt sick.

"What about my grandmother? She knows about fairies. Is she in danger?"

Jack shook his head. "Not for the moment. The Fury don't know about your grandmother. If they did, she would be dead already."

"But you know about my grandmother," Nelly said in a quiet voice.

Fig pursed her lips. "We have no intention of telling the Fury anything. We are not supporters of them or their policies. More to the point, both Jack and I have breached the law. To turn you in would be to turn ourselves in, and we are not about to do that."

"This doesn't make any sense. None of this makes any sense," Nelly said, mostly to herself. "Didn't you say this place was safe, given its history? If these Fury people know about my family, then they know about this farm, they know about this house!"

"That's true," Jack said. "But the Fury consider the case against the Morighans closed. They believe all members of your family to be dead. They can't set foot on this property without reopening the case."

"And to do that, they must have cause and evidence enough to convince the Debates," Fig said. "As of now, they have neither."

"–Th-The debates?" Nelly said and then held up a hand for them to say no more. "No, stop. Don't explain. It's too much." She sat back in her chair. Her head was spinning again. She was having a hard time accepting any of this. A part of her was still hoping this was all just a very intense dream.

"Here, eat something," Fig said, pushing a bowl of pomegranate seeds toward Nelly. They looked like little red drops of dew. Without thinking about it, Nelly picked up a single pomegranate seed and put it into her mouth, just as she would have if it had been Grandmother telling her to eat.

Nelly had always loved pomegranate seeds, the pleasant, mildly sour flavor. But this was different from any pomegranate seed she had ever tasted. It was better. Much better. It was the tart, sweet taste she remembered magnified and heightened tenfold.

"How old are you?" Jack asked.

"Sixteen. I'll turn seventeen in December," Nelly said. She felt a tingling sensation run through her body. It wasn't alarming. In fact, it felt good. It felt better than good.

"How many members of the Morighan family still live?" Fig asked.

"Just my grandmother, my father, and me," Nelly said, sitting up straighter. She felt strong, healthy, full of energy, as though she had recovered from a long illness she hadn't even known she had.

"How did they escape the Fury's notice?" Fig said.

"I don't know. I didn't even know the Fury existed," Nelly answered before realizing that the question had been directed at Jack. He shook his head, and then the fairies both turned their eyes to Nelly once more.

"Is your father like us?" Jack asked.

Nelly popped several more seeds into her mouth, wanting another shot of whatever that was. These were even better. The sensation of strength, of energy, magnified yet again. "I don't know," she said again. "He seems human to me. But I seemed human to me until I met you two."

"What about your mother?" Fig asked, sliding Nelly a bowl of cherries.

"My mother?" Nelly said over a mouthful of pomegranate seeds. She felt so good now, she thought she might be drunk, though she had never been drunk before and wasn't sure what it felt like. "She did teach me the language we're all speaking. What's it called again?"

"Eldritch," Fig said, and again exchanged glances with Jack.

Nelly finished the pomegranate seeds and moved on to the cherries. And like the pomegranate seeds, these were the best she had ever tasted. Each bite was more wonderful than the last and she felt stronger and stronger the more she ate.

"Where is your mother now?" Jack asked, pushing a cup of tea toward Nelly.

Nelly picked it up and drank deeply. It tasted of pumpkin, ginger root, and cinnamon bark. She looked up at the fairies and smiled in spite of herself. They were smiling, too, but their smiles were more shrewd than kind.

"I don't know," Nelly said. With a sudden tingle of nerves, she thought of that stuff like blueberry syrup Mother had forced her to drink. She sat up straighter. "What's in this tea?"

"You don't like it?" Jack said. "It's a standard late-summer blend."

"No, no, it's not that. It's wonderful. It's just ... strange." It suddenly occurred to Nelly that the fairies had been asking her questions and she had been answering them, truthfully, without a second thought. "Did you drug me?"

"No, no," Jack said with a laugh. "That's fairy food. Food for the spirit. All those years on human food will have dulled your senses, weakened you. What you feel now is how you are supposed to feel. We have healed you."

Nelly stared into her teacup, at the ghostly steam swirling from it. What Jack said certainly felt true. She did not feel drugged. She felt better than she ever had before. "But—"

"You're one of us," Fig cut in, as though reading her thoughts. "You feel compelled to answer our questions because of the bargain we made, just as we feel compelled to answer yours."

"Where is your father, Nelly?" Jack asked. He had dropped the friendly tone and the pretense that this wasn't an inter-rogation.

"In the hospital," Nelly said immediately. "That's where humans go when they are sick."

"What's the matter with him?" Fig asked without missing a beat.

"I don't know," Nelly said, trying to think up a question to ask them, so she could be the one doing the interrogating. Instead, more answers came spilling out. "He fell sick years ago, right around the time my mother left. He doesn't speak, doesn't react. Now I think a fairy might have struck him. I think it was my mother."

The fairies looked at each other, wide-eyed.

"He's human then?" Fig said.

Several things happened at once. The table rattled, chair legs screeched against the floor, Jack shot up, Fig reached for Nelly, and—

"Morag Fie!" Jack shouted.

Fig froze. She turned a look of outrage on Jack. Then her eyes went wide. "Jack," she muttered and gasped. Two tears, one then the other, rolled down her cheeks. She collapsed. Jack was next to her in a heartbeat. He caught her before her now unconscious body hit the floor.

"–Wh-What just happened?" Nelly asked, standing up.

Jack laid Fig down on the floor. "She was about to kill you," he said. "I stopped her."

"What?" Nelly said, stepping back. "Why?"

"Because of what you are," Jack hissed. "A thing like you, a fairy born of human blood, you are not supposed to exist. Please don't ask me to explain. Fig could wake at any time and when she does, she'll be in a blind rage. You must leave. Now!"

A kind of webbing was spreading out from under Fig's clothing. It crawled over her skin, up her chest, toward her neck and face.

Nelly hesitated. "But ... but what about my grandmother?"

"I'll help you retrieve your grandmother's spirit," Jack said. "We both will, once I've reasoned with her. But only if you leave now!"

The webbing was spreading over Fig's face and threading itself into her hair.

"And my father and Orson?" Nelly said.

"You must go now," Jack said, standing up.

"A bargain?" Nelly said, still hesitating.

"Yes, yes, all of them, fine," Jack said, now physically pushing Nelly toward the basement. "Go back the way you came. Turn the night key. It knows the way. It will take you back."

Behind them, Fig groaned. Jack shoved Nelly into the basement stairwell and slammed the door. Nelly stood there for a moment, frozen. Then what Jack said finally sunk in. Fig had been about to kill her.

She ran for the cellar.

CHAPTER FIFTEEN

YELLOW PAINT, GRAY WOMAN

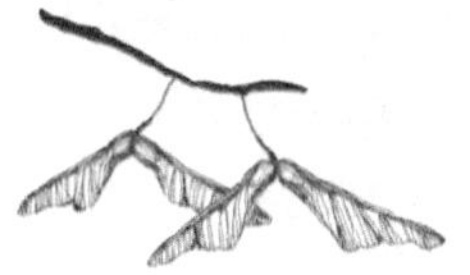

After a turn of the key, a loud *POP*, and the scent of beeswax and burned matches, Nelly found herself back in the janitor's closet at the Priory House. It was so dark she could hardly see. Her cell phone was still unresponsive. It appeared that technology and fairy magic didn't mix.

She groped for the door but hit a shelf instead. Something on the shelf wobbled and tipped over. Cold, gloopy liquid ran over her head and down her back. Ugh! What was this stuff? She touched her hair and something wet and slimy came away on her fingers.

The door opened. Light flooded into the room. The groundskeeper stood in the doorway, gaping at her. Nelly blinked against the light and then looked down at her hands. They were covered in electric-yellow paint.

The groundskeeper marched Nelly to Ms. Kennedy's office. It was after last period and students crowded the halls. They gawked as Nelly walked by. Her hair and uniform dripped with paint, and she left a trail of yellow footprints in her wake.

Ms. Kennedy would not allow Nelly into her office. She lectured her out in the hallway instead; a five-minute diatribe about the seriousness of entering rooms without permission and vandalizing school property. Nelly did not protest. She did not tell Ms. Kennedy who had locked her in the janitor's closet; it would only make things worse with Alexis. In fact, Nelly didn't offer any explanation at all for her bizarre predicament. Her mind was still reeling after what had happened in the Morighan House. Coming up with a convincing lie at that moment was too much to ask.

Ms. Kennedy suspended Nelly for three days. It was an in-school suspension. This meant Nelly wasn't allowed to visit the farm over the weekend and had to attend detention all day Friday instead of classes. Had this happened the day before, Nelly would have been fuming, especially at the way Ms. Kennedy had seemed to relish denying her request to spend the weekend on the farm.

But Nelly had been to the farm, thanks to that weird key. What had Jack called it? A night key? She had confronted the fairies, too, as she had planned. She even had an explanation for what was wrong with Grandmother and a potential solution. As for everything else she had learned, Nelly tried not to think about it as she trudged up Maple Hall's narrow staircase toward her dorm room on the third floor.

The third-floor corridor was empty, much to Nelly's relief, but as she neared her room, she noticed her door was ajar. Voices were coming from inside. She recognized one voice immediately as belonging to Bianca. Nelly sighed. She didn't want to face anyone right now, let alone Bianca with company.

"Oh please, do not start," Bianca's voice barked as Nelly paused outside the room. "I told you I did not want to hear the words *Morighan* or *ghost* this year. It's tired, it's stupid, and I think we're all a little old for ghost stories, don't you?"

"That's just it, Bianca, they are not stories," a male voice said. Nelly recognized it as belonging to Grady Pipes. Grady Pipes, whose very presence made Nelly's stomach flutter with nerves, was in her room while paint congealed on her forehead. "Pretty much everyone at this school except you has experienced something real." he continued, his voice sharp with irritation.

"What are you even talking about?" Bianca snapped.

"He's talking about the cold spots in Chapter Hall," a third voice said. This voice belonged to Alexis. Nelly clenched her paint-smeared hands. "The weird smells of smoke or sulfur and soil in the library, the handprint on the north range window that keeps coming back no matter how many times the groundskeeper cleans it."

"You guys seriously think this school is haunted?" Bianca scoffed. "Like ... seriously?"

"Are you telling me you haven't noticed anything unusual at this school?" Grady said.

"Aside from Charmaine's haircut? No."

"Hey!" Charmaine's voice said.

"Then you, Bianca, are the only one," Grady said.

"Maybe she's too close to the source," Alexis muttered.

Nelly clenched her hands tighter.

"You know something happened to me?" Grady said. "I was hanging out with the guys after hours in the quad. The moon was full, and we had these long shadows on the grass. We started joking around, right? We were making shadow puppets, and that's when I saw it. There were five shadows, but only four of us."

"Oh, please," Bianca said and scoffed again.

"Are you saying I'm lying?" Grady asked, aggressively.

"No, I'm saying you can't count."

"That's so weird," Charmaine said in a breathy voice. "I haven't seen anything like that, but one night I was up late, and I heard something outside my room. It sounded like a woman muttering about something, angry. I opened the door, and the hall was empty."

"I've heard the muttering, too," Grady said. "And I've seen her and I'm not the only one."

"Her?" Bianca said, still sounding unconvinced. "Who?"

"The bell woman," Grady said. "She's this crazy-looking woman in old-fashioned clothing, all gray. I was walking down the east cloister a couple days ago. It was dark out and raining, but I swear I saw a woman standing in the old bell tower, the one under renovation. That's where she lives. I know other people who have seen her, too, out in the quad, standing there, staring up at the school. But all of that is nothing compared to what's been happening to Alexis."

"Are you guys kidding?" Bianca said. "Seriously, Lex, what's he talking about?"

There was a long silence. When Alexis finally spoke, her voice quavered.

"Someone has been calling my name at night over and over. Not like a whisper or a growl, but a voice calling out. I've tried following it a few times, but it always wants to lead me outside onto the grounds, and then I don't know where. I don't want to know."

"Oh my God," said Charmaine.

"Once," Alexis continued, sounding like she was holding back tears, "I decided to block the voice out completely. I put on my headphones and turned up my music and stayed in bed. After a while, my bed jumped as if someone kicked it. I looked up and there was this shadow on the wall that couldn't have been caused by anything in the room. It was the shadow of a body ... hanging."

Bianca gasped. "Are you serious?"

"I don't understand why this keeps happening to me," Alexis went on, her voice thick. "I just know it's gotten worse since *she's* been back in town."

Nelly's skin prickled and not because of the ghost stories. Stories like these didn't frighten her. She'd been hearing them her entire life. Things other than ghosts could explain most of them. Take the cold spots in Chapter Hall: the building was old and drafty; there were bound to be spots that were cooler than others. As for the voice Charmaine had heard: the Priory House had over four hundred students, and sometimes people muttered to themselves, big deal. And as for the bell woman and Alexis's alleged experiences, well, people were certainly capable of lying. None of this was evidence of ghosts. *Fairies, on the other hand ...* Nelly kneaded her paint-covered hands. *Forget the fairies*, she told herself. Her biggest concern at this precise moment was the *she* the people in her bedroom were referring to, and if they were planning to do anything more to her than lock her in a closet.

"Get out of our way, Bianca," Grady said, his tone threatening.

"So you can search through my roommate's stuff?" Bianca said. "What do you even think you're gonna find?"

"I don't know," Grady said, exasperated. "Information, evidence, the kind you found in her diaries but won't tell us about."

"I told you I gave her diaries to her grandmother."

"But you won't tell us what was in them," Alexis snapped. "It's like you're loyal to her or something."

"I don't know what was in them!" Bianca said. "I didn't

read them. I have better things to do. Gawd, this is so stupid! Even if this place is haunted, I really don't see how *she* has anything to do with it."

"You don't get it, Bianca," Alexis said. "You're not from Nothing. It's that family. They're into something. I don't know what it is—witchcraft, Satan worship, some kind of cult—but I'm telling you, all the weird stuff in this town, it's their fault."

"We're running out of time," Charmaine said. "She's got to be out of that closet by now. She could be back any minute!"

"We're doing this, Bianca," Grady said. "Either help us or get out of the way. Charmaine, check the hall. Tell us if you see her."

Nelly stifled a gasp. For a moment she considered running back down the hallway and ducking into the stairwell, but the trail of paint would give her away for sure. There was nothing else to do. She took a deep breath and pushed the door open.

The silence in the room was absolute.

"–Oh ... my ... God," Bianca said. "What happened to you?"

"Someone locked me in the janitor's closet," Nelly said, her voice remarkably steady. "Not anything supernatural."

Bianca snickered, but she was the only one to do so. "And the paint?"

Nelly did not respond. She walked as calmly as she could to her closet, leaned her violin case against the wall, and pulled out a towel and a change of clothes.

She faced them. Bianca was standing next to her bed between Nelly's half of the room and the others. Alexis stood near Bianca, glaring hatred at Nelly. Charmaine stood next to Alexis, blushing and staring at the floor. And Grady, adorable Grady, was standing by the door, blue eyes piercing Nelly from behind his glasses.

"For the record," Nelly said, her cheeks burning, "I've had

nothing to do with whatever strange things you think are happening at this school. So please, just leave me alone."

Nelly stood as tall as she could in the silence that followed, hoping the others couldn't hear her heart hammering in her chest. Finally, Grady turned and left the room. The others followed in single file, avoiding eye contact. Only Bianca remained.

After a few moments of awkward silence, Bianca pointed at the yellow handprint Nelly had left on the door, and said, "Um, you're gonna clean that, right?"

That night Nelly was so exhausted she fell asleep the second her head hit the pillow. In her dream, there was running and shouting voices. Something hit her on the back of the head. Her stomach lurched. She fell and jerked awake.

BANG! Nelly sat bolt upright. The sound had come from the floor above. Rapid footsteps were vibrating the ceiling.

Bianca groaned under her canopy. "What's going on? I am trying to sleep!" she shouted at the ceiling.

More pounding footsteps. *BANG! THUD! CRASH!*

Bianca let out an annoyed sigh and put a pillow over her head. "Cam you tewl vem to SHU UB?" she shouted, her voice muffled. Bianca looked out from under her pillow and gave Nelly a pleading look.

Nelly looked back in disbelief.

"Pleeeeeaase!" Bianca said in a whiny voice. "I need to sleep. I have a quiz first period. Can you tell them to be quiet?"

Nelly's expression did not change. Did Bianca think they were friends all of a sudden? Were they trading favors now?

Bianca gave a pouty smile in return as if that was exactly what she thought. "I swear, Nell, if-you-do-me-this-favor-this-one-time-I-will-owe-you-forever!" Bianca stuck out her lip and batted her eyelashes.

Above, there was another *CRASH!*

"I need the flashlight on your cell," Nelly said, throwing off her covers. "Mine's dead."

"You're the best! I love you!" Bianca chimed, holding out her phone. As Nelly took it, Bianca blew her a kiss.

Nelly shook her head and smiled a little against her will. Bianca had this magical ability to make Nelly both hate her and like her at the same time. It was annoying.

Nelly slipped on sneakers, threw a robe over her pajamas, and crept out into the hallway.

Moonlight beamed in through casement windows, splashing the floor in silver squares. Nelly moved soundlessly up the dark stairwell and onto the fourth floor, where the ruckus seemed to be coming from.

But the fourth floor was quiet. She scanned the hallway with Bianca's phone light. There was no sign that anyone was awake, much less running around. If there had been trouble up here, it appeared to be over. She was about to head back downstairs when she noticed an open door farther up the corridor.

Nelly approached it with cautious steps. As she got nearer, she thought she could hear whispering and someone crying. She shut off the light and pushed at the door with her fingertips.

A bright light shone into her face. Someone screamed!

"Shh!" Nelly said, shielding her eyes.

"Who's there?" a frightened voice asked.

"It's Nelly ... Morighan."

A gasp. "Nelly?" The light lowered, and Nelly could see two

girls huddled together. It was Ramona and Gwen, the girls who had questioned Nelly in the library for the school paper. They were both in pajamas. Ramona held her hand over her own heart.

"You scared us half to death," she hissed. "For a second, it looked like your eyes were glowing!"

Nelly remembered how the fairies' eyes had reflected the light that night in the farmhouse, like animal eyes do. She looked at the floor. "Um, it must have been a trick of the light," she muttered. "What's going on?"

"It's my sister," Ramona said. "Something's wrong with her."

"Where is she?" Nelly groped along the wall for the light switch. She flicked it up and down. Nothing happened.

"Power's out," Ramona said and motioned toward a figure sitting on the floor. Nelly switched on the phone light.

There in the corner was Alexis. She wore white pajamas with little red hearts on them, her brown hair loose over her shoulders. Her face was in her hands.

"What's the matter with her?" Nelly asked.

"We don't know," Gwen said, her eyes wide. "She texted Ramona, said something was in her room, so we came up and found her like this."

Nelly swept the room slowly with her light. It was identical to Nelly's minus Bianca's decorating. There were two beds, both empty, both a twirl of sheets. "Where's her roommate?"

"Pauline went home for the weekend early," Ramona said. "Alexis is alone up here. She saw someone in Pauline's bed. A ... figure."

Nelly's eyebrows went up. The bed across from the girls was empty. But the comforter was bunched up in such a way that a person could be hiding under it. Behind the bed, several books lay open face down on the floor along with a spray of broken glass, which glittered in the phone light. It looked like Alexis had been throwing things at whatever she had seen.

Nelly walked over to Pauline's bed. The form under the comforter did look disturbingly human like someone was under there curled up in the fetal position. But it was probably a pillow or a trick of the shadows. She took a deep breath and yanked the comforter back.

There was nothing there. She looked over at Ramona and Gwen, who now stood shoulder-to-shoulder.

"–Wh-What about under the bed?" Gwen asked.

Nelly dropped to her knees and swept the light under the bed. Nothing but dust bunnies. "There's nothing," she said.

Ramona stepped forward as if emboldened by this. "What about the closet?"

Nelly glanced at the closet. She had an interesting relationship with closets these days. She walked over, took another bolstering breath, and threw the door open wide.

It was an ordinary closet. She swept aside dangling dresses and school uniforms to prove this to the other girls. She even put her hand flat on the back wall and patted it. "All clear."

Ramona squatted down next to Alexis. "Lex, did you hear that? We've checked everywhere. There's nothing here. You're safe."

Slowly, Alexis lowered her hands. Her face was deathly pale; her lip was trembling. "I saw it," she said. "It was there, in the bed. It looked at me." Then Alexis's eyes fell on Nelly. "You! It's your fault! You did this! You let them in!"

She grabbed a snow globe from her bedside table and hurled it. Nelly ducked. The snow globe smashed on the wall above her head, exploding in a rain of glass, water, and glitter.

"Alexis!" Ramona shouted as a tiny plastic fairy spun

across the floor. "I'm sorry, Nelly! She didn't mean it. Are you OK?"

"I did mean it!" Alexis shouted. "Get out! Get out of here!"

Nelly wiped glittery water from her cheek as heat surged into her face and neck. She suppressed the urge to hurl Bianca's phone back at Alexis and started for the door.

"Wait!" Gwen called. "Don't leave! Do you hear that?"

"Hear what?" Nelly snapped. She had tried to help, and Alexis had chucked a snow globe at her. She was in no mood to stick around.

"I hear it, too," Ramona said, moving closer to Gwen. "It … it sounds like a voice, whispering."

Nelly listened. She was starting to think these girls were playing a prank on her. There was nothing on or under the bed, nothing in the closet, and she couldn't hear any whispering. She listened deeply, intently, focusing all her energy on it. Sounds rose out of the silence. The girls' hearts, she could hear them beating. Water sloshed in the pipes behind the walls. Someone was padding around in slippers several floors below. A bird, perhaps an owl, landed on the roof, claws scratching. And then she heard it: a voice rose out above the other sounds. It was so faint it wasn't much more than a breath. It said one word. "Revenge."

A cold chill rushed over Nelly's skin. She stepped in front of the girls and faced the doorway where she thought the voice had come from. The door was ajar. The air smelled earthy. Nelly held up the phone like a weapon while Alexis, Ramona, and Gwen cowered behind her.

The light flickered.

"Who's there?" Nelly demanded. She made a fist with her free hand. It was enough that there were fairies. Too much. If there were ghosts too, if they were haunting Alexis and the town of Nothing, as the townspeople had always claimed, then they had ruined Nelly's life.

"Leave," Nelly said. "Now."

The phone light stopped flickering. There was a surge of electricity and the light in the room flooded back on, bright and blinding. The door creaked wide open.

A woman was standing on the other side.

CHAPTER SIXTEEN

THE DIARY OF MADGE MORIGHAN

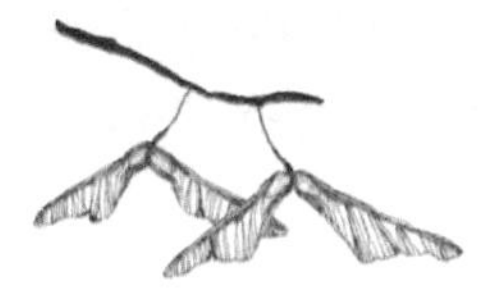

"What is going on here?" the woman said.

It was Maple Hall's middle-aged housemother, Mrs. Dunch, a puffy-faced woman dressed in a robe covered in cartoon cats.

"Girls, explain what is going on. Why is Alexis crying? Why are you four out of bed?"

Alexis seemed to regain herself. She wasn't as pale as she had been before, but there was still a look of horror on her face.

"Attacked," she said in a quavering voice.

"What?" Mrs. Dunch said. "Who attacked you?"

Nelly, Gwen, and Ramona turned their heads toward the empty bed on the other side of the room, which was still surrounded by books and broken glass. But Alexis did not look toward the bed. Instead, she raised a single, trembling finger and pointed it at Nelly.

Nelly blinked in disbelief. "No ... That's not true."

Mrs. Dunch's small, suspicious eyes shifted from Nelly to the others. "Gwen, Ramona, what happened here?"

For a long moment, neither Ramona nor Gwen spoke.

Mrs. Dunch put her hands on her cat-covered hips.

"Someone had better tell me what happened, and it had better be good or I'll be marching the four of you to Ms. Kennedy's office first thing in the morning. Gwen?"

Gwen didn't speak for a long time. Her eyes shifted from Alexis to Ramona to Nelly. She had a tortured expression on her face.

"Well?" Mrs. Dunch said, tapping a slippered foot.

"It's true," Gwen said, finally. "Alexis is telling the truth."

Nelly's mouth dropped open. "But I didn't—"

"I don't want to hear it," the housemother said in a huff. "Nelly, you will report to Ms. Kennedy's office at eight am tomorrow. Alexis, Gwen, Ramona, you three had better be there as well to explain whatever happened here. In the meantime, all four of you get to sleep. Eight o'clock comes early."

Mrs. Dunch ushered Nelly, Gwen, and Ramona out of the room. It wasn't until Nelly was back in her dorm room that her disbelief at what had happened fermented into anger.

Revenge, a voice in her head said. *Revenge.*

Nelly hardly slept that night. When she arrived at Ms. Kennedy's office a few minutes after eight, she felt numb. She was sure Ms. Kennedy would believe Alexis and not Nelly, the girl who had maybe, possibly put her son in the hospital. But Ms. Kennedy wasn't in her office. The secretary said she was away at a conference and that Nelly was to see Mr. Haley in his office instead.

Nelly navigated the corridors to Mr. Haley's second-floor office, feeling like she was on the way to her execution. She thought she had about as much of a shot with Mr. Haley as she had with Ms. Kennedy. She could only hope that Gwen or Ramona had gained a spark of conscience in the light of day and would tell the truth about what happened.

But just as she reached Mr. Haley's office, his door swung open and out walked Alexis, Gwen, and Ramona in single file. Alexis glared at Nelly while Ramona and Gwen avoided eye contact. It was a very bad sign.

Mr. Haley ushered Nelly into his office and shut the door. The office decor said "stuffy professor." Bookshelves, leather furniture, and dark woodwork sat atop a wall-to-wall Persian carpet. There was a sweet and dirty scent in the air, like burned coffee or cigar smoke. Mr. Haley looked out of place in the room with his rockstar good looks and tattoos peeking just a tad from under his dress shirt. He sat behind his desk, the leather seat creaking, and gazed at Nelly with his hangdog eyes.

Nelly dropped her backpack on the floor and took a low seat facing Mr. Haley. Staring up at him across his desk, she felt like a peasant petitioning a king or a judge. She launched into her defense. "Sir, I swear I didn't attack Alexis. I only went up there because—"

"I know, Nelly," Mr. Haley said. "I interviewed each of those girls separately before you arrived, and each one told me a different story. Not one of them made any sense."

Nelly felt a swell of hope. A paperweight shaped like a bird sat on the desk next to Mr. Haley. He picked it up.

"Unfortunately," he said, passing the bird back and forth between his hands, "I can't guarantee Ms. Kennedy will see things the same way. Alexis's allegations are serious. You could be expelled, I'm afraid."

Which was exactly what Alexis wanted. Nelly sank lower in the already low chair. But why was she upset? She had never wanted to come to this stupid school. Maybe getting expelled was the best thing for her. She had other, bigger problems to deal with.

"You don't say much, do you?" Mr. Haley said, looking Nelly over. "My mother always told me to be careful of those who don't say much. They are either very, very stupid or very, very smart."

Nelly shot Mr. Haley a hard look. That was a weird thing for a teacher to say.

Mr. Haley leaned back in his chair. "You know I went to school with your father."

Nelly blinked, surprised. "You did?"

"He was a few years older than me," said Mr. Haley. "I didn't know him personally. I knew of him, of course, Merritt Morighan of the infamous Morighan family. What's the old saying? Mad, missing, or ..." He trailed off and gave Nelly a probing look as if prompting her to finish his sentence.

She did not. Something the fairies said echoed in her mind. *No human may know of our existence and live.* She shifted in her chair.

"Merritt was bullied back then, just as you are now," Mr. Haley went on. "The other students feared him. I feared him, too. I suppose we all thought the Morighan curse was contagious." He laughed a little as if the idea was funny. Nelly did not see the humor in it.

"I often wonder," Mr. Haley continued, fidgeting with the bird figurine, "if the fears the people in this town have of the Morighans are justified. I'm curious what you think about that."

There was an awkward silence. "Um, well, there are a lot of superstitions about us, that's for sure," Nelly said, stating the obvious, and not really answering his question. She didn't have an answer. She wished she did. She wished she could say with confidence that the townspeople had nothing at all to fear from Nelly or anyone related to her. But she couldn't, not with a couple of possibly homicidal fairies squatting in the Morighan House.

Mr. Haley didn't push the issue, for which Nelly was grateful. Instead, he changed the subject. "We have someone else in common. Gilbert Glanville. He's my uncle."

"Mr. Glanville?" Nelly repeated, surprised again. Grandmother's husband had never mentioned a nephew before. And then, for the first time, she noticed the nameplate on Mr. Haley's desk. ROGER HALEY. "You're Roger!"

Mr. Haley nodded. "Yes, though I prefer students not call me by my first name. I have to say, I'm surprised Uncle Gilbert mentioned me at all. He and my mother had a falling out some years ago, around the same time he married your grandmother, as a matter of fact."

Mr. Glanville had never mentioned Mr. Haley, but Nelly didn't want to offend him by saying so. She watched him, trying to read him. There was an aggressive undertone to his voice as if he blamed Grandmother for whatever had gone wrong between his uncle and his mother. But he also seemed nervous, the way he kept passing the bird figurine between his hands. If Nelly was going to probe him for more information, she would have to be delicate.

"My grandmother did mention something about you and a - a diary."

Mr. Haley glanced toward one corner of the room and then his eyes were on Nelly again.

"I was just wondering if - if ..." Nelly trailed off.

Mr. Haley was glaring at her. "She told you about the diary, did she?" he said, holding eye contact.

He put the bird figurine down on the edge of the desk. It tilted and fell to the floor. He made no move to retrieve it.

"Would you pick that up for me, please?" he asked.

Nelly glanced at the figurine. It was closer to him than it was to her. Was this a show of his authority? He was the teacher, she was the student. He was the adult, she was the teenager. His authority was obvious.

"Er ... OK," Nelly said, shooting him a disapproving look.

As she reached for the figurine, a commotion erupted outside the office. Voices were shouting. She paused inches from the fallen bird. Mr. Haley stood up.

"Stay here," he said. "And don't touch anything until I get back."

"OK," Nelly muttered as he strode across the room.

The second the door clicked shut behind Mr. Haley, Nelly shot out of her chair.

Find Roger, Grandmother said. *Get the diary.*

Fingers clumsy with urgency, Nelly searched through the stack of books on Mr. Haley's desk: *Sweet Nothing: A Little History of a Little Town*; *Spooked: A Haunted History of Nought County*; *Nothing Daunted: A Town in Crisis (1822 – 1885)*; *The Ghosts of Nothing: Exploring the World's Most Haunted Town.*

A folder fell from the desk. Its contents went sliding across the floor like a snake unfurling its tongue. Nelly gasped, dropped to her knees, and frantically began gathering up the loose notes and newspaper clippings. As she stacked them together, she paused, realizing that they were all about the Morighan family. Various mysterious incidents related to the Morighans—missing persons reports, unusual deaths—were all there in black and white. And there was a record of Grandmother's real estate holdings.

Nelly frowned. *If Grandmother knew this man was keeping track of her finances like this, she'd hit the roof.*

A sound from the corridor made Nelly jump. Boys were shouting. Mr. Haley's voice rose above the commotion. He was trying to calm some situation down. Nelly put the folder back on the desk and listened. The arguing in the hallway continued.

Nelly took another chance. She rushed around the desk and tried the drawers. *OUCH!* The drawer handle had shocked her. Nelly touched it again cautiously. And again it shocked her. She squeezed her fingers to relieve the pain. Then something occurred to her. The drawer handles were antiques. They were probably made of iron. She recalled Fig's violent reaction to Grandmother's kitchen shears back at the farm. Fairies hated iron. And Nelly was one of them. Trying not to dwell on how she felt about this, she covered her hand in her sleeve and tried the drawers again. They were locked.

There had to be a key around somewhere.

She searched the desk, under files and books, inside a cup filled with pens and paperclips, but found no sign of anything resembling a key. She thought about the maple keys in her pockets. If she used one, would it unlock the drawer, or transport her to the Morighan House again?

Frustrated, Nelly blew out some air. Her breath misted. Only then did she realize how cold it was in the room. Had Mr. Haley turned the air conditioning up full blast?

THUD! Again, Nelly jumped. That sound hadn't come from the corridor but inside the room. A painting on the far side of the room had fallen off the wall. It was a painting of fairies in a garden. Disturbed to find anything having to do with fairies in Mr. Haley's office, she took tentative steps toward it.

A card tucked into the frame identified it as a print of The Fairy Feller's Master-Stroke by Richard Dadd. Nelly stared at it. Mr. Haley had glanced in this direction when she had mentioned the diary. On a hunch, she picked up the painting and turned it around. A small antique key was taped to the back of the painting.

Iron.

Nelly put her hand in her sleeve again and pulled the key from the back of the painting. The ruckus continued in the hallway. She dashed back to the desk as Mr. Haley's voice rose outside in a lecturing tone, jammed the key into the lock, and turned. The drawer slid open. It was filled with dried yarrow and little bags of rowan berries, their contents half spilled. Under yarrow stalks and rolling berries was a small, antique-looking book bound in cloth. Gingerly, Nelly brushed past the yarrow and the berries and picked up the book. She flipped it open to the first page. There, in messy handwriting, was the word *Diary*.

She couldn't believe it. She found it. She had actually found it.

The hallway had gone quiet. Then there were footsteps, getting closer. A wild panic set off in Nelly's stomach. She froze for a second of indecision and then committed to something risky. She tossed the diary into her open backpack, closed the drawer, and locked it. As quickly as she could, she dashed back across the room, stuck the key where she had found it, and straightened the painting with treacherously trembling fingers.

After a running slide, she fell back into her chair. The diary was peeking out from inside her backpack. She zipped it shut.

Mr. Haley wasn't back yet. She had done it. She had gotten away with it.

The bird figurine was still on the floor. Nelly reached for it. *OUCH!* The bird shocked her. She blinked in surprise. *Iron.* The bird figurine was made of iron. Had Mr. Haley dropped it on purpose? Had he wanted to see what would happen when she picked it up?

There were footsteps just outside the door. She put her hand back in her sleeve, scooped up the bird, and put it back on the desk. The door swung open just as she fell back in her chair.

Mr. Haley leaned into the room. "Nelly, I need to deal with this." His eyes paused on the bird figurine on his desk and were on her again. "I'll schedule you an appointment with Ms. Kennedy on Monday. In the meantime, room 101."

Room 101 was detention hall. It was a wide, sparse room with rows of single desks set well apart. Nelly was the only student in the room for the first fifteen minutes until two senior boys she didn't know walked in. It was their fight in the hallway that had drawn Mr. Haley from his office. It was a silly fight. One boy had accused the other of stealing his watch. The other denied it. That was the extent of it, as far as Nelly could tell. She was grateful, even so. Without their fight, she never would have found the diary.

But she hadn't found it, really. It had found her. That fairy painting had practically jumped off the wall. Nelly tapped the cover of the book. What if the people of Nothing were right? What if the town *was* haunted? Fairies were real, after all. Why not ghosts?

Nelly's gaze drifted out the window. The day was windy. Clouds scuttled across the sky, maple keys and leaves sailed in the air, and a construction worker chased a tumbling hard hat at the foot of the bell tower.

The diary called for Nelly's attention. It almost seemed to be speaking to her somehow, just like the strange key that belonged to the fairies had done. With careful fingers, she opened the first brittle pages and started to read.

My name is Madge Morighan. I thought if I wrote the name

down, it would feel like mine. It is not mine. My husband, Eoin, chose it for me when we landed. I much prefer the name I had in Ireland. Máiréad Ó Muireagáin. It was a strong name, but Eoin says we cannot expect the people here to navigate Irish names. He goes by John now. I could insist he call me Máiréad, but he has a devil in him, and I dare not wake it. Máiréad will have to become my secret name. The name of my heart and soul.

Nelly looked up from the page. Margaret "Madge" Morighan was her great-great-great-grandmother. She and her husband were the first Morighans to settle in the county all the way back in the 1800s.

So, her real name was Máiréad, Nelly thought, running a finger across the word. It was a pretty name, though Nelly couldn't say the same about her handwriting.

She kept reading, struggling to decipher Madge's messy scrawl. From what Nelly could tell, Madge was an ordinary woman. She was thoughtful, lively. She'd loved her children and her husband, though they'd all gotten on her nerves at times. She liked to read and to walk in the woods, to sing at the top of her lungs and even to play the tin whistle like Nelly! But there was a note of frustration in her writing. She wasn't fond of Nothing. She complained often about local attitudes—overbearing, she called them; gossips and busybodies. They put ideas into her husband's head.

It is as if my poor Eoin has lost all sense. These backward farmers have never met an educated woman; it is no wonder they think me peculiar. My father thought Eoin peculiar and not at all fit to marry his daughter. We defied him and I'm glad we did, but now what has become of us? A new life, a new world, and all Eoin wishes is to be like all the rest. I will not say I love him less for his behavior, but he is not the man I once admired.

It was interesting, in a kind of historical way, but Nelly couldn't figure out why Grandmother had wanted her to find this. But then, as Nelly reached the halfway point, an entry came up that explained everything.

Something happened today. I met someone out in the woods. She was beautiful. So beautiful I can hardly describe her, like a creature from a dream. When I found her, she was sitting in a patch of bluebells weeping like a child. She wore a ruffled dress that billowed around her like mist and from head to toe, she was covered in powder, like she had been doused in dyed flour.

"Pardon me," I said to the woman. "But why are you crying?"

She looked up at me with eyes like amber glass. Her beauty was stunning. It drew me in and repelled me both at once.

"I've lost my key," she said, tears streaking her powdered face. Though her accent was foreign, her voice was full of innocence and youth, and I suddenly needed to help her, to protect her, to rescue her, whatever the cost.

"Oh, my poor dear thing," I said, sitting down next to her. "Don't cry. I'll help you find your key."

"You will?" the girl said, blinking her fathomless eyes. She embraced me. She was so delicate. It was as if I held a bird in my arms. At that moment, I knew I loved her, and I would love her for the rest of my life.

Nelly stopped reading. Unless she was mistaken, her great-great-great grandmother had met a fairy. This must have been the fairy Jack and Fig mentioned in the Morighan House. They said a fairy came to the human world years ago and met one of the Morighans. So, Madge was the one, Nelly thought, regretting all the times she had drifted off when Grandmother had talked about the family history.

Nelly read on and what she read played out like a kind of strange love story. Madge bonded with the fairy. They sat together in the boughs of oak trees or in fields of wildflowers and had long conversations. Madge did most of the talking. The fairy would ask questions about life in the village, fascinated by the most ordinary of details, like how Madge washed her clothing or stored preserves. It soon became obvious that the fairy was as taken with Madge as Madge was with her.

Soon, Madge began to document unusual details about the fairy. The fairy had an aversion to iron and collected maple keys. She followed a strict set of rules that didn't seem to have any logical reasoning behind them. She couldn't, for example, cross a line of rowan berries or disturb yarrow flowers. If she heard a cowbell ring, she would stop dead in her tracks. And she treated bargains, agreements, and promises as things of deadly seriousness and would stick to the letter of them.

Was this why Grandmother had wanted Nelly to get hold of this diary? So Nelly could figure out the rules and tricks for dealing with fairies?

Nelly kept reading. It wasn't long before Madge's story took a turn for the worse. One spring afternoon as thistledown floated through the forest behind the farm, Madge's husband saw her with the fairy. He saw them both—Madge as she leaned back against a tree; the fairy as she leaned in close and stole a kiss.

Eoin flew into a rage. He forbade Madge from ever seeing the fairy again. He said Madge had been tricked or cursed or mesmerized or stolen; the accusations seemed to change depending on the day. He dragged her to church and forced her to confess.

Sensing the danger, the fairy told Madge the villagers were right to be afraid. "I am a monster," the fairy said. "You should stay away."

But Madge refused. "You could never be a monster. Not to me," she said. For Madge knew that even if she did agree to stay away from the fairy, it wouldn't make a difference. The damage had been done. Rumors were spreading through the village that Madge was a wanton woman and a witch. The villagers now blamed her for everything that went wrong in Nothing—missing items, failing crops, even bad weather.

Why must it be this way? Why must they hate me so much? I don't understand how I can be this person I am, a person who loves and wants to be loved, who feels the pain of others as if it is my own, who would never harm anyone for all the world, and yet inspire rage and violence and cruelty in others. They wish for my destruction when I have done nothing, when I want nothing but to be left in peace.

Nelly looked away from the page. This passage had hit a little too close to home. As she gazed out the window, lost in her thoughts, a shadow fell over her.

It was Mr. Haley.

CHAPTER SEVENTEEN

FRIENDS ... AGAIN?

The bell rang. Nelly glanced at the clock. School was out. She had been reading Madge's diary all day.

A vein throbbed on Mr. Haley's cheek as he glowered down at her. He scooped up the diary and stormed out of the room without a word.

Nelly grabbed her backpack and hustled after him. In the corridor, she weaved among the throngs of students pouring out of classrooms.

"Mr. Haley!" she called out, now at his heels. "Mr. Haley, that doesn't belong to you!"

"Oh? Who does it belong to, then?" he said, without slowing his pace.

"It says so right there inside. Morighan. Not Haley."

Mr. Haley scoffed and continued walking. "And you think, as the last Morighan standing, you have some sort of claim on it?"

"My ancestor wrote it," Nelly said, ignoring his last-Morighan-standing comment.

"This book has been passed down through my family for generations," Mr. Haley said, speeding up. "My ancestor—"

"Stole it from mine!" Nelly cut in. That book might be Nelly's best chance at helping Grandmother. She wasn't about to let it go without a fight.

Mr. Haley stopped in front of his office and whirled on her.

"Did you ever wonder why my uncle married your grandmother?" he hissed, leaning toward her. "Uncle Gilbert never mentioned her, never once in all the years I've known him. And he was like a father to me. Then suddenly they were engaged. Moira Morighan and the richest man in the whole county. Doesn't that strike you as odd?"

"He loves her," Nelly said, standing her ground.

"You're naïve." Mr. Haley held up the diary. "My ancestor might have taken this old book from yours, but your grandmother stole *everything* from me. I'd like to say we're even, but we both know you came out ahead."

Nelly glared. "I need that book, Mr. Haley."

"I am your teacher. Try to take this book again and I will make certain you're expelled from this school ... if you're not expelled already."

With that, he marched into his office and slammed the door. Nelly raised her fist, about to slam it against the door, but she stopped herself. She stood there with her fist in midair and then unclenched her hand and looked at it. When Nelly had smacked the desk in the library, her hand had left a burn mark on the wood. And when she had slapped Orson Kennedy ...

There were eyes on her. The students milling in the corridors had stopped their conversations and were staring at her. She held her hand to her chest and then ran.

That night, Nelly lay awake in bed, staring at the ceiling. The wind was still howling outside, rattling the windowpanes. Sometimes on stormy nights like this, when Grandmother couldn't sleep, she would make herself lavender tea. Nelly would sit with her in the kitchen while lavender steam swirled in the air, and they would chat about things Grandmother had read in the paper until the old woman's eyes started to droop.

If Grandmother couldn't sleep in the psych ward, there would be no one to sit with her, no one to make her lavender tea. Nelly's thoughts drifted to her father, silent and staring, and then to Orson. She held up her hand and stared at it. The school lights through the window cast her hand's shadow on the wall, making it appear warped and monstrous.

She pulled her hand to her chest and then buried herself under her covers. She wanted to hide there forever, away from warped shadows and the reality of what she might be. *A fairy. A monster.*

A few minutes later, Nelly was too warm and kicked the covers back. The room smelled of beeswax candles and lit fireworks. She sat straight up in bed. Across from the bed, her closet door stood shut and silent. Bianca snored; the pipes gurgled.

Then ... a clicking sound.

The sound was coming from Bianca's closet on the opposite side of the room. The doorknob was turning.

Nelly shot out of bed, rushed into a shadowy corner, and pinned herself to the wall. Bianca's closet door swung open and several little lights the color of the moon whizzed into the room. Behind them in the closet stood the fairies, their heads draped in a couple of Bianca's school uniforms. Jack was looking as strange and confused as ever, blue jeweled eyes glittering behind wire-rimmed glasses, while Fig, her burnished face framed by piles of fiery hair, looked like a wild ghost, and glowed like a faint ember.

As the fairies moved into the room, silent and fierce as tigers, Nelly held her breath, hoping they wouldn't notice her, wishing she wasn't wearing blaring red pajamas.

Her heart hammered. Fig had tried to kill her the last time they met. Jack said he would try to reason with her, but what if Fig had changed *his* mind instead?

The shadows seemed to retreat from the fairies as if in deference. Then Fig tripped. She lost her footing on one of Bianca's many pairs of shoes and fell flat on the floor. *THUD!*

This stunned Nelly. It was like watching a prowling predator trip over a tree branch. It wasn't supposed to happen.

Bianca stopped snoring. "Are you serious right now?" she said, sitting up and tearing off her sleeping mask. In that same instant, faster than Nelly could gasp, Fig was back on her feet and at the end of Bianca's bed like some preternatural thing. There was the flash of a snuffbox in Fig's hand and then a burst of powder. Bianca stiffened and fell backward on the bed, eyes closed.

"What did you do?" Nelly said, stepping out of the shadows. The fairies both turned to look at her with that eerie synchronicity they so often had.

"Nelly?" Bianca muttered, lying on her back.

Fig's eyebrows shot up. "Oops," she mumbled and started patting at her pockets.

"*Oops?*" Nelly said, alarmed, and rushed to Bianca's bedside.

Bianca blinked and looked deeply into Nelly's eyes. "You ... you ... you ... you're beautiful," she said, her voice breathy.

Nelly would have been less surprised if Bianca had slapped her across the face.

"What?"

Bianca took Nelly's hand in hers and sat up, eyes locked on Nelly. "I've always thought so. I should have told you before. You make me feel like ... like ... like ... bubbles!" A big goofy grin spread across her face, and she laughed as though drunk.

Nelly gaped. She looked at Fig, who had another snuffbox in her hand.

"Step away from her," Fig said.

Nelly tried to pull away, but Bianca was clutching tightly to her hand.

"Where are you go—" Bianca started, but a puff of white powder on her face ended her sentence. She fell back on her pillow. A few seconds later, she was snoring.

"I mistook love dust for sleep dust," Fig said, waving a cloud of powder away from her own face. "A mistake, you understand. I am not at my best."

"Love dust?" Nelly said.

Jack stood over Bianca, shaking his head and clicking his tongue. "Nasty stuff. I don't recommend it myself."

"It won't last," Fig said after a panicked look from Nelly.

"How long?" Nelly asked.

"Maybe a few ... two or three ... months," Fig said.

"Months!"

"Or so," Fig said. "The dosing is different with humans. It's difficult to predict."

"—So, Bianca is in love with ..." Nelly couldn't believe this was happening. "Isn't there some kind of antidote?"

Fig shrugged, shook her head. She was staring at Nelly intently. So was Jack. And suddenly, Nelly remembered why she had been hiding.

"Why are you here?" she asked, backing away from them.

Jack shot Fig a look.

Fig shook sparkly white dust from her fingers and cleared her throat. "I'd, uh, I regret my behavior back at the house," she said, sounding more than a little reluctant. "I should not have attempted to harm you. I made a bargain with your grandmother, as Jack reminded me. And now I've made a bargain with Jack. I won't try to harm you again."

Nelly didn't know what to say to this.

"If you need more reassurances, you have Fig's true name now," Jack said. "The words I spoke, back at the house, that stopped Fig before she could grab you."

"If you remember them," Fig added with a sly smile. "I certainly won't be repeating them and Jack, I'd rather you didn't."

Nelly thought back to the Morighan House. She had been eating that wonderful fairy food, food so good that even thinking about it made her mouth water, and then she was answering questions, and then suddenly Fig was on her feet and then Jack shouted something and then Fig was on the floor. What had he shouted? Morris Fis ... Merry Mie ... something like that? "–So, if I say—"

Fig held up a hand. "Don't say it. You don't have to prove you remember. I believe you."

"If I say ... those words, you'll faint?" Nelly said.

"Ah no," Fig said, sitting down rather heavily on the edge of Nelly's bed.

"Fig fainted because of an unrelated personal matter," Jack said, adjusting his glasses.

"It happens sometimes," Fig said, seeming tired. "I can't control it."

"For our people, hearing our true names causes a shock at first and then great weakness," Jack said, staring curiously at the still-snoring Bianca. "Fig remains weak even now from the ordeal. So, you have both Fig's word now and, if she should break it, her name. Say it and she won't have the strength to harm you. So there, now we can be friends again." He clapped his hands and smiled as if that settled the matter.

Nelly didn't move. "But you know my name."

"Nelly is not your true name," Fig said, stroking her temple as if nursing a headache. "You haven't got a true name, not yet. You have to earn that."

Nelly frowned. The fairies had a knack for answering questions in a way that only raised a dozen more. "But how—"

"Do you want to put your grandmother back together?" Fig asked, crossing her arms.

Nelly felt a surge of hope. "You'll help her, then? You'll fix her?"

Jack nodded. "We have a bargain."

"What about my father and Orson?"

The fairies exchanged glances. "A bit of a problem there," Jack said, leaning against Bianca's bedpost. "Fig was the one who struck your grandmother, which means she is the only one who can retrieve her spirit. We need her cooperation."

Nelly looked at Fig, who looked away.

"I've already agreed to help," Fig said. "As I said, I'm in hiding, so it will be a significant risk for me to return home. But I owe Jack a favor, always a dangerous thing. I will do it."

This was a relief. The fairies were both staring at Nelly now with their shattering eyes. It took her a moment to realize why. "I'm the one who struck Orson ..."

The fairies nodded.

"You're the only one who can retrieve him," Jack said.

Nelly felt a shiver run through her whole body. "–B-But I can't go to another world."

"It's up to you," Fig said, with a wave of her hand. "How much do you like this Orson fellow?"

"I don't," Nelly said automatically. "I mean, I don't know. He was awful to me, but we were just kids." Nelly thought about Ms. Kennedy. Orson was her son, and he would be stuck in a psych ward for the rest of his life if she, Nelly, didn't do something about it. Then she thought about her father, what it felt like to visit him, to hope year after desperate year, for some response from him, some sign of life. No one deserved that.

"My father," she added, her voice small. "We don't know who struck him."

Fig cocked her head. "We can only deal with what we can deal with. We'll fix your grandmother and ... the other one and then ..." She trailed off and began stroking her temple again.

"Fig's right," Jack said, and the little lights zipping above his head gave his eyes an inhuman glow. "If it's possible to help your father in the future, then we will. But we can help your grandmother and Orson right now."

That seemed sensible enough. Nelly nodded her agreement.

Fig clapped her hands together and leaped to her feet. A second later, she and Jack were striding into Bianca's closet side by side. The little lights followed them in, and the room's shadows began to reassert themselves. Then the fairies turned together and stared at Nelly, their faces expectant.

"Now?" Nelly asked, an explosion of nerves setting off in her stomach. "–B-But I can't. I mean, I'm in my pajamas—"

"You can't wear human clothing where we're going," Jack said, his hand on the closet doorknob. "We'll get you something to wear."

Nelly stood frozen. A million things were rushing through her head. She was about to go to another world. Shouldn't she tell someone? But who would she tell and what would she say? The only people who cared about her were in the psych ward. Would anyone even notice if she disappeared from school? Would anyone care?

She glanced around the room. She couldn't take her cell phone. It was dead anyway.

Shoes, she told herself.

She walked to the end of her bed and slipped on a pair of sneakers. Then, taking a deep breath, she walked into the closet with the fairies.

The closet smelled like cedar and crisp autumn air. Tiny lights danced above their heads. Jack shut the door behind them and pulled something out of his pocket. It was a maple key.

He told Nelly to hold on to one end of it and he held onto the other. Then he wrapped a piece of blue thread around the key and both their fingers. "Think of the place where your grandmother is," he said. Nelly was about to ask why but thought better of it. She thought about the psych ward. And suddenly, the maple key glowed an odd, luminescent blue. Then, just as quickly, it faded.

"Good," Jack said. He unwrapped the thread, broke open the seed pod, and pulled out a tiny skeleton key. He stuck it into the closet door and *POP!*

The room changed. They were still in a closet, but it did not belong to Bianca. Thanks to the little lights, Nelly could see a neat row of clothing hanging behind Fig. She recognized the clothing. Not because of how they looked, but how they smelled. Like her father.

Jack cracked open the door and then signaled for Nelly and Fig to follow. Nelly recognized the room immediately. They were in her father's room in the psych ward. He lay asleep in the bed in the corner. She walked to his bedside and stared down at him. He looked like he could wake up at any moment, animated and alive. But he wasn't really there, was he?

"What are we doing here?" Nelly whispered.

"We need an item from each of those whose spirits we wish

to retrieve," Jack said. "Something the spirit can attach itself to for the journey back from our own. Is that your father?"

"Don't hurt him," Nelly said, immediately standing between her father and the fairies.

"Why would we?" Fig said. She and Jack both considered Nelly's father, their eyes roaming over his features. They exchanged meaningful looks.

"You are certain this man is your father?" Jack said.

"Well ... yeah," Nelly said. What kind of question was that?

"Hmm," he said, leaning past her and plucking a hair from her father's head.

"Why do you need his hair?" Nelly asked.

Jack did not reply.

"Look, I'm a human!" Fig said. She had put on Nelly's father's old glasses, the pair with the hairline crack, and was making silly faces.

Nelly scowled. "Don't touch those!"

Fig glared at Nelly with a ferocity that made Nelly's blood run cold, but then the fairy took off the glasses and held them forward for Nelly to take.

"We might use these to retrieve your father's spirit," Fig said. "If we ever manage it."

Nelly took the glasses from Fig.

"Oh, uh, thank you," Nelly said, but Fig had already walked away.

"I assume your grandmother and Orson are around here somewhere?" Jack asked. He was on the other side of the room now, near the door.

"Yes," Nelly said, clutching her father's glasses. "But we have to be careful. We can't let anyone see us."

"We'll take your lead," Jack said, holding out a hand. After a pause, Nelly walked over and took his hand. It was cold and coarse, the bits of paint and powder stuck to his hand giving it a calloused texture. Fig took Nelly's other hand, so the three of them formed a chain. Fig's hand was cold, too, like a winter stone.

Nelly led the fairies into the corridor and hurried them along next to the wall, like scurrying mice. She felt horribly exposed under the glaring hospital lights, dressed in red plaid pajamas, a fairy in each hand.

She pulled at them both to stop when they reached Grandmother's room and the three of them slipped inside. Grandmother was asleep in the bed in the corner. Nelly tried to think of an item of hers they could use to ... whatever Jack had said.

Grandmother's wrought iron bell necklace, the one she always wore, was sitting on the bedside table. Nelly reached for it.

"I wouldn't touch that if I were you," Jack said.

Nelly paused. *Iron.*

"No spirit will attach itself to cold iron," Jack said. "It is an offense to us."

"Us?" Nelly repeated, but Jack looked away from her, his eyes darting toward Fig like a pair of glistening fish in dark water.

Fig had opened the closet and was shuffling through the items inside. Nelly jumped to join her. She didn't like the idea of strangers rifling through Grandmother's things. Fig got the idea and let Nelly take over.

There were a bunch of outfits hanging there that Nelly recognized. Mr. Glanville must have brought them over. She flipped through them until she found a black jacket pinned with a weird black brooch made of feathers and sequins. She unpinned it and held it up for the fairies, who nodded their approval.

Back in the corridor, Nelly and the fairies scurried along the wall. It was past midnight, and the hallways were deserted.

But the overhead fluorescents were relentlessly bright, and Nelly kept expecting a nurse or an orderly to come waltzing around every corner.

They made it to Orson's room without incident. But he wasn't in bed. He was sitting in a chair, staring out the window at the clouds drifting across the moon. Nelly took a tentative step toward him while the fairies hung back in the shadows.

"Orson?" she whispered, but he did not acknowledge her.

"Everything's going to be OK soon. I'm going to help you," she added, knowing he probably wasn't aware of her.

A squeaking sound came from the corridor, like the rolling of grocery cart wheels. Jack popped up at Nelly's side. He took her hand. His was covered in dust. Fig took Nelly's other hand. Hers was also covered in dust.

Then the entire room flipped upside down. Nelly's back was suddenly pinned to the floor. The fairies were with her, holding her hands tightly. She looked up and there was Orson, still sitting in his chair. But he was upside down, attached to the ceiling, seemingly defying gravity.

No, that wasn't right. Nelly and the fairies were the ones on the ceiling. She was looking down, not up. The door beneath Nelly and the fairies opened, and a man walked in, pushing a cart of medical supplies. He was a nurse, wearing scrubs.

"Come on, Orson," the nurse said. "You can't keep getting out of bed every night." The nurse led a blank-faced Orson to his bed and tucked him in. All the while Nelly watched from the ceiling, holding her breath, in total disbelief that this was happening.

The nurse walked out of the room a few seconds later, taking his trundling cart with him. As soon as the nurse closed the door, the room flipped again, and Nelly and the fairies were back on the floor.

The room spun. Nelly stumbled to one side and fell.

"A rare dust, that one," Jack said with a little grin. "Give it a moment. You'll get your legs back."

Nelly wasn't the only dizzy one. Fig took a few wobbly steps and dropped to the floor as well, her raggedy dress billowing around her.

Jack held out a hand for Nelly. She was about to take it, but a flash of yellow caught her eye. She reached under the bed and pulled out a small, yellow bouncy ball. It was the same ball Nelly had found outside Orson's room at the beginning of the summer.

"This is Orson's," she said.

"Good. Then let's get out of here," Fig said, picking herself up. "Let's get out of this whole world."

Nelly felt cold and shivery. But there was no turning back now. She stood up and followed the fairies into the closet.

CHAPTER EIGHTEEN

AWAY WITH THE FAIRIES

There was one last stop before the fairy world: the Morighan House, for a change of clothes. There, Fig gave Nelly a crazy, raggedy dress stitched with too much thread and bits of ivy and flower heads. It fell in uneven layers that Nelly quickly discovered, concealed dozens of pockets. Fig said the pockets were for dusts, tinctures, night keys, or elfshot.

"What's an elfshot?" Nelly asked.

Jack pulled a tiny flint arrowhead out of one of his own concealed pockets. "We use them to deliver the effects of a dust or tincture from a distance."

This, of course, only raised more questions. Why did fairies use dusts and tinctures and elfshots?

"Elfshot," Jack said, correcting Nelly's Eldritch grammar. The word *elfshot* did not need to be pluralized, and fairy magic only worked by contact, he explained. A fairy had to touch another, skin-to-skin, to deliver any sort of blow, magical or otherwise.

"We get around this by infusing objects with various prop-erties," Jack went on, animated as Nelly had never seen him.

"Dusts work best since they are easy to deliver, if not always accurate. Tinctures are more concentrated and powerful, but harder to deliver. Elfshot is best for stealth, but we consider it underhanded unless there's no other choice."

"Jack is a spinner," Fig chimed in. "He's trained over many years to spin magic into objects. It's considered an art form back home. And Jack is one of the best."

Jack gave an embarrassed smile. "When we get back, I'll show you my workshop."

Standing alone in one of the Morighan House's abandoned bedrooms, Nelly shivered at the thought of what she was about to do. She slipped the hooded jacket Fig had given her over her dress and looked at herself in an old cheval glass mirror.

She didn't look like a fairy from a storybook, that was for sure. They always seemed to have exquisite gowns and flashing jewels and coiffured hair. Nelly moved the mirror into a beam of moonlight to get a better look at herself. She tugged at her dress. She looked slouchy and raggedy and just weird. But not quite human either, and that was what was really bothering her.

Had she always looked this way? Had her eyes always gleamed like this in the moonlight? Had her hair and skin always been so ghostly? No wonder the people of Nothing stayed away from her.

The door opened, and Fig stuck her heart-shaped face into the room. "It's time."

On the main floor, Nelly found the Morighan House kitchen returned to its former condition: broken tiles, spider webs, and boarded windows. Once again, the door to the basement was a splintered wreck. Had the restored kitchen she'd seen before been some kind of illusion?

Jack was at the table packing a bag, and Fig was nowhere to be seen. Instead, an old woman stood in the corner next to an unlit lantern, popping cherries into her mouth.

Nelly caught Jack's eye and motioned toward the woman.

His eyebrows went up. "Oh, that's Fig. It's dangerous for her to show herself back home so she's under a glamour."

"A glamour?" Nelly repeated.

"A disguise," Jack said with a wink.

Nelly looked the old woman up and down. If this was Fig, the transformation was remarkable. There was no trace of Fig's living-doll beauty in that old, wizened face. Even Fig's hands had aged, her knuckles knobby and pulsing with blue veins as she fiddled with a cherry stem. If she were human, Nelly would have guessed she was at least a hundred.

The old woman grinned and suddenly Nelly did recognize her. She had the same dark, sad eyes as Fig had, eyes that stayed sad even when she smiled.

"You mustn't call me Fig, either," Fig said, her voice still sounding like her own. "That name of mine is known back home."

"How about Nettle?" Jack said and grinned mischievously.

Fig crossed her arms. "Are you saying I'm prickly?"

"Of course not," Jack said with a wry smile. He strapped his bag over his chest. "Let's go then, prickly."

Fig gave Jack a mock-annoyed look and then pushed

herself from the counter with the agility of someone much younger than a hundred. Nelly wasn't sure what to make of this back-and-forth between the fairies. They seemed to have let their guard down in front of her for the first time. For a moment they had not been strange, predatory fairies, but a pair of old friends.

This didn't last. Outside, under the eerie glow of the moon, they became strange and predatory once more. The night was cold. Nelly's ragged fairy clothing whipped against her legs in the biting wind.

Jack held out a hand. "We'll move quickly now."

Nelly's heart hammered wildly. She took his hand and immediately pulled away. His hand was colder than the night. He grabbed her hand again and held firm. The cold of it was painful. Fig took Nelly by the other hand. Her hand was even colder.

The fairies took off at a run, pulling Nelly along with them. They raced toward the forest at a pace that felt like flying. Nelly's hair lashed her face. Her eyes stung with tears. She was running her legs as fast as she could to keep up with the fairies, but her feet were barely touching the earth. They burst through clawing branches into the dark forest. The fairies moved confidently, never stumbling or slowing despite the darkness and the trees. They veered this way and that around obstacles, sending up a spray of mud and leaves. They leaped over fallen logs, through bogs, over hedges and ditches. It was both terrifying and exhilarating to run this fast and with so much certainty. It was like a dream. Nelly had a roller-coaster feeling in her stomach. Each long bound was a leap into darkness and potential disaster, but they always landed safely and then immediately leaped up again into the cold unknown.

Water rushed somewhere nearby. It was the only sound Nelly could make out over the wind in her ears. The fairies made no sound. They were as silent as ghosts. Then they stopped. They let go of Nelly and she flew forward, landing down hard in a splash of mud and roots and acorns. Black water rushed by. She was on a riverbank. It had to be the bank of the river Nought, the only river that ran behind the Morighan farm.

Trees swayed in the wind overhead. Nelly got up, wiping her muddy hands on her fairy coat. "What ... are ... we ... doing ... here?" she managed between breaths.

The fairies didn't appear out of breath or tired in the slightest.

"We must cross the river," Jack said, his eyes flashing, his skin gleaming faintly.

Fig's old lady face was livid in the darkness. She pulled a key out of one of her pockets and held it between her gnarled fingers. It was a skeleton key like the ones they had used to pop between closets, but much larger. Like those other keys, this one gave Nelly a shivery feeling, as though it were alive and whispering about dark things.

Fig dropped to her knees, right into the mud on the river-bank. She held the key out in front of her like a knife and plunged it into the damp earth. Then she twisted it as if it was in a lock. *CLUNK*! There was a sound like a lock sliding open.

Jack dropped to his knees next to Fig. Together, they took hold of a tree root protruding from the ground. They yanked on the root and an enormous chunk of earth separated from the riverbank like a trapdoor. Jack and Fig heaved this door-like chunk of earth upward and then pushed it back until it fell with a great *SPLUNK* on the riverbank. Where the chunk of earth had been, there was now a deep, dank hole.

Nelly stepped to the edge of the hole and peered down into darkness.

Fig whistled. A few seconds later, several tiny lights

whizzed toward them between the trees. Fig held up an unlit lantern, and the lights flew inside it, lighting it up like super-charged fireflies.

She held up the lantern, her eyes reflecting the light like a cat's. "I'll go first," she said and casually stepped over the edge of the hole.

Nelly gasped as the light of Fig's lantern fell and fell and fell, getting smaller and smaller until finally, fathoms below, it stopped.

Nelly's mouth hung open. "Is Fig—"

"Nettle," Jack interrupted. "You must remember to call her Nettle from now on. "

"Ready!" came Fig's voice, echoing up from below.

Jack handed Nelly a bag of powdery dust. "Take this. Count to ten, pull the string, and clap it between your hands."

Nelly looked over the edge. "No, no, no. I can't. It's too far. It's not—"

"Sure, you can," Jack said and shoved her.

With a small yelp, Nelly plunged into the dark. The smell of damp earth enveloped her. Wind roared. Fig's lantern hurtled up toward her.

She was going to die, wasn't she? What had Jack said, count to ten? She hadn't been counting. She pulled the string on the bag of dust and clapped the bag between her hands. Her stomach lurched. The whole world seemed to flip as it had in the psych ward.

Her back smacked into something cold and damp. She thought for a moment that it was some kind of ceiling. She stared down a long tunnel that led to branches and a starry sky below her. No, she wasn't upside down. She was lying on her back on the ground.

Fig stepped into view above her, raised her lantern, and gazed down at her. The fairy held out a hand. Nelly took it and allowed herself to be pulled to her feet. Fathoms above them, the earthen door slammed shut, blotting out the stars.

"Everyone all right?" Jack's voice said. Nelly spun around. Jack stood behind her, his face eerily lit by Fig's lantern. He brushed dirt from his trousers.

"How did you ..." Nelly stopped mid-sentence. The ground below her was shifting. It slid downward as if they were in an elevator.

"What's happening?" Nelly asked. And then she realized they *were* in an elevator. They weren't in a hole in the ground anymore, not strictly. They were in a small room made entirely of green glass and the room was moving downward. She could see through the glass to the earthen walls, which were stuck in places with roots and small lights. She touched the green glass. It was smooth and solid.

"–H-How is this possible?" she asked the fairies, one of whom was glamoured to look like an old woman, and immediately realized it was a silly question.

As the room descended, they passed what appeared to be graffiti scrawled here and there on the earthen walls. Nelly tried to read the graffiti but could only make out a few sentences: YOU ARE LOST. CROSSING MEANS DEATH. WE WILL FIND YOU.

"That's the Fury," Jack said, nodding at the graffiti. "Threats, warnings for those who cross to the human world."

"Or promises," Fig said, her voice grim. "We'll hope not."

After what felt like a long time, the glass room lurched to a stop.

Jack shot Nelly a look. "Oh, can you swim?"

"Why?" she asked, and the floor fell out beneath them.

Nelly managed a panicked gasp before water swallowed her whole. The cold of it shocked every nerve in her body. She reached upward, grasping for the surface, but only found more water. In a panic, she drove herself upward, grasping, reaching, expecting with every horrifying second to hit the floor of the green glass elevator. But there was only more water, black as ink. She climbed and climbed. She needed air. Her lungs were screaming for it. She saw pinpoints of light, flickering and foggy. She was going to lose consciousness. Air, air, she needed air!

The surface broke. Nelly gasped. Oxygen and relief flooded her lungs.

THUD!

Something hit her on the head. Something grabbed the collar of her dress. Something lifted her out of the water like a dead fish and dropped her flat on her stomach, on the deck of a boat.

Nelly coughed and gasped, spitting water out of her mouth. She tried to lift herself, but her limbs gave out beneath her.

Then something spoke.

"You've killed our fish," a voice said. It was hollow and faraway sounding.

Nelly tried again to move, to see who or what was speaking.

"It's moving," a second voice said, also sounding distant and reedy.

Nelly forced herself to her hands and knees, blinking water from her eyes. She turned around and immediately recoiled. Sitting side by side across from her in the bow of a small fishing boat were two *things*. The things sat hunched, dressed in tangled rags, their faces covered by masks shaped like angler fish. Where their eyes should have been, there were deep, black holes.

"It's stronger than we thought," one voice said, the fish mask bobbing as it spoke. "I don't feel as hungry as before."

"Yes, stronger," the second voice said. "It will make a good meal."

Nelly cried out in horror. She was about to jump out of the boat when something leaped high out of the water like a shark, grabbed one of the things, and yanked it over the edge.

"Nelly," a voice said. It was Jack. "Glad you made it." He picked up an oar from the deck and swung it at the remaining thing. The oar sailed right through the thing, as if through air.

Fig, still looking like an old woman, climbed into the boat next. It was Fig who had yanked the first thing out of the boat. Whatever those things were, they were gone. Empty rags swirled on the water and two fish masks spun on the surface like children's toys.

Nelly found her voice. "What were those?"

"Shh," Fig said, eyes flashing.

"Dead things," Jack whispered. "Let's not speak of them."

Nelly sat in the stern and hugged herself as the fairies picked up oars and plunged them into the water, rowing with determined vigor. Soon they were gliding forward.

They appeared to be on a lake, or maybe something much bigger. Mist hung over the water. Their little boat cut through it like a knife through cream. Through the mist, dozens and then hundreds and then thousands of lights hovered just above the surface. It was as if the night sky had fallen, and they were drifting through it.

Behind the boat, a wake of phosphorescent light rippled in the water as if the boat and the oars were leaving bioluminescent trails behind. Nelly reached over the edge of the stern and stuck her finger in the water. Around it swirled rings of luminescent color.

THUNK! The boat ran aground. The fairies jumped out into shallow water and dragged the boat up onto the muddy shore with easy strength. Nelly followed them, jumping out into the water, her splashing strides producing more luminescent rings.

They were on a long beach. The fairies signaled to Nelly and then moved quickly and quietly along the shore. Fig held a lantern. Nelly had no idea how it had survived the water. It swung at Fig's side, casting a small circle of light around them. Nelly did her best to keep up with the swift fairies and the swaying light.

Behind the beach was a dark forest of twisted trees and undergrowth. Light flickered between the trees, giving the impression of a city somewhere within the forest. Nelly could hear things, too, as they hurried along the beach. Bells ringing here and there, sticks knocking together, wind chimes, disembodied whispers, and rattles.

The fairies led Nelly up the side of a bluff where the strangest house she had ever seen came into view. It was a sort of treehouse. Not a house built into a tree, a house that somehow was a tree, or many trees that each looked to have spontaneously grown house parts. Trunks grew into moss-covered walls and awnings dripped with ivy. Lanterns dangled from curving branches and round windows sat inside giant knots in the bark. The trees themselves were crooked and windswept, leaning dramatically to one side as though about to dive from the bluffs into the water. The house jutted in uneven levels into the treetops and pulsed with a weird glow in the moonlight.

The fairies made their way along a mossy path to the house's arched front door. Nelly, who had stopped to stare at the house with her mouth hanging open, had to run to catch up to them.

Fig opened her lantern and nodded as the lights inside flew free and whisked away into the woods.

"Doed left the lights on again," Jack muttered as he opened the front door.

He ushered them into a small entrance hall where lights dangled from fishing wire. A large map hung on the wall. On it in big letters were the words *Weird Wood, Southwest Corner*. Notes were scrawled all over its surface. On either side of the entrance hall, archways led to dark corridors.

Jack shut and bolted the front door when they were all inside.

"Doed!" he called out. "Where is that boy?"

He eyed Nelly and went from serious to smiling. "Where are my manners? Welcome, welcome. This is my home. I'll show you around, but let's all change into dry clothing first. I'll put on some tea. I think we could all use some. Nettle, your glamour's slipped."

Fig looked like herself again, young and doll-like. But her face and clothing were now smeared in messy blotches of what appeared to be makeup or paint. It was as if the old-woman disguise had been nothing more than an elaborate makeup job and now was running.

Jack led Nelly and Fig down a gloomy hallway. The floors were creaky and uneven with frequent random steps up and down, seemingly to navigate over tree roots. They scaled a spiral staircase built around a tree trunk.

On the next level, the floors slanted starkly to one side. Jack showed Nelly to a low doorway crisscrossed with branches. They ducked under the branches and into a small bedroom that hung out over the bluffs. Nelly could see the water through a large, round window that waves sprayed periodically. Jack opened a closet full of clean clothing and linens and told her to make herself comfortable.

Alone now, by the light of a table lantern, Nelly changed out of her wet clothing into a nightdress and cozy socks. She gazed out the window at lights bobbing over the waves and breathed in the scent of sea and cedar.

She couldn't believe she was here. Another world. Was she insane to have done this? To have trusted these fairies who had threatened her life and hurt her grandmother?

Yes, she decided. This was insane. But that didn't matter. She wasn't about to let her grandmother or even Orson rot away in an institution for the rest of their lives, not if she could do something about it.

Nelly met Fig in the hallway, though Fig didn't look like Fig or even an old lady anymore. Now she looked like a teenage girl with tangled hair and sunken cheeks, dressed in a nightgown. But her voice was the same. So were her dark, sad eyes.

She led Nelly back down to the main floor and then to a round room that appeared to be some sort of library. Shelves made of branches stuffed to the brim with books lined every inch of the place from floor to ceiling. More books were jammed into oddly shaped corners or stuffed into hollows in the tree bark walls. In the middle of the room, there stood a fireplace with a merry fire crackling inside.

Nelly and Fig sat on matching ruby-red armchairs by the fire. Jack served them tea that smelled of cinnamon and cloves, and cakes that tasted like pumpkin pie. It was all very warm and comforting, especially after the cold and horror of the water, and Nelly soon found her mind going fuzzy and her eyes drooping.

"What do we do next?" she asked, forcing herself to stay awake. "How do we get Grandmother's and Orson's spirits back?"

Jack sat on the floor by the fire, picking a few notes out on a fiddle. "There's nothing to be done tonight. We need to rest. We'll all be suffering from the drag for a night or two. That's a kind of tiredness caused by crossing from one world to another."

Nelly found her eyes drifting back to the fire as Jack plucked on the fiddle strings. The sound was hypnotic. She forced herself to concentrate. "But once we've recovered, how do we—"

"Tomorrow," Jack said and yawned. "Tomorrow ..."

Nelly yawned, too. Her eyes drifted again, this time to the books lining the walls. Titles were visible on their spines: *Stoat's Guide to Spinning; Key Craft: Advanced Studies; Life in the Days of Thistle and Rime; Great Debates of the Past 1000 Years; The Human Threat: Yesterday's Crisis, Today's Distraction; The Weeping Wars Volumes 1–50.*

"What're the Weeping Wars?" Nelly asked, trying to keep herself from nodding off.

"Hmm?" Jack said, looking up from his fiddle. "Oh, they were a series of great battles that almost destroyed our people. But they ended thousands of years ago. Nothing to worry about now."

"Oh," Nelly said, still gazing at the titles. "The human threat? Do the fairy people see humans as a threat?"

"Some do," Jack said. "It's a controversial matter."

Nelly found this bizarre. "I don't think humans are a threat to fairies," she said. "Most humans don't even believe fairies exist."

"Well then, that settles the matter, doesn't it?" Fig said, folding her arms. "Perhaps we should have Nelly testify in debate, convince the Fury?"

The Fury, Nelly thought and felt a chill. She remembered what the fairies had told her about them. The Fury enforce the law. *And no human may know of our existence and live.*

Fig and Jack were exchanging grins. Fig had been mocking her, Nelly realized.

"But it's true," Nelly said, indignant. "Humans are not a threat to fairies."

"If only the truth mattered," Fig said.

"It doesn't?" Nelly said. The idea of a world where truth didn't matter sounded terrible, and suddenly Nelly wanted to do what she came here to do as fast as she could and get back home.

"The truth matters," Jack said. "Of course it does, but there are people who believe that truth matters less than ... other concerns. Dangerous people."

"You mean like the Fury," Nelly said.

There was a heavy silence. Fig leaned back in her chair. "Let's not speak of such things," she said, now looking deeply tired. "Play us a song, Jack. One for forgetting all that's wrong and dark and sad."

Jack stood up and then dragged his bow across his fiddle strings, releasing a plaintive sigh. He launched into a slow, haunting melody that was itself wrong and dark and sad in ways Nelly could not explain. But it was lulling, too. As Jack played and the fire sent shadows dancing along the walls, she could no longer resist the fog descending over her.

She closed her eyes and fell asleep.

CHAPTER NINETEEN

JACK'S WORKSHOP

The next morning, Nelly woke to warm sunlight on her face. As she lay in bed, cozy under the covers, she blinked open her eyes, and for a brief moment, she thought everything she had experienced with the fairies had been a crazy dream. Then sea water sprayed against the window over her bed, and the whole room bobbed up and down. Branches creaked.

She sat up. She was in the fairy world. In Jack's house. She was here to get her grandmother's spirit back. And Orson's, too.

A raggedy dress hung from a hook by the door. Nelly got herself washed and dressed. She was surprised to find that the fairies had indoor plumbing in a washroom down the hall. There were taps in the room over a basin, each made of a glass-like material she could not identify. They poured water in gentle streams like soft rain. She wasn't sure why this had been so surprising to her. She had learned in history class that the ancient Romans had indoor plumbing. Why shouldn't the fairies? Maybe it was because everything about the fairies was mysterious and magical. But plumbing wasn't mysterious. It made sense in a concrete, mechanical way and she wondered if the fairies weren't so different from humans after all.

The scent of spiced tea and baking honey cakes wafted up the stairs. Stomach growling, Nelly crept down the spiral staircase in her socks. On the main floor, she could hear the sounds of pots and pans and the low murmur of Jack and Fig in conversation. She followed the sounds around a bend, up and down crooked steps, and past round windows until she spotted a triangle-shaped doorway. Ivy the color of autumn leaves dangled everywhere. Sun catchers suspended in the doorway sent splashes of light rippling across the floor and up the walls.

Nelly hesitated. She had the urge to explore this weird house, to poke around a bit on her own, away from watchful fairy eyes. But as soon as she had the thought, Grandmother's voice was in her head. *"You mustn't snoop, Nelly. It's rude."* Then the voices of Jack and Fig became clearer.

"Doubts," Fig was saying. "Serious doubts. Are you sure we can trust her?"

"No. But I don't see that we have a choice," Jack said. "She knows something. She must. We'll get it out of her. One way or another."

Nelly backed away from the doorway. If the fairies didn't trust her, then she didn't trust them, she decided. Perhaps a little snooping was in order, after all.

"Best check on the girl," Fig said.

How did the fairies do that? It was like they had a sixth sense!

Nelly looked around for a place to hide. A low curtain of ivy hung from the side of a staircase. The ivy, she saw, concealed a crawl space under the stairs. Nelly ducked into the dark space and crouched there, silent and still.

The space was cramped and smelled of earth and forest resin. Jack's shadow swept across the floor on the other side of the ivy. He had not noticed her. Nelly grinned a little, proud of herself. When she had appeared in the basement of the Morighan House, the fairies had found her with supernatural ease. Maybe she was getting better at fairy stealth.

There was dust on the floor, fairy dust, in an array of colors. A trail of it led to Nelly's left, where splatters of it ran up what she could now see was a small door. The tarnished bronze lock on the door was shaped like a monstrous face yawning wide. The handle above it was shaped like a tail.

"This way," the lock whispered.

Nelly blinked. "Did ... did you just speak?"

The lock winked and clicked its tongue. The tail-like handle lowered, and the door opened. Nelly peeked inside. The trail of dust continued beyond the door, where a root ladder led down into a basement.

Nelly crawled through the door and lowered herself onto the ladder. The fairies would probably find her any second. But this was an opportunity, and she didn't want to pass it up. Jack and Fig weren't telling her the whole truth, of that much she was certain. Maybe on her own, she could find some clue, some stray piece of information that would reveal their secrets.

Climbing down the root ladder, Nelly found herself in a room that wasn't really a room at all. It was a tangled labyrinth of tree roots splattered with fairy dust. Above her head, roots dangled apart like an elegant canopy, while, throughout the room, bulging roots twisted from ceiling to floor like stalactites in a cave. She worked her way around them, ducking and weaving until she found a spot where they grew apart like drapes that had been opened. She walked through this archway into a second, larger space.

This next room was an enormous subterranean hall. Its

walls curved up to an arched ceiling at uneven heights, as the room appeared to have been built underneath the bluffs. There were skylights on the ceiling. Sunlight beamed from them like spotlights.

But what was in the room was even more bizarre.

Spinning wheels. Dozens of old-fashioned spinning wheels, each a different size. The wheels were linked up to form a giant spinning contraption that rotated like an orrery made of spinning wheels instead of model planets. Colorful threads ran through wheels and around hooks that jutted out of the floor or ceiling, giving the place the look of a spider's lair.

On the floor, around and between this shifting mass, were dozens of wooden buckets. Each bucket contained vials or pouches of powder. The buckets had labels, such as SLEEP DUST, GROUND FIRE, TRUTHWORT TINCTURE, or FOG FLOUR.

Every surface of the entire room, the floor, the walls, the ceiling, was covered with blotches of glittering color, like the studio of the messiest painter in the world.

Nelly marveled at the room, ducking as one of the spinning wheels rotated past her. She ran her hand through a fractured sunbeam, which seemed to pour through her fingers like water. She slid past threads and buckets and wheels, exploring more of the room and the weird contraption.

"What are you?" a voice said.

Nelly whirled around. A boy about her age stood in the shadows. He was tall and slender, with dark hair, pale skin, and sunken eyes.

He stepped toward her, passing under a skylight, and the sun lit up half his face, showing an eye that was a shocking shade of gold.

"You're not ... right," he whispered.

Then he fainted.

Nelly stood there for several surprised seconds. Then she turned and ran.

On the main floor, Nelly found Jack and Fig in a half-moon-shaped room that appeared to be a kitchen. Jack was pouring a cup of tea while Fig, who still did not look like Fig, was sitting at a table reading some sort of newspaper.

"Oh Nelly, there you are," Jack said, and then his face changed. He put down his tea and Fig stood up.

"What's the matter?" they said in perfect, synchronized unison.

Nelly led the fairies to the crawlspace where the talking lock said, "He's really done it this time," in a clattering voice, and laughed. The lock's laughter followed them as they climbed down the ladder, into the room of roots, and then into the room with the churning contraption of connected spinning wheels.

The boy was where Nelly had left him, passed out on the ground beyond the spinning wheels. Jack spotted him and was at the boy's side as quick as a thought.

He patted the boy's cheek. "Doed," he said again and again.

The boy's eyes were closed, his mouth was slack. His skin, which had already been frighteningly pale, was almost blue.

"You've got to give him something to counter whatever he's done to himself," Fig said. She stood nearby, hugging herself. She didn't look like the old woman or even the teenage girl she had appeared as last night. Now she looked like an elegant woman in her thirties with black hair and a graceful neck. Her face was a worried frown.

"–I-I don't know what he's taken," Jack muttered, shaking

the boy. "Fig, look around. See if you can find an empty vial or—"

The boy gasped. His strange golden eyes flew open. "Fig?" he said, grasping Jack by the shirt. "She's dead!"

"No, Doed," Jack said. "She's here." He pointed at Fig, who was ducking under rotating spinning wheels, eyes darting back and forth, searching the ground.

"NO!" the boy shouted. He scrambled away from Jack, golden eyes wide in hysterical panic, only stopping when his back hit the wall. He closed his eyes and covered his ears.

"Not listening. Won't listen. Go away, go away," he repeated, rocking back and forth.

Nelly, wanting to help, started searching around as well, though she did not know what to look for. Then she noticed a little glass bottle partially hidden by a bucket, close to where she stood. The bottle was on its side, a dark liquid dribbling from its mouth.

Nelly grabbed the bottle and was about to call out to Jack. But she stopped. There was a smell wafting from the bottle, a smell she recognized. A memory flooded her senses. It was night. She was on the Morighan House porch while the door creaked in the wind. She held a dark blue bottle in her hand. Her mother stood across from her and told her to drink.

The boy let out a petrified scream, jolting Nelly back to where she was and what was happening.

"I found something!" she said, holding up the bottle.

"Toss it here!" Jack said.

Nelly threw the bottle to Jack, through a gap between the spinning wheels and connecting threads.

Jack caught it, took one look at it, and muttered, "Piper's dew ... Fig, the white bottles over there!"

Fig scooped up a bottle filled with milky liquid from a bucket marked MILK OF THE DEAD and tossed it to Jack.

The boy struggled against Jack, who forced him to drink from the bottle. Jack plugged the boy's nose and held a hand over his mouth. As soon as the boy swallowed, he immediately calmed. His breathing slowed. He stopped shivering. Color came to his cheeks. His skin was now less blue and more naturally pale. He opened his eyes, blinking, and his pupils, which had been gigantic, shrank down to normal size.

"You're back," he said, looking up at Jack.

"Where did you get this, Doed?" Jack demanded, holding up the little blue bottle.

The boy, Doed, glanced at it. He tried to stand. Jack took him by the arm, but Doed pulled away.

"I'm fine," he said, one hand on the wall for support.

"You are not." Jack held out the bottle with the white liquid.

"Drink."

"I said I'm fine," Doed snapped and pushed the white bottle away. Then, wobbly on his feet, he shoved past Jack and weaved around the spinning wheels toward the root room.

"I want to talk about this, Doed," Jack called after him.

Doed waved a dismissive hand over his shoulder. As he passed Nelly, he glanced at her with those strange golden eyes but did not stop. He disappeared into the room of roots.

"He hasn't changed," Fig said to Jack. She frowned and shook her head when a door above them slammed shut.

Jack rubbed the back of his neck. "I promised Birdy I would watch over him."

"What kind of apprentice is he, anyway?" Fig asked, picking up a cloth pouch from a bucket marked TIPSY TONIC. "I'm sure he takes more than he makes."

"He has the talent."

Fig dropped the bag back into the basket, and a puff of glittery dust wafted into the air. "He squanders it."

"He's my brother," Jack said.

"In name only," Fig said.

"Yes, but he's still ..." Jack paused and glanced over at Nelly as if just remembering she was there. "Nelly. I apologize for that. Family matters, you know."

Nelly shifted awkwardly. She knew she had just witnessed something private. It was strange to see the fairies this way, so vulnerable and worried, and to think that even they had family drama. But it wasn't their family drama that was on her mind. She couldn't keep her eyes off the blue bottle in Jack's hand. What was that stuff the boy had taken? And why had Nelly's mother given the same stuff to her?

"Well, now that you're here, what do you think of my workshop?" Jack said, slipping the bottle into his pocket. "It's my own design. A demonstration?"

"A demonstration?" Nelly repeated and nodded immediately. She wanted to know about whatever was in the blue bottle, but she wasn't about to pass up a chance to see how this crazy room worked.

Jack clapped his hands together. "Yes, yes! A demonstration! Nettle, if you would? And Nelly, this way, this way!"

Jack moved between threads and ducked under wheels as giddy as a kid at a carnival. Nelly trailed after Jack, around and under and between the parts of the rotating contraption.

Jack called it a "spinnery." Under the administration of a trained spinner like him, a spinnery could extract the magic that is particular to one fairy and transmute it into a dust or a tincture that anyone could then use.

"You see, there are certain skills we all share as People, such as the ability to strike or spark a glamour, for instance," he explained. As he moved, he made adjustments to the spinnery, rolling the wheels this way or that, shifting threads from hooks to wheels or one wheel to another. "But there are many more abilities that are unique to specific individuals or peoples."

Clouds of powder puffed from the threads as Jack manipulated them. They stained his fingers and clothing with what looked like dusty paint splatters. Nelly found she had to stay close to him to avoid the crisscrossing parts of the spinnery flying every which way. Jack seemed to know just where to step. She was mesmerized, watching his fingers dart around, deftly handling the threads and wheels. It was like watching a spider at work or a master musician.

As he worked, he told her a list of traits some fairies had that others did not. The Nodding People of Dousy Way could put you to sleep with a touch. From them, spinners could extract sleep dust. From the Blue Men of the Western Moors, he could extract a smoky mist called flash fog that could drop any glamour. Buttery Sprites produced truthwort powder, which acted as a truth serum. While the Love Talker of the Dim Evenings was unique and was the only one from whom spinners could extract love dust.

"But he's trouble, that one," Jack said, as he gathered up a handful of threads. "Very difficult to get his cooperation. And even if you do, half the time you'll end up in love with him, for months on end, and no one wants that. Some spinners have taken to knocking him out and extracting the dust against his will. I don't work that way myself. I prefer willing subjects. They produce more potent dust."

Fig came into view. She was standing at the center of the spinnery, her feet inside an empty bucket.

"Ah, and here is our willing subject," Jack said, smiling. Then he spun the threads he had gathered around Fig's arms. "Nettle, as you know, is a Fire Sitter," he said, winding threads around her. "Fire Sitters have the ability to produce fire and soon, so will I." He winked at Nelly.

He wrapped more thread around Fig's arms down to her fingertips and then fed the threads back into the spinnery so that she now almost seemed a part of the thing. Then he led Nelly out of the spinnery to a lever on the wall. He pulled the lever and the spinnery ground to a halt. "Stand behind me," he added, sapphire eyes glittering behind his glasses.

Nelly immediately ducked behind him, bracing herself for whatever was about to happen.

Jack pulled down the lever on the spinnery, and it creaked back to life. It spun counterclockwise in the opposite direction it had been moving before. Fig, at the center of the contraption, went stiff. Then, something remarkable happened. Sparks flashed from between Fig's fingers and smoke rose in long tendrils.

The spinnery picked up speed, rotating faster and faster. Lights flickered and flashed, sparks flew, glittering dust wafted into the air, and gusts of wind from the thing blew Nelly's hair back.

Fig held her arms up in the air now, perhaps because the spinnery was forcing her to do so. Her glamour slipped several times, her face shifting back and forth from her doll-like self to her dark-haired-woman disguise. Then her whole body lifted into the air until her feet were hovering above the bucket. After about 30 seconds, Jack pulled the lever and the whole thing slowed to a stop. Fig dropped back down into the bucket.

"Now look, look!" Jack clapped his hands together in excitement.

He rushed over to Fig, who lowered her arms. The threads that had been cocooned around her dissolved into dust and poured down into the bucket. Fig shook herself off and then stepped out of the bucket.

"Now over here, over here," he said, pushing the bucket

toward a table wound around with thread and smeared with so much paint-like dust it looked like a modern art project.

Nelly followed Fig, whose footprints across the floor smoldered like embers. On the table sat a mess of brushes, bowls, and bottles of various colors. Jack stood behind the table, glasses low on his nose. He dropped a pinch of the newly minted black powder into a bowl.

There was a minor explosion. Sparks crackled inside the bowl, smoke rose in a cloud and then a small flame, like one on the end of a candlestick, danced at the bottom of the bowl.

Jack grinned. "You see! Now I, a humble Night Stealer, can produce fire just as well as any Fire Sitter. What do you think of that?"

Nelly stepped forward. The flame danced at the bottom of the bowl with no source; no wick, no ember, no wood, keeping it lit. *Magic.*

"Can I do that?" she asked, thinking of the burn mark her hand had left on the library table at school.

"You're part Fire Sitter," Fig said. "You don't need ground fire to produce a flame. Just rub your fingers together and think warm thoughts."

Nelly held up her hand. She wasn't sure about this. She was here, in the fairy world, in a fairy's house, standing next to a spinnery. And yet she hadn't quite accepted any of it. It all felt like a weird dream. But if she rubbed her fingers together and produced a flame, would it feel real then? Did she want it to?

She rubbed her fingers together, a part of her hoping it wouldn't work and another part hoping it would. She thought of warm things, of the fireplace in Jack's library, of a cup of fairy tea, of Grandmother, at home and healthy again. And it happened. Sparks flickered from her fingertips and smoke twirled. She stopped.

"Why did you stop?" Fig asked.

Nelly held her hands to her chest. "Back home, you said I wasn't just a Fire Sitter. You said I was something else, too."

Fig nodded, her mouth grim. "A Wight. Doed is a Wight. Perhaps he can tell you more about it. But those abilities might not be ones you want to explore."

"Oh? Why?" Nelly asked and then shook her head. "But there was something else, too. Jack said it in the Morighan House after you fainted. You said I was a fairy of … of..."

Jack's eyes went wide. He held up a finger for silence. "You must not mention that here."

"Here?" Nelly repeated, whispering because he had. "You mean in your workshop?"

Jack and Fig exchanged glances. "No," Jack said. "Here in this world."

"But—" Nelly started, but Jack cut her off.

"You must trust us," he said, looking deadly serious. "Not here."

Then his expression changed. He clapped his hands together, sending up a puff of colorful dust, and in a normal voice said, "Breakfast?"

CHAPTER TWENTY

WISP HUNTING

Through the triangle doorway, the room Nelly thought was a kitchen, was indeed a kitchen. It was shaped like a crescent moon around a central tree. Pots and pans, strings of garlic, and dried lavender dangled from ceiling branches. A huge round window revealed a spectacular view of the water and the bluffs.

A breakfast fit for fairy royalty was spread out on the kitchen table. There were bowls of raspberries and sliced apples, steaming seed bread and honey cakes, walnuts, cherries, and chocolate.

Nelly took a seat at the table across from Fig, who returned to the newspaper she had been reading earlier, while Jack busied himself with the teakettle. The boy, Doed, was nowhere to be seen.

Nelly helped herself to apple slices and seed bread, and because they were fairy food, they were more delicious than any she had ever tasted.

"After breakfast," she said over a mouthful of apple, "will we look for my grandmother's and Orson's spirits?"

"We can't leave the house until nightfall," Jack said, pouring Nelly some tea that smelled of spices. "It's not safe for Nettle to be out during the day."

"Oh," Nelly said. She glanced over at Fig, who wore a pair of reading glasses that made her look like an otherworldly librarian. She had her nose stuck in her paper. It said DEBATE CIRCULAR on the front.

"Debating is practically a sport around here," Jack said, noting Nelly's gaze. "The circular holds the results of all the latest arguments to come out of the Glass Gallery. That's where we make all our major laws and agreements."

"This is plain silly," Fig said, lowering the paper. "You know they have us bowing before we eat blueberries now?"

Jack's eyebrows went up. "What's that?"

"It's a new bargain. We must now bow before we eat blueberries at the request of the ..." Fig squinted at the page. "Hedge Sparrows of Dunnock Way. I've never even heard of them."

"Let me see that," Jack said, reaching for the paper.

"You're ... you're supposed to bow before you eat blueberries?" Nelly asked, bewildered.

"*We* must bow before blueberries. You're one of us, Nelly," Fig said, handing the paper to Jack.

"But why?"

Fig shrugged. "No good reason. It's infuriating, really. These agreements are supposed to be meaningful, especially those that pass through the Gallery. They're supposed to be made in good faith. But there are all sorts in the wood, you know. And some just want the pleasure of making the rest of us dance."

"Is that why you're not allowed to cross a line of rowan berries? Because of an agreement?" Nelly asked, thinking of the rules she had read in Madge Morighan's diary.

"Rowan berries are sacred to the Hag of the Black Reels," Fig said, absently picking up a handful of berries. "And, to be fair, no one wants to anger her." Fig noticed there were blueberries in her handful and dropped them all in disgust.

"And what about yarrow stalks? I read that you're not allowed to disturb yarrow stalks."

Fig leaned back. "Yarrow stalks are sacred to the Moss People. They won't break you into bits and bone like the Hag would, but they'll start litigation, claims for damages, and that's a whole other nightmare."

"We follow hundreds of agreements like these," Jack said, looking up from the paper. "To keep the peace. And more are added every year. They're easy enough to remember once you get used to them. But Nettle is right, this one is ridiculous."

Nelly thought about that night at the farm with Grandmother, how the fairies had stopped just short of the line of rowan berries she had dropped on the ground but had still reached across it. "But are you forced to follow these agreements?"

"Forced?" Fig repeated. "No. We feel a certain compulsion to honor our bargains, but we can't be forced or bound except by choice or cold iron."

"So, if the Hag of the ... of the ..."

"Black Reels," Jack said.

"Yes, her," Nelly said, straightening in her seat. "If she wasn't around, you could cross a line of rowan berries if you really wanted to?"

"We could, yes, of course," Fig said, pulling the paper out from under Jack's elbows. "But we are People. We always try to honor the spirit of our arrangements. Whether the Hag is around to witness it is not the point."

"That, and you never know who's watching," Jack added.

"A reputation as a bargain-breaker is not one you want around here."

"Even when the bargain was made on your behalf," Fig muttered, her eyes back on the circular.

Jack tapped a finger on the table and shot Nelly a quizzical look. "Did you say you *read* about the yarrow stalk agreement? Where did you read about that?"

Nelly wasn't sure she should tell the fairies about Madge Morighan's diary. They probably wouldn't be too happy to hear that a human had written down all their secrets.

"Nowhere," Nelly lied. "I mean, I heard about it—from my grandmother."

Nelly sipped at her spiced tea while Jack watched her, his eyes slits of suspicion. She had never been a very successful liar.

After breakfast, Jack took Nelly on a tour of those parts of the house she hadn't yet seen. There wasn't much more to it. The upper levels had only bedrooms, with Jack's private room at the very top. He said the bobbing of the branches helped him sleep. There was a sitting room she hadn't seen by the entrance hall. This was where Jack met with those he called *Sloes*, an Eldritch term Nelly didn't know. These were fairies from whom he could extract his dusts and tinctures, for a price. He met with buyers there as well, who would trade fairy gold or sometimes favors or promises for a dust or tincture. He said favors were in most cases more valuable than gold.

Behind the house, down the sloping bluff, was a greenhouse surrounded by maple trees. This was where Jack grew the night keys that allowed them to pop from one enclosed place to another. This was called key craft, an ancient art only Night Stealers like Jack were capable of, and only after much training.

Trees infused with Night Stealer magic grew keys in their nuts, seeds, catkins, or pinecones. Maple trees were preferred because their seed pods made perfect incubators and produced friendlier and more pliable keys.

Jack said night keys even grew in some trees in the human world because once a tree had been doused in Night Stealer magic, then it and all its offspring would produce keys for all time. But these keys were mostly useless. Without a Night Stealer to lock them, that is, to instill in them specific destinations, the keys remained wild and would transport those who used them to any random place, as long as it was enclosed. That meant you could end up in the boiler room of a sunken ship, a volcanic grotto filled with lava, a snow cave on a mountain peak, anywhere.

"It's beyond foolish to use the wild ones," Jack said to Nelly as they stood under the swaying trees next to the greenhouse. "They've got minds of their own. Some are practical jokers, others are malicious. It depends on the temperament of the tree they sprouted in."

Jack seemed to enjoy talking about keys or dusts. He had a kind of geeky, encyclopedic knowledge of it all and would go into animated, excessive detail. But whenever Nelly asked him about something more consequential, such as how they would retrieve Grandmother's and Orson's spirits, he would clam up or change the subject.

Fig, meanwhile, kept to herself. She stayed in the house and stared out the window at the sea or sat in the library and gazed into the fire, her eyes far away and sad. The boy, Doed, was nowhere to be seen at all.

When darkness fell, it was finally time to venture into the

woods to do whatever they had to do to retrieve the lost human spirits. Jack said it was important Doed come with them, but this had taken convincing.

Nelly hadn't taken part in this herself, but she'd heard Jack and Doed arguing on the floor above as she'd sat waiting in the library with Fig.

"Why is it so important that Doed come with us?" she asked Fig, impatient to get moving. "Can't we find the spirits without him?"

Fig, who now looked like a kindly, older woman with rosy cheeks and white hair, said they didn't need Doed for that at all. "But Jack wants to consult with someone who may give us direction. That someone is Doed's mother."

Nelly, who had been pacing, stopped. "But aren't Jack and Doed brothers?" she asked, recalling what Jack had said earlier.

"Only in name," Fig said, cracking open a walnut with a nutcracker that looked to be made of blue glass. "Jack is an orphan. Doed's mother adopted him. But Jack and Doed weren't raised together. They only met a few years ago. So, I suppose in a way they are brothers, but in name only."

This made sense, Nelly thought. Jack and Doed certainly didn't look alike.

Fig shot Nelly a cold look, as though she was losing patience with all the questions. Nelly shrank under Fig's stare. A bargain was the only thing keeping Fig from attacking Nelly again. And fairies could break bargains. She thought back to that moment in the Morighan House when Jack had said Fig's true name. What was it? Murray something? Nelly wracked her brain. She needed a way to defend herself if Fig turned on her again.

A few silent minutes went by. Nelly couldn't help herself. She asked another question. "If this woman we have to consult is Jack's adopted mother, then why does he need Doed to talk to her? Why can't he—"

"She's upset with Jack," Fig cut in. "She won't see him unless he brings Doed along."

"Why?"

"Because I tried to break her out of prison," Jack said, walking into the room with three cloaks over his arm. "Unsuccessfully." He tossed Fig and Nelly each a cloak. "I've filled Doed in on all the details. He's agreed."

The forest was black as the night sky, the darkness punctuated only by the lights twinkling like stars between the trees. The lights were everywhere throughout the forest, hovering between trunks as tall as redwoods. But aside from the lights and the stark silhouettes of trees, there wasn't much to see.

But there was much to hear. The forest echoed with overlapping sounds; the snapping of twigs, the dropping of tree nuts, a sprinkle of wind chimes here, the jingling of bells there, the rattle of a snake, far too close.

As they continued forward, each holding a lantern, the sounds became more distinct and deliberate. There was a rhythmic tapping to their left. A clattering like marbles dropped on rocks followed. And then there came snippets of haunting music: violins, cellos, tin whistles, drums, and a child's voice singing, distant, but wrenching and clear.

Nelly and the fairies didn't speak. Before they left the house, Jack said Fig should avoid speaking in the wood for fear her voice might be recognized. The others could speak, but it was better to stay silent to avoid drawing unnecessary attention. Each of them wore a hooded cloak as well so that Fig wouldn't stand out.

Nelly watched Fig as she strode forward, her lantern casting a blue glow over her glamoured body. Her changing looks were hard to get used to. Fig's by now familiar sad eyes staring out of a parade of new bodies was surreal to behold. She looked almost like Mrs. Claus in this latest disguise, if Mrs. Claus had been transported to a haunted forest and dressed to match it. Nelly wondered about Fig, not for the first time. Why was she hiding out in the human world? Why did they need so many precautions to keep her from being recognized?

Looking away from Fig, Nelly caught Doed watching her, his golden eyes gleaming in the dark. He looked away immediately. She wondered what Jack had told him about her, if anything. Jack certainly hadn't told Nelly anything about Doed. But maybe this was the way with the fairies. You needed to press them to get any real answers.

Nelly blew out a breath, ghostly white against the cold darkness. She reminded herself of why she was here. *Grandmother and Orson.* They were all that mattered. And her father, of course, though if Jack and Fig were right, and they needed whoever struck him to retrieve his spirit, then he would have to wait.

She glanced at Doed again and once more found his eyes on her. Again, he looked away. Watching him now, she felt herself blush and immediately realized why. Doed was shockingly handsome. Shocking because she hadn't noticed it until now. She wasn't sure how she could have missed it. Maybe it was because he had been ill when she'd first seen him, and then unconscious, and then panicking and pale. But now that his features were relaxed, she could see how soft they were in the glow of the lantern light. He had a constellation of birthmarks on his cheek next to a sharp jawline; his eyes under thick, graceful brows were deep and searching.

He looked at her again, and now it was her turn to look away. She felt her cheeks go hot, tried to repress a smile, and then wondered if he was smiling, too.

Soon they came to a clearing filled with so many floating lights, it was like the air had been decorated for Christmas. It felt like a wonderful, magical dream.

Nelly couldn't help herself. She twirled around and tried to memorize the moment so she could return here again, if only in her imagination. Jack handed her a butterfly net. At least it looked like a butterfly net.

"Catch as many as you can," he whispered. And he was off.

Nelly stood there for a moment, holding the net, watching as Jack and Fig, each with their own net, chased lights around the clearing. The lights were reflected on their shining faces and pulled away from the fairies like fish underwater. An incredulous smile spread across Nelly's face.

She rushed out into the clearing, exhilarated, and chased after the lights. The music of the forest seemed to chime along with their flashing, with their sparkling. They felt warm against her skin whenever she neared them. Nelly threw her head back. The sky above was a riot of stars. And down here on the forest floor, she was chasing stars.

She caught one! As it landed in her net, a trail of what she imagined to be stardust shimmered across the air. She caught another and another. Inside the net, the lights appeared as luminescent glass spheres, glowing with phosphorescence. For a moment she thought she could hear voices from inside the lights, whispering to her, reaching out from a great distance, lost and forgotten.

Then she saw them—hands pressed against the inside wall

of one sphere. A tiny face emerged from the cloudy light. It was screaming. Nelly gasped and dropped the net.

A hand landed on her shoulder, making her jump. It was Jack.

"Something wrong?" His eyes glowered wolf-like in the gleam of the lights.

"I ... I saw something," Nelly said, her heart thundering. "In one of the lights."

Jack's eyes narrowed. He scooped up Nelly's net and examined the three lights inside it. "Ghost lights," he said and released them. "We don't need those. We need wisps. They look similar. It's difficult even for us to tell them apart. But Nettle and I have caught as many as we need."

"What are ghost lights?"

"Spirits," Jack said, directing Nelly toward a dark grove where Fig and Doed stood waiting.

"You mean like Grandmother's and—"

"Yes," Jack cut in, whispering. "Like them, but not them. Be patient. This way." He cocked his head.

Nelly hesitated. That face inside the light had looked terrified. Was that what Grandmother was experiencing, trapped and terrified inside some tiny sphere, floating around a world she didn't understand?

She hurried to catch up with Jack. "How do we save my grandmother and Orson?" she asked, keeping pace with him. "What do we need to do?"

"Hush," Jack said, reminding Nelly of her mother.

She swallowed. There was no other option. She followed the fairies between the trees, the sense she was being led astray clanging inside her like a warning bell.

Jack led them to a tree so twisted and haunted-looking that if it were in the human world, it would have a reputation. He took out a night key and stuck it into a yawning hole in the gnarly bark. He turned the key, and a hidden door on the side of the trunk swung open. He ushered them inside.

They had barely squeezed inside the cramped and musty tree when Jack shut the door. There was a loud *POP!* And they were somewhere else.

Nelly's first impression of this somewhere else was wind and a spray of water, and a shifting floor as if they were on a boat.

But they were not on a boat. They were on the topmost level of a stone tower, its walls overgrown with moss. Above their heads was the starry sky. Below their feet, the wooden floor, made of broken, rotting planks of wood, was indeed shifting. But this was because the whole tower was shifting back and forth, battered by wind and waves.

"Where are we?" Nelly asked, her teeth chattering with the cold and the damp.

"Owl Island," Jack said, putting his lantern down. "Inside Rime's Tower. Rime was a great general during the Weeping Wars. He died here. Out of respect, most avoid it. It is one of the few places I know of remote and deserted enough to do what we are about to do."

"What are we about to do?"

"Contact my mother," Jack said as a wave shouldered the tower, sending spray high up the walls. The tower moaned and swayed back and forth.

Nelly held the wall for support. "I don't understand. How—"

"My mother is in Walls prison," Jack said, now untangling a pair of lights, the wisps, he had called them, from a mesh bag.

"A terrible place," Fig said, gazing out a window at the churning black waters below.

It surprised Nelly to hear Fig speak, but she figured it must be safe for her here since Jack did not object. "But how—"

"You'll see," Jack said. He instructed them to douse their lanterns and sit back from him, with their backs to the stone walls. Jack sat in the middle of the room, holding the two shining spheres in his hand. The lights were about the size of small marbles and made a faint bell-like tinkling sound when they moved.

Examining them more closely, Nelly could see forms at their centers that looked like dragonflies. Jack whispered something to them and then pressed the little round entities closer together and spun them both on his palm like tops.

The lights spun and spun. Then one light separated from the other and flew into the air. It continued to rotate in a wide circle around Jack as if attached to the wisp that remained in Jack's hand by an invisible string. Still circling, the airborne wisp flew farther and farther away until it soared out a window and flashed around the outside of the tower like a tiny lighthouse beacon.

Inside the tower, the remaining light had a strobe effect, spinning faster and faster in Jack's hand as the other light faded away outside.

Nelly looked over at Fig, who was staring forward, stone-faced as the light flashed. Doed was staring at the floor or perhaps his eyes were closed. It was hard to tell. The strobe effect was overwhelming. Nelly blinked as light and shadow warred all around her.

Then a fifth pair of eyes appeared in the dark.

CHAPTER TWENTY-ONE
MAD AS BIRDS

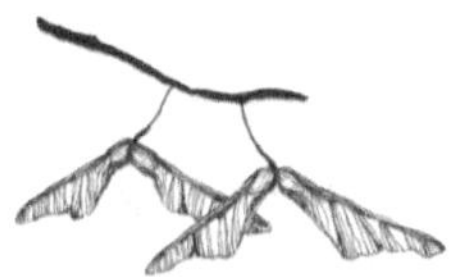

The light in Jack's hand slowed down its spinning, and then it stopped altogether. In the shadows, someone or something else was now holding the second light. It was a small girl, maybe ten-years-old, a startlingly beautiful little girl with freckles, dark hair, and golden eyes.

"Been a while, Jack," she said. Her voice did not sound like that of a child. It was gruff and gravelly, like an old witch in a fairy tale. Her golden eyes shifted from Nelly to Fig to Doed, where they paused. Then they flicked back toward Jack.

"What do you want? I was rotting. You're interrupting."

Jack shifted; the light cupped in his hands bounced off his skin. He seemed nervous.

"Mother," he said, nodding.

Nelly did a double take. *Mother?* This little girl was Jack and Doed's mother? The girl was glaring at Jack, the devouring stare of someone much older than she appeared. Someone dangerous. It was glamour, Nelly told herself. This girl was not a girl at all.

"Careful, Jack," the girl said. "My patience, even with you, has limits."

Jack looked at the floor. "You've forgiven me, then?"

"Forgiveness is not a sentiment I know," the girl said. "Perhaps if you give me what I want, then we could talk."

"You know I can't. I almost died last time and now ..." Jack did not meet her gaze. "I did everything I could—"

"Not enough," the girl cut in fiercely.

Jack frowned. "You're not being fair."

"NOT ENOUGH!" the girl screamed, standing over him like an angry ghost. A wave crashed against the tower, tilting the room. The lantern next to Nelly fell over and rolled straight toward the girl. She didn't move to avoid it.

It rolled right through her like she *was* a ghost.

Surprised, Nelly looked at the lights, one cupped in Jack's hand, the other cupped in the girl's. Jack had said his mother was in prison. Maybe she was still there, and what they were seeing now was some sort of illusory projection.

"You are mad, Birdy, to think Jack could break you out of Walls prison," Fig said, making Nelly think her guess was right. "You know it's impossible. If he had done anything more than he did, he'd be in a cell next to yours. Unless that's what you want."

The girl, who Fig had called Birdy, turned her head slowly in Fig's direction. A hungry smile spread across her face. "I know that voice," she said and chuckled. "Never one without the other."

Jack shot Fig a scolding glare. His tone held a warning. "Birdy, this is important. More important than you can possibly realize. Important enough for us to take this risk."

Nelly felt an onslaught of nerves. She had a bad feeling about this. Something told her this meeting wasn't about Grandmother and Orson.

"So why bring this one along?" Birdy asked, sweeping a hand in Doed's direction. "You know I can't stand to look at him."

This surprised Nelly. What a thing for a mother to say. But Doed didn't seem bothered by it. He pulled at a loose thread on his sleeve as if bored.

"To remind you of your obligations," Jack said.

Birdy pursed her lips. "Fine. You've piqued my curiosity. You have one minute to impress me." She sat down in front of Jack, cross-legged, the light held cupped in front of her casting her features in an eerie light.

Fig and Jack exchanged meaningful looks.

He lowered his voice to a whisper. "This girl, she calls herself Nelly Morighan ... Fig found her in the Other, on the Morighan farm. She is ... *of human blood*."

Birdy whirled around to face Nelly. Her mouth dropped open. "You're sure of this?"

"Reasonably," Jack said.

"He did it," Birdy muttered, eyes wide.

"Did it?" Fig asked. "Are you suggesting someone created this girl on purpose?"

Before Nelly could wonder what that meant, Birdy was right in front of her, Nelly, inches from her face, looking with laser intensity into her eyes. "She is still weak ... relatively. She must face the Piper. Now. Before she gets any stronger."

"Do you think that's a good idea?" Fig asked.

"She must know herself, claim herself," Birdy said. "This is her birthright. Would you have missed the opportunity if you could do it again?"

"I admit I wouldn't have," Fig said. "But this is different. Nelly is different. She may be better off not—"

"Aren't you supposed to be dead?" Birdy said, glaring over at Fig with a ferocity that could wither an oak.

Fig folded her arms. "You're changing the subject. Why?"

"Why is Morag here, Jack?" Birdy said, whirling on him. "You think you can trust her with this? She's not one of us."

Morag! Nelly thought, after seeing Fig wince. That was the first part of Fig's true name. The name Jack had called her in the Morighan House.

"How can you say that?" Fig said, her eyes too bright. "After all I've done? After all I've sacrificed?"

Birdy waved a dismissive hand. "It's true you were useful once. But what good are you now to the cause? Morag Fie, deader than dead."

Morag Fie, that was it, that was Fig's true name! Nelly repeated it to herself several times, memorizing it.

"Fig is the only reason we know of Nelly's existence," Jack said, clearly trying to diffuse the situation. "She told me about Nelly and only me. Of course, we can trust her."

"Who else would she tell?" Birdy said, walking a slow, predatory circle around Jack. "We here in this room are the only ones left who wouldn't kill or arrest her on sight. But perhaps that should change. Perhaps I should let it slip to my jailers that Morag Fie isn't near as dead as rumored."

"Bluffs don't become you," Fig said quietly.

"The girl must face the Piper!" Birdy shouted, pointing at Nelly.

"But what does that mean?" Nelly said, speaking up for the first time. Her heart quickened as all eyes turned on her.

"It's something all our people do," Jack said, his face back to gentle. "The names we give ourselves, the names our parents give us, are not our true names. You must earn your name by facing the Piper. It is a ritual of a kind. Once you have earned your true name, you'll have access to all your power. And then ... then you'll be able to identify and rescue Orson."

"So, if I do this ritual, then I can get Orson's spirit back?"

Something felt off about this, but it was also the first time the fairies had given Nelly any kind of direction. A ritual. This was something she could focus on. Something she could do.

"But why did we have to come here, then?" she asked, shooting Birdy a sideways glance. "Why can't I just face the Piper or whatever? —A-And what did you mean when you said I'm of human blood? Is that because my father is human?"

"All good questions," Fig said, folding her arms. She turned a hard stare on Birdy. "And here's another one. What do you know about this girl? How is it she exists?"

"Morag Fie!" Birdy snapped. "Even dead, you talk too much."

Fig winced. "Enough of that."

Birdy's smile had a vicious curl. She repeated, each time louder than the next, "Morag Fie. Morag Fie. Morag Fie! MORAG FIE!" Fig winced and flinched. Tears filled her eyes.

"Birdy, stop!" Jack shouted.

Birdy would not. Fig, her body trembling, covered her ears.

"MORAG FIE!" Birdy shouted again and Fig's glamour slipped away, streaking down her face in a cascade of colors.

"The girl will face the Piper," Birdy said, standing over Fig, who was now curled up in a ball on the floor. "Or you will face the Fury. That's not a bluff, that's a promise. Now get out."

Fig looked up at Birdy, rage and pain in her eyes. With some effort, she stood and wobbled on trembling legs toward the opposite side of the room, where the outline of a trapdoor showed on the floor.

As Fig passed Nelly, she stumbled and fell to her hands and knees. Nelly reached out to help her, but a look from Fig warned her away. At the same time, Nelly noticed something dangling from around Fig's neck. Something she had never noticed before. It was a necklace. It must have slipped out from under her clothing when she fell. It was almost identical to the necklace Nelly's mother wore. A glass acorn. But Mother's was an amber color, and this one was foggy white.

"Birdy," Jack said as Fig opened the trapdoor and descended the stairs beneath it. "We came to you for help. If this is how you are going to behave, then—"

"You say Morag has been hiding in the Other place?" Birdy asked. "Fine. I'll keep that secret. But I don't want to see her or speak to her again. Send her back to the Other and we will deal with this, you and I."

Jack scowled at her. "Oh, it's you and I now, is it? All is forgiven, then?"

"Not forgiven, never forgiven." Birdy pointed at Nelly. "But this is how you earn a reprieve."

"No," Nelly said. Her heart was pounding, but not from fear anymore, so much as anger. She and Fig might not have been friends, but she didn't like the way Birdy had treated her.

"No?" Birdy said, her eyebrows raised.

"Fig can't go back," Nelly said. "She's the only one who can help my grandmother. And Fig's already got a name, so she doesn't have to do any ritual to find her, right?"

Birdy cocked her head. "She's willful, this one. Clever, too. That will have to be dealt with. Take her to the Bone King. There is a Piper on Brittle Island that does namings. The Bone King will hold her name secret from the registry, for a price. I'll contact him and make the deal. In the meantime, keep her hidden. There is much planning to be—"

"Stop talking about me like I'm not here!" Nelly shouted. "I don't understand any of this! And I don't care. I don't care about your plans. I don't care about whatever you think I am. I only want my grandmother, my father, and Orson back safe. And if you can't help with that, then there's nothing more for us to talk about."

There was a ringing silence. The face of the ten-year-old

girl standing over Nelly seemed to grow old and skeletal in the play of light and shadow. Birdy considered Nelly for a long moment and then her gaze seemed to soften. "I knew your great-grandmother, you know."

This was the last thing Nelly had expected her to say.

"More greats than that," Jack said.

"More? Has it been so long?" Birdy asked. She looked at Nelly again, eyes flashing in the darkness. "I can't see her in you. She is not in your face. I don't see her in your eyes. But you are one of us. That must be it. Yes, that's the reason. She was willful like you. Always asking questions. I taught her many things about our people, many secrets. She wrote them down."

"In ... a diary?" Nelly asked, the pieces coming together in her mind.

Birdy nodded. Her tone was distant, mournful. "I told her not to. I told her, 'You mustn't write such things down. The wrong people might find it.' But she didn't listen."

Nelly couldn't believe what she was hearing. "–Y-You're talking about Madge Morighan. You're the fai—I mean, you're the one she met! But that was two hundred years ago."

"I loved her," Birdy said. "And love made me weak. Her husband and his friends from *that town* found her diary. They discovered my secrets. They tricked me into an iron cage. And then they hanged her; they hanged her from a red maple tree while the leaves fell down."

Nelly blinked. The townspeople killed Madge Morighan?

"I did not scream. I did not protest," Birdy went on, staring into the shadows. "I did not give them the satisfaction. I only watched them, memorizing their faces, memorizing their names. Even as they tossed me in the river, still inside that cage, I watched them. As the dark water swirled around me, I watched and I repeated, *Abner, Kennedy, Pipes, Glanville.*"

Birdy turned away and gazed out the window at the rolling

sea. All was silent except for the waves. "I escaped with a night key, a wild one. I crossed back to our own through the gate under the river. Then I went back to the Other for revenge. The Fury followed me, stopped me, put me in this cell ... but it's not over."

The rage in Birdy's eyes as she turned back toward them made Nelly's blood go cold. "What do you mean?"

"The debt is not paid," Birdy said, half her face shrouded in shadow. "The Morighans were punished. I killed Madge's treacherous husband myself. But Abner, Pipes, Kennedy, Glanville, they have not known justice. And they must pay in blood and body and bone. When I escape this cell, I will find them. Abner, Kennedy, Pipes, Glanville. I will find them, I will grind them into litter and leaves! ABNER, KENNEDY, PIPES, GLANVILLE! Revenge. REVENGE!"

Birdy squeezed the light in her hand so hard it burst, sending daubs of glowing liquid splattering across the room.

She vanished.

CHAPTER TWENTY-TWO

DOED

The wisp in Jack's hand floated away from him and then zipped over to one of the glowing splatters dripping down the wall. It buzzed around, jingling furiously, and then flew out the window.

The room became dark. Doed lit a lantern with a pinch of ground fire while Jack opened the trapdoor and signaled for Fig to return.

Fig, who had been sitting on a set of steps below the trapdoor, lifted herself back into the room. She did not look well. Her glamour had streaked away entirely, and she was back to her doll-like self, but her eyes were red, and she was unsteady on her feet.

Jack helped her stand. "Can you hold a glamour?" he asked her.

She shook her head, no.

"I have death's milk back at the house," Jack said. "I'll wrap you in a cloak. I'll carry you. We'll rush. We'll make it."

Fig objected, saying it was too dangerous, but Jack

wouldn't hear it. He tossed Doed a night key and told him to wait here with Nelly for a time before returning.

Nelly, nervous about staying alone with Doed, asked why they couldn't all return together. Jack said that if Fig was discovered, anyone in her company would suffer for it. And he wasn't willing to risk all four of them.

He wrapped his cloak around Fig, hiding her face like a shroud, and led her to the trapdoor. Once they were both below, the trapdoor pulled shut behind them, Nelly heard a soft *POP*, caught the scent of fireworks, and knew they were gone. It all happened in a few seconds.

Doed stood in the shadows, leaning against the decaying old wall. He stared at her, eyes smoldering like embers in the darkness.

Nelly's stomach fluttered. She did not know what to say to him. But he spoke first.

"You look like a ghost."

Nelly fiddled with her hair. "Uh, yeah, it's the hair."

His eyes were locked on her. "It's more than that," he muttered, and stepped forward, the shadows rippling across his features. "We haven't been introduced."

Nelly gave a nervous laugh. "No, I guess not. I'm Nelly and you're ..."

"You know what I'm called," he said, his voice rich and sonorant. "Rhymes with Toad. Doed the toad. That's what my mother named me in the full, and it stuck, as names do. She has quite the sense of humor," he added, though it was obvious he didn't see the humor in it.

Nelly didn't either. "Your mother's in prison."

Doed answered with a faint smirk. "Yes."

"But we could see her, speak to her here," Nelly said. "Was that because of those little lights?"

"Wisps," Doed said, now drifting in and out of the shadows. "They can cast a living spirit across a great distance as long as there is a second wisp on hand to receive the projection. It was working well until Birdy killed one of them."

"Birdy killed one? You mean when she squeezed the light and it ... it ..."

"She's not the soft and gentle type," Doed said with another smirk. "That's going to cause us some trouble in the future. We can't communicate all that well with wisps, but they talk among themselves. They won't be keen to help us again after this. Not for some time." He lifted himself onto one of the crumbling windowsills, which didn't seem safe at all, and crossed his legs.

"Oh," Nelly muttered, feeling bad for the little wisp. "So, I guess Jack told you about me ... and where I come from and stuff." Nelly tried not to cringe. She had never felt more awkward.

Doed's strange eyes were still on her. He nodded. There was a weighty silence. Nelly tugged at her dress. She didn't want the topic of this conversation to be *her*.

"So, uh, Birdy, why is she in prison?"

"Because she crossed to the Other and was careless enough to get caught. Though, what she said about falling in love with a human and getting herself trapped in a cage and *revenge*, *revenge* was news to me." Doed's tone was bitter. "Who knew my mother was capable of love? You learn something new every day."

There was another charged silence. Nelly leaned against the wall and tried to put everything she'd learned together. "Madge Morighan died two hundred years ago. Does that mean Birdy has been in prison for all that time?"

Doed nodded. "Festering like an old sore."

"How long is her sentence?"

"She'll never get out," he said, rocking on the windowsill.

"Not in her lifetime. She crossed to the Other, fraternized with humans. It's a serious offense and the Fury don't mess around."

Nelly thought about this. "Does that mean you, I mean we, I mean fairies, aren't immortal?"

Doed raised his brows. "Immortal? No. But we have long lifespans compared to the humans, or so I'm told. Humans live a hundred and fifty, a hundred and eighty years, no?"

"More like a hundred," Nelly said. "And it used to be much less."

"Hmm, that's all?" Doed said curiously. "Well, we live to be around a thousand, on average."

"A thousand years old?" Nelly said, eyes widening. "So ... how old are you, if that's not a rude question."

Doed shrugged. "I'm eighteen. Amongst our people, I'm considered a kid."

This surprised Nelly. She had been expecting him to say he was three-hundred and forty or something, even though he did look eighteen. Looks could be deceiving around here, after all. This meant she was a kid, too, in this world. Though she supposed teenager and kid weren't so far apart, even in the human world.

"What about Jack and Fig? How old are they?"

"They are both two hundred and twenty-two," Doed said, uncrossing and recrossing his legs. "They were born around the same time. They'll probably die at the same time, too, knowing them. At their age, they are considered young adults. My mother is somewhere in her five-hundreds, middle-aged."

"Oh," Nelly said, thinking this through. Did this mean that she, Nelly, wouldn't age in any significant way for the entirety of a human lifespan? *Good luck explaining that to the towns-people,* she told herself. Then something else occurred to her. If

Doed was only eighteen and Birdy had been in prison for two hundred years, then ...

"I was born in prison," Doed said as though reading her mind. "I lived there until a few years ago when Jack saw it in his heart to take me in."

Nelly didn't know what to say to this. Doed's tone was so acerbic she didn't want to press him on what was clearly a sensitive subject. And yet, he was open, he was answering her questions without any prodding or deals. She was learning more here, now with Doed than she had the whole time with Jack and Fig. She decided to try for more.

"Out of curiosity, what did Fig do? I mean, why does she have to hide all the time?"

Doed's dark eyebrows went up. "They didn't tell you?" He scoffed. "That's typical. The inseparables and their secrets."

"The inseparables?"

Doed nodded. "A nickname Jack and Fig have had since they were kids. Believe me, it's fitting."

"Are they ... together?"

"Together?" Doed asked, cocking his head. "They left together."

"No, I mean, are they a couple? Are they in love?"

"Ah," he said, nodding. "No, not in that sense. They are friends. As close as friends can be, and more loyal to each other than anyone else, even family." There was bitterness in Doed's voice again. There was a history there.

"And Fig, why is she—"

"Attempted murder," Doed said matter-of-factly.

Nelly blinked. "Murder?"

"She claims she's innocent, falsely accused. And of course, Jack believes her."

"You don't?"

Doed pursed his lips. "What I believe doesn't matter. She

was tried by her peers in the Glass Gallery and found guilty. They sentenced her to execution. Obviously that didn't take, though everyone thinks it did. You and I, Jack and now Birdy are the only ones who know she's still alive."

There was another heavy silence. Nelly thought back to when Fig had rushed at her in the Morighan House, and to when Fig had slapped her and sent the worst pain of her life shooting through her body. It wasn't that hard to believe that Fig had tried to murder someone. *Attempted*.

"So, whoever she tried to kill is still alive?"

"In a sense," Doed said ominously. "All four of them—"

"Four of them?" Nelly cut in, incredulous.

Doed nodded. "They all live in an asylum now. They survived what happened to them in body, but not in spirit. They can no longer speak. They can't communicate. They can only weep. Whatever they were before was destroyed. Hence the harsh sentence." Doed's voice cracked as if the thought of what had happened to those people upset him. He looked away into the darkness.

And so did Nelly. It was disturbing to hear. She didn't like the idea that there were asylums in the fairy world, either. This was the place she had come to find a cure for whatever had landed her father in a psych ward. The idea that there were fairies in asylums, fairies whose spirits had been destroyed beyond saving, filled her with dread. What if the same thing happened to her father or Grandmother or Orson? What if she couldn't save them, no matter what she did?

The wind howled up through the tower like it was a throat. A muscular wave crashed into the outer wall and the room swayed. Doed gripped the windowsill for support.

"Maybe you should get down," Nelly said, feeling like a surfer on the tilting floors.

He raised his graceful dark eyebrows, and she was once

again struck by how handsome he was. Not just handsome; beautiful, like a painting. Droplets of water from the spray sat on his hair like dew. His cheeks were ruddy, and his breath blew steam. His strange eyes glittered at her. A smile played on his lips.

"Does this make you nervous?" He stood up on the windowsill and let go of the wall, balancing like he was on a balance beam. The wind tore at his hair and jacket.

"That's not funny," Nelly said.

Doed's smile widened. He tilted back into the darkness outside the tower, with the water swirling fathoms below against a cascade of jagged rocks. If he fell, she didn't see how he would survive.

"Don't," Nelly said, stepping toward him. "It's really not funny."

With a sly smile, Doed leaned back even farther, as if enjoying her concern.

Then, a wave struck the tower.

CHAPTER TWENTY-THREE
PIPER'S DEW

The force of the wave threw Nelly to the floor. She gasped and sat up. Doed was still in the tower, on the windowsill, hugging the wall, his hair and jacket soaked through.

He tossed back his wet hair and with a wild, gleeful "Wahoo!" put his hand on his chest. "My heart is beating! Come and feel it!"

Nelly didn't move. "Doesn't it always?"

Another smaller wave hit. Doed held the wall again. The wind roared, billowing his jacket up over his head like a hood. Something fell out of his pocket.

The object dropped to the floor of the tower and rolled around in a wide circle. It was a tiny blue bottle, like the one Nelly had found on the floor in Jack's workshop. The same memory she'd had in the workshop hurtled into her head again. *It was night. She was on the Morighan House porch. She held a blue bottle in her hand. Her mother stood across from her and told her to drink.*

Now, Nelly watched as a bottle, much like the one her

mother had given her years ago, rolled around on the floor and came to a stop. And so did Doed.

He jumped down from the window, snatched it up, and winked. "Don't tell Jack."

Nelly got to her feet. "What is that?"

"Nothing," he said, slipping the bottle back into his pocket. He tossed his wet hair out of his face, sending droplets spraying. "We've been here long enough. We should return."

Nelly didn't move. "That's the same stuff you took in Jack's workshop. You passed out, you—"

"That was personal," Doed flared.

Nelly frowned, feeling chided. "That's fine, fair enough. I'm not trying to pry. I just want to know what that stuff is."

"Why do you care?"

"What's the difference? I won't say anything to Jack."

Doed scoffed. "You sound like the inseparables. All secrets and lies."

"I'm not the one keeping secrets," Nelly snapped back.

"It's my secret to keep!" Doed said, raising his voice. "Why does it matter to you?"

"It just does," Nelly said, not wanting to share the story about her mother. It was far too personal, and she'd only really met Doed five minutes ago. "Can you please explain to me what that stuff is? Please. I promise I won't tell Jack. We can make it a deal."

Nelly realized she was pleading. But she had to know what her mother had given her. Just the thought of it, of that night, had her blinking back tears. *Mother stood over her, told her to drink. The liquid in the bottle smelled pungent, narcotic. It looked like blueberry syrup.*

Doed's breath misted on the air. He raked back his damp hair. "A deal then. I'll tell you what it does, and you won't tell Jack or Fig you've seen me with it, now or ever."

Nelly nodded. "OK, yes, I agree."

"It's called piper's dew. It's poison."

Nelly felt like the tower had just crumbled beneath her feet. "Poison?"

"I'm not trying to kill myself if that's what you think. In small doses, it's not deadly. In small doses, it has a tempering effect, it dampens certain ... traits," said Doed.

But Nelly barely heard him. There was a kind of thrumming sound in her head, blocking out everything else. *Poison!* Her mother had given her poison? The room was spinning. Her whole world was spinning. It couldn't be true, it couldn't be.

"–Y-You're lying," she said.

Doed's cheeks flushed. "No, I'm not."

But he had to be. "Tell me the truth," Nelly demanded.

Doed glared at her, his eyes two smoldering cinders. He picked up a lantern, marched over to the trapdoor, and stuck a night key into its lock. *POP!* The room changed.

They were inside the cramped, musty tree again, so close his hair dripped on her cheek. Doed threw open the tree door and stormed out into the wood. After a startled pause, Nelly followed.

"I'm sorry," she said, catching up to him as he veered around dark trees and brushed aside hovering ghost lights. "I didn't mean—"

He whirled on her. "I could lose you in this wood if I wanted to. But I won't because Jack wouldn't forgive me. That's the only reason. I kept my part of the deal. I expect you to keep yours. Don't talk to me again."

He turned and marched away. Nelly followed him and his swinging lantern, keeping a few paces back. His reaction surprised her. Then again, she supposed no one liked to be called a liar. She hadn't meant to hurt his feelings. She had only been shocked. *Poison?* It couldn't be true.

When they arrived back at the house, Doed disappeared immediately down a winding hallway. Nelly found Jack in the kitchen putting together a late supper. Fig was there, too, sitting at the table, glamour restored. She had a quilt around her shoulders and was sipping at a cup of tea like she was nursing a cold. They had both made it back without incident.

Fig's latest glamour (a pretty redhead in her twenties) was closer to her actual appearance than any of the others had been, perhaps because she was still too weak to create anything elaborate.

Nelly sat at the table. She thought it odd that fairies' true names had the power to weaken them so much, and wondered what the point of having one was, anyway, if it could make one so vulnerable.

"Oh, but you need a name," Jack said, though he didn't elaborate much. He only said that if Nelly wanted to do anything or be anyone in the fairy world, she would need a name.

"But I don't want to do anything or be anyone here. I only want to find my grandmother and Orson," Nelly protested. "And my father, too, eventually."

"Well, that's *doing something*, isn't it?" Fig quipped, looking up from her tea. There were dark circles under her eyes.

"Don't worry. No one will discover your name," Jack said, putting steaming bowls of butternut squash soup on the table next to a plate of seed bread, grapes, and cheese. "Not unless you tell someone."

Nelly glanced at Fig, who did not react to this comment. Did this mean Fig had told people her name? Why would she have done that? But before Nelly could ask, Jack launched into an explanation of what it meant to "face the Piper."

The Blue Piper was a type of predatory fairy, he explained. There were only a few of them left, and each one was strictly monitored and contained. Pipers were leeches. They fed off the power of others.

"Like the dead," Fig said as if this cleared things up. She shot Jack a quizzical look. "The humans know this, yes? It's common knowledge."

Nelly stared at them, bewildered.

"It would seem not," Jack said, taking a seat at the table. "The dead feed off the living. They need our presence to sustain themselves. But they prefer our people to the humans. We make them a better meal, so they congregate around us. That's why there are so many of them here. The ghost lights in the wood and on the water are all dead things. Many are human spirits, drawn to this world by our presence."

Nelly cupped her hands around a bowl of soup and glanced out the great round window, where ghost lights drifted over the water.

"But they aren't dangerous," Fig said. "The dead can't drain you so much that you would be weakened by them or even notice you were being drained, unlike the Piper, who can drain you to death."

"To death?" Nelly said.

Jack shot Fig a scolding look. "But that won't happen. The Piper is held in controlled surroundings. All you have to do is let it touch you. Through a barrier. It's perfectly safe."

"I just have to let it touch me?" Nelly asked, thinking there had to be something more to it. "And then I'll have a name?"

"It's as simple as that," Jack said with a smile that did not reassure Nelly at all. "We'll do it tomorrow."

"And then I'll be able to get Orson's spirit back?" Nelly asked.

Jack smiled again. His glasses reflected ghost lights floating by the window. "Of course."

Nelly couldn't sleep. She sat on the bed in her room in Jack's house and gazed out the round window, trying to put her fears about the Piper and the fairies out of her mind. The sky above was a crowded mess of stars. Hovering over the wide ocean, thousands of ghost lights reflected on the water below, giving the illusion that Jack's treehouse was floating in space.

It was strange to think that most of the lights out there were spirits. Some human. Nelly tracked the path of one of the ghost lights on the windowpane with her finger. She once read somewhere that all the ingredients of a star were inside a human being. If human spirits ended up here in the fairy world, floating in the wood or on the water as glowing spheres, did that mean they became stars again when they died?

It was a nice thought. She wondered if it was perhaps the same with the fairies. She lay her head down on the windowsill. From this angle, she could see a large branch that curled out from the side of the house and hung over the bluff. Doed was out there, sitting on the branch, his feet dangling over the water.

She sat back from the window. Should she go out there and talk to him? Try to patch things up? Her heart quickened at the thought of it. He had been so angry with her; she wasn't sure she wanted to face him. And then there was that stuff her mother had given her. *Poison*, he had said. If he was telling the truth, did she want to know it?

Nelly made a decision. She got up, wrapped a sweater around her nightgown, and slipped into the hallway. She followed it around a bend until she found an open window. Through the window she could see Doed still sitting on the branch, his face tilted upward, looking at the stars. Nerves fluttered in her stomach.

It was an awkward thing to climb out a small window onto a branch, no matter how big and sturdy the branch was. Nelly had to turn around and lower herself onto the branch backward to avoid losing her balance. When she was finally on the branch, she turned around. Doed was standing there, glowering at her.

Nelly didn't move. There was no other way back into the house for him now but through her. "I want to talk."

"I don't," Doed said. Then, all at once, Nelly felt hands on her shoulders. She was lifted, spun, and released. And now Doed was where she had been standing, climbing back inside through the window.

"—M-My mother gave me that stuff," she blurted.

Doed paused, looked at her. "You mean piper's dew?"

Nelly looked down at the branch, nodded.

"Why would she?"

"I don't know," Nelly said. "I thought you could tell me."

Doed's dark brows knitted together. "I wasn't lying when I said it was poison."

There was a pause. Nelly said nothing. She couldn't. There were too many emotions churning inside her.

"But ..." Doed added. "But I take it. Regularly. And I'm still here."

"Why do you take it?" Nelly asked.

Doed rubbed the back of his neck. "You know that piper's dew comes from the Blue Piper, right?"

"The Piper?" Nelly muttered, surprised that she hadn't

made the connection herself. "The same one I'm supposed to see tomorrow?"

"Maybe not that one specifically," Doed said.

"What does it do?"

"The Piper drains the power of others into itself. That's how it's able to figure out your true name. As it drains you, it can see inside you, into your spirit. It can read things about you, hidden even from yourself."

"So, you take piper's dew to learn things about yourself?"

"No, no, it doesn't work like that." Doed looked away. "I take it ... I take it to suppress things about myself."

"Like what?"

"Is this about me?" he snapped.

"I'm only looking for an explanation. Why would my mother have given me that stuff? I don't understand." Her voice cracked with emotion.

The ensuing silence was thick. When Doed spoke again, his voice was gentle. "I know what you're thinking, but your mother's one of us, she's People. If she had wanted to kill you, there are much easier ways than slow poisoning with piper's dew."

This was not comforting. Nelly couldn't hold back her tears any longer, so she turned away from him. She walked along the branch to the part hanging over the bluffs, sat down, and stared out at the water and the ghost lights.

"I can communicate with the dead," Doed said.

Nelly wiped her eyes and looked up. Doed was standing over her, a breeze blowing his dark hair across his face.

"Or, I should say, they can communicate with me," he added.

"What do you mean?" she asked.

Doed sat down next to her. "I'm a Wight. It's something we can do. Each of those lights out there on the water is a thing, a dead thing. You see lights. I see something more. White forms, faces, terrible faces. The lights are sometimes lodged in their chests, sometimes in their temples or eye sockets." Doed paused and shuddered. "They speak to me. I'd rather they didn't. When I take piper's dew, they stop for a while. That's why I take it."

Nelly looked out at the lights. She imagined spirits, ghostly and frightening, materializing around them. It was a disturbing thought. She couldn't blame Doed for wanting to block that out.

"But Jack said I was part Wight," Nelly said. "I only see lights."

Doed stared at her. "Jack said that? Are you sure? You don't look like a Wight."

"Why, what are Wights supposed to look like?"

"We all look different," Doed said unhelpfully. "Except for our eyes."

Nelly looked into Doed's eyes, two shining spheres of gold. They were certainly distinctive, like glowing rings deep in a pool. After a long moment, she realized she was staring and looked away.

"Maybe Jack's wrong," Nelly said, hoping Doed wouldn't notice her blushing. "My eyes don't look like yours and I've never seen a spirit, even though the town I'm from is supposed to be haunted."

"Jack is rarely wrong," Doed said and crossed his legs. "But there's your answer. This town you're from is haunted. You are part Wight. Your mother gave you piper's dew to spare you the torment of dealing with the dead. She did you a favor."

Nelly thought about this. It made sense, and she liked it better than the alternative explanation. But there were some holes in the theory.

"The thing is, I haven't seen my mother in years. I haven't taken that stuff in years, and I still don't see any spirits."

"Maybe you're too weak," Doed said. He leaned in and whispered in her ear. "All that time you spent with *them*, eating their food." His breath moved her hair and gave her a shiver. He smelled like the wind before a storm. He leaned away and spoke in his normal tone again. "That and the piper's dew will have suppressed your abilities."

"Oh," Nelly said, still feeling shivery. She hugged herself, intensely aware of how close he was to her. She searched for something to say. "I ... uh ... in the town I'm from, the people there, they complain about ghosts all the time. I always thought they were making up the stories as an excuse to attack me and my family. They blame us for the hauntings. They think we're cursed."

"I don't know about any curse," Doed said, leaning a hand on the branch and gazing at her, his head crooked. "But the hauntings are very likely because of you. Well, you, and my mother, and your mother, and Jack, and Fig, and any other fairies that have been hanging around your town. The dead are drawn to us, to our people, like wasps to honey. Wherever we are, so are they. You've lived in that town all your life? Then it is haunted. It must be."

Nelly looked out at the ghost lights. There were noticeably more of them around her and Doed and Jack's house than there were far out on the water. She thought about the towns-people, the rumors, the whispers, the suspicious stares, the accusations hurled at her in the schoolyard growing up. All this time, Nelly had thought the townspeople superstitious and unfair. But they had been on to something. How did they know? Could they sense something about her? Could they tell on some level what she really was?

"It's a difficult thing to be mistreated," Doed said with a

sigh. "Even more so when you deserve it." He gave her a dark look, and she had the feeling he wasn't talking about her.

"I'm sorry I called you a liar," Nelly said as Doed stood up.

He held out a hand to her. She took it and allowed him to pull her to her feet.

"Don't apologize," he said, a faintly devilish smile playing on his lips. "I am a liar. I just wasn't lying then."

And with that disquieting statement, he led her back into the house and they went their separate ways.

CHAPTER TWENTY-FOUR

THE GROVE OF THE BONE KING

As the sun set the next evening, Nelly stood in her room in Jack's house. She was wearing a long white dress with too much material and a multitude of concealed pockets. A sewing box sat on the bed, its contents spread out on the coverlet—buttons, thimbles, feathers, shells, and acorn tops. Fig, glamoured to look like a young woman with blonde hair, stood behind Nelly, making adjustments to the dress with a needle and thread.

The dress belonged to Fig. She had worn it herself at her own naming ceremony years ago, although she didn't appear to have any attachment to it.

It was tense. Things were always tense when Nelly found herself alone with Fig. Out of the fairies Nelly had met so far, excluding Birdy, Fig was the strangest and the most intimidating. Of course, Fig had tried to kill her and possibly four others and had put Nelly through the worst pain she had ever experienced, so perhaps this was to be expected.

It was more than all that. All the faces, the names Fig took on, made her seem less human-like than Jack or Doed, more alien. It was hard to get a handle on her.

Fig would not be accompanying them to the naming ceremony. Jack had made the declaration earlier that day. It was too dangerous, he'd said, and Fig had taken too many risks as it was. She should return to the Other without delay.

"After she finds my grandmother," Nelly had piped in.

Jack looked at Nelly as if for a moment he had forgotten she was there.

"Well, yes, of course, after that. Naturally," he said with a smile.

This had not been reassuring.

Nelly could see a faint reflection of herself and Fig in the window overlooking the sea. They both looked foggy and ethereal in the glass, not human at all.

"Nettle," she ventured, breaking the silence. "You have a name."

Nelly felt Fig's fingers pause, needle poised. "Yes. And I know it very well, thanks, you don't have to remind me."

"No, I mean, you don't have to face the Piper or anything. You can find my grandmother's spirit now. So ..."

"So?" Fig repeated as she sewed buttons into the material that lay between Nelly's shoulder blades.

"So, why don't you?"

Fig sighed. "I can't go out until dark. But after nightfall, after you and Jack have gone, I'll be sure to do ... everything I'm supposed to do. Does that satisfy?"

It did not. Nelly frowned. She couldn't shake the feeling that the fairies were lying to her, that they had no intention of helping her find Grandmother and Orson, that there was something else going on here she couldn't begin to guess.

Nelly tried again. "When we were talking to Birdy, you said I might not have to face the Piper. You said—"

"I was wrong," Fig cut in, voice tinged with impatience. "Birdy was right."

"You're only saying that because she threatened you," Nelly muttered.

Fig let go of the dress. Nelly faced her warily.

"Are you calling me a coward?" Fig said, her eyebrows raised.

Nelly's heart started to pound. Fig sneered and began gathering up her sewing instruments. As she bent over the bed, her acorn necklace slipped out from under her shirt. Smoke seemed to swirl inside the glass like an imprisoned whirlwind.

"Are you?" Nelly said, standing up straighter. Her mouth had gone dry. The last thing she wanted to do was offend someone like Fig, but she was fed up with all the secrets.

Fig didn't seem offended. Instead, she seemed to think the question over.

"Maybe," she said and latched shut her sewing box. "I don't know. I don't know what I am anymore."

Fig's dark eyes burned into Nelly as she continued, "I used to take stands on all sorts of things. That upset people. So, they took me down. They took my name. They took my life. All I have left is my freedom, such as it is." She indicated her glamour disguise. "And I intend to keep it."

She picked up her sewing box. There was obviously more to that story, but it was equally obvious she didn't want to go into that.

"Your necklace," Nelly blurted. "Does it mean something?"

Fig shot Nelly a look. "No." And she turned to leave.

"I only ask because ... because my mother has one just like it."

Fig stopped so abruptly, it was as if Nelly had said her true name. "What did you say?"

Nelly could feel herself shrinking under Fig's gaze. "Just

that my mother has the same necklace. A glass acorn. Except hers is a kind of yellowish color."

"Amber," Fig said, and her glamour began to slip. "Your mother? Are you certain?"

"Why? Does that mean something to you?"

Before Fig could reply, there was a rap on the door. Jack stuck his head into the room. "It's time," he said.

Nelly felt a thrill of nerves. She turned back toward Fig, who had a peculiar expression on her face. Fig gasped. Two tears, one then the other, rolled down her cheeks.

She fainted.

Jack caught her in his spidery arms before she hit the ground, and with careful gentleness, laid her down on the bed.

"Is she OK?" Nelly asked.

Jack nodded. "Oh yes, very much so. It happens sometimes, as you know. She can't control it." A kind of webbing was spreading over Fig's hands and face. "She'll wake soon. Good as always. Quick now. We can't delay."

Jack turned on his heel and ducked his lanky body through the low doorway.

After a brief hesitation, Nelly followed.

Jack led Nelly out into the woods, bound for the Piper and whatever that entailed. Doed was with them. They needed him, Jack said, in case something went wrong.

"But what could go wrong?" Nelly asked as Jack handed her an unlit lantern.

"Oh, this or that," Jack said with a dismissive wave. "It's always best to travel in threes."

Nelly wasn't sure how she felt about this. She wasn't sure

how she felt about anything at the moment—Jack and his cryptic, non-answers; Fig and whatever was going on with her; Doed and his eyes, on her and then not; the Piper—it all felt wrong in so many ways.

Grandmother and Orson, she reminded herself for the hundredth time. They were the reason she was here. She could never forgive herself if she lost her chance to rescue them.

She followed Jack and Doed between gnarled trees in the purple evening. Jack's stride was long and somewhat clumsy. He was tall and seemed always on the verge of stumbling, but never did. Doed's stride was cautious and quick, his head down and his shoulders tense, as if anticipating a blow.

The fairies led Nelly through bush and briar as if on an invisible forest path. Some roads were tunnels of green, as if the trees had grown around the paths on purpose, knowing fairies would pass this way. As they moved, forest noises whispered and rang. Faces seemed to shift in tree bark, moss, and fungi.

Soon they reached a door built into the wall of a mossy ravine. Behind the door was a shallow cave. After the turn of a key, a *POP*, and the now familiar scent of honey and fireworks, they were in another compact, muddy hollow underneath the roots of a tree. They climbed out of the hollow one by one, Jack leading the way.

As Nelly stepped into the dim evening, she could tell at once that they were far away from where they had been.

They were still in a forest, but the trees had changed. Here the trees weren't hunched together and haunted-looking, and tangled up with vines, but straight and smooth as pillars, bone-white, and joined at the canopy in a way that gave the impression of a great cathedral. It was a quiet, eerie place. The earth sloped downward as if they were standing on the side of a forested mountain. There were ruins scattered about, parts of a wall here, a crumbling tower there, sections of a stone staircase that curved up between the trees and then dropped off into thin air.

Jack gave a small bow, as if out of respect, and then muttered that these were the ruins of Mag Dún, which, in the old tongue, meant *black ring*, a once mighty fortress destroyed during the Weeping Wars. He lit his lantern with ground fire and led them down the slope.

It was a tricky descent. Slippery things blanketed the ground, leaves, mossy rocks, and toadstools, and it took all of Nelly's concentration and several close calls not to slide down the incline on her backside.

They reached a cramped clearing surrounded by thick brambles. Between the brambles was an opening like the mouth of a cave. Wisps buzzed around this opening and a sweet smell wafted from it: a mix of pine resin, lemon, and dark chocolate.

Jack raised his lantern. Through the opening, stone steps led down into darkness. He motioned for Nelly and Doed to follow him and then bent his spidery body almost in two to duck through the brambles. Nelly followed.

On the other side of the opening, Jack descended stone steps overgrown with moss and lichen, and could soon stand up straight. They were in an earthen tunnel that sloped sharply downward. The light of their lanterns bounced off the walls and steps, which were covered in what appeared to be polished sapphires. The sapphires glinted, sending a kaleidoscope of light dancing through the darkness.

That sweet smell of pine sap, lemon, and chocolate intensified as they descended. It reminded Nelly of the smell of an old church. After walking down what must have been a hundred steps, they reached a stone archway. Carved into the wall of the arch were the words: *A monster dwells in the deep. It is the lamp-bearer.*

Nelly wondered what it meant. Beyond the arch, three tunnels branched off in different directions. There, Jack stopped. It was cold and his breath fogged.

"I have to speak with the Bone King," he said to Nelly, his glasses glinting. "Doed will take you the rest of the way. When the Nivduhene come for you, go with them, memorize everything they say, and follow their instructions to the letter."

Nivduhene. This was an old Eldritch word Nelly didn't know and couldn't translate in her head. Jack said it meant psychopomp, but she didn't know what that meant either. Before she could ask for clarification, he was off down the tunnel on the left while Doed slipped ahead of her down the tunnel on the right.

Doed held up his lantern and signaled to her. He flashed a smile that was beautiful and sinister all at once. Not at all reassuring.

She hurried to catch up with Doed, and then immediately started asking questions. What was a Nivduhene? Sort of a guide, sort of a priest, sort of an acolyte, was Doed's unhelpful answer. And the Bone King? Not really a king, Doed said, even more unhelpfully. What did the words on the arch mean? Was the Piper a monster? Where were they, anyway, and where were they going?

Nelly stopped asking questions, partly because Doed was now giving the same kinds of non-answers Jack and Fig always gave and because she had become distracted by their surroundings. As they moved along, the earthen tunnel was becoming crammed with thorns, branches, and brambles, gray-green in the low light. Wild mint and asphodel flowers grew between the thorns in long, encroaching spires.

Their lanterns created the look of halos around them. The

tunnel sloped upward and expanded. The brambles were parting to reveal tree trunks and eventually they were back in the forest and came upon three towering stone statues of women, crowned and veiled, facing in opposite directions.

As Nelly and Doed approached the statues, all was silent except for the distant hooting of an owl. But when they passed under the stone ladies, everything changed.

There was music and smoke and swirling dancers. A hand grabbed Nelly by the wrist and yanked her into a crowd. She tried to pull away, but then other hands grabbed her and whirled her until everything became a blur. Faces materialized out of the smoke. Torches twirled. That smell of pine, lemon, chocolate, and now firewood flooded her senses. Violins whined. Cellos moaned. Drums pounded. Bells jangled. Voices sang, wrenching and pure. And it was cold. So very cold.

Then someone grabbed her arm and pulled her close. It was Doed. He held her tight. He felt warm compared to the others.

"What's happening?" she asked, trying to regain her bearings.

They were in a clearing, surrounded by thick forest and stone ladies. Cobwebs dangled from the trees like disintegrating curtains. Ghost lights hovered in the air. Bonfires sprayed sparks into the treetops. And there were fairies. Fairies in every direction; sitting in the trees, chatting and swinging their legs, swaying, dancing, or whirling on the ground, or flying through the air in impossible acrobatics. Fairies, young and old, of every shape and size, some tiny as pea pods, others tall and skinny as trees, some grotesque and hunched, others regal and beautiful. It was as if Nelly had stumbled into a mad, gorgeous, terrifying carnival hidden in the woods.

Doed leaned in close. "It's tradition," he said, his breath on her neck. "All those in white are initiates, like you."

Nelly spotted a boy, perhaps ten, dressed in white. He had chestnut hair and a puckish face and swayed, entranced by a bonfire. Nearby a girl with skin so dark it was almost blue, also dressed in white, swirled with the crowd. This girl had eyes like Doed's, which meant she must have been a Wight.

Another boy dressed in white with blond hair and icy eyes was being pulled to-and-fro by the crowd. Tears were running down his face.

"What's happening there?" Nelly asked.

Doed glanced at the boy and shrugged. "He's about to face the Piper. He's frightened."

"But Jack said there was nothing to worry about," Nelly said, her voice coming out higher than she had intended. "Jack said the Piper is behind a barrier. He said it was safe."

"Jack says a lot of things."

Nelly tried to pull away, but Doed pulled her closer. His eyes were mischievous, sinister. "Stay close to me," he said. "You must be careful not to be swept up in the party."

"Why not?" Nelly asked.

"Because this party never ends. Enjoy yourself too much and you can get stuck here, whirling forever in eternal celebration. See the looks on their faces, the ones that are not initiates? What you see is pain, not joy."

Nelly looked again at the smiling, laughing faces swirling around her, and she saw, along with the smiles, exhaustion, tears, faces twisted in pain.

"Dance with me," Doed said, his breath in her hair. Nelly held onto him, her hands clammy, and he whirled her around and around.

"What if I don't want to go through with it?" Nelly said, her lips next to his ear. "What if I say no?"

"It's your choice. No one will force you," Doed said. "But Birdy's right. You should face the Piper. If you don't, you'll always be at a disadvantage. The nameless are weaker than everyone else. Their power is erratic, uncontrollable, unpredictable. You need a name. And this may be your only chance."

"Why? Why is this my only chance?"

"Because of your age. Initiates must be below the age of seventeen. You only barely make the cut. Any older and you become too strong. The Piper is a leech. If it drains someone too powerful, it could gain enough strength to escape. And that would be dangerous."

"Why? What would it do?"

"Kill."

He danced her toward the edge of the clearing. His hand was on the small of her back. Masked beings stood on the sidelines. They were like the dead things that had fished her out of the water when she'd first come to the fairy world. These wore masks shaped like animal or bird heads. They bobbed back and forth, eyes empty black holes.

"I'm frightened," Nelly admitted.

"If you weren't, you'd be a fool," Doed said. "The Piper is terrifying. That's the truth if you want it. But it wasn't so bad for me. It took a while for it to even take an interest in me. When it did, it grabbed my arm, said my name, and dropped me. Then it said I was pathetic. Insults are quite common. And that was that. I left, and I had my name."

"That doesn't sound so bad."

"It's different for everyone."

The music changed. The sound of a single flute or perhaps a tin whistle rose above the rest. It was haunting, yearning, at once ancient and plaintive. It made her crave her own tin whistle. The music she pulled from that instrument was more meaningful to her, more bone-deep than anything she could draw from the more sophisticated violin. As the fairy flute hit a pure, shattering note, something even deeper stirred inside

Nelly, something long asleep like the return of a forgotten dream. The crowd stopped swirling and parted.

Three women had arrived in the grove, dressed in robes of whispery blue. Their faces were shrouded behind veils that hung from jutting headdresses made of branches or maybe antlers. They each held a staff that seemed to be made of a long branch that ended in a cluster of points. A hovering blue light glowed at each of their staff's many points. The crowd and even the smoke parted for them wherever they moved. They seemed to float, their robes running over the earth like water.

"The Nivduhene," Doed whispered, sending a shiver up Nelly's neck.

The Nivduhene approached the boy with the puckish face and surrounded him. The boy went pale. Tears hung in his eyes. But he went with them without protest.

When the boy and the Nivduhene had disappeared down a slope on the far side of the clearing, the crowd resumed its hypnotic swirling. The Nivduhene returned to the clearing twice more after long intervals, first to collect the girl with the bluish skin, then to collect the blond boy, who wailed and screamed before finally agreeing to go with them. It could have been several hours that had passed during this time, though Nelly was having a hard time keeping track.

She and Doed danced, twirling to the music, and for a while, it was as if there was no one there but the two of them. He smelled like the wind before a storm. Electric. His irises glowed. He smiled at her sometimes, but only for a flickering moment. His smiles were beautiful things that appeared briefly and then vanished like shooting stars. They made her feel warm inside.

Ghost lights pulsated all around them. Doed was wary of them but much more concerned with the robed beings in masks that stood on the outskirts of the crowd. They were dead things, he said. Powerful ones. When a creature died, whether animal, fairy, or human, it lost its form and became spirit only. But over time, it could gain some of that form back, first as an orb, weak and vanishing, then as a ghost light, and finally as one of those masked things.

"They'll speak to me if I get too close," he said in a low voice, his cheek almost brushing against hers. "But they'll let me be as long as we're dancing."

It surprised Nelly to find herself disappointed that he wasn't dancing with her simply because he wanted to. He looked into her eyes. The air seemed to crackle. But then his hand fell from her waist, and he stepped back.

Again, she was surprised at her own disappointment. She was so aware of where his hand had been. She wanted to keep dancing with him. He lowered his eyes.

The music changed. Something was happening. As the dancers parted, Nelly realized what it was. The Nivduhene had come for her.

CHAPTER TWENTY-FIVE

THE PIPER

The Nivduhene surrounded Nelly, one ahead and two behind. She glanced at Doed for reassurance, but his eyes remained focused on the ground. Nelly steeled herself and went with them, following the one in front out of the clearing and down a short flight of stone steps that jutted out of the earth. They passed beyond the stone ladies and emerged into a dark silence.

The lights on the tips of the Nivduhene's staffs shone like foxfire. The silent women led Nelly to a beach lined on the shore side with trees. Sand, white as ground seashells, glinted in the foxfire lights. Nelly's feet slowed in the soft sand, but the Nivduhene did not. Their forms wavered as they drifted forward like liquid.

The air was full of the smell of the sea. Rhythmic black water slid onto the sand. It could have been a lake or an ocean that stretched out before them, but Nelly couldn't see much of it in the dark. There was no moon.

She shivered, wondering what had happened to the initiates who had gone before her. Not one of them had returned to the clearing. Had they gone to another clearing after facing the Piper? Was there another group of dancers and bonfires and masked dead things somewhere in the forest? Had they simply gone home? Had they returned at all? Visions of monsters and human sacrifices flashed into her mind.

The Nivduhene stopped at the edge of the water. They surrounded Nelly, driving their branch staffs into the sand. Then they lifted their shrouded faces to the sky and began to sing in pure, clear, haunting voices.

"The spark that stings rises from the deep.
Go with the Riverman and do not speak.
Follow along the island's spine.
Pluck a seed from the withered vine.
Face the monster, say its name,
feel the bellows, douse the flame.
Then to stop the clutch of death,
rip its hand back from your chest.
Eat the seed when all is dark,
New alive, you'll know the spark."

Their voices pierced the air with a chanting, droning melody that cut into Nelly's soul. Her eyes filled. The Nivduhene repeated the song and circled her, their robes rippling over the sand, leaving a wavelike pattern but no footprints. As they sang and circled, they anointed her skin with oil and stuck small silver stones to her in groups of three: her face, neck, chest, arms, anywhere her skin was exposed. The stones were cold and smooth, like marbles. Once the Nivduhene had completed this, they stopped circling. A pair of hands landed on Nelly's shoulders and forced her to her knees. Silver censers billowing incense swung out from under their robes. The old church smell, pine resin, lemon, and chocolate, was now overwhelming. They resumed the circling and the singing, repeating the refrain in their soaring, shattering voices.

Nelly didn't know what to think of this, but it felt very important. She tried to remember as much of the song as she could, repeating it in her head along with the Nivduhene. After some time, the women stopped singing and stood still. Each woman picked up a branch staff and pointed it toward the water.

There, floating over the waves, a face materialized out of the darkness. It was the face of a wizened old man with a long beard. As he came closer, his gray robes became visible. He was standing in the bow of a small rowboat, which bobbed in the water. The Nivduhene were pointing to the boat with their staffs.

Go with the Riverman and do not speak, Nelly thought, still repeating the Nivduhene's song in her head. *This must be the Riverman.*

Nelly got up, picked up her skirts, and waded into the water. No one protested so it seemed she was doing the right thing. She climbed into the stern of the boat and sat, hugging her knees to her chest. Immediately, the boat began to move. It was fast, cutting through the water like a motorboat, and yet there was no motor, or none that Nelly could see. There were no oars either. The Riverman stood in the bow, staring at her. His eyes gleamed. She looked back toward the shore. There was nothing there now but darkness and a spray of water. Behind the boat, a wake of bluish light frothed like bioluminescent plankton. She guessed that this resulted from some sort of magic dust or powder, like the ones Jack cooked up in his workshop.

She hugged her knees again and continued to repeat the song of the Nivduhene to herself. She was grateful to have this to focus on.

Up ahead, an island rose out of the darkness. It was a great, tangled mass of darkness as if a black hole was devouring what light was around it. There were no ghost lights around this island at all, and Nelly wondered why, though she wasn't sure she wanted to know the answer.

The Riverman brought the boat ashore at the edge of the island and made it fast, then he stared at her with his gleaming eyes. Nelly guessed this was her signal to move and climbed out of the boat. The water did not ripple with bioluminescence as it had in the waters near Jack's house. Instead, it remained black as ink. Only the Riverman's boat left a luminescent wake.

Nelly trudged out of the water onto a stony shoreline. *OK, now what?* She could barely see more than a few feet ahead. And it only got darker the farther she went from the boat and the shining wake it had left on the water.

What had the Nivduhene said, follow the island's spine? What was that supposed to mean? She hesitated, not wanting to plunge into the darkness and unknown. Should she turn back? Ask the Riverman what she was supposed to do? The Nivduhene's song said, *do not speak*, but this was asking the impossible. How was she supposed to follow the island's spine if she couldn't see a thing?

Then she remembered what she was. *Fire Sitter*. Nelly rubbed her fingers together as Fig had taught her and thought warm thoughts. She thought of being on the other side of this initiation, of the relief of having faced the Piper and survived, of finding Grandmother's and Orson's spirits, of her father recognizing her one day and saying her name. Sparks flew from her fingertips and a flame bloomed. It was a tiny flame, but it was a flame even so. It danced above her finger, glowing with a pleasantly warm heat.

In the flame's light, Nelly could see something shiny nearby on the ground. She approached it and found a cluster of silver stones, like the ones the Nivduhene had stuck to her skin. She touched one stone, and it immediately became a glowing ember, but a ghostly blue. Not only did it light up, but so did all the surrounding stones. Then more stones lit up and more and more. It was as if she had set off a trail of illuminating dominos and soon a path of pulsating blue stones appeared out of the darkness.

The island's spine. This had to be it. The moment she stepped onto the path, the flame on her finger went out and the silver stones that were stuck to her skin lit up. Clusters of three shone on her arms, her neck, and her face. The stones did not emit any heat.

The illuminated path led toward a series of low mountains, where the mouth of a dark cavern yawned wide. Nelly followed the trail of lights into the cavern. Tree roots dangled from the cavern's ceiling. To comfort herself, she kept repeating the Nivduhene's song out loud. The cave gradually narrowed until it encroached on her shoulders on either side. She reached what appeared to be an ornately looped garden gate. But the gate wasn't made of iron. It was made of something else, like carved obsidian. It appeared to be locked, but the moment she touched it, it clicked and swung open wide.

Nelly stepped past it and the gate swung shut behind her, the lock clicking into place. Again, she reminded herself of why she was doing this. She pictured her grandmother stuck in the psych ward and kept moving, following the trail of glowing stones deeper into the tunnel. Past the gate, the ceiling sloped farther downward. Nelly had to hunch to continue.

"Lucky I'm not claustrophobic," she muttered to herself, following the tunnel's narrowing twists and turns.

The glowing path stopped abruptly at a stone wall with a ladder carved into it. The ladder led straight up what looked like the inside of a vertical tunnel as if she were at the bottom of a well looking up. There was nowhere to go but up.

She climbed. Now the only light was coming off the stones

on her skin. She reached a second gate, this one positioned horizontally above her head like a trapdoor. She pushed it open with some effort and continued her climb. Above the second gate, desiccated-looking white roots grew from cracks in the walls and seemed to reach for her with skeletal fingers. Miniature white sacks dangled from the roots. At first, she thought they were cocoons and looked around for any insects, but then she realized they weren't cocoons at all. They were seeds.

Pluck a seed from the withered vine.

Relief flooded her. Pieces of the Nivduhene's song were unfolding little by little. This meant she was on the right track. She picked a seed, it was soft and somewhat squishy, and slipped it into one of her many pockets. She continued to climb with a new sense of confidence. Maybe she would get through this in one piece after all.

She reached the top of the ladder and lifted herself into a small cave. The light from the stones on Nelly's skin lit up cave walls that were covered in drawings. The images were primitive-looking and depicted what appeared to be hunters navigating a labyrinth. At the center of the labyrinth was a monster holding a light.

On the far wall was an opening big enough to walk through. It was completely covered by a third ornate gate. Nelly pushed the gate open part way and took one step out of the cave. She felt open air and realized immediately that she stood inside a large outdoor cage. Her stones illuminated its ornate metal bars. The bars surrounded her on every side, except for the side with the gate that led back to the cave behind her. On that side, the bars drove into the rock and stone on the outside of the cave. This meant the only way into this cage was through the cave.

The cage looked like a massive, iron birdcage. The cage itself was lodged in a grove of trees whose black finger-like branches clutched at the sky. Far above their branches, stars blinked like pinpricks in a black sheet.

But why was she in a cage? She tried not to jump to any conclusions. Jack said that the Piper was kept behind a barrier. Was this what he meant? She looked back at the gate she had just come through. It was still ajar, exactly as she'd left it. She wasn't completely trapped. She could get back into the cave at any time.

"OK, think this through," she said out loud. One way to keep yourself separate from a predator was to lock yourself inside a cage. Thrill-seekers sometimes did this when they wanted to get up close and personal with a shark. So maybe this was like a shark cage?

Oh, God.

A freezing wind sailed through the cage bars and sent her teeth clattering. She hugged herself. Was she just supposed to wait here for the thing to show up? How long would that take? She started to pace to warm up and walk off her nerves, repeating the Nivduhene's song to herself. She pictured her grandmother and her father and Orson and kept telling herself that all she needed to do was let whatever-it-was touch her through the bars. She could do it. She could do it. She had come this far. Everything would be fine.

She walked the length of the cage, but as she turned back to retrace her steps, she saw something out of the corner of her eye. She spun around.

Someone was standing outside the cage. It was a girl dressed in white with pale skin and white-blonde hair and ...

Nelly almost laughed out loud. She was looking at her own reflection. She could see little clusters of glowing stones on her reflection's skin, mirroring her own.

She stared at herself. Her hair looked wild and windswept like Fig's often did. Her eyes reflected the shine of the stones.

She had never looked less human. At least, not that she was aware of.

But what was casting this reflection? There was no outline of a mirror or any kind of reflective surface.

She took a step closer to the bars. The reflection mirrored her movements. She waved at herself, waggled her eyebrows, stuck out her tongue. All these things were perfectly mirrored back. And yet something felt wrong about it, something about the eyes. They were emotionless, dead, like the eyes of a shark.

"You're not a reflection, are you?" Nelly muttered.

"You're not a reflection, are you?" the reflection repeated after a pause.

Nelly stepped back from the bars. The reflection, or what-ever it was, stepped forward.

"What are you?" Nelly whispered.

"What are you?" the thing repeated like a child playing a game. It cocked its head and smiled a little, though its eyes remained lifeless and cold.

Nelly recoiled. This was wrong. It wasn't normal. It wasn't right!

"–A-Are you the Piper?" she asked, reminding herself she was in a cage. She was safe.

"–A-Are you the Piper?" the thing repeated, even imitating Nelly's nervous stammer. Its voice sounded just like Nelly's, but its tone was mocking.

Nelly's heart was a jackhammer against her chest. This thing had to be the Piper. What else could it be?

She resisted the urge to turn and run. "I'm here because I … I need a name."

"I need a name," the Piper repeated, cocking its head in the other direction, a strangely animal-like movement.

Something about this thing revolted Nelly. Every instinct

was telling her to run. She wanted this over with now. She took a step toward the bars. "I'm supposed to let you –t-touch me."

"–T-Touch me," the Piper repeated, walking right up to the bars and staring at her with disturbingly hungry eyes.

Nelly stepped forward. Its eyes were concentrated completely on her. It seemed less and less human, or less and less fairy, the closer she got to it. Its face grew gaunt and skeletal, its teeth sharpened, its skin took on the luminous gray pallor of the moon. And yet it still looked like her, like Nelly, a monstrous version of her, but her, nevertheless.

With a lunge like a striking snake, it grabbed her arm. Its touch was so cold it burned. Nelly yanked her arm back, but the Piper held her firm. It pulled her toward the bars until she was almost touching them. Then it wrapped one of its hands around the back of her neck.

Its hands were ice. She tried to scream, but all that passed from her lips was her breath, which turned to white mist in the air. Another sensation took over. A tingling at first, then a leaden heaviness that seeped through her entire body. She knew this feeling. She had felt it after drinking that blueberry syrup stuff that Mother had forced her to drink. *Piper's dew.*

Thoughts of her mother; her gaze, her touch, her smell, flooded Nelly's senses, and she released an anguished sob.

The Piper smiled. It pulled her closer to the bars. Nelly could see the veins under its skin, delicate blue lines like rivers on a map. It gasped suddenly and threw its head back like it was experiencing a deeply pleasurable sensation. The blue lines under its skin went bright, electric until every vein was visible, even the ones in its eyes.

"What are you?" the Piper said. Its voice still sounded like Nelly's, but there was another tone underneath it, guttural and reptilian.

Nelly felt weak, lightheaded, like she was giving blood.

"What are you?" she heard herself repeat.

"Fairy? Human? Neither?" the Piper said, its voice a hissing whisper. "Of human blood ..."

"Of human blood," Nelly repeated against her will. Why was she repeating what it was saying?

"Monster," the Piper hissed, eyes glittering with pleasure as if it knew this was an insult that would sting.

"Monster," Nelly repeated, her voice small and weak.

Then the Piper released a sound so chilling, some primal part of Nelly woke up. She felt the bone-deep terror a prey animal must feel at the call of a predator. The sound was both shrill and guttural: the screech of an owl, the cry of a hawk, the moan of a loon, and the bellow of a crocodile all together at once, like some nightmare bird of prey.

And Nelly knew now why it was called Piper.

She couldn't think. If she could have run, it was all she would have done, forever. But she couldn't run. She couldn't move.

The thing stopped piping. "What's your name?" it asked, now looking her in the eye.

"What's your name?" Nelly repeated, though her voice was so thin with fear, only a whisper of sound came out.

"My name is Piper," the Piper said.

"My name is Piper," Nelly repeated. The light from the stones on her skin was dimming.

"Your name is ..." The Piper paused. "Winnow Fie."

"Winnow Fie," Nelly repeated and felt an immediate surge of strength. Winnow Fie, this was her true name! She knew it like she knew the sky was blue and the grass was green. It was a simple fact written on her bones, and she wondered how she could have been unaware of this before. Her name was Winnow Fie. Of course it was.

The Piper smiled. "You taste like destruction," it whispered, a guttural crocodile growl in its voice. "Stay with me. Let me drink you away. I can give you peace. They will make you a weapon."

Nelly did not repeat this. The heavy sensation returned. She had a name now. Wasn't it supposed to let her go? She tried to pull away, but she was so weak. Her knees hit the ground. The stones on her skin had faded to struggling embers. The Piper piped, and it was chilling and rapturous and terrible. That sound hit her like a gut punch. She was going to die here, wasn't she? Nelly forced herself to focus. She recalled the Nivduhene's song. *To stop the clutch of death, rip its hand back from your chest.* She summoned all her strength, grabbed the Piper's hand—it burned so much she screamed—and tried to wrench it from her chest.

The Piper pulled her forward, its smiling face pressed against the bars. White smoke billowed in tendrils from the thing's face wherever the iron bars touched it. "It doesn't matter. None of it matters. We'll be together soon. We are inevitable, you and I."

It released her. Nelly fell to the ground and immediately scrambled back from the bars. She was trembling with such violence that her teeth chattered. Tears covered her face. The stones on her skin flickered and went dark, and so did the world. She couldn't see anything now, not the bars, not the Piper, not the way out, only the stars high above, pinpricks of light in a black curtain.

Then she saw something, a very faint light coming from one of her pockets. She stuck her hand inside and found the seed she had plucked from the vine in the tunnel. *Eat the seed.* This was the last part of the Nivduhene's song.

She popped the seed into her mouth and bit into it. A flood of liquid burst onto her tongue. It had a pleasantly thick, sweet taste that reminded her of eggnog. It felt hot going down and warmed her insides. The stones on her skin flashed back to life again, brighter than before. And she felt her strength and her courage returning. She had done it! She had faced the Piper. She had a name!

Winnow Fie.

Nelly got back onto her feet. She could see the gate she had come through to enter the cage. It was over. Then a screaming sound like twisting metal scraped across the silence. She looked up. There was a hole in the top of the cage. The bars were mangled and bent, as though something powerful had ripped them apart. But if the bars had been breached, then ...

Something giant rose between black branches. A monstrous thing, pale as the moon, with a cobweb of electric blue veins under its skin.

Nelly saw gleaming eyes, a flash of teeth, a glint of claws, and nothing more. She had already turned and started to run.

CHAPTER TWENTY-SIX

BLOOD IS THICKER THAN ...

Nelly bolted back toward the gate. Metal groaned behind her. She pulled the gate shut after her and then heard it rip from its hinges. She leaped into the tunnel and down the ladder. Dirt rained on her as the thing forced its way into the too-small opening above her head. She lost her grip on the ladder and fell hurtling past branches and seeds.

SMASH!

She landed hard on the second trapdoor-like gate. Above her, dirt and seeds poured, and jaws snapped. She lifted herself onto the ladder and yanked open the gate below her. Sliding past it, she scraped her skin on the bars, pulled the gate shut behind her, and dropped. A second later, the tunnel vibrated with the force of the thing slamming itself into the gate. More dirt rained down as Nelly hit the ground. There was a grinding sound as the thing dislodged the gate.

She scrambled to her feet, ducked, and ran hunched through the low tunnel. The walls shuddered and cracked as the thing forced its way after her. Chilling piping sounds roared from its throat. The tunnel was collapsing, hailing stone and earth, as the monster forced its way through like a drilling machine.

Nelly shoved through the first gate and burst out into the night air. Black water crashed on the shore. The Riverman and his boat bobbed nearby, surrounded by bioluminescence.

"Piper!" she screamed. Behind her, the mountainside burst, and she was thrown forward. Nelly flew through the air and into the water along with a shower of rocks and chunks of earth. The sloshing sound of water enveloped her and muffled everything. Something else splashed into the water after her. It was so large it set off high waves and pushed her deeper into the watery darkness.

She swam for the surface, her dress tangled in her legs, and broke through. Lights were streaking over the water and popping like fireworks in the sky. The Riverman had set off some kind of flare. He had turned his boat around and was racing back for land at an incredible speed. He was leaving her behind!

Then the boat and the Riverman vanished. Something from beneath had pulled it under and left only a pool of bubbling, glowing water in its wake.

Nelly was alone. There was only water and darkness and the sound of her own gasping breaths. Her panicked mind told her to swim for the shore. But before she could find it, something grabbed her by the back of her dress and plucked her out of the water like a rag doll. She slammed onto the floor of a rowboat. She spun around, coughing and sputtering, expecting to find dead things in masks and robes. But she found Fig in her old-woman glamour.

"Fig!" Nelly said without thinking.

"Shh!" Fig hissed, a finger to her wrinkled lips. "Pull the glow stones from your skin and throw them in the water."

Nelly did as she was told. She ripped the stones off her skin like sticky bandages and then hurled them into the inky depths.

"It doesn't see well in the dark," Fig whispered and held out an oar. "Gently, quietly."

Lights streaked over their heads like the aurora borealis. Nelly and Fig dipped their oars into the water as quickly as they dared. The black water around them rippled and splashed. With every plunge of their oars, Nelly thought the Piper would find them, leap up like a sea monster, and swallow them whole. Soon, the beach and the dark forest grew visible beyond the waves.

The boat ran ashore, sending Nelly lurching forward. Fig hopped out and Nelly followed, leaping into the knee-deep water.

"Nelly!" a voice called. Doed came running out of the darkness.

"Where's Jack?" Fig asked him.

Doed gave Fig a confused look. "What are you doing here?" he said and then shook his head. "The Bone King has him."

"What do you mean?" Nelly said, wading out of the water.

"We can't help him now," Fig hissed. "We have to go."

"What about the Piper?" Nelly asked. "It's loose! We have to warn—"

"They know," Fig said, and pointed at the lights streaking the sky.

Nelly, Fig, and Doed raced up the bank and into the dark forest. Fig's boat had drifted far to the right of the spot where Nelly had set off with the Riverman. And so, the trio did not follow tunnels made of thorns or stone steps to get back up the incline. Instead, they scaled it, scrambling step after laborious step, up the steep slope through bush and bracken, as quickly as they could manage.

Nelly had a much easier time keeping up with the fairies

this time, though the terrain was more difficult, and they were climbing and not descending. This wasn't the only thing that had changed. Her senses felt sharper somehow. She could see better in the dark. Whereas before the forest at night had been a devouring darkness, now it was bathed in a faint blue light, as if she were wearing night-vision goggles. She could see the trees and the tangled thicket even outside Doed's circle of lantern light. Was this because she had a name now? Nelly thought she could hear better, too, but did not like what she was hearing—screams of terror, people running, the Piper piping.

She hurried to catch up with Fig and Doed, who were a few meters ahead. The fairies moved quickly but were quiet as ghosts. Doed's lantern showed ruins and bone-white trees. The Piper piped again, sending a chill through Nelly's heart. That sound was getting closer. She glanced back over her shoulder and ran right into Doed.

Both he and Fig had stopped cold.

"What's wrong?" Nelly asked, and they shushed her. She listened. People were screaming, running. The Piper piped. But there was another sound, too, a sound she hadn't heard before. It was close, but faint and out of place. It sounded like someone was whistling.

A glittering mist rose out of the darkness. Thick and swirling, it engulfed them like an avalanche. Fig's glamour poured from her skin and splashed to the ground in a pool of swirling colors. She gasped and stumbled back against a tree. Her true form was now exposed. Streaks of color on her face and clothing were all that remained of her disguise.

"What's happening?" Nelly asked.

Fig's eyes were wild. "The Fury," she whispered.

"It's flash fog," Doed said. He had gone sheet white. "The

Fury use it. It drops all glamours, renders all powders and potions useless."

Fig held on to a tree for support. "They're here for the Piper, but they'll take us, too." She was trembling. She looked at Nelly. "Get away from me. If they find us together—"

"Can't we do something?" Nelly cut in. "Use one of those night keys?"

Doed shook his head. "Night keys won't work in the fog. We're in the Fury's path. The fog is the first wave. The scouts will be on us soon. We can't outrun them or evade them."

"We can hide!" Nelly looked around. She recognized this place. The ruins of Mag Dún, Jack had called them. "That tree we came through is right near here. There's a hollow under it!"

"It's too late," Fig said, staring into the darkness. "There's no hiding from the Fury."

"We have to try! Doed, please!" Nelly said, grabbing him by the arm.

"Yes ..." he said as though shaken from a trance. "You hide. I'll try to lead them away. I'm a lowly Wight. They have no reason to bother with me. And the Piper is loose. They may be too distracted to notice you."

"They won't find us," Nelly said with false confidence. She urged Fig to follow, and the fairy woman did, pushing herself from the tree. A glowing handprint, the remnants of Fig's glamour, remained on the bark where her hand had been and then faded away.

They ran for the tree with the hollow under its roots and climbed down inside. When Nelly and Fig were safely below, Doed covered the entrance with branches and leaves and was gone.

There wasn't much space in the hollow. Fig sat in the corner, squeezed under dangling roots, trembling like a frightened rabbit. She was rocking herself. It was disturbing to see her this way. Nelly was reminded of Grandmother and her episodes and how she would hide in the basement and rock back and forth on the floor.

Nelly crouched next to Fig. She held out a hand, and to Nelly's surprise, Fig took it.

A whistling sound rang out. *WHIP, WHIP, WOOOEEE!*

Fig clapped a hand over her own mouth.

WHIP, WHIP, WOOOEEE! It trilled again, closer now.

A tear ran down Fig's cheek.

A cacophony of other sounds rose out of the silence. Wolves howled, crows croaked, owls shrieked, a hunting horn whined. There was a chilling, furious scream. The air became heavy with the smell of charcoal. Nelly held her breath and Fig became perfectly still as the sounds of a great host moved overhead. Hooves and paws and runners' feet rumbled the ground. The roots in the hollow trembled and dirt pattered down on them. Strange insects, shaken loose by the dirt, dropped into Nelly's hair, and scurried down her neck and back, making her skin crawl. But she dared not react to them. The tree above them creaked and lurched as though something large had landed in its branches. But still Nelly and Fig stayed quiet and still.

Soon the noises above faded and then petered out entirely. Nelly and Fig sat in silence, barely breathing, hand in hand, squeezing tight. Then something changed. The air didn't feel as heavy and the charcoal smell began to lift. Nelly glanced at Fig. She still looked like herself, but her hair had streaks of gray in it. Not wanting to risk speaking, Nelly picked up a strand of Fig's hair and showed it to her.

Fig's eyes went wide. Immediately, she shoved her hand into one of her pockets, pulled out a night key, and jammed it into the dirt. There was a *POP*, and then the complex smell of honey and fireworks. They weren't in the hollow anymore.

They were in a shallow cave with a door on one side. Fig flung open the door.

"Quickly," she whispered and pulled Nelly out into the woods. Quickly was an understatement. Nelly had never in her life moved so fast under the power of her own two legs. Fig whisked Nelly between trees and under ghost lights like a blast of wind. They burst free of the forest in a swirl of leaves and then raced along a beach at the edge of the sea.

Soon they came to a great pile of twisted driftwood that lay on the sand like the skeletal remains of a washed-up sea monster. The wind off the water was wet and rough, and tore at their clothing, sending Nelly's wet dress flapping around her legs. Fig led her ducking and climbing into the very center of the pile of driftwood. There, a trapdoor lay hidden. Below the trapdoor was a small, wood-lined room buried under the sand. Once Nelly had jumped down inside it, she asked where they were going, but Fig only hushed her.

Fig pulled the trapdoor shut above their heads and then pulled out a large, stylized key. *POP!* The room changed and then lurched upward like a fast-moving elevator. The walls were made of green glass.

As they moved upward, they could see earth shot with scattered lights through the green glass walls. Nelly watched Fig. The fairy's face was streaked with the remnants of her glamour and grimy tears. She was taut as a stretched elastic, her hands balled into fists at her side. She looked like a survivor of a war or a disaster. Nelly caught a hazy glimpse of herself in the green glass and realized she didn't look much better.

The room jerked to a stop. Fig pushed open a heavy trap-door in the ceiling, which thudded on the ground above, and heaved herself out into the open air. Nelly followed her, climbing out of the room with some effort. They stood in a completely different forest now.

Fig dropped to the ground. She put her hands on her head and released an audible sob. Then she clutched at the earth like a sailor who had found land after months at sea.

Nelly looked around, confused. Something had changed. This forest felt smaller, grayer, less haunted than any of the forests in the fairy world. Even the air seemed to have changed. It was duller, less electric.

"Where are we?" Nelly muttered though she had already guessed the answer.

Fig sat back on her heels. "Back among the living," she said, wiping tears from her face.

They were back in the human world.

"No ... no ... not yet," Nelly said. "We haven't found Grandmother or Orson—"

"Be grateful," Fig said, getting to a shaky stand. "You do not know what we just escaped." She started away between the trees, limping slightly.

"But we're going back, right?" Nelly said and hurried after her. "We have to go back! What about my grandmother?" Nelly was fuming. She wasn't about to give up now, not after everything she had been through.

Fig stopped and pulled something from one of her pockets.

"Here," she said and thrust a small jar into Nelly's hands.

Nelly held up the jar. Two ghost lights were floating inside it. "What's this?"

"Look closely."

Orson's yellow ball and Grandmother's broach sat at the bottom of the jar. Above them, the two ghost lights pulsed faintly. Perfect spheres. Inside the spheres, miniature worlds seemed to be playing out. In one, a boy about Nelly's age sobbed in the corner of a dark room. In the other, an old woman ran terrified through some sort of labyrinth. Was that Grandmother?

"You see? They're fine," Fig said. "We'll put them back in their bodies and all your problems will be solved, trivial though they may be."

Nelly scowled. "My problems aren't trivial."

"Depends whose problems you compare them with, doesn't it?" Fig said.

Nelly squinted at the lights inside the jar. "I don't understand. I thought—"

Fig was once again walking away from her. Nelly hurried after her, weaving around trees. Soon, the Morighan House rose between the trees, black and still as it always was. They were back on the farm.

"But I thought you needed me to find Orson," Nelly called after Fig. "I thought—"

"We lied," Fig said without slowing her pace. "Anyone can retrieve a lost spirit. It's a simple matter. We could have done it at any time."

Fig broke from the forest and walked straight toward the Morighan House. Nelly caught up just as Fig limped herself onto the Morighan House porch.

"Why did you lie?" Nelly said, trying to catch her breath.

Fig pushed open the creaky back door and paused, raising her brows as if surprised Nelly hadn't figured it out. "So, you wouldn't put up a fuss when we kidnapped you."

CHAPTER TWENTY-SEVEN

OF HUMAN BLOOD

Nelly stood there for a moment in silence. "What?" she said and hurried up the porch steps and into the house.

Fig was in the kitchen lighting candles with her fingers. The house was dark and dank, though not nearly as intimidating as Nelly remembered it. It felt smaller, somehow, too, as if she had grown since the last time she'd been here.

"What did you just say?" Nelly said again.

Fig looked up, the candle flames reflected in her eyes. "We stole you," she said in a matter-of-fact tone. "We could not take you by force because of the bargain we made with your grandmother. We needed your cooperation. And you made it very easy for us if you want to know. Never trust a fairy who offers help for no reward. There is always a catch."

"But why?"

"That ... is complicated," Fig said. Then she pounced.

Nelly cried out, but before she could even think to defend herself, she found herself tied to a chair.

"This is for your own good," Fig said, putting a final knot in Nelly's bonds. "I can't have you following me."

Nelly struggled against the rope. "Why? Where are you going?"

"Back to our own," Fig said, brushing dirt from her own hair and skirts. "To send some wisps after Jack and Doed, make sure they survived the Piper and the Fury."

She put the jar with Grandmother's and Orson's spirits in it on the dusty table and then held up a night key.

"This will take you to the asylum where your grandmother and Orson are being held. Go there and release the lights. When they are close again to their bodies, they'll return of their own accord. But you should move quickly. The longer a spirit is separate from its host, the more likely there is to be permanent damage."

"What kind of damage?" Nelly asked, alarmed, but Fig did not reply.

She put the night key on the table next to the jar and pulled a small tin box out of her pocket.

"This is gnomish healing ointment," Fig said. "Dab it over the injuries on your face and arms. It will fix you up."

Nelly glanced at her arms, which were scraped up badly from her ordeal with the Piper. Fig put the tin on the table and turned to leave.

"Wait! Don't leave!" Nelly shouted. "Morag Fie!"

Fig stopped. She turned a fierce stare on Nelly.

Nelly shrank. "—Y-You can't just leave me here like this," she mumbled.

"You'll get yourself loose soon enough," Fig said, rubbing her fingers together. Sparks flashed and a tendril of smoke rose between them. "Remember what you are."

"No, you explain first. Why did you kidnap me?" Nelly cringed at how weak and whiny her own voice sounded.

Fig once again turned to leave.

"Morag Fie!" Nelly called again in a loud, clear voice.

Fig winced but did not stop.

"Morag Fie! Morag Fie! Morag Fie!" Nelly shouted.

Fig, almost at the door, crumpled to the floor and then smacked it in frustration.

"I'll say your name again and again if I have to," Nelly said. She didn't want to hurt Fig, but she wasn't about to be left here alone in the dark. Not again.

"You're not leaving. Not until I get the truth."

"Nelly, please," Fig said, her voice small. She turned and her eyes were bright with tears.

"Why did you kidnap me? What was your plan?"

Fig sat on the floor, shoulders slumped, legs straight out in front of her like a giant rag doll.

"Once you had gained your name, we planned to hand you over to the Bone King. He wants someone like you, one who is neither quite fairy nor quite human, neither quite here nor quite there."

"Why?"

Fig blew her hair out of her face. "I don't know. I can only guess."

"Your guess will be better than mine," Nelly said. "So guess."

Fig looked at the ceiling. "Our people do not come here, to this Other place, without reason. Whatever happened between Birdy, your ancestor, and this town years ago, she initiated by coming here. The question is, why? Why did she come here at all? Only Birdy can answer that."

A shadow cast by the flickering candles passed over Fig's face. She seemed disturbed. But she hadn't said anything Nelly couldn't have worked out on her own. Nelly was about to say as much when Fig spoke again.

"It doesn't matter," she said, her wild hair falling back over her face. "Whatever Birdy has cooked up, it doesn't matter anymore. I won't let them have you. You are safe now. You can go back to your life."

"I don't understand," Nelly said. "You're helping me now?" She paused as something else occurred to her. "You ... you were there waiting for me at the island of the Piper. You weren't supposed to be there. You kidnapped me, you were going to hand me over to the Bone King, then you risked yourself to find me, bring me back here, and - and give me healing ointment? Why? What's changed?"

There was a long silence.

"Morag Fie!" Nelly shouted.

"You are my niece," Fig said, wincing.

Nelly would have been less surprised if Fig had transformed into a giant toad.

"What?"

Fig pulled her foggy acorn necklace out from under her shirt and held it up. The candlelight refracted inside it and sent a shard of light dancing across the floor. "You said your mother has a charm like this one, but amber. There is only one charm like that in either world, and it belongs to my sister. I know because I gave it to her. I may be on the outs with our family, and you as well, but I will not allow a single one of you to be harmed if I can prevent it."

Nelly sat in stunned silence. Her mother had a sister? And that sister was Fig? Was it possible? She gazed at Fig's strange features and the more she stared, the more she saw it. The familiar slope of Fig's nose, her graceful eyebrows, the red of her hair, so like Mother's and yet different. And all at once, all the emotion Nelly felt about her mother flooded through her.

"So, you're my aunt," Nelly said, her voice cracking. "And you're, what, protecting me now?"

"You are my family."

"You tried to kill me!"

"A mistake," Fig said, lifting herself to a shaky stand.

"Where is she? Where's my mother?"

"I don't know—I'm telling the truth!" Fig snapped as Nelly began to say her true name. "I haven't seen her in years. I didn't know she came here. I didn't know you existed. I certainly didn't know she had been with a ... with a *human*." She paused and shook her head in disbelief. "But I do know she wanted you kept away from this." Fig patted her own chest. "From our world and its politics and its problems. Why else would she have left you here? Let me go, Nelly. You have your life back now, your grandmother who loves you, your other-worldly concerns. Forget about us and be happier for it."

"Forget?" Nelly said, tears in her throat. "How am I supposed to do that?"

"It's better if you do."

Nelly couldn't believe what she was hearing.

"Better? Better for me not to know you, not to know my own family or who or what I am? To live a lie?"

Fig took a single step and then stumbled into the wall like a drunk. "There's safety in lies," she said, leaning against the peeling wallpaper.

"I don't want safety. I want the truth!"

"And I don't want to argue with you."

"Then don't abandon me!"

Fig's eyes smoldered. "I am your aunt, not your mother. Saying to me what you want to say to her won't accomplish anything."

Nelly wanted to scream. "You don't know what it's like!" she shouted, tears falling freely now. "My mother left, my father's in a hospital, Grandmother is all I have left. The people here, they know I'm not like them. They can tell and they hate me for it. They'll never accept me! That's what you think is best for me?"

"It's better than the alternative."

"Which is what?"

"Death," Fig said, dropping the word like an anvil. "If you spend too much time in our world, the Fury will find you. It's inevitable. Secrets this big cannot be kept for long. Eventually, they will find you, just as they will find me if I keep pushing my luck. But if they find me, I alone will suffer. If they find you, they will kill *everyone*. You and everyone you've ever met, anyone who's heard even a rumor of your existence, the humans in your school, your town, all the surrounding towns. They will drop down on you like a star from the sky and the impact will extend for miles. They will take no risks with one such as you. You are not allowed to exist. That is the truth."

"One such as me? You mean because I'm ... of human blood," Nelly said, recalling the words she had now heard several times. "You were going to kill me when you heard those words. The Piper said them, too."

"The Piper said them?" Fig dragged a hand down her own face. "That means it's true."

"I don't understand. Doesn't that just mean I'm part human?"

Fig was shaking her head. She was turning away. She wasn't going to tell the truth. She was going to change the subject or walk out like she always did. "Morag—"

"Nelly!" Fig snapped. "Having power over someone is a responsibility. It's not right to abuse it."

Nelly clapped her mouth shut. There was another long silence.

Fig pulled a chair over and sat down heavily. She watched Nelly. She seemed to be struggling with something. Finally, she spoke.

"When one of our people and one of theirs creates a child, normally, not that it's normal, but normally such a child is born fully human. The human blood is insidious, it over-whelms our own so that most children born of these unions bear no trace of our blood, our abilities, our lifespan. These humans born of fairy blood may be more connected to our people than other humans, but they are not *us*. There are no half-fairies. You either are one of us or you are not."

"So, I'm ... I'm ..."

"You are one of us, even though your father is human. You are a fairy born of human blood. There is no being more rare or more feared amongst our people. We are told stories of fairies of human blood from the time we are small children. There hasn't been one like you for many thousands of years. It is said that you, that those like you, present a deadly danger to our people, that you are destined to rain destruction down upon us."

"Destruction?" Something the Piper had said rattled in Nelly's head. *You taste like destruction.* "But that can't be true. I'm only, I'm just ... me. I couldn't destroy anything, even if I wanted to, which I don't." There were tears in her eyes. The people of Nothing feared her and maybe they were right to, but fairies, too?

"I believe you," Fig said gently. "I know you now a little. I'm sorry I tried to harm you. I won't ever again. We're family and that means something to me. Human blood or not, I'll protect you. With my life if necessary. That's a vow. But please don't make it more difficult for me than it has to be. Stay here and live your life with the humans. Safely. Quietly. Our people don't need to know about you."

"But Jack and Doed and Birdy and—"

"I'll deal with Jack and Doed. The Bone King has never met you, never seen you. We'll tell him you don't exist, that you're a figment of Birdy's incarcerated imagination. As for Birdy, we'll tell her the Piper got you. She's hardly in a position to check."

Nelly lowered her gaze. Maybe Fig was right. She'd already had a taste of how dangerous the fairy world could be. That she, Nelly, could be a danger to beings as formidable as fairies was not something she wanted to face. The very idea made her want to climb into a closet and hide there forever.

"What about my father?" Nelly muttered.

"I tried to find his spirit, but he has been lost for too long," Fig said. "I'll keep looking and you, you will be a human. Deal?"

Nelly hesitated. She looked away from Fig, her mother's sister, emotions still churning inside her. The sun was rising, sending the shadows into retreat.

"Try forgiveness," Fig said.

She nodded toward the jar with Grandmother's and Orson's spirits. "Start with yourself."

Nelly looked at the floor.

"And once you've done that," Fig continued, "move on to the humans in your town, your mother, and, in time, your silly old aunt."

Fig's eyes glittered with a smile, and for a moment they didn't seem as sad as they normally did. Nelly couldn't help it and smiled back.

Fig's eyes turned sad again. "Forgiveness is better than anger, better than righteous fury," she said, leaning back heavily in her chair. "And always better than revenge."

Nelly nodded. Fig could be comforting when she wanted to be, even wise. Maybe it wouldn't be so bad having her for an aunt.

Fig pulled a small vial of milky liquid from one of her pockets.

"What's that?"

"Death's milk. A strengthening concoction. The seed you ate after facing the Piper contained the same stuff. It fortified you after the Piper drained you." Fig rubbed her forehead as though nursing a headache. "I don't normally take this stuff, but after hearing my name so many times …"

"Oh, uh …"

"Don't apologize." Fig pulled the cork on the vial and drank half the bottle. The color rushed back into her cheeks and her eyes began to faintly glow. She stood up and changed as she did so. She was now a regal-looking woman with dark skin, short hair, and a slender neck. Glamour. At some point, Nelly had to figure out how to do that.

Fig put the half-empty bottle of death's milk down on the table and turned to leave.

"Fig?" Nelly said. "Will you … will you visit me?"

Fig paused and looked at Nelly with her sad eyes and, for a brief moment, some other emotion passed behind them.

"I'll be here whenever you need me. Right here. Don't talk to the cat."

She turned to leave. And this time, Nelly let her.

CHAPTER TWENTY-EIGHT

HUMAN AGAIN

Don't talk to the cat. That wouldn't be too difficult since the cat that wasn't a cat was still down in the basement, locked in an iron cage. As Nelly burned her bonds apart with her fingers, she wondered if she should check on Trouble, at the very least. They had been away for several days. How long could a fairy cat go without food and water? Did it even need food and water?

She stood up. The ropes that had bound her to the chair fell to the floor, ends burned black. There was something satisfying about that. Unnerving, but satisfying. She grabbed the night key and the gnomish healing ointment Fig had left her and slipped them both into her pockets. Then, with a delicate touch, she lifted the jar containing Grandmother's and Orson's spirits.

The cat would have to wait. Nelly didn't have any food or water to give it, for one thing. She paused. Fig's half-drained bottle of death's milk was still on the table. Somehow she doubted the fairy woman had left this behind for her. She pocketed it anyway and hurried out of the Morighan House and across the field to the farmhouse. The sun rose behind it, giving it a halo-like glow in stark contrast with the shadowy Morighan House.

Nelly slipped the jar into one of the many pockets in her garb, climbed the oak tree next to the back door, forced open her bedroom window, and crawled inside. She thought it best not to alert Mr. Glanville to her presence. There would be explaining to do, and she wanted to avoid questions she couldn't answer.

Her room was as she'd left it, but like the Morighan House, it seemed different somehow, smaller. Had the room changed, or had she?

Nelly couldn't wait to change out of her dress. It was torn and damp and covered in mud. There were handfuls of dirt and rocks in the pockets, left over from her encounter with the Piper. She placed the jar on the table and emptied the pockets onto the floor. Dirt from the fairy world, and the Piper's island, was in her bedroom. She could hardly believe she had survived that island. The memory of it and the Piper's chilling call sent a shiver all over her skin.

She crossed to her closet, pulled out a pair of jeans and a sweater, and turned around.

Her stomach turned over.

A girl with fierce eyes and wild, white hair was standing in the shadows, staring at her. The Piper!

Nelly recoiled and tripped over the edge of her bed. The room spun. She crashed to the floor and then held still.

The room was silent except for the breeze coming in from the window, moving her curtains in and out like breath. How could the Piper be here? It wasn't possible. Nelly mustered up the courage and peered up over the mattress. Her cheval glass mirror stood in the shadows on the other side of the bed. A wave of relief washed over her. The Piper wasn't in her room. It hadn't followed her. Her own reflection had spooked her.

She stood up and stared at herself in the mirror. Her hair was as wild as the Piper's had been, her eyes held an intense internal light, and her skin had a slight tinge to it as if her image had been lifted from an enhanced photograph. She did not look human.

Nelly touched the dirt streaks on her face. A nasty bruise was rising on her cheekbone. It must have happened when she fell down that vertical tunnel on the Piper's island. She shuddered at the thought and then pulled tidbits of leaves and twigs from her hair. She had to clean herself up, change into some human clothes. That would fix things. Well, maybe not fix, but improve.

She took a shower and got dressed. The healing ointment Fig had left her, a blue substance that glowed when it made contact with her skin, healed all of Nelly's wounds. It was unnerving but satisfying.

Mr. Glanville wasn't at home. He may not have been at home for some time. There was a layer of dust on all the surfaces, and she found nothing but condiments in the fridge. Had he gone on a trip and thrown everything away? That couldn't be right. Why would he go on a trip so soon after Grandmother had been hospitalized?

Nelly found a jar of mixed nuts and dried fruit in the pantry, the only trace of food in the kitchen. She walked around the house with no particular purpose, crunching almonds that tasted of cardboard. Fairy food had apparently ruined her for anything human.

Back in her bedroom, she caught a glimpse of herself again in the mirror. The light had faded from her eyes and her skin had dulled. It was an improvement, she supposed. She sat down on the end of her bed, feeling tired and empty and alone.

But why did she feel so alone? She was better off now than she had been before she'd met the fairies. Grandmother would be better soon, and there was hope for her father. And she had an aunt now, too. She had never had an aunt before. Fig was strange and frightening, it was true, but she was on Nelly's side now; she would be there for her as her mother had never been. There was comfort in that.

Nelly fell back on the bed, exhausted. It was like gravity was pulling her down into the mattress. She had to get Grand-mother's and Orson's spirits back to their bodies right away, but it couldn't hurt if she closed her eyes for five minutes first. She thought of the fairy world. She'd had the barest glimpse of it, and yet she knew it contained horrors and wonders she couldn't begin to imagine. It seemed a shame to give up on ever experiencing any of it again, to become Nelly Morighan, though she had only just earned the name Winnow Fie.

It was a strange name, but it felt like hers. Right but strange. The second part of it was like the second part of Fig's true name. Morag Fie and Winnow Fie. Was that because they were related? As these thoughts flowed by like a stream, she drifted and began to dream.

In her dream, she was running through an autumn wood. People chased her, shouted at her, hissing and spitting like angry geese. Objects flew at her, whipping between falling leaves; apples and stones. An apple hit her in the back of the head. She stumbled and then fell. Hands grabbed her, lifted her, dragged her as she struggled and screamed toward a three-legged stool and a noose dangling from a red maple tree.

"Revenge," a voice whispered. "REVENGE!"

Nelly woke up. It took her a second to realize where she was—in her bedroom on the farm. How long had she been asleep? She glanced at her bedside table where the jar that held Grandmother's and Orson's spirits sat waiting.

Grandmother!

She shot out of bed. The clock on her bedside table flashed 2:30 p.m. She had slept all morning and into the afternoon. She scooped up the jar, the night key, the death's milk, and the healing ointment but had no convenient pockets to stash them in. Human clothing was so impractical. She found an old backpack from middle school at the bottom of her closet. She had stopped using it because it had sparkly stars all over it that left a trail of glitter wherever it went. But her other backpack was in her closet at school. This one would have to do.

As she stuffed the jar into the backpack, she heard a sound. A car was pulling into the driveway out front. *Mr. Glanville?* She slung the backpack over her shoulder, walked into the hallway, and peeked out the hall window.

An expensive-looking car was parked in the driveway. A woman with coiffed hair, wearing smart business attire got out on the driver's side, while a man in a suit got out on the passenger's side.

Strangers on the farm? This was highly unusual. The people of Nothing never set foot on the Morighan farm. It was haunted. It was cursed. It was ...

Nelly noticed something on the lawn as the two strangers strode up the walkway. It was a sign that read FOR SALE.

For sale?

A key jiggled the front door lock. A second later, the strangers were walking inside. Nelly held her breath, crept along the corridor, and then peered down the stairs toward the front hall, careful to stay out of view.

"This house was built in the 80s," the woman said as she sauntered into the front hall, her voice chipper and booming.

"The other one has been around for over two hundred years. The history of the property is ... interesting, to say the least—"

"I'm aware of the history," the man said, talking over the woman. He sounded terse and bored. "The buyers I represent are not looking for a residence. They will likely tear down both houses. All they are interested in is the land, which they plan to use for the production of animal feed."

Animal feed?

Nelly couldn't believe what she was hearing. Mr. Glanville couldn't sell the farm! Grandmother would never allow it. How could he even consider it? Grandmother had only been sick for a week.

Nelly crept back into her room as the strangers prattled on about commodity crops and arable soil.

We'll see about that, Nelly thought. When Grandmother was back to herself, this sale didn't stand a chance. She climbed into her closet and stuck her night key in the door.

POP!

The air smelled of honey and fireworks, a scent Nelly was starting to enjoy. She was now in a small room with buckets and mops and cleaning bottles. A janitor's closet.

The door wasn't locked. She slipped out into one of Nought County Hospital's brightly lit corridors. The corridor was empty and silent. One of the ceiling lights was flickering, giving the place an eerie feel. A rush of cold air rose the flesh on the back of her neck and blew her hair forward. She turned around. But there was no sign of where the cold air had come from.

Nelly walked quickly to the end of the corridor and peeked around the corner. The front reception area buzzed under fluorescent lights. This meant she was on the main floor, which was not where she needed to be. The psych unit, where Grandmother and Orson were held, was several floors up. It was also a secure ward with guards and locked doors. When she was here last with the fairies, the night key had deposited them into the ward itself, bypassing all the security. Now she would have to find her own way up. Unfortunately, she could only think of one sure way to do that.

Nelly flattened her wild hair, straightened her sweater, and approached the reception desk. There were several small groups of people in the waiting area, each engaged in their own conversation. None of them paid Nelly any attention.

The woman behind the reception desk tapped away at a computer with long, pink fingernails that clacked against the keyboard.

Nelly cleared her throat. "Excuse me." It was strange to speak English again. Nelly had to concentrate to get her tongue around the words.

The receptionist did not look up from the computer. Instead, she held up a just-a-minute pink-nailed finger and returned to tapping.

Nelly stood with her backpack between her knees, feeling strangely exposed and vulnerable.

"Yes?" the receptionist said finally, still staring at her screen.

"I'd like to visit my grandmother, please," Nelly said, keeping her voice low.

"Name of patient," the receptionist said, her voice ringing with impatience.

"Moira Morighan," Nelly muttered.

"Say again?"

Nelly cleared her throat and spoke a little louder. "Moira Morighan."

"What's that?"

"Moira Morighan!"

The receptionist looked up. Nelly glanced around, aware that the room had fallen silent. Everyone was staring at her.

"–J-Just a moment," the receptionist said, now sounding nervous. "Have a seat."

The receptionist dialed a number into the desk phone, turned around in her chair, and then spoke under her breath into the receiver. That was concerning. Nelly had been banned from the psych ward back in June for *causing a disturbance*, but the ban was only meant to last the summer. It was September now; the ban was over. They couldn't keep her from seeing her grandmother now, could they?

Nelly took a seat, trying not to make eye contact with any of the gawkers in the waiting area. A little boy, around four, was playing nearby with a wind-up toy car. The car buzzed over and hit Nelly on the foot. She picked it up and held it out for the boy, who wandered over, his hand outstretched.

A woman Nelly assumed to be the boy's mother pulled him back by his sweater and shot Nelly a dirty look. The boy started to cry. "Leave it," the woman said. "I'll get you a new toy."

Nelly rolled her eyes and put the car on the side table. Sometimes, in Nothing, being a Morighan was like having the cooties. The side table was covered in magazines. Nelly picked one up absently and flipped it open.

A slip of loose paper fell from between the pages and drifted to the floor. Nelly stepped on it to stop it. The paper was blank except for a single word written on it in jagged pencil. *Revenge.*

She stiffened, reached for the paper, and held it up. The word *Revenge* was written diagonally across the page, but this was not the most disturbing thing about this slip of paper. Held up to the light, Nelly could see an image printed on the other side of the page. It was an image of her own face. She turned the page over. A photocopy of her school photograph from last year was staring back at her from the page. Above her photo, words were written in red block letters.

MISSING: NELLY LOUISE MORIGHAN. PLEASE CONTACT NOUGHT COUNTY POLICE WITH ANY INFORMATION.

A shadow fell over her. She looked up. A man she didn't know stood, towering over her. He was wearing a police uniform.

"Nelly Morighan," he said. "Come with me."

CHAPTER TWENTY-NINE

IN PRISON AIR

Nelly's glittery backpack, the night key, the healing ointment, the death's milk, and the jar that held Grandmother's and Orson's spirits were spread out on a table at even intervals like pieces of evidence. Nelly sat on one side of the table under a bank of blinding overhead lights. She was in a police interrogation room. Across from her stood the policeman who had detained her at the hospital. He was an ogreish man with a bald head and a brick-like frame.

He glared at her with small, beady eyes. "Where have you been for the last month and a half?"

"Month and a half?" Nelly repeated, unable to contain her surprise. She had not been away for a month and a half. It had only been a few days. Unless ...

Nelly sat back in her chair. Was it possible time ran differently in the fairy world? If the fairy tales Nelly had read as a child had any basis in reality, then ...

Uh oh.

"You've got some nerve," the policeman said. "You know

there was a county-wide search for you? We thought you'd been kidnapped, or worse."

Well, technically she had been kidnapped, Nelly thought, though *kidnapped by fairies* was probably not what the policeman wanted to hear.

"So, you gonna admit the truth?" the policeman asked, crossing his arms over his wide chest.

"The truth?" Nelly repeated.

The policeman put his hands on the table and leaned toward her. "You ran away, didn't you?"

It was as good an explanation as any.

Nelly looked down and nodded.

"I knew it!" he said, clapping his hands together. "Wasting our time. Typical Morighan."

Nelly shot the man a look. "What's that supposed to mean?"

"Oh, so now you're gonna cop an attitude?" he said, shaking the jar with Grandmother's and Orson's spirits in it.

Nelly cringed as the lights shifted back and forth, but stayed safely locked in the glass container. The policeman didn't appear able to see the lights. He could only see Grandmother's broach and Orson's ball at the bottom of the jar, the items Fig said grounded their spirits and prevented them from escaping.

"You know how many false alarms we've had to deal with over the years because of your family?" the policeman went on, putting the jar back on the table.

"This whole town's on edge because of you. Just last week they had us searching the Priory School cause some kids got it in their heads there was an intruder in the bell tower. There was no intruder. The kids were spooked because of you."

Nelly glared at the man. She'd been on the receiving end of these sorts of wild accusations her whole life. Her impulse was to protest, but she held herself back. The man had a point, after all, even if he didn't know why. Ghosts were drawn to fairies. She was a fairy. The town was haunted because of her.

A policewoman opened the door and stuck her head into the room. "I've got Glanville on the phone."

The policeman took the phone from the other officer, put it on speaker, and then set it on the table in front of Nelly.

"Nelly? Nelly! Is that you?" came Mr. Glanville's worried voice over the phone. "Oh, thank God, thank God you're all right!"

"I'm so sorry, Mr. Glanville. I never meant to—"

"The important thing is you're safe," Mr. Glanville said as Nelly's insides twisted with guilt.

The policeman leaned forward. "Mr. Glanville, sir, this is Deputy Andrews at the Nought County police station. We've got you on speaker."

"Ah, Deputy Andrews, thank you, thank you for all your help. Nelly, are you still there?"

"Yes," Nelly said, leaning toward the speakerphone. "Where are you, Mr. Glanville?"

"In the city, but more importantly, where have *you* been?"

That question again. The policeman was glaring at her.

"How's Grandmother?" Nelly asked. "I went to the hospital. They wouldn't tell me anything."

"She's no worse than she was, no worse. But tell me where you've been. Where have you been living? What have you been doing?"

Deputy Andrews shot Nelly a probing look. "I, uh, well, the thing is ..." she started, and then changed track.

"Is it true you're selling the farm?"

"How do you know about that?" Mr. Glanville asked.

"I saw the FOR SALE sign."

"Oh, well, I'm sorry you had to find out that way, but—"

"You can't, Mr. Glanville, you can't. Grandmother would never—"

"I'm doing it for your grandmother," Mr. Glanville cut in. "If—*when* she recovers, she'll understand. That farm has brought you and your family nothing but misery. And living alone in that house, well, it was downright eerie. It was an easy decision. I was hoping to tell you about this in person, but there's no point in holding back now. Nelly, I've made arrangements to move both your grandmother and your father to a long-term care facility here in the city. They'll have the best doctors, the best treatments. And I'm looking at buying a house here, too. Still working out the details. It'll be a fresh start for us all. I'll enroll you back at Mountain Wood Academy. You can even take my name if you'd like. You'll be Nelly Glanville. No more Morighan family baggage weighing you down. What do you think of that?"

"Nelly Glanville?" Nelly realized she was shaking her head and had been for some time. If Mr. Glanville had proposed this only a few months ago, she would have jumped at the chance to move to the city permanently, to leave Nothing behind and all the rest of it, but now ...

She realized at that moment that she didn't want to let go of the name Morighan or the baggage that came with it. It wasn't baggage; it was a part of her and so was her family history, no matter how miserable it was. And then there were the fairies.

"Mr. Glanville, I appreciate what you're trying to do, but—"

"You're upset," he said, cutting over her again. "Once you start up again at your old school, get settled, you'll see. It's for the best."

It's for the best. Fig said something similar. And yet this didn't feel like it was for the best. None of it felt *for the best.*

"For the time being, I've made arrangements to have you placed back at the Priory House," Mr. Glanville said. "It'll only be temporary until I work out the details of the move. The principal there, Ms. Kennedy, has agreed, though it took a sizable donation. I don't think she's much fond of you, to tell you the truth."

That was an understatement. But this was good news. This meant Nelly would remain in town for a little while, at least. There was a window of opportunity to make things right.

Nelly stared at the jar and its two floating spirits as Mr. Glanville continued on about the move. She'd stopped paying attention. After dark tonight, she would use the night key Fig had given her to get from the school to the hospital and return Grandmother's spirit to her body. Once Grandmother was back to herself, she would put a stop to all of it—the sale of the farm, the move, the transfer of Nelly's father to the city. Everything would go back to the way it was. With the addition of a fairy aunt.

An hour later, as the sun set, the policeman dropped Nelly off at the Priory House's front gate. Nelly stared up at the school. It looked even grimmer and grayer than she remembered it.

Ms. Kennedy herself met them at the gate. The policeman handed the principal the glittery backpack that held her own son's spirit, trapped in a jar, and then drove off.

The principal didn't say a word to Nelly. She led her at a brisk pace into the school and then down the bleak and empty hallways, the backpack leaving a trail of glitter bits in its wake. Classes were done for the day. The students would all be in their dorms or at dinner. Nelly was glad about that. She wasn't looking forward to facing her classmates anytime soon.

There were posters on the wall for the annual Halloween dance. A cheesy illustration of a jack-o'-lantern hovered over the words, *All Ghouls Gala, October 31, in Chapter Hall. Live Band "Ghost Town" will perform.*

Ghost Town? Nelly had never heard of them, but the name was certainly appropriate. It was strange to think it was only a few days until Halloween already. Losing all that time in the fairy world was discombobulating.

Ms. Kennedy led Nelly into her office and shut the door. She dropped the glittery backpack on her desk and crossed her arms.

"Well. We are both about to get what we want," she said through her teeth. She was angry. Angrier than Nelly had ever seen her.

"You will be transferred out of this school and out of my hair as soon as humanly possible, but between then and now, there will be rules. You will be escorted to and from every one of your classes and remain in your room at night. When you are not in class or your room, you will be in detention. Is that clear?"

It was as clear as it was unfair. Nelly would have protested but decided now was not the time to challenge Ms. Kennedy. She nodded.

"What's that?"

"Yes, Ms. Kennedy."

Someone knocked at the door.

"That's your escort." The principal took a seat behind her desk.

Nelly reached for her backpack, but before she could grab it, Ms. Kennedy slammed her hand down on top of it. "This will remain with me until your transfer."

Nelly felt the blood rush into her cheeks. "–B-But I need that. There are some things in there that—"

"There's nothing in here you need, Nelly," Ms. Kennedy snapped. "But I see you care about the contents of this bag. Good. That means you'll be on your best behavior if you want to earn it back."

Nelly stared at Ms. Kennedy, trying to come up with some brilliant excuse for why she needed that bag now, but nothing sprang to mind. This was going to be a problem.

Gwen Praveen stood waiting for her in the hallway. Gwen was friends with Alexis's younger sister, Ramona. One look at Gwen's guilty face and everything that happened before Nelly had run off with the fairies came rushing back. A sequence of scenes popped into her mind: Nelly had found Gwen and Ramona trying to help a panicking Alexis in her room in the middle of the night. Nelly had tried to help and for her trouble, Alexis had thrown a snow globe at her. Then something strange happened, and the housemother had shown up. And Alexis, Gwen, and Ramona had all blamed Nelly. They said she had attacked Alexis when she had done no such thing. They almost got her expelled!

"I'm supposed to escort you—" Gwen started, but Nelly walked past her before she could finish her sentence and ducked into the stairwell.

"I'm sorry," Gwen said, at Nelly's heels as she leaped down the stairs. "But Ramona's my best friend. Alexis is her sister. I had to back their stories."

On the main floor, Nelly increased her pace, pushed open the double doors that led to the quad, and marched outside.

She didn't have time for this. She had to figure out a way to get her backpack back from the principal and get Grandmother's and Orson's spirits back in their bodies. This high school drama didn't matter.

"Listen, I'm trying to apologize here," Gwen said, out of breath.

Nelly made a beeline for Maple Hall. Up ahead, the dorm house slouched under the evening sky. Like the rest of the school, it seemed grayer, bleaker than it had before she'd left. Why did everything seem different now? Was it the contrast with the fairy world? Or had she changed in some way she didn't understand?

"Right, I forgot," Gwen said. "Nelly Morighan doesn't need any friends. You're so above everyone else. You're above this whole town."

Nelly stopped. "What?"

"You heard me. Look, I know I lied, and that was wrong, I admit it, but it all worked out, didn't it?"

"How did it work out, exactly?"

"You're fine. I knew you'd be fine. Alexis's father is on the Priory House board of directors. He's obsessed with being all normal and upstanding. All he cares about are appearances. And honestly, he's kind of scary. If he knew what's been happening with Alexis, he'd freak. I was only trying to protect my friends."

"Right," Nelly said. "Because nobody thinks I'm normal anyway, so what does it matter if I get blamed for something I didn't do?"

Nelly pushed open the doors to Maple Hall and then took the stairs two at a time up to the third floor.

"I get it. What I did sucked," Gwen said, still at Nelly's heels. "But if you ran away because of that night, because of what we said—"

"What? No," Nelly said, stopping in front of her dorm room. "That had nothing to do with you. I've just been dealing with ... stuff."

"Well, if you ever want to talk," Gwen said.

Nelly shot her an incredulous look.

"We don't have to be best friends or anything. It's just, what you did that night ... all three of us were freaking out and you stayed calm. You were trying to protect us. I thought you were brave, that's all."

Nelly blinked. Did someone from Nothing just pay her a compliment?

"I want to make it up to you. We should hang out sometime," Gwen said, following Nelly into her room. "It would be nice to hang out with someone calm for a change. You know, someone who hasn't completely lost it."

"Lost it?" Nelly said, flicking on the lights.

Her dorm room looked just as it had before she'd left, Bianca's side of the room a lacy explosion, her side of the room sparse and bare.

"You do not know what this school has been like since you've been gone," Gwen was saying. "It's like the whole place has gone mental."

Nelly noticed something on her bedspread. It was a powder-pink envelope sealed with a lipstick kiss. OK, that was unusual. She opened the envelope and pulled out the letter folded inside.

Ever dearest Nelly,

I can't believe you're still missing. It's been more than a month. I've been thinking about you every day. I wanted to text you, but I don't have your number or email or anything. Isn't that weird?

I hope you come back soon. I swear this place is like a living Hell without you. I miss you more than chocolate right now (I'm trying to lose three pounds). Come back soon! MIIISSSS YOOOUUU!!!!!!!!

xoxo

Bianca

Nelly lowered the letter. *Ever dearest? XOXO?* Then she remembered what happened the last time she had seen Bianca.

Love dust.

Uh oh.

The door to Nelly's dorm room swung wide and a loud squeal issued from the doorway.

Bianca was standing there, her mouth gaping.

"You're baaack!" She ran at Nelly and tackled her, sending her flying back onto her bed. Bianca wrapped her arms around Nelly's neck and squeezed tight, tight, tight. "I've missed you sooooooo much!"

"Bianca!" Nelly gasped, "I—can't—breathe!"

Bianca let go. "I'm so sorry. Are you OK? I can't believe you're back. I thought I would never see you again! You should have heard the stuff people were saying about you. They said you were dead, or that you had been kidnapped and I was so worried. And then Alexis was like, 'Why would anyone want to kidnap her?' And I was like, 'Excuse me? You do not get to speak about my best friend like that.' And she was like, 'Since when is Nelly Morighan your best friend?' And I was like, 'Since always, bitch.' I said that, yeah. And she was like 'Whaaa! I'm gonna start crying now 'cause I'm a pathetic little baby.' And she *actually started crying.* And everyone's like 'Bianca, you're so mean. You offended Alexis and made her cry.' And I'm like, 'Those aren't even real tears, you idiots. She's pretending to be upset so she can get her way.' I swear, people are so gullible. Um, hi, can we help you with something?"

Bianca had noticed Gwen, who was still standing by the door, looking awkward.

Nelly cleared her throat. "Er, Bianca, this is Gwen Praveen."

Bianca looked Gwen up and down. "Aren't you, like, in middle school?"

Gwen's face went pink. "No, ninth grade."

Bianca's eyebrows went up. "OK, well, this is a private conversation, so ..."

The pink in Gwen's face deepened. "I was just leaving."

"That's a great story," Bianca said without missing a beat and glared until a sheepish Gwen shuffled toward the door.

Well, Bianca hadn't changed.

"Hey Gwen," Nelly called out, now feeling sorry for her. "We'll talk later."

Gwen nodded, smiled a little, and left.

Bianca spent the rest of the evening updating Nelly on all the school gossip—against her will. Pauline Davis had asked a popular senior boy to the Hallowe'en dance, and he'd said no in front of everyone, totally humiliating her. Charmaine Torres had over-plucked her eyebrows and now looked constantly surprised. Alexis Abner and Grady Pipes had broken up and gotten back together. Twice. And so on and so forth.

Thankfully, Bianca didn't ask why Nelly had left or where she had been all this time, which Nelly appreciated. Who knew total self-absorption could be a good thing?

As Bianca prattled on, Nelly tried to come up with a way to get Grandmother's and Orson's spirits back from Ms. Kennedy, but she wasn't having any workable ideas.

After nightfall, when Bianca finally stopped talking and started snoring, Nelly got out of bed as quietly as she could. She glanced at Bianca sprawled under her covers, her eyes hidden by her *Beautiful Dreamer* sleeping mask.

The love dust would wear off eventually, she told herself, and then ...

Nelly remembered the Piper, how it had risen above that iron cage and transformed into a monster. Nelly had survived that, hadn't she? She could survive Bianca's inevitable wrath.

Maybe.

Nelly crept over to the door but found it was locked from the outside. She leaned her head against it. Ms. Kennedy wasn't taking any chances.

Now what?

She patted her pajama pockets.

Maple keys!

After she'd first met the fairies, they had stuffed dozens of maple keys in her clothing and suitcase. Maple keys had night keys hidden in them!

She opened her drawers and went through all her clothes. Nothing. Then she tried her suitcase. But every corner, every crease, was maple key free. Had Bianca cleaned? She sat back on her heels.

Moonlight streamed through the open window. She got up, crossed to the window, and gazed outside. There were stars in the clear night sky, but none were visible over the trees or hanging above the river Nought, which flowed behind the school like a black ribbon.

The lights that hovered low in the fairy world were not stars, she reminded herself. They were dead things. Doed said they tormented him. He feared them. He weakened himself with piper's dew to keep them away.

But Nelly didn't fear them, she realized. Maybe she didn't know enough to. Actually, she missed them. The world here felt empty without them. She missed the others, too, Fig and Jack and Doed. She felt empty. It was like she had left a piece of herself in the other world.

Nelly leaned out the window and breathed in the night air. Dead leaves had lodged in the decorative grill around the window ledge. She picked a few out and then noticed something else protruding. With gentle maneuvering, she slid it out. It was a maple key.

CHAPTER THIRTY

THE MISTAKE

There was a loud *POP!* and Nelly was inside a small, dark room. The familiar scent of honey and fireworks drifted into the smell of rot. She was in the Morighan House basement, in the cold cellar. The last time she had been in this room, the darkness had blinded her. But now she could see shelves and glass jars filled with distorted preserves and that there was a door a few paces ahead. Yet more evidence that her vision had mysteriously improved.

Or maybe not so mysterious. She had a name now. Maybe that came with perks. She pushed open the cold cellar door and stepped out into the main part of the basement. It was nighttime, so the room was as dark as the cellar had been, and still, she had no trouble making out the objects scattered around, odds and ends, pieces of old furniture, coats dangling from ceiling beams.

Nelly wove her way around these objects toward the stairs at the far end of the basement. The house was silent and still, but that didn't mean Fig and the other fairies weren't here.

Whispering voices rose out of the silence.

She stopped in her tracks. There were ghost lights in the room. Unlike the ghost lights in the fairy world, which were the size of tennis balls, these were tiny as pinpricks. And yet Nelly could see them clearly. They stood out, glowing against the darkness. She counted eight of them. They glided toward her and then away like curious fish.

"You see them," a voice said.

Nelly whirled around. In the far corner, under a dingy window, cat's eyes glowed from inside an iron cage.

"Trouble?" Nelly said.

She approached the cage, wary. A form coalesced around the pair of eyes. It was not that of her cat. It was a boy. He looked to be around ten. He was gaunt, dressed only in a pair of gray breeches like he was a survivor of a famine in the 19th century. He had curly hair and a mischievous face that made Nelly think of a puck or a faun from Greek mythology. He did not look human.

"The ghost lights," the boy said with a fey grin. "You can see them now. They are the ghosts of nothing. I've watched them flutter around you for years like moths, begging for your attention, but you've never noticed them before."

"You're Trouble," Nelly said, still trying to get her head around this. "You're my grandmother's cat."

"I am not and never was your grandmother's anything," the cat that was not a cat said, his voice a strange, soft purr. "But, yes, I am a cat. I am the prince of cats if you want to know."

Prince of cats? OK. "What are you doing here?"

"Watching over you," the boy-cat said. "I owe a debt to your mother."

"My mother? My mother asked you to watch over me?" Nelly said, stunned.

"Watch you, track you, drug you," the boy cat said. "Whatever the moment required. Here as a cat, there as a mouse, everywhere as a crow. Wherever you are, there I go in one form or another."

"–D-Did you say drug me?"

A sly grin crossed his face. "With piper's dew. A little in your food, a little in your tea. Once a day to keep you weak."

Nelly couldn't believe this. "My mother wanted to keep me weak?"

"You're supposed to be a human. You've got to blend in," he said, unfolding his skinny limbs and standing up. "Not blending in so well now, I see. That may not work out for you."

"What are you talking about?"

"You're quite strong. You can see the ghost lights. They're mad, you know. All dead things are. They don't mean you well."

Nelly watched the lights as they drifted through the darkness, shedding light across her skin as they passed, light that bounced off the boy-cat's eyes.

"Fig told me not to talk to you."

"Good advice," he said and grinned again. "But curiosity and all."

He had her there. Nelly watched him. "If you can change into a mouse, why don't you escape?"

"Glamour is an illusion. The way others perceive me changes; I do not. I can appear to have shrunk, but I cannot shrink."

"Oh ..." Nelly said, thinking of the Piper and how it had appeared initially to be Nelly's size until it had broken through the bars of the cage. Then it was twelve feet tall. She suppressed a shudder.

"Has Fig come back yet?"

The boy cat shrugged, a strangely feline maneuver. "I doubt she ever will."

"Why do you say that?"

"She takes too many risks, that one. She's supposed to be dead, and yet I know she's alive. If I can find out the truth, so can less desirable sorts."

Nelly eyed the boy. It was suddenly very clear why Fig was keeping him in a cage. "Do you, uh, need anything? Water, food ... a litter box?"

"Are you proposing a deal?"

"I'm not going to let you out."

He folded his arms. "But you want something from me?"

"No ... Well, maybe one thing," Nelly said. "When Fig comes back, you could give her a message for me. You could tell her I've got a problem and I need her at the school right away."

"What sort of problem?"

"Nothing you can help me with," Nelly said. She needed another night key, one that could get her out of her room but not out of the school. Then she'd at least have a fighting chance of getting Grandmother's and Orson's spirits back from Ms. Kennedy.

"I will deliver your message. In exchange, I want information."

"What kind of information?"

"I want the location of my brother Nimble."

"How am I supposed to—"

"Ask Fig. She'll help you. You are her niece. That has weight."

"What if I can't find him?"

"Fig is resourceful. She'll ask Jack and Jack will ask his contacts and in time, the information will make its way to you."

Nelly thought about this. Jack and Fig said bargains with fairies could be broken, so even if she said yes, she didn't have to follow through. Find a cat. It certainly sounded innocent enough. But it didn't feel right.

"No thanks. I'll ... write her a note," she said, backing away from the cage.

"I don't ask for much," the boy-cat growled after her. "Here's another deal. You leave me now in this cage and the moment I get out, I'll kill your grandmother."

Nelly stopped. "What? No!"

The boy-cat smiled a mouth full of sharp teeth. "Pick which deal you prefer."

"If I take the first deal, you'll leave my grandmother alone?"

He nodded as ghost lights drifted past his face, casting it in strange shadows.

"All right, OK, you tell Fig I need her at the school and ... and I'll find out where your brother is."

"Deal," he said triumphantly.

Nelly closed her eyes, hoping she wouldn't regret that. When she opened her eyes, the boy was gone. A cat the color of smoke sat in his place.

Back in her dorm room, Nelly tried her best to fall asleep, but her mind was racing. It was hours before she could finally drift off, and when she did, it was to the same dream she'd had the day before.

Again, she was running barefoot through an autumn wood. She wore a white nightgown. People chased her, shouted at her, hissing and spitting like angry geese. An apple hit her on the back of the head. She fell. Hands grabbed her and dragged her as she struggled and screamed to a three-legged stool and a noose that dangled from a red maple tree.

"Revenge," a voice said. "REVENGE!"

She woke up.

"Morning, sleeping beauty," Bianca chimed. She was sitting at her desk in front of a mirror, putting on eye makeup. "Bad dream?"

"Uh ... yeah," Nelly said, blinking away her grogginess. *The same dream twice in a row. Weird.*

"Aw, you look so cute right now," Bianca said. "Get up and I'll do your hair!" She smiled and held up a pink hairbrush.

Nelly raised her brows. *What* wasn't *weird at the moment?*

Later, still half asleep but with an elaborate fishtail braid in her hair, Nelly walked the halls of the Priory House. If her classmates had stared at her before she went missing, it was nothing compared to the way they stared now. The news that Nelly Morighan had been found safe and alive was all over the school, along with the news that she had run away. Maybe they thought a Morighan had no right to go missing for such a mundane reason, or maybe they thought she had no right to come back at all. Either way, their stares were not friendly.

Nelly attended all her classes, not that she had a choice. Gwen Praveen escorted her to all her morning classes, while Sophie Lloyd, a senior girl Nelly didn't know, took over in the afternoon. Her teachers each had a pile of work for her to do to make up for lost time, although the only one to give her a hard time about it was Mr. Haley. Nelly assumed he was still upset because she had taken Madge Morighan's diary from him, however briefly.

This annoyed her. That diary had belonged to her ancestor. He had no right to it. And he certainly had no right to be upset with her for having taken it. Or maybe he did. He said it had been in his family for generations, and she had stolen it. She was a little mixed up on that one.

In the meantime, Nelly still did not know how she was going to get Grandmother's and Orson's spirits back from Ms. Kennedy, not without Fig's help. It was almost like Ms. Kennedy had planned it this way. Every second of Nelly's day was scheduled and monitored. And when she wasn't being monitored, she was locked in her dorm room like a convicted felon.

Her last class that day was music. Mr. Nottingham, the watery-eyed teacher the students called *the sheriff*, had assigned each of the students a midterm piece to practice and perform in front of the class. Today was the last day of performances. The sheriff pulled Nelly aside at the start of the class and told her that if she had something prepared, she could perform a piece, otherwise, he would have to fail her on this term's work. Nelly had automatically agreed to play. She knew plenty of pieces by heart and she didn't want to fail. But as the class moved forward, as other students performed their pieces, some awkwardly and some adequately, as Alexis Abner and Grady Pipes sat snickering a couple of rows back, she wondered if she should have taken the failing grade.

What did this class matter right now, anyway? Grandmother was lying in a hospital bed, possibly being damaged in some mysterious way because her spirit wasn't in her body. Nelly should be helping her, not wasting time in this classroom playing around on the violin.

Something whizzed past Nelly's cheek and landed on the desk in front of her. It was a bottle cap. Nelly turned and spotted Alexis and Grady sniggering to themselves. Grady was holding a bottle without a cap. Her ears went hot. She stared forward again and tried to focus on Ken Higuchi, who was squeaking through an unidentifiable piece on his clarinet.

Why couldn't Alexis just leave her alone? Nelly held her violin in her lap. Her hands were hot and sweaty. She shouldn't even be in this class with Alexis and Grady, she told herself. She should be in the advanced class. She could play rings around any of these students. She was good, and she'd worked very hard to become so. If people wanted to mock her because they thought she was a weirdo and a ghost magnet, then so be it, but she was a talented musician and she was about to prove it.

Her heart started thumping. Nelly had made a decision. She was going to play. She was going to play the way she really could, in front of everyone. She was going to show them all what she could do.

Then something hit her on the back of the head. For a split-second, Nelly was back in her dream. *An apple hit the back of her head ... she fell to the ground ... hands grabbed her arms ... they were dragging her toward a three-legged stool and a noose dangling from a maple tree.*

"Nelly Morighan!" Mr. Nottingham called. "Whenever you're ready."

Nelly was back in the room. Ken Higuchi had finished his performance. Everyone was looking at her. One half of a big rubber eraser shaped like an apple fell to the floor at her feet. She looked at Alexis. The mousy-haired girl was holding the other half of the eraser, a cruel and satisfied smile on her lips.

There was a sound like a crackling sparkler. Her violin was on fire! Nelly gasped and jumped out of her chair. Her violin fell to the floor. Flames engulfed the instrument. Smoke billowed. The fire alarm beeped. Students screamed and lurched away in a commotion of bodies. Mr. Nottingham rushed over. He held a fire extinguisher. White foam shot out onto her burning violin. The fire hissed angrily at him and then died, smothered under a mountain of foam.

Smoke rose around Nelly and Mr. Nottingham like a mist. The room was silent. It was as perfect a silence as Nelly had ever experienced. Everyone was staring at her, eyes wide. Mr. Nottingham looked furious.

"Ms. Morighan," he said quietly. "Go to Ms. Kennedy's office. Now."

After a brief, stunned pause, Nelly did as she was told and walked between the desks toward the back of the class. As she walked, she was aware of the *clap-clap* of her dress shoes against the floor and the smell of smoke and fireworks.

The second she stepped into the corridor, the class behind her erupted into a buzz of frantic conversation. Nelly had a pretty good idea of what they were saying.

In a kind of daze, Nelly walked the empty corridors to Ms. Kennedy's office. What had she done? She had meant to play her violin in front of the class, not set it on fire. *Her violin.* She loved that violin, and now it was nothing but blackened splinters and fire retardant. She didn't see how she could ever play it again.

The corridor outside the principal's office was empty. The students were all still in their classes. She approached the office and looked through the little window in the door. There were a couple of construction workers in the office, deep in conversation with Ms. Kennedy and the secretary. The renovations on the bell tower must have still been underway.

Nelly did not want to go in there but didn't see that she had a choice. She was about to knock when she noticed something.

Inside the office, a trail of glitter sparkled on the floor. There was only one thing that left a trail like that. Her middle school backpack!

The glitter led to an archway on the far side of the principal's office. This meant someone had carried her backpack through that archway. There must have been a second room beyond that archway, connected to the principal's office. Could that room be accessed from the corridor?

Something dawned on Nelly. She was alone. *No escort.* She stepped back from the little window and speed-walked down the corridor, in the direction the trail of glitter had gone, to a second door. This door had a window. She peered in.

This room appeared to be a conference room and was indeed connected to the principal's office by an archway. There was a table in the middle surrounded by chairs and a white-board pushed up against the wall. Beyond the table, she could just make out a straggly line of glitter that led to a cabinet in the far corner. It was a good bet that her backpack was in that cabinet along with Grandmother's and Orson's spirits. Now it was just a matter of finding a way into this room. And she knew how to do it.

Nelly bolted down the second-floor corridor. This was her one chance to do what she was about to do, and she was not about to miss it. She leaped down the stairs to the first floor and then walked at a fast pace, but not so fast she'd draw attention to herself, down several more corridors until she found the janitor's closet in the east range. Having been locked in it at the start of the semester, it wasn't hard to find. She tried the door. It opened. And she slipped inside.

There were rings of keys hanging from hooks on the wall. Each ring was marked with a number. Nelly grabbed the ring marked 2 under the hook marked W. She guessed that this ring held the keys to every lock on the second floor of the west range, including Ms. Kennedy's office and the room next to it.

The bell rang. Nelly covered her ears. Why were school bells so much louder inside janitor's closets? When the bell finally stopped blaring, Nelly pocketed the keyring and slipped out into the corridor just before the students poured out of their classrooms.

She suppressed a triumphant smile. The Hallowe'en dance was tomorrow. Tomorrow was the night. If Ms. Kennedy was at the dance and not in her office, which she likely would be, and if Nelly lost her escort, then—

A hand grabbed Nelly by the arm before she could finish her thought and yanked her into the girl's bathroom.

CHAPTER THIRTY-ONE

THE DISTRACTION

"**W**hat did you do to Bianca?" It was Alexis. She had Nelly by the arm.

"What is your problem?" Nelly shook out of Alexis's grip.

Alexis looked awful. Nelly hadn't been able to see this in music class, but up close, the mousy girl was looking pale and almost haggard. She had dark circles around her eyes as if she hadn't slept in days.

"Well?" Alexis said, a tinge of hysteria in her voice. "What did you do to her?"

"Nothing!" Nelly said although she was sure her guilt had to be showing. Just then, a couple of ninth-grade girls walked into the room.

"Get out!" Alexis shrieked.

The girls jumped. Startled eyes darted from Alexis to Nelly and back again, and then they both backed out of the room. Alexis locked the door behind them.

"Now," Alexis said, grabbing Nelly's arm again. "You're going to tell me what you did to Bianca or—"

"But I haven't—"

"Don't lie!" Alexis shouted, looking insane. "I know you did something to her and I'm going to find out what, so you might as well confess!"

Alexis's nails were digging deep into Nelly's arm.

"Alexis, you're hurting me."

"Bianca always hated you and suddenly now she's your best friend?" Alexis said, her nails piercing farther into Nelly's arm. "It's impossible. I want to know what you did to her, and what you've been doing to me, to this whole school!"

"I haven't done anything!" The pain in Nelly's arm was making her angry. "Let go of me."

"Tell me! Tell me now or I swear I'll—"

"You'll do what?" Nelly said, locking eyes with her.

"I'll make sure you end up like everyone else in your freaky family."

Nelly's eyebrows went up. Now this human was threatening her? Really? If she only knew what Nelly could do to her with a simple slap across the face.

"I'd like to see you try," Nelly said and pushed her away.

Alexis stumbled back. She clutched her chest where Nelly's hand had made contact. A swirl of smoke rose there between her fingers. She looked at Nelly, afraid.

Good, Nelly thought and glared back. "Stay away from me. And Bianca, too, or I'll make sure you regret it."

Nelly unlocked the door and walked out. She'd had enough of this school, of this whole stupid town. She'd been back for less than two days, and she'd already been arrested, interrogated, locked in her room, and threatened. What was wrong with these people?

Farther down the hall, she spotted Sophie Lloyd, her afternoon escort, flagging her down. It was time for detention. And Nelly still had to see Ms. Kennedy and face the music about her ruined violin. She scowled. She wasn't sure how much more of this she could take.

There was no explaining the violin incident, so Nelly didn't try. She told Ms. Kennedy she did not know how or why her violin had suddenly burst into flames. This part was a lie. The next part was the truth: she loved that violin and would never have damaged it on purpose. Ms. Kennedy didn't seem remotely convinced, but there wasn't much more the principal could do about it, short of expelling her, which wasn't an option at the moment. So, Ms. Kennedy piled yet more detentions onto Nelly's already packed schedule.

The next day was Hallowe'en. There was no sign of Fig. Nelly couldn't count on her returning soon, or at all. But she was starting to think she didn't need fairy help. There was an ordinary human way to get Grandmother's and Orson's spirits back.

That evening was the Hallowe'en dance, the Ghoul's Gala. Nelly was given permission to attend, probably because Ms. Kennedy wanted to keep an eye on her. This meant Nelly would be out of her room, in a crowded hall, with opportunities to slip away. She just needed a distraction.

Nelly and Bianca got ready for the dance in their dorm room. Bianca had put together a last-minute costume for Nelly, who hadn't prepared at all to dress up. Nelly stood in front of Bianca's full-length mirror in a pale pink blouse and tie under a deep maroon suit jacket and matching pants. On her head, two weirdly shaped branches attached to a headband gave the impression of horns.

Bianca stepped into the reflection next to her. She wore a

cream-colored dress with a puffy tulle skirt. A pair of gauzy, glittery wings sprung from her shoulder blades, and her hair was braided around her head like a halo.

The angel and the devil.

"We look so good right now. I'm just saying," Bianca said, putting on some red lipstick.

Nelly adjusted her "horns." "I'm not sure how this is a devil costume."

"It's fashion," Bianca said. "You don't want to be obvious, you want to be subtle. Red suit, cute little horns. You still look beautiful, but there's a hint of the monster inside."

"Right," Nelly muttered, uncomfortable. She tugged at her tie.

"Don't pull at it!" Bianca swatted Nelly's hand away and pushed her tie back in place.

It felt like a noose. How did guys wear these all the time?

"I still can't believe your violin is ruined," Bianca was saying, brushing lint from Nelly's shoulder. "It would have looked so perfect with your outfit."

Nelly sat down on the edge of Bianca's bed. She had no desire to parade her violin around the school dance, but she missed it all the same. "I guess I could bring my tin whistle," she said.

Nelly pulled her tin whistle out of her side table drawer. This was the first instrument she had ever learned. It wasn't as difficult or complex as the violin, but she had a soft spot for it.

"Oh, yes, bring that!" Bianca said, spritzing a puff of strawberry spray in the air and twirling into it. "You should totally play it, too. It's magical what you can do with that thing. Seriously."

Nelly raised her eyebrows. "I didn't realize you had ever heard me play."

"Are you joking?" Bianca said. "We lived together for like a year. Of course, I've heard you play. You're fantastic on the violin, like a professional. But when you play the tin whistle, I don't know. It hits differently. It's like, from another world or something."

Nelly smiled. A warm feeling settled on her.

Bianca sat down next to her, a tube of pink lipstick in her hand. "Do this," she said, parting her lips. She dabbed at Nelly's lips with the lipstick tube.

Their eyes met. The air turned tense.

"Bianca," Nelly said, looking away. "You know the things you're feeling right now about me, about our friendship, they're not real."

Bianca's eyes went wide. She stood up, put the lid back on the lipstick tube, and walked over to her desk, where she rummaged in her makeup drawer.

Nelly's insides squirmed with guilt. "I didn't mean—"

"I'm not mad," Bianca said tersely, slipping on a pair of ballet flats. She was blinking too much. She wouldn't meet Nelly's eyes. She crossed to the door.

"Bianca," Nelly started. She didn't know what to say. Love dust was awful stuff. It wasn't right to mess with people's emotions like this, even Bianca's.

Bianca opened the door and screamed!

Nelly shot to her feet.

Sophie Lloyd stood on the other side of the door dressed as a creepy ghost woman. It was a good costume—a little too good.

Bianca scowled at her. "Can you not?"

Sophie grinned. "I'm Bloody Mary. You know, the vengeful ghost?"

"Right, 'cause we really need more vengeful ghosts around here," Bianca said, rolling her eyes.

"Ms. Kennedy wants me to walk Nelly down to the dance,"

Sophie said.

"Whatever," Bianca said. She glanced back in Nelly's direction but would not meet her eyes.

"Wear those," she said, pointing at a pair of white, high-top sneakers by the door. She was still blinking too much. "I'll wait for you outside."

Nelly was relieved to hear it. She needed Bianca if her plan was going to work. If only she could have gained her help without this. Without breaking her heart.

Nelly put on the white sneakers.

Chapter Hall pulsated with lights and music and costumed bodies. Student council had outdone themselves on the decorations. Shiny confetti blanketed the floor and black and green balloons bounced around the dancing feet. Jack-o'-lanterns, dozens of them, lined the walls on tables of various heights and seemed almost to float in the darkness. And from the ceiling, cobwebs, spiders, and glow sticks dangled and spun like supernatural things.

Nelly marveled at it all as Bianca, who appeared to have forgiven her, dragged her onto the dance floor.

The band Ghost Town was onstage thumping out upbeat synth-pop while their lead singer, a punk-rock princess with dark skin and a faux hawk, chimed in with haunting vocals. Nelly was impressed by how good they were and surprised to see Mr. Haley up there on stage with them. He was dressed as a skeleton man, tattoos on full display, and was plucking away at a bass guitar.

She had heard Mr. Haley was in a band. This must have been it. She felt a knot in her stomach as she watched him, remembering their confrontation over Madge Morighan's diary.

Bianca took Nelly by the hand and pulled her between dancing bodies. She bounced and smiled and spun, and Nelly found herself swept away by Bianca's enthusiasm and the music and electricity of the crowd. She smiled back despite her worries and danced, jumping up and down to the beat.

As she danced, the costumed figures shifting around her reminded her of the naming ceremony in the fairy world. And for a moment, spinning on the dance floor, she felt that a part of her was still there in that other place. Faces flashed around her. Masked figures, like the dead things, appeared and vanished. It was as if she were back there. That other place was real. This wasn't, it was just makeup and dress-up, an imitation of the real thing—Faerie, her home, her essence, her reality.

Bianca pinched Nelly's arm, bringing her back to the room, and nodded toward the doorway. Bianca's friend Charmaine Torres had just walked in dressed as Red Riding Hood in a blonde wig and a hooded cloak. Close to Charmaine stood Ms. Kennedy, surveilling the room.

Nelly nodded to Bianca. "It's time," she said, having to speak directly into Bianca's ear to be heard over the thumping music.

Charmaine was making her way over to Bianca and Nelly. The dark-haired girl, who as usual wore too much makeup, was terrified of getting on Bianca's bad side, and had agreed to help them out. With no questions asked.

"I'll switch costumes with Charmaine," Nelly said, repeating the plan to Bianca. "Then you distract Kennedy while I slip out the back doors."

"Nope, no way," Bianca said. "You be the distraction. I'll slip out."

"What? No, no, that's not the plan," Nelly said. She had gone over this plan with Bianca three times. Bianca was meant to talk to Ms. Kennedy, to complain to her about something as only Bianca could, while Nelly slipped out the door on the far side. The plan was simple. It was perfect. It was going to work.

"It has to be me," Nelly said. "I'm the only one who knows what—"

"Glittery backpack. Conference room. Cabinet," Bianca said, interrupting. "I know what to do."

"No," Nelly said firmly.

"You're the one Kennedy's watching, not me," Bianca said, slipping her hand into Nelly's jacket pocket and pulling out the janitor's keys. "You know this makes more sense. And I have the perfect idea for a distraction."

Bianca whirled around.

"Wait, what kind of distraction?" Nelly called after her, but the music drowned her voice.

Charmaine stopped next to Nelly. "What's going on? What's Bianca doing?"

"I have no idea," Nelly muttered, a tight feeling in her stomach.

Bianca was weaving through the crowd toward the stage. Nelly watched her, baffled, hoping Bianca wasn't experiencing some unpredictable side effect from the love dust.

Bianca passed by Alexis and Grady, who were both sipping fruit punch from plastic cups. Grady was dressed as a pirate. Alexis was dressed in white. A golden "halo" made of wire and fake gems sat on her head. Another angel. Nelly wondered if Alexis and Bianca had planned matching costumes before fairy love dust had broken up their friendship. Guilty, Nelly looked at the floor.

Bianca was by the stage now, smiling and flirting with a guy dressed as a zombie. He seemed to be with the band. She said something to him, and he said something to her, and she laughed, throwing her head back and touching him on the arm.

Bianca looked pretty, Nelly thought against her will. Much more than pretty. Her cheeks were pink, her smile was dazzling, and her angel wings shimmered in the lights. Bianca leaned in close toward the zombie guy, maybe too close, and again said something in his ear. At the same time, the band on stage came to the end of their song. The room cheered.

Nelly fiddled with her tin whistle as the zombie guy got up on stage and had words with the lead singer. Bianca signaled to Nelly with a wink and a nod. Nelly's heart was pounding.

"Where's Nelly Morighan?" the lead singer asked into the mic, her voice filling the room.

Nelly's face went hot as heads turned and voices murmured. Charmaine stepped away from her, and so did the rest of the crowd. It was as if a spotlight had beamed down on her and her alone.

What had Bianca done?

The singer pointed at Nelly. "I hear you've got skills on that thing. Come on up here. Jam with us!"

The singer was pointing at the tin whistle clutched in Nelly's hand. Bianca meant for Nelly to play her tin whistle. *In front of everyone.* Nelly's face was burning. She was sure she was as red as her outfit.

She glanced toward the door, where Ms. Kennedy stood, eyes transfixed on Nelly, along with everyone else in the room. This was one hell of a distraction.

Nelly's mind went blank. In a kind of thudding fog, she made her way through the crowd toward the stage, mouth dry, fingers trembling. Bianca told them she could play. But she had only ever been able to play in private. Not in front of all these people.

As Nelly walked up on stage, Mr. Haley gave her a side-eyed glance, half annoyed, half curious, from behind his bass guitar. The zombie guy Bianca had talked to put a second mic on the stage for Nelly. It looked like a hanging tree.

The lead singer covered her mic and leaned over. "We're gonna do an old cover. You know 'A Forest' by The Cure?"

"Yeah, I think so," Nelly said, her voice high and small.

The lead singer grinned. "Jump in where you can and try to keep up. If you can't, get off the stage."

The singer signaled to her bandmates and with a one, two, three, and four, they started to play.

Nelly didn't move. The thumping sound in her head got louder and louder. The audience stared up at her, faces floating in the darkness. She couldn't do this. She couldn't play in front of all these people. There was only fear, fear of all those eyes on her, of her hands shaking her tin whistle from her lips, fear of humiliating herself.

Nelly reminded herself what this was all about. *Grandmother*, she told herself and pictured the old woman helpless in a hospital bed.

She lifted the tin whistle and started to play. She tried to ignore the audience and focus on the music, but she was so nervous she could hardly get any air through the instrument. The sound it released was so weak it could barely be heard. The lead singer shot Nelly a look, unimpressed.

Calm down, Nelly told herself.

Bianca stood near the stage. With a subtle motion, she directed Nelly's attention to the back of the room. Ms. Kennedy was there. She was leaving, walking through the crowd toward the door.

Nelly stepped up close to the mic. If she was going to be the distraction, she was going to be the distraction. She took a deep breath, closed her eyes, and started to really play. As she could. As she played when no one was around. Notes flowed from the instrument, clear and sonorant. She improvised around the band's melody, twisting and turning around the notes, complementing them, teasing them, dropping in unexpected and complex combinations.

Nelly dared to open her eyes. The lead singer was looking at her. This time she nodded, impressed. Ms. Kennedy had stopped next to the door. She turned around and watched as Nelly continued to play. At the same time, Nelly spotted Bianca slipping out one of the rear doors.

Emboldened by this, Nelly stepped up her playing, improvising an entirely new melody around the song. She added in bits of melodies she had heard in the fairy world—haunting trills, strange dips, and shatteringly clear notes that soared into the rafters. More teachers and chaperones came into the room from outside. The lead singer had stopped singing altogether while the band continued the song's simple baseline, allowing Nelly the freedom to experiment around it.

Ms. Kennedy stepped away from the door. Her eyes were fastened on Nelly. They weren't as stern as they normally were. They weren't hot or cold. They were worried. No, it was more than that. They were scared.

Nelly stopped playing abruptly, and the band followed her cue. She lowered her tin whistle. The room was quiet. Ms. Kennedy's eyes bore into her, and the others, too. Mr. Haley, the band, the audience. Eyes, dozens of eyes, stared at Nelly, stunned, scared.

They knew.

Then hands went up in the air and clapped, obscuring Nelly's view of Ms. Kennedy. The crowd was cheering. The lead singer clapped Nelly on the shoulder.

"That was awesome, seriously," she said, shaking Nelly's hand. "We should talk."

"Uh, OK. After the show," Nelly muttered, distracted.

She couldn't see Ms. Kennedy anywhere. It was time to go. She thanked the singer and then jumped down from the stage as the band regrouped and launched into one of their originals.

Weaving through the crowd, Nelly was surprised by how many people patted her on the shoulder or smiled at her or gave her a thumbs-up. It was a strange and foreign experience.

Sophie Lloyd was tracking her. Nelly moved farther into the crowd until she found Charmaine Torres in her red riding hood costume.

"OK, let's switch now," Nelly said to Charmaine.

"You still want to?" Charmaine asked. "What happened to Bianca?"

"I'll find her," Nelly said, ducking beneath the heads of the dancing crowd and pulling off her jacket and headband. "We'll meet you later. OK?"

Charmaine shrugged and nodded. She put on Nelly's jacket and headband as originally planned and handed Nelly her Red Riding Hood cloak.

Now disguised under the long cloak and deep inside the hood, Nelly made her way to a door at the back of the room. She chanced a backward glance and spotted Sophie Lloyd and then Ms. Kennedy both watching Charmaine, whose "devil horns" bobbed above all the heads. Nelly frowned. This was proof her original plan for a distraction would have worked just fine. She hadn't needed to make a spectacle of herself up on stage. *Thank you very much, Bianca.*

But then Nelly realized she *was* grateful. She had played in public. She had played as she really could. She had just broken through a lifelong fear that had been holding her prisoner. Bianca had given her a gift. *Thank you very much, Bianca.*

Marveling at how strange life could be, Nelly slipped out of the room.

CHAPTER THIRTY-TWO
AWAY WITH THE HUMANS

Nelly took the stairs two at a time up to the second floor. The corridor was empty, lit only by the school's low nighttime lights. As she turned the corner toward Ms. Kennedy's office, she ran headlong into Bianca.

"Oh my God!" Bianca said, clutching her chest. "You scared me!"

A smile spread across her face. She held up Nelly's glittery backpack.

Now it was Nelly's turn to smile. She took the backpack from Bianca and opened it. Inside was the jar with Grandmother's and Orson's spirits, still glowing, still intact, as well as the night key to the asylum, the healing ointment, and Fig's vial of death's milk.

"Bianca, I love you," Nelly said and pulled her in for a hug. Had she really just said that? Was she really hugging Bianca?

"Shut up, I know," Bianca said, hugging her back.

"Shh," Nelly said, pulling back.

Someone was coming. She could hear high-heeled shoes

clapping against the floor. Ms. Kennedy was on her way back to her office.

Nelly took Bianca by the hand and pulled her into a run. They raced down the corridor toward a second staircase at the far end. Then they pushed through the doors and leaped down the stairs.

Back on the main floor, they ducked into a bathroom close to Chapter Hall. The door banged shut behind them and they stood still and listened for signs they had been spotted.

"Do you think she saw us?" Bianca whispered, breathing hard.

Nelly didn't reply. She walked the length of the bathroom stalls, ducking to check for shoes. None. They were alone.

"I don't think so," Nelly said.

"I swear I almost had a heart attack," Bianca said, leaning against the wall. "When I heard those shoes, the Wicked Witch of the West song went off in my head. Dun-duh-nun-dan-nuh-nuh!"

Nelly looked at Bianca and they both burst out laughing. They laughed and they laughed, half out of relief and half out of picturing Ms. Kennedy as the Wicked Witch of the West. By the end, they were both leaning against the counter for support, tears streaming down their faces.

"It really wasn't that funny," Bianca said when they'd finally stopped laughing, and that started them both up again.

"Thank you ... for helping me," Nelly said seriously when they'd finally laughed themselves out. She leaned back against the counter, her tin whistle in one hand, her glittery backpack in the other.

"What are friends for?" Bianca asked. She looked into Nelly's eyes. "You've got something, just there ..."

She plucked something from Nelly's cheek. She held up her

finger and a tiny square sparkled there. "Glitter," she said and kissed Nelly on the mouth.

Nelly was so surprised she didn't move, didn't react. The kiss didn't last very long, only a few seconds. Bianca pulled back, her face pink and her eyes cast down.

"Don't tell anyone," she whispered, looking up through her lashes.

The door swung open. Bianca jumped back. Relief flooded through Nelly as Gwen Praveen walked in. She wore a pair of bunny ears in her hair, a pale blue dress over horizontal-striped tights, and a giant stopwatch hung from her hip.

"Nelly!" she said, a hand on her chest. "I've been looking for you everywhere. Ramona and I, we did a seance and we—we contacted something. I think ... I think ..."

"What?" Nelly asked.

"I think it took Ramona."

"What do you mean, it took Ramona?" Nelly repeated.

Gwen shifted and kneaded her hands. Her eyes were wide. "We were by the river. You know that creepy oak tree?"

"No," Nelly said. She'd only been at this school for a couple of weeks altogether. She probably knew the fairy world better than she knew this place.

"What were you doing all the way out there?" Bianca asked, shooting Nelly a look as she retouched her lipstick in the bathroom mirror.

Nelly glanced at herself in the mirror and saw that some of Bianca's bright red lipstick lingered on her mouth. She pressed her lips tightly together and covered them with her fist as Gwen explained.

"I dunno. It's Hallowe'en. It felt appropriate. It doesn't matter. We did a seance. We were trying to contact the ghost."

"Ghost? What ghost? What are you talking about?" Bianca said.

"The ghost," Gwen said, waving a hand around in the air. "The one that's haunting this school and probably the whole town. Well, one of them, anyway."

"Not this again, *puh-lease*," Bianca said, rolling her eyes.

"It's real. Nelly knows it's real," Gwen said and pointed at Nelly. "You were there that night. You heard it. I know you did!"

Bianca folded her arms. "What night? What's she talking about?"

Nelly stood there for a moment before responding. "It was before I ... went missing. I went up to Alexis's room."

"You were in Alexis's room?" Bianca repeated, sounding jealous.

"It was the middle of the night. I heard a sound. You heard it, too, remember?" Nelly said defensively. "You were the one who asked me to check it out."

Bianca frowned. "So, what, you found a ghost wrecking up the place?"

"No, actually it was Alexis who'd wrecked up the place," Nelly said. "She threw a snow globe at me."

"She what?" Bianca asked, her eyes going wide. "I swear, that girl has been getting on my last nerve. She's been acting like a complete nutcase for weeks now. And she's all, 'Bianca, why don't you want to hang out with me anymore?' and I'm like, 'cause you're a psycho.' It's not rocket science."

"She's not a psycho," Gwen snapped. "She's just ... she's being haunted."

Bianca's brows shot up. She looked at Gwen as if the younger girl had just dribbled on her shirt. "Um, Nelly, can I talk to you for a second? *In private?*"

Gwen looked on the verge of tears. "No, Nelly, no. You were there. You know Alexis wasn't imagining things. You heard it. You felt it!"

"That's funny," Nelly said, raising her chin. "Because that's not what you told Mr. Haley."

Bianca pursed her lips and glared cooly at Gwen as if daring her to respond.

"—I-I'm sorry I lied, but please, please," Gwen said, now practically begging. "That night, you told the ghost to stop, and it did. I know you can help. You're the only one who can. I'm telling you, it took Ramona!"

Gwen was right, even if she didn't understand why. If she was telling the truth, if a ghost had done something to Ramona, then she, Nelly, was the only one at the school who could do anything about it. She was a fairy, after all. Not just a fairy, but a Wight. And Wights could see and communicate with the dead. Or so she'd been told.

But she didn't have time for all this right now. She had a grandmother to save.

"Please, Nelly," Gwen pleaded, her lower lip trembling.

Nelly sighed. "OK, take me to this creepy tree."

Nelly, Bianca, and Gwen snuck out of the school through a side door. They hurried along, sticking to the shadows to avoid being seen. They passed the dorm houses and soon the scattered trees on the grounds grew more plentiful. Only then did they feel confident enough to switch on their cell phone lights and speak normally.

"It's not much farther," Gwen said, leading them toward the river that marked the end of school property.

"It better not be," Bianca muttered, walking close to Nelly.

As they approached the river, Nelly knew at once which tree had earned the "creepy" moniker. Up ahead, an ancient oak twisted toward the moon. It was hunched and hairy with moss, weird growths, and fungus. Its protruding roots looked like a pile of snakes, its branches like a witch's fingers. A cluster of half-melted pillar candles sat next to the tree and nearby was an old three-legged stool.

"This is it. This is where we held the seance," Gwen said. "We were right here, sitting down next to those candles. We held hands and closed our eyes. Ramona found the instructions on the internet."

As Gwen spoke, Nelly put her tin whistle in the glittery backpack. She pulled off Charmaine's Riding Hood cloak and wrapped it around the jar that held Grandmother's and Orson's spirits. Then she placed it with care back in the backpack. If there was a ghost out here, she wanted to be ready.

"And then what?"

"We were concentrating, trying to make contact, you know, and then I sneezed," Gwen said.

"You sneezed?" Bianca repeated in disbelief as Nelly placed her backpack in one of the tree's many crannies, just to be safe.

"Yes, I sneezed," Gwen said. "And I let go of Ramona's hands, just for a second. When I opened my eyes, she was gone."

Bianca put her hands on her tulle hips. "She's obviously playing a prank on you! Did you even bother to try her cell?"

"Yes, of course. I'm not stupid!" Gwen snapped back.

"OK, OK," Nelly said, stepping between them. "Maybe Ramona *was* playing a prank. But then you left, and she went looking for you. Why don't you try calling her again?"

Gwen scowled. She pulled out her phone and tapped the screen rather harder than she had to. A few seconds later, something vibrated against the ground.

"Over here," Nelly said and led them through an overgrowth of weeds by the river. There, a cell phone lay vibrating in the mud.

Gwen picked it up. "This is Ramona's cell. She would never have left this here!"

"OK," Nelly said, now getting concerned. "Let's spread out, look around for her."

Bianca and Gwen swept their phone lights over the ground. Nelly still didn't have a phone. Hers had never recovered from its night-key journey to the Morighan House. But she could see well enough now in the dark that she didn't need one. She scanned the shadows while Bianca and Gwen called out Ramona's name. All that came back was silence and darkness and the occasional gust of wind.

"Over here!" Gwen cried out, her voice high and panicked.

Nelly and Bianca rushed to her side. Gwen's cell phone lit up a single, black, Mary Jane shoe stuck in the mud.

"That's Ramona's. She's Alice. I'm the white rabbit," Gwen said, picking up the shoe. "Something took her! Something took her!"

"We should tell Ms. Kennedy," Nelly said reluctantly. Telling Ms. Kennedy would mean raising questions about herself. What was she doing out here? How and why had she slipped her chaperone? And then there was the glittery back-pack Nelly was not supposed to have in her possession. But something was very wrong here, and she wasn't yet convinced it was supernatural.

A blast of icy wind whipped at their clothes and hair. Gwen screamed and took off, racing back across the grounds toward the school. Nelly started after her.

"Wait, Birdy, don't leave me," a voice said.

Nelly stopped, looked at Bianca. "What did you say?"

"I said, let her go," Bianca said. "This is a prank. I promise you, Ramona is at the dance right now, having a good laugh."

"No," Nelly said, shaking her head. "You called me something, you said *Birdy*."

"No, I didn't."

Nelly glanced around. Something weird was going on. "I'm gonna get my backpack," she muttered.

She walked back toward the creepy tree. Bianca hurried alongside her, slipping her arm under Nelly's and holding her close.

The three-legged stool came into view. Sitting on top of it was Fig's vial of death's milk.

Nelly stopped cold. That vial had been in her backpack.

She ran over to the tree and stuck her hand into the cranny where she had hidden the glittery bag. It was still there and so was the jar containing Grandmother's and Orson's spirits, safe and sound. Nelly breathed a sigh of relief. But how had the death's milk moved from the bag to the stool?

Bianca picked up the vial of death's milk and held it up to the light of the moon. The liquid inside shimmered like quicksilver. "What's this?"

Nelly stuffed her backpack back into the cranny. "That's uh, that's ..."

Fig said death's milk was a strengthening concoction. If there was a ghost here, maybe Nelly was too weak to see it. If what the cat said about drugging her food was true, then those mixed nuts she had eaten on the farm had been laced with piper's dew.

Maybe the ghost was trying to send her a message. Maybe if she took that stuff, she would be strong enough to see it, to communicate with it, to ask what happened to Ramona. It couldn't hurt to try.

Nelly took the vial from Bianca.

"It's nothing," she muttered, turning away to surreptitiously down what was left in the vial. The milky liquid tasted of eggnog and made her think of the Piper and that black island. And yet it warmed her right down to her belly.

She shoved the empty vial into her pocket and glanced around.

Bianca gasped. "Your eyes," she said, her hand over her mouth. "They're glowing."

Nelly looked away immediately. Fig's eyes had glowed after she had taken the death's milk. How could Nelly have forgotten that?

Bianca stepped forward. "You're not human, are you?"

Nelly's mouth dropped open. "What? Of course, I am. Of course. –W-Why would you—"

"It's OK," Bianca said, reaching for Nelly's cheek. "You don't have to hide from me. I've known all along, from the moment I first laid eyes on you. The way you move, the way you stand, like a wild deer, the way your eyes catch the light."

Nelly pulled away. This wasn't right. Bianca couldn't know. She couldn't have just figured it out. Nelly hadn't even figured it out herself before a few months ago, and that was only because a couple of fairies had walked out of her closet.

But Nelly had known right away that Jack and Fig weren't human, hadn't she? Was it possible everyone in Nothing saw her the way she saw the fairies? Eyes too bright, cheeks too pink, skin that seemed almost iridescent.

Bianca reached out for her. "I'm not afraid. I want to know you, the real you."

Nelly backed away. No. No. She couldn't tell Bianca the truth. She couldn't tell anyone. She wasn't like them. They couldn't handle it.

"Look at me," Bianca whispered.

Nelly shook her head.

"Is it because you're afraid of what I'll see? I'm not afraid. I know you're not human, but so what? That doesn't make you a monster."

"And what if it does?" Nelly said, the words slipping out.

"You could never be a monster. Not to me."

Nelly faced Bianca. She crossed the space between them and embraced her. She wasn't sure why. It was an impulse, sudden and irresistible. There were tears in her eyes. Bianca hugged her back. But something was wrong. Something felt strangely familiar about all of this. It was like this—Bianca realizing Nelly wasn't human, their conversation up to this moment, this embrace—had happened before in one of Nelly's dreams. *No, not in a dream.* She had read something like this, *exactly* like this, in Madge Morighan's diary.

Bianca had called her *Birdy*.

Nelly pulled back.

Birdy, Doed's mother, the woman who had appeared, projected by a wisp from prison in the fairy world. Birdy had been here, in the human world, two hundred years ago and met one of Nelly's ancestors, the same ancestor who had written the diary in Mr. Haley's possession. *Madge Morighan.*

It was only then that Nelly noticed how strange Bianca looked. Her face was a war of waxy white skin and skeletal shadows. Her eyes were gleaming like the moon.

"They're coming," Bianca whispered with a voice that was not hers.

Something hit Nelly on the side of the head. It felt like a tennis ball. An apple lay at her feet, its flesh crushed on one side. Figures rose out of the darkness. They were coming from the direction of the school.

"RUN!" Bianca screamed.

CHAPTER THIRTY-THREE

WEAPON

It was like Nelly had fallen into her recurring nightmares. She and Bianca ran for the edge of the school grounds, where the tree growth thickened into a forest.

People chased after them. Nelly could hear their footfalls pounding the earth, their panting breathing, their shouts. Lights flashed in the darkness. Bianca's hand slipped away.

"Bianca!" Nelly cried. Something hit her again on the back of the head. It was another apple. Pieces of its rotten flesh splattered around her like hail. She tripped on a tree root.

She fell.

Hands grabbed her by the arms. Light flashed around her, boots in the dirt. They heaved her up. She tried to pull herself away, but there were too many of them. They had her. They were dragging her back toward the river and the creepy tree. Moonlight hit their faces. She saw men with tangled beards and yellow teeth, dressed like 19th-century farmers. But then the light changed, and they weren't men anymore. They were students dressed in school-issue black jackets, hoods up. Scarves hid their faces, but under their long jackets flashed hints of Hallowe'en costumes—the knee-breeches of a pirate, the stained dress of Bloody Mary.

The twisted tree loomed. Hands shoved Nelly forward. She fell to her knees. Lights flashed in her face.

"Her eyes! Look at her eyes!" a voice screamed.

She recoiled, trying to block the harsh lights with her arm.

Her eyes! How could she ever explain them?

She squinted through the lights and spotted Bianca. The dark-haired girl was crying; makeup rivulets streaked down her cheeks. Two black-clad figures held her by her arms like a prisoner of war.

Nelly tried to stand.

WHAM.

A fist came out of nowhere and slammed into her face. She fell backward. One of her cheeks hit the earth, the other was on fire. She tasted blood.

"I knew it!" a voice shrieked. It was Alexis. "Look at her eyes! That's proof! She's the one behind it all! Everything that's been happening at the school! It's her! It's been her all along!"

Alexis stepped forward. She was dressed in white. The halo from her angel costume glittered in the light. She grabbed Nelly by the tie.

"Where's my sister?" she hissed, her face wild and enraged. "Where is she, you freak? WHERE IS SHE?"

Voices shouted Ramona's name. Searchlights swept the grove.

"I don't—I don't know," Nelly said, her hands on Alexis' forearm.

"LIAR!" Alexis hit Nelly again, a sharp *SLAP!* Right across the face. "Where is she?" Alexis screamed. "I'll kill you! I'LL KILL YOU!"

"Alexis!" someone shouted. "Look!"

Alexis, who had been about to strike Nelly again, stopped,

hand in midair. Nelly blinked tears from her eyes and followed the lights. They all pointed at the same thing—a noose dangling like a fishhook from the creepy tree.

Nelly's stomach turned over.

She tried to stand. Alexis kneed her in the stomach. Nelly crumpled. She couldn't breathe.

"Help me!" Alexis shouted.

Hands grabbed hold of Nelly and held her down. A knee drove between her shoulder blades. Alexis loosened Nelly's tie and pulled it roughly over her head.

"Grady, take this! Tie her hands!"

Hands pulled Nelly's wrists together behind her back and tied them tight. She struggled to breathe, to free herself. Alexis's halo fell off and landed in the dirt at Nelly's chin.

Hands forced her upright. They dragged her to the three-legged stool. The noose dangled over her head, swaying back and forth like a ringing bell.

Bianca screamed.

Nelly made a desperate attempt to free herself from the hands and the black-clad bodies. Another blow to the side of her face stopped her.

Pinpricks of light blinked at the corners of her vision. Her knees wobbled. Hands forced her onto the stool. The rope, thick and rough as twine, dropped around her neck and tightened. And then she was alone.

Nelly stood on the stool, hands tied behind her back, the noose tight around her neck. If she stepped off the stool, she would hang.

She could hardly see. A dozen lights were still shining right in her face. But she could hear them whispering to each other, coughing, panting. And she could smell them, their perfumes, their colognes, their sweat.

A ghost light drifted toward her. Color twisted inside it like an underworld version of a bubble in the sun. It was beautiful in a way, amidst all this darkness.

"Revenge," a voice whispered.

"Tell me what you did to my sister?" Alexis shouted, spittle flying from her mouth. She put her foot on the stool. "Or you'll regret it."

"Leave her alone!" Bianca screamed. Lights shifted to Bianca as she squirmed away from the people holding her.

Bianca marched over to Alexis.

"Shut up, Bianca," Alexis said, turning on her. "You can't defend her. Look at her eyes!"

"Those are contacts, you moron! It's Hallowe'en," Bianca said, whirling on the others.

Yes, contacts, Nelly thought, hope rising. But would they buy it?

"Look at yourselves!" Bianca said. "Look what you're doing! You kick that stool away, that's murder! *Murder!* What do you think this is, eighteen-hundred and, like, something? You won't get away with this! This is the twenty-first century. We have forensics! You'll all end up in prison for the rest of your pathetic lives. And I will happily testify against every single one of you. Grady Pipes in your pirate pants; Sophie Lloyd in your Bloody Mary costume; Pauline Davis, I can smell your coconut body spray from here. Your stupid scarves aren't fooling any—"

Alexis slugged Bianca across the face. Bianca fell. No one caught her. There was a rock. Her head smashed into it. Her eyes fluttered closed. She stopped moving.

In that moment, everything seemed to slow down. Nelly's face went hot. Her fingers tingled. Her stomach twisted with fury. She touched the tie that bound her wrists together and burned through it like a hot poker through paper. Hands free, she grabbed the noose at her neck. Smoke billowed from between her fingers and rolled past her eyes. Someone screamed.

The noose seared apart. Nelly was loose. She leaped down from the stool, grabbed Alexis by the front of her dress, and slammed her against the creepy tree.

The crowd scattered. Voices cried out in panic. Dark figures raced back toward the school, cellphone lights bouncing.

Nelly locked eyes with Alexis and raised her hand for a strike. Then a face formed out of the darkness. The face was blue-gray like a corpse. Tangled hair hung over sunken eyes that burned with a stony glitter in the moonlight. The face appeared in a flash and then vanished.

A hand grabbed Nelly by the wrist.

"Killing humans now?" a voice said in Eldritch.

Nelly turned around. Fig was standing there, looking like her unglamoured self, wild and inhuman. She turned an icy stare on Alexis, who screamed at the top of her lungs. Nelly let go and Alexis hurtled back toward the school, tripping and falling clumsily as she went.

"I wasn't going to kill her!" Nelly shouted, her body buzzing with adrenaline and rage.

"You're humming with death's milk," Fig said, releasing Nelly's wrist. "If that strike had landed, that girl would be dead."

"Dead?" Nelly repeated. A body lay motionless on the ground. "Bianca!"

Nelly rushed to the unconscious girl's side. There was blood in her hair. She wasn't moving. Her face was ghostly white. "She's not breathing!"

"Let me see." Doed stepped out of the shadows.

He kneeled next to Bianca and examined her, checking her wound and peeling back her eyelids like a doctor.

"How long has she been this way?"

"I don't know," Nelly said. "Not long, a few seconds."

Doed looked at Fig. "Healing ointment may still work."

Fig looked at Nelly, whose eyes widened. She dashed for the creepy tree, stuck her hand into her backpack, and pulled out the tin Fig had given her. Doed held up his hand, and she tossed it to him.

After catching the tin deftly, Doed opened it and dipped his fingers inside. They came out covered in a substance that glowed faintly blue and looked to be both powder and liquid at once. He brushed the substance over Bianca's wounds and then over her lips, making them shimmer.

Doed emptied the entire tin of ointment on Bianca's wounds. A few seconds later the dark-haired girl's chest rose with a deep breath. Her eyes opened. She looked from Nelly to Doed and narrowed her eyes. "Who's he?"

Doed blew a puff of white sleep dust at her, and she immediately started snoring.

"Will she be OK?" Nelly asked.

"She should be," Doed said, wiping a streak of glowing blue across his chest. "Gnomish healing ointment works well enough on our people, even in dire conditions, as long as it's used soon enough. Should work even better on one of them."

"Nelly, what has happened here?" Fig was staring at the burned noose.

Nelly stood up. She was trembling all over.

"They attacked me," she said, her voice emotionless.

They had attacked her. Alexis and the others had put a noose around her neck. Her classmates. Her neighbors. She had grown up with these people.

Nelly picked up Alexis's fallen halo. "But it was like they weren't in control," she said, thinking out loud. "It was like they were repeating something that happened in the past. Madge Morighan—the townspeople hanged her and forced

Birdy to watch. If Birdy was free, she said she would come back here and get revenge on the people who hanged Madge Morighan."

"But Birdy isn't free. She won't ever be. No one escapes from Walls Prison," Fig said.

"What about Madge, or ... or the ghost of Madge?" Nelly said. "What if she's here? What if she's always been here? The townspeople have always said the ghosts of dead Morighans are haunting the town. What if they're right? What if it isn't many Morighans, just one?"

"There is a ghost here," Doed said, his eyes seeming to float in the darkness. "I can smell it."

"What does it smell like?" Nelly asked. She smelled only the wind and the grass and the faint electric smell that seemed to always accompany the fairies.

"Turned earth," Doed said. "And roses." He pointed at the noose. "And its fingerprints are all over that."

The noose was now only a burned piece of rope dangling from the tree. Nelly couldn't see fingerprints on it. But Nelly was a Wight. Shouldn't she see what Doed was seeing?

She hugged herself against the chill. "But that means my great-great-great grandmother was trying to kill me."

Doed shook his head. "You're its descendant. And you're People. It would want you alive, to feed off you. Your presence is the reason it has the strength it has."

"And the death's milk will have compounded that twenty-fold," Fig said, frowning.

"But if she wasn't trying to kill me, then ..." Nelly paused as something dawned on her.

"She was trying to kill the humans," Doed said, finishing Nelly's thought. "You're the weapon."

Nelly thought of that moment when she had been holding Alexis by the dress, hand raised, about to strike. She had been beyond angry. But of course, she had been angry. They had put a noose around her neck; they had hurt Bianca. But, no, it had been more than that. For a few seconds, as she stared into Alexis's eyes, her anger had melted away. She had felt ... nothing. She had been focused, pitiless. Alexis had been an ant, and she had been about to squash her. She had felt nothing.

Nelly hugged her arms, disturbed. How could she have been so cold?

"It wasn't you," Doed said as though reading her mind. "This is the way of the dead. They can influence us even without our knowing it."

Realizing she was still holding Alexis's halo, Nelly tossed it aside. She concentrated on the rope hanging from the tree. She needed to see what Doed was seeing. She wanted to see it, whatever the consequences. Then, just like that, a scent swirled upon the wind. It was the smell of turned earth and roses. Pale gleaming fingerprints crystalized on the rope.

"The dead are bent on revenge," Doed was saying. "If they think they can use one of us to get it, they will."

Nelly gasped. The livid fingerprints weren't just on the rope, they were on the tree, too, all around the hollow where she had hidden her backpack. Something dawned on her. When she had searched for the healing ointment, in her panic to help Bianca, the backpack had been strangely empty.

She rushed over to the tree and stuck her hand in the hollow. The backpack was still there. It, too, was covered in vivid ghostly prints. She opened it wide.

Her tin whistle was there and so was Charmaine's Red Riding Hood cloak. But the jar that held Grandmother's and Orson's spirits was gone.

CHAPTER THIRTY-FOUR

THE LULL BEFORE THE STORM

The fairies looked lustrous against the dull darkness.

"Why would a ghost care for what's inside that jar?" Fig said, looking wild and windswept. "Why would anyone? Present company excepted."

Nelly flushed. "My grandmother—"

"Is also the ghost's descendant," Doed said. "Fig is right. No ghost wants to harm its progeny."

"But ..." Nelly paused, remembering something Birdy said. "Glanville, Abner, Pipes, and Kennedy. Birdy said those were the names of the townspeople who killed Madge Morighan. Orson's spirit is in that jar, too. Orson's last name is Kennedy!"

The fairies exchanged glances.

"There's your answer," Fig said with a sweep of her hand. "The ghost wants to destroy Orson Kennedy, along with Glanville, Abner, and Pipes."

"Can it do that?" Nelly asked. "I mean, can a ghost harm Grandmother's and Orson's spirits?"

"It cannot destroy them. There is no force we know of strong enough to destroy a spirit," Fig said. "But ..."

"But?" Nelly repeated, alarmed.

Fig's face darkened. "But if it smashes the jar, it will fling the spirits inside to the ends of the earth. Finding lost spirits in our world is one thing, but finding them here? We don't know this world. It could take years to track them down, decades, even centuries. And by then ..."

"We have to find the ghost. We have to get that jar back!" Nelly said.

The fairies didn't move.

"We shouldn't interfere with the affairs of the dead," Doed said, his golden eyes like ghost lights in the darkness.

"Doed is right," Fig said. "This is not our concern."

"But my grandmother—"

"There's nothing we can do for her now. The humans angered the ghost. They must suffer the fallout."

"But they didn't," Nelly said. "The humans who hanged Madge Morighan are all dead. Their descendants are innocent. You can't punish people for things that happened hundreds of years before they were even born."

"We shouldn't interfere with the affairs of the dead," Doed said.

"A crime was committed," Fig said. "Someone has to pay the debt."

"We shouldn't interfere with the affairs of the dead," Doed said again.

"What about all the stuff you said about forgiveness?" Nelly snapped.

Fig shrugged. "There's a point when it becomes too late to forgive. Madge is dead."

"We shouldn't interfere with the affairs of the—"

"WHAT ABOUT MY GRANDMOTHER?" Nelly shouted.

The fairies regarded her with cool stares.

Nelly threw her hands in the air. "Fine. Don't help me. But I am getting my grandmother's spirit back, with or without you two."

Nelly turned on her heel and stormed back toward the school. She didn't have a plan. She didn't know what she would do. She only knew she couldn't look the fairies in their cold, emotionless faces anymore. How could they be so heartless? It was like they weren't even human. Just as Nelly realized what a silly thought she'd had, the fairies appeared next to her, one on either side.

"There are only two ways to fight a ghost," Doed said.

Relief blossomed inside Nelly. They were going to help her. She wasn't alone.

"The first is to weaken it," Fig said. "The ghost will be strong. With our presence here and you on death's milk, it will be very strong. So, we cut off its food supply. We weaken it by weakening ourselves. The fastest way to do that is with piper's dew. But I don't keep that stuff."

Nelly glanced at Doed, who shot her a hard stare. He and Nelly had that deal. She had promised him she wouldn't tell either Jack or Fig that he had piper's dew. "What else can we try?" she asked, honoring the deal.

Fig shrugged. "Say my name enough and I will fall, but I don't think it's me or Doed the ghost is feeding from."

Nelly stopped walking. She had an idea. Probably a bad idea, but Grandmother's life was on the line. "What if ... I told you *my* name?"

"No, Nelly," Fig said immediately, whirling on her. "You must never tell anyone your true name, not for any reason."

"But you told Jack yours and—"

"No, I didn't," Fig said, her eyes flashing. "My name was released against my will as part of a criminal sentence. The whole world knows it. And even my friends can't resist the temptation to use it."

Nelly felt a twinge of guilt. She had used Fig's true name herself to get information out of her.

"That's the trouble with power," Fig said, her face grim. "Hardly anyone can resist abusing it, which is why you must never, never allow anyone power over you like that. No one can be trusted with it. No one."

"OK," Nelly said, seeing the sense in this. "What's the other option?"

"We move it," Doed said. "To our own. It won't be able to do any damage there. Once in our world, it won't want to return."

Nelly started walking again. "OK, so how do we move it?"

"Like with your grandmother and Orson, we need an object, something Madge was attached to while she was alive," Fig said, striding at Nelly's side. "We'll use it to draw the ghost in and then trap it."

Nelly paused. "Would a diary work?"

Nelly, Fig, and Doed snuck into the school through a side door. It was strangely quiet as they crept down the corridors. Although they had chosen an entrance far removed from the dance and Chapter Hall, they should have been able to hear Ghost Town's synthetic beats. Nelly paused for a moment to wonder about it, but no longer.

She led the fairies to Mr. Haley's office and tried the door. Locked. Nelly patted her pockets for the keys she had stolen from the janitor's closet.

"Bianca has the keys," she said, stomach sinking. They had left Bianca in a deep, snoring slumber by the creepy tree on the grounds.

"Keys?" Fig said, eyebrows up. She took hold of the door handle. There was a sizzling sound like meat on a skillet. Sparks flew from around the knob.

THUD.

The doorknob had dropped to the floor like a lead weight. There was only a hole now where the handle and its mechanism had been.

"No locked door is fairy-proof," Fig said.

Nelly touched the charred hole. "Can I do that?"

Fig grinned and pushed open the door with a finger.

The room was dark, quiet, and frigid, so cold it was as if Mr. Haley had left the air conditioning on despite the chilly autumn weather.

They searched the room, behind every painting, inside every drawer, but found no sign of the diary. As Nelly shifted books around on the bookshelf, footsteps clapped against the hallway floor. She glanced at the fairies and found they were already hiding in the shadows. Nelly followed suit, slipping between a bookshelf and the painting of fairies in a garden.

The door opened. Mr. Haley stood there, holding the fallen office doorknob. He stepped into the room, cocking his head in a weird way, and dropped the doorknob.

The door swung shut behind him. Mr. Haley spun around. The slamming door seemed to have snapped him out of a trance. Something strange happened to him. He swayed on his feet and then blinked as if confused.

He turned around again. "Who's there?" he said, squinting into darkness.

Nelly stepped out of the shadows. And so did the fairies.

The second Mr. Haley laid eyes on them he went sheet white. He stumbled back, pointing from Doed to Fig to Nelly. "–I-I know what you are," he said, his voice trembling. "Fairies!"

Nelly froze in place. The word was directed, not just at Fig and Doed, but at her, Nelly, as well. And a minor electric jolt rippled over her skin. It wasn't terribly painful, but it hurt enough to set her teeth on edge. The fairies stopped, too, and both glared at Mr. Haley, but only momentarily.

"I said your name, you have to answer my questions!" Mr. Haley said, backing up behind his desk and almost falling over his chair. "Fairies!" he said again.

Again, Nelly felt a jolt of pain, like a full-body static shock.

"We don't have time for this," Fig said in Eldritch. Then, in English, she added, "Should I poke his eyeballs out?"

"No," Nelly hissed.

Mr. Haley knew what Nelly was. There was no point trying to hide it. "Mr. Haley, we're not going to hurt you," she said softly. "We're here for the diary. Madge Morighan's diary."

Fig and Doed began advancing on him again.

"That's what you want?" he said, opening his desk drawer and fumbling with something. "I don't have it." He pulled out a cloth bag.

Fig leaped onto the desk and Doed pushed aside the desk chair.

Mr. Haley backed into the wall and poured the contents of the bag out on the floor in front of him.

Rowan berries.

Fig stepped off the desk and landed on the floor as lightly as a ballerina, right at the edge of the line of berries. "Doed," she said, glaring at Mr. Haley.

Doed reached across the rowan line and grabbed Mr. Haley by the throat.

"Don't hurt him!" Nelly said.

The fairies both glanced at Nelly and then in unison turned their attention back to Mr. Haley.

Doed wrapped his hand around the back of Mr. Haley's neck.

"What are you doing? Get away from me!" Mr. Haley tried to push Doed away, but it was like he had pushed a moving statue. "Help! HELP!" the teacher shouted.

Then Mr. Haley stopped struggling. His eyes widened. He gasped. Not with pain, but with something like pleasure. His whole demeanor softened. His hands, which had been gripping tight to Doed's arm and shirt, fell limply to his sides.

Doed wrapped both his own hands around the back of Mr. Haley's neck now and looked into his eyes. Mr. Haley gazed back, his expression vulnerable, desperate.

"Tell me where you've hidden Madge Morighan's diary," Doed said, his voice a caressing whisper.

Mr. Haley's mouth hung open, slack as though they had drugged him. There was the faintest smile on his lips. "In town. In the bank. In a safe deposit box."

Fig looked at Nelly. "Bank? A riverbank?"

"Uh ... no," Nelly said, finding it hard to think of anything other than whatever Doed was doing to Mr. Haley. "A bank is a place where ... we can't get it there. There's no way. Mr. Haley has to get it for us."

Doed closed his eyes for a moment, concentrating.

Mr. Haley gasped again. His expression was one of pure ecstasy.

"Bring us Madge Morighan's diary," Doed whispered, his voice soothing. "Let nothing and no one stand in your way."

Mr. Haley nodded. He was staring into Doed's eyes as if he wanted to crawl inside them. He grabbed Doed's arm, this time not to push him away but to pull him closer. Doed stepped back. And Mr. Haley stepped forward, across the rowan line.

Now it seemed to be Doed who was struggling. His hands

slipped from around Mr. Haley's neck to the man's shoulders. Doed was trying to hold the teacher back.

"Don't ..." Doed muttered, swaying as if about to faint, but Mr. Haley only pulled him closer.

Nelly was getting concerned. "Is he—"

Fig held up a hand. "We can't interfere."

Doed seemed weak now, not a strong statue anymore, but fragile as a human boy.

"Stop," he muttered. "Get off me!"

With obvious effort, he shoved Mr. Haley away, sending the man stumbling into the wall. Doed's legs buckled. He held onto the desk to stop himself from falling.

Mr. Haley stiffened, stood up straight, and then made a beeline for the door. Neither of the fairies moved to stop him.

The door swung on its hinges after Mr. Haley walked out. His footsteps clapped against the floor, receding down the corridor.

"What happened? What did you do to him?" Nelly asked.

"Doed lulled the human," Fig said, walking around the desk. "It's something Wights can do."

"I thought Wights could communicate with the dead," Nelly said.

"They can do more than one thing," Fig said as if this was painfully obvious. "Though lulling is illegal. And draining besides. It makes you vulnerable. I wouldn't recommend it."

"Vulnerable how?" Nelly asked as Doed collapsed into Mr. Haley's chair.

Fig frowned at him. "You should not be this weak, Doed. It was only a human. Perhaps you should lighten up on all the recreational poisoning."

Doed shot Fig a sour look.

Nelly thought this through.

"So, what you did to Mr. Haley," she said, thinking out

loud. "Lulling. That weakened you. I'm part Wight. If I lull someone, will that weaken the ghost?"

"No. Lulling involves a transfer of power," Fig said, picking up and examining the odds and ends on Mr. Haley's desk. "You gain control over the one you lull, temporarily. In exchange, they take your strength into themselves. The power doesn't diminish as it does with piper's dew; it still exists as it did, but it's in someone else. That's why your Mr. Haley appeared to be enjoying that so much. He got a massive dose of Doed's power. Even for our people, it's an intoxicating sensation. For a human, think fairy food magnified, perhaps as much as one hundred times."

Fairy food magnified by a hundred? Nelly could not imagine it.

Doed slumped in his chair. When he spoke, his voice was a hoarse whisper. "The point is, lulling will not weaken the ghost. But it doesn't matter. Mr. Haley would walk over his own mother now to bring us that diary. All we have to do is wait."

"But we can't just wait," Nelly said. Her mind was racing. "What if the ghost smashes the jar? We have to find it. We have to stop it!"

"Well, if you have any suggestions," Fig said, holding up a pair of Mr. Haley's headphones, her face quizzical.

At the moment, Nelly did not. She shivered. Why was this room so cold? She started to pace, recalling everything she knew about the ghost, what she had read in the diary, what Birdy had said, the rumors she'd heard around school.

She stopped and looked out the window, hopping against the chill. The quad stretched into the shadows below, still and silent. On the other side of the quad stood Chapter Hall, windows lit up with Hallowe'en lights. Beyond the hall loomed the bell tower, and at the top, the ribs of its dome were like a giant birdcage.

"The bell woman," Nelly muttered. "It's in the bell tower."

THUD.

Nelly spun around.

Fig was on the floor.

She had collapsed.

CHAPTER THIRTY-FIVE

THE STORM

"What happened?" Nelly cried, rushing to Fig's side.

Fig was unconscious, sprawled on her front next to Mr. Haley's bird-shaped paperweight. The paperweight was made of iron, but iron caused fairies a shock of pain, as Nelly knew firsthand, not unconsciousness.

"She fainted," Doed said, his eyes shrouded. "She faints."

This was true. Fig had fainted twice in the short time Nelly had known her, for no apparent reason.

Nelly rolled Fig over onto her back. The fairy seemed OK. Her chest rose and fell with her breath. She looked like she was sleeping.

"There's powdery stuff on her face," Nelly said. "I don't remember that happening last time she fainted. Do you think—"

Nelly's breath caught in her throat. Doed stood by the window, staring out at the bell tower. The full moon lit his forehead and cheekbone and the constellation of birthmarks near his jaw. He looked like a painting.

He turned his head, and the light shifted across his beautiful features.

"The bell tower," he said and held out a hand to her.

Nelly blinked. Doed's eyes swam like liquid moonlight. She put her hand in his and allowed him to pull her to her feet.

"What about Fig?"

"Someone must wait for the diary," he said. His hand was cold.

"But—"

The sound of screaming cut Nelly's sentence short. From the window, she could see dozens of students pouring out of Chapter Hall, running as fast as they could in the paraphernalia of their costumes, escaping across the grounds like the place was on fire.

Alarmed, Nelly turned and rushed into the corridor, Doed close behind her. But once they stepped outside Mr. Haley's office, everything went silent. It was as if they had walked into a sound-proofed bunker.

Nelly and Doed exchanged glances. They walked down the silent corridor toward the stairwell. As they moved, the electric lights overhead flickered and then blinked out.

Nelly's heart was pounding. The darkness was total. Even her recently improved fairy sight couldn't penetrate it. She backed into the wall.

"Doed?"

No answer.

Don't panic, she told herself. She concentrated on warm things and then snapped her fingers, imagining she was striking a match. Her forefinger sputtered and smoked, and then a crackling flame appeared and danced above it.

Something was different. Nelly realized immediately what it was. The corridor had changed. It was like she had slipped back in time. The Christian iconography on the walls was no longer aged and faded but brand new. The floors appeared to be their original oak rather than the linoleum that had since covered them. Her flame reflected in stained glass windows that looked to have been installed yesterday.

A group of Christian monks walked past her, their robes sweeping the floor. They didn't appear to notice her. Nelly held her breath and stood still as they walked by. An icy wind accompanied them.

The monks walked toward the end of the corridor, where Nelly spotted Doed. He was standing in the shadows, his eyes alight like twin moons. Doed did not move out of the path of the monks, and they walked right through him as if they were made of smoke. They vanished. Doed did not react.

Nelly stepped toward him, her voice tentative. "Doed?"

A blast of cold air slammed into Nelly, sending school papers whirling around her and dousing her finger flame.

A hand grabbed her shoulder. She spun around. But there was no one there. Fingers brushed her arm. She spun back the other way. Still no one. Something touched her face ... then her back ... then her hair.

What was happening?

A face materialized out of the darkness. "Freak!" it shrieked and then vanished.

Another face appeared. "Creature!"

Then another. "Thing!"

And another. "MONSTER!"

Nelly recoiled, moving away from the faces as they appeared, pale as corpses. They appeared again and again, reaching for her, screaming in her face. She broke out into a desperate run.

"Doed!" she called out.

Cold laughter rang out. Objects whizzed past her—rocks and rotten apples that smashed apart when they hit the walls.

She stumbled.

She lost her footing.

She fell.

But when she hit the ground, she did not land on linoleum or even hardwood; she landed on the earth, soft and damp, and inhaled the smell of soil and dead leaves.

Hands grabbed her, lifted her to her knees. A tree loomed overhead, a noose dangling from its branches like a fishhook.

No. Not again.

"LET ME GO!" she screamed in a burst of desperation and fear.

The lights flashed back on.

She was on the linoleum floor in the school corridor. She was in the present. The hallway appeared as normal as ever. She stood up, breathing hard.

What was going on?

She was in the north range of the school. An arched doorway, which was covered over by plastic sheeting, led to the bell tower.

"Help me!" a voice called.

"Doed?"

The voice sounded like it had come from inside the bell tower. Nelly didn't know what else to do. She set off the flame at the end of her finger again and followed the voice into the dark tower.

Behind the plastic sheeting left from the construction work was a narrow stone staircase that climbed up and up and up. Nelly scaled the spiral staircase until she reached a boarded ceiling with a trapdoor.

"Help me, please!" the voice cried from the other side of the trapdoor.

A heavy, rusted padlock dangled from the trapdoor. The lock hung open as if someone had left it that way on purpose.

She touched the metal lock. It shocked her and made her fingers smoke. *Iron.* She tapped at it again several times, until it slipped from the latch and fell, bouncing down the spiral stairs.

Heaving open the trapdoor, Nelly lifted herself into a musty belfry. The room was frigid, even colder than Mr. Haley's office. Moonlight streamed in through three arched windows. As she stood up, the flame at her finger cast long shadows on the walls. A giant bell hung from the rafters. Cobwebs thick as lace looped across ceiling beams.

She stepped forward. Dried flowers, bluebells she noted, crunched under her feet. The light of her flame quivered over piles of junk; buttons, shells, shiny pieces of jewelry, broken kites, guitar strings, and a gold watch. More odds and ends of the same sort hung from nails on the wall. Silvery spider webs cluttered with moths ran from object to object. It was like the nest of a scavenger bird.

A life-sized doll dressed in white sat by a window on the far side of the bell, its hair pinned to the wall. As Nelly moved around the bell, a figure came into view. A boy stood on the windowsill next to the doll. He was facing the outside as if he was about to jump. He turned his head to look at her.

Nelly's light illuminated the features of Grady Pipes. Tears streaked his face.

"Help me," he whimpered.

The trapdoor slammed shut. Nelly whirled around. A figure sat hunched in the darkness. It appeared to be a woman, dressed in rags, with stringy hair that dangled over her face. Behind her hair, a pair of eyes peered out, white in the shadows.

Nelly stiffened. "Who are you?"

The figure cocked its disheveled head, its eyes darting about like a fish underwater. The figure stood up. With strange, halting movements, it stepped forward into the light of Nelly's flame. At first, as the light fell on the figure, a woman's face appeared, blue-gray like a corpse. But then, with another step, the face changed and became Doed's. His face was livid, and his eyes were wide. His irises, white instead of gold, burned with an unnatural glimmer.

"Three of four will have to do," he said, his voice a silky whisper.

Nelly stepped back. "What do you mean?"

"Abner," he said, cocking his head toward the doll.

Nelly glanced again at the doll and did a double-take. The doll wasn't a doll. It was Alexis! She was pale as death and barely moving except for the streams of tears pouring from her eyes.

"Pipes," Doed said, pointing at Grady still shivering on the windowsill. "Kennedy ..." He pulled the jar with Grandmother's and Orson's spirits inside it from behind his back and held it up high. "But, alas, no Glanville." He patted his own chest.

"This one filled him with too much power. He is beyond my influence."

Doed was talking about Mr. Haley, Nelly thought. Mr. Haley was a Glanville descendant.

"No matter," Doed said, again cocking his head grotesquely. "His time will come. And now I have you."

"Me?" Nelly said, backing away.

"Without you, none of this would be possible," he said, still holding the jar high. The moving shadows cast by Grandmother's and Orson's spirits fell across his face.

Nelly backed up into the wall. Doed stepped up close to her, reached out, and touched her face, dragging all five of his icy fingers down her cheek.

"You like this boy," he said. "You shouldn't. He's weak. Too weak to resist his own darkness. Too weak to resist me. He'll betray you as he's betrayed others."

A tear fell from Doed's eye as he smiled, strange and incongruous.

"You are not Doed," Nelly said, her voice quavering. "You're Madge Morighan."

The wind blew. Dead leaves swirled outside the windows in mini cyclones.

Doed leaned in close. He smelled of turned earth and roses.

"Revenge," he whispered.

"Madge, please don't do this," Nelly said. "The people who killed you—"

"MURDERED!" Doed screamed, and his voice was suddenly that of an enraged woman.

"Yes, murdered," Nelly repeated, trembling. "I know what happened to you. Birdy told me."

Doed pulled back at the mention of Birdy. The shadows rolled across his face, and again, he became a woman with tangled hair and sunken eyes.

"I know the townspeople murdered you," Nelly said. "But Abner, Pipes, Kennedy, Glanville, they're all dead. These people are only their descendants. They didn't hurt you. They are innocent."

The room around Nelly swirled into vivid scenes from her own past. Orson Kennedy ground her diary into the mud with his sneaker. Alexis Abner called her a freak. Grady Pipes turned away from her, pretending she wasn't there.

The memories evaporated in a white mist, and she was back in the bell tower once more.

"Innocent, are they?" Madge said, now using Doed's voice. "I have seen them, watched them as I have watched over you. There is hate in their hearts. They deserve to die."

"And what is in your heart?" Nelly snapped, anger

bubbling up inside her. Her classmates may have tormented her growing up, but they had only done it because Madge had been tormenting them.

Doed laughed with Madge's hollow voice an echo after his.

"Why do you defend them after all they've done? They look at you and see only a monster."

"I know," Nelly said, her voice cracking. "But I'm not what they think I am. I'm not a monster. That's why I can't let you hurt them."

"Let me?" Madge said. "You are my accomplice. Everything I do here, I do with your permission."

Madge stepped back toward a window and held up the jar with Grandmother's and Orson's spirits. It lit Doed's beautiful features.

"Even this. You don't want her back. You are freer without her. Why not let her go?"

Madge balanced the jar in Doed's upturned hand, perched near the end of his fingertips, and held it out the window.

"No," Nelly said, stepping forward. "Please. Don't."

"I will. And you'll let me." Madge pointed one at a time at the room's three windows. "Three windows, three choices. You won't be able to save them all."

What happened next seemed to play out in slow motion. Madge threw the jar up in the air and then melted into shadow. Nelly ran for the window and the jar still spinning in midair outside it with a speed only a fairy could muster.

Madge ran at Grady and Alexis. Aware the others were in danger, Nelly leaped onto the windowsill. She grabbed hold of the wall and stretched her hand out in midair to catch the jar.

The jar hit her palm and bounced. She fumbled it ... again ... and again ... but then she had it. Her fingers closed around its base. Nelly pulled herself back inside the tower and jumped to the floor.

Madge pushed Grady from the next windowsill.

As Grady fell, Madge grabbed Alexis by the hair and yanked her to one side. Nelly raced for Grady, the jar under her arm like a football. She lunged, reaching over the windowsill. Grady was still out there, hanging from a piece of scaffolding. It groaned and cracked under his weight.

"Don't let me fall, Nelly!" he screamed. "Help me, please!"

Nelly reached for him. She dropped the jar. It fell to her feet. *CRACK*. Grady grabbed her hand. The scaffolding teetered and fell with a groan of snapping planks.

Nelly heaved Grady up with a strength she didn't know she had. He put his elbow over the windowsill. When he seemed to have a firm hold, Nelly looked around for Madge.

Madge stood by the last window, her eyes glittering behind Doed's. Above her, Alexis stood on the windowsill, dress and loose hair blowing in the wind, tears falling freely.

"Máiréad, don't do this," Nelly said, using Madge's true name.

"A shame names don't have the same effect on humans as they do on fairies," Madge said and pushed Alexis.

Once again, everything seemed to unfold in slow motion. Nelly bolted to the window and leaped over the sill. With half her body hanging over the ledge, she reached for Alexis. Alexis reached back. Her fingers grazed Nelly's. But there was no scaffolding on this side of the tower, nothing to stop her.

She fell.

Her eyes were full of terror. Her hair and her white angel dress fluttered around her. Her mouth opened in a silent scream.

She fell. Down and down. Fathom after fathom until the darkness swallowed her with a sickening *THUD!*

Nelly pulled herself back inside. She stumbled back from the window.

Madge, in Doed's body, smiled.

"Good choice," the ghost said.

Fury exploded inside Nelly like a time bomb. She saw white hot flames and blue veins.

She screamed.

And the scream that bellowed from inside her was visceral, primal, the fury of a thousand hurts, a million crimes unanswered, eons of suffering spirits crying out for revenge. The only sound even close to it was the cry the Piper had released on Brittle Island when it had escaped.

There was a flash of white light. The tower shook.

Beams, dust, bird's nests, and spiderwebs fell from the rafters.

The bell cracked in two.

Grady fainted.

And so did Doed.

Nelly stopped screaming. Dust billowed around her in clouds. The room was a disaster area, as if a missile had hit it. Her breaths came in short, shallow bursts.

She had done this.

She felt numb. She made her way over broken beams and pieces of stolen jewelry to Doed. He was still breathing. She peeled back one of his eyelids. His unconscious eye was gold once more, confirming what she already knew. The ghost was gone.

A vial of piper's dew lay next to him. It must have fallen from his pocket. She pocketed it herself and then checked on Grady. He was breathing, too. Still alive.

Something glowed faintly from beneath the wreckage. She pushed aside rubble and fallen beams until she uncovered the jar holding Grandmother's and Orson's spirits, cracked but still intact. Nelly picked it up, dusting it off.

The whine of sirens rose in the distance.

CHAPTER THIRTY-SIX

FAIRY AND HUMAN BOTH

Nelly walked the long corridors of the Nought County psych ward, holding a cracked jar with two spirits glowing inside it. She had used Fig's night key to transport herself here. Though she made no attempt to avoid security, they avoided her. It was as if some instinct for self-preservation kept them from turning down the hallway where Nelly Morighan walked, slowly, determinedly, as if in a dream.

Grandmother's room was right across the hall from Orson's. She flung open both doors wide. The wind fluttered the curtains. She stood in the middle of the corridor, between the two rooms, and opened the spirit jar.

The lights inside flew out. Each one floated toward its body. Nelly followed one into the room where her grandmother lay. This light buzzed around Grandmother's head like a honeybee, illuminating a frozen, fretful expression. Then it flew directly into the old woman's chest and vanished.

Grandmother breathed deeply, her features relaxing. A smile appeared on her face. She rolled to one side and, still sleeping, nuzzled deeper under the covers. And Nelly knew she was healed.

Nelly left the room. She wandered the corridors alone until she found her father's room. She had no spirit in a jar for him, but she wanted to see him all the same. She stood at the foot of his bed like a specter.

There was a mirror on the wall. She saw her reflection. Her eyes burned with an otherworldly light. She did not look human.

She sat in the chair next to her father's bed. On the table next to him was a piece of paper. The word REVENGE was written on it in messy scrawl. Nelly touched the paper and it shriveled into ashes.

She pulled the vial of piper's dew she had taken from Doed out of her pocket and thought of her mother. Mother had forced Nelly to take this stuff and had asked the cat to sneak it into her food. Had she done it to protect her, Nelly? To keep her from seeing the ghosts that haunted the town? Or had she done it to protect the town ... from Nelly?

Nelly pulled the cork. The syrupy elixir inside smelled heavy, bitter, acidic. It made her think of a cage.

She drank it.

Everything went dark.

Nelly woke the next morning with the sun on her face. Her father wasn't in his bed. She looked around, groggy from the piper's dew, and found him sitting in a chair by the window.

"Dad?" she said, but he only stared forward.

There was a commotion in the hallway. Nelly followed the ruckus out of the room and down the corridor.

"This is ridiculous. I feel fine. I demand to see the doctor in charge," a voice was saying.

A smile spread across Nelly's face. That voice belonged to Grandmother.

"And get my husband on the phone at once. At once, do you hear?" Grandmother went on, sounding like her old self. "And I want to see my granddaughter."

Realizing she had no good explanation for being here, Nelly pulled Fig's night key out of her pocket. Then she heard another voice she recognized.

"Where is he? I want to see him!" It was Ms. Kennedy.

"Right this way," came another voice.

This one Nelly recognized as belonging to the crotchety nurse who had Nelly banned from the ward at the start of the summer.

"But don't expect a miracle," the nurse was saying. "His condition has improved, yes, but he's not—"

"Mom?" another voice said.

Nelly couldn't help herself. She peered around the corner. A few meters away, she saw Orson, lucid and alert, run into his mother's arms.

"Orson?" Ms. Kennedy said. "You know me? You know me?" She hugged her son back and released a joyful sob.

Nelly could see Orson's face as he hugged his mother back. There were tears in his eyes. He looked up and saw Nelly. She was about to duck away, but he didn't shout for the nurse or make any moves to expose her. Instead, he smiled a little and nodded.

"Thank you," he said, mouthing the words.

Nelly blinked. How much did he remember?

She smiled and nodded back. Then she slipped away.

There was a funeral ceremony at the school for Alexis a few days later. Nelly attended, dressed in black. Bianca wept on her shoulder. Orson was there, too, completely recovered, standing at his mother's side. Ms. Kennedy made a speech. She said classes would be canceled all week and counseling would be made available to all who wanted it. Nelly considered this. But what would she say to the counselor? What could she say?

Alexis's friends erected a shrine for her at the base of the bell tower. Grady Pipes put bluebells on it. He seemed to have recovered from his experience in the belfry, physically if not mentally. Nelly did not know what he and her classmates remembered from that night, from Nelly's attempted hanging to the supernatural activity around the school. No one seemed to want to talk about it.

Ramona Abner, whose vanishing had started the confrontation with Alexis and the others, had been found, alive and well, sleeping off spiked Hallowe'en punch in her dorm room. She blamed Nelly for her sister's death, but no one else seemed to.

The police ruled the death accidental. Grady said he and Alexis had gone up the tower on a lark, and she had fallen. He didn't mention Nelly or anything else. No one doubted his story. There was no reason to.

Nelly found the fairies at the Morighan House later that day. They had Madge Morighan's diary in their possession. Mr. Haley had brought it to them shortly before being arrested for breaking into the bank and his own safe deposit box. More collateral damage.

"We'll take this back with us," Fig said, holding up the diary. "As a precaution."

And only as a precaution. There was no ghost attached to the diary now, they told her. There was no ghost at all anymore. As far as Doed could tell, Madge Morighan, along with every other ghost that had existed in Nothing when Nelly screamed in the bell tower, was gone. Just gone. Snuffed out of existence. He couldn't explain it. He only said that, despite their presence, Nothing was now the least haunted town in the world. He would no longer meet Nelly's eyes.

"Why do you have to go back?" Nelly asked Fig. The farm was safe. Grandmother had put a stop to Mr. Glanville's plans to sell it. Fig could stay for as long as she wanted.

"Jack's in trouble," Fig said. "He made a bargain with the Bone King. I can't abandon him."

"So, you'll help Jack and ... and then you'll come back?" Nelly said, desperation edging her voice.

Fig met Nelly's eyes and nodded. "Then I'll come back."

Before it was time for the fairies to leave, Nelly sat with Fig on the Morighan House porch. Together, they chatted and sipped spiced fairy tea.

"Did you really try to kill four people?" Nelly blurted during one of many awkward silences. Fig was her aunt, after all. Nelly had a right to know what had happened.

"Who told you that?" Fig asked, eyebrows shooting up.

Nelly didn't reply and Fig didn't press her for the answer. Instead, she leaned back with a heavy sigh.

"I did not," Fig said, gazing at the thick forest beyond the farm. "Before my disgrace, I was involved in politics, something I don't recommend. There's very little meaning in it. But I had some influence then, and with influence come enemies. They wanted me out of the way. They got their wish. Someday I'll tell you the whole story. But not today."

Fig wasn't ready to open up yet, and that was OK. Nelly wasn't either. But there was something she had to get off her chest and no one else she could talk to about it.

"When I was in the bell tower with the ghost," she said, squeezing her teacup between her palms, "it—*she*—gave me a choice. I could try to save the lives of Alexis and Grady or protect Grandmother's and Orson's spirits. I chose my grandmother. I didn't even think about it. I got lucky with Grady. If it hadn't been for the scaffolding, he would have died along with Alexis."

"You chose one you love over two you did not," Fig said. "A natural decision. Most would have done the same in your place."

"But you said if the jar smashed, Grandmother's spirit would be lost, but she would still be alive. That means I chose my grandmother's sanity over two people's lives. Doesn't that mean ... I'm a bad person?"

Once again, Fig exhaled a heavy sigh. "There are no good or bad people. It's a mistake to think such qualities are innate. In my experience, the most dangerous people in the world see themselves as innately good. The pure don't feel compassion for the impure. They don't show mercy. They don't forgive."

Start with yourself, Fig said the last time she mentioned forgiveness. She was probably right, but it wasn't all that easy.

Fig put a hand on Nelly's shoulder. "Good or bad is a choice we must all make, day to day, hour to hour. It's never simple or obvious; it's usually difficult. You didn't kill that girl; you tried to save her. In that instance, it seems to me your choice was good."

Nelly nodded. She could get used to having a fairy aunt.

That evening, Nelly brought her tin whistle onto the roof of her dorm building and stood under a firmament of stars.

"Start with yourself," she said, facing the bell tower. And then she played. She played a song for Alexis. It was a piece she had written herself, sad and beautiful and strange. As she played, dorm room lights flashed on beneath her like ghost lights and some of her classmates leaned out their windows and listened.

As the music rose into the sky, a figure dressed in white appeared in the bell tower.

The specter of Alexis rose onto a window ledge of the tower and gazed out at Nelly and her tin whistle. So there was a ghost left in Nothing after all.

"Revenge," it said.

Nelly lowered her tin whistle. The wind blew at her hair and her jacket as she gazed across the grounds at the ghost. She was glad to see it. There was something comforting about a ghost lurking about in Nothing. It was as it should be.

"I wouldn't if I were you," Nelly said back, both as advice and a threat she now knew she could deliver on.

Alexis's ghost seemed to understand. It shrank back, growing more translucent as it did. "Forgiveness?" it said.

Nelly smiled a little and nodded. "Forgiveness."

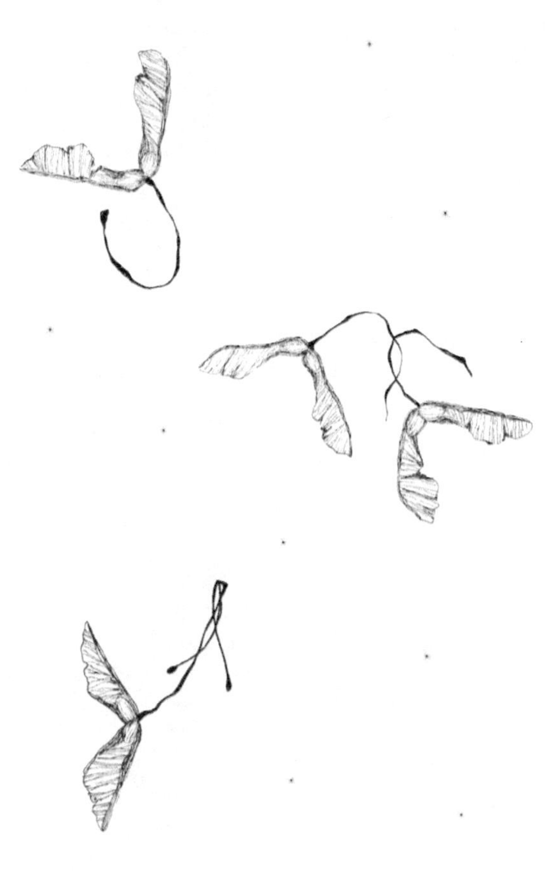

A MESSAGE FROM THE AUTHOR

Dear Reader,

I hope you have enjoyed your journey with Nelly into the world of the fairies. Nelly and her story have been flittering through my imagination for many years now. The fairy world has, for too long, been my secret, my getaway from the trails of the real. I spent far too much time hesitating to share this world, fearing that it was fragile as a glass sphere and might be shattered under the eyes of others. But I know now a world is no good unless it's shared, and my deepest hope is that you have been as enriched by this world and this story as I have been.

If you enjoyed this book and would like to visit Nothing and the fairy world again, I have good news. I am working on book two in the series as we speak. For updates and sneak peaks about book two or about my youtube channel, please visit cecilywalters.com and join my mailing list. You can write me a message there, too, if you'd like. I'd love to hear from you.

But before you go, I would like to ask you for a favor. It would be so helpful to me and the future of this book series if you'd leave a review of The Ghosts of Nothing wherever you purchased your copy or on GoodReads, your book blog or BookTube channel. Reviews can be difficult to come by, but they make all the difference to first-time authors like me. And readers like you, really do have the power to make or break a book. Your reviews are like fairy dust, spreading the magic of

this book far and wide. So thank you so much in advance if you
do take the time to do so. It really means a lot.

With gratitude and a sprinkle of fairy dust,
    Cecily Walters

Website:
cecilywalters.com
Newsletter:
The Shaken Tree

ACKNOWLEDGMENTS

Bringing this book to fruition has been a long and twisty road through a seemingly endless fairy forest. Thankfully, there were lights in my life that helped to guide me through the dark.

I would like to thank my parents, Don and Ellen Walters, for their unwavering support and encouragement throughout the writing process. Your belief in me means the world.

Special thanks to Fred Ward, who sadly isn't with us anymore. Fred was a writing mentor to me and helped me with early drafts of this novel. He was also one of the kindest men I have ever met.

I am grateful to those who gave me editorial advice, including Sarah Patterson, Maya Rock, and Lucia Ferrara.

While this isn't a screenplay, the encouragement and feedback of my screenwriting teacher, Michael Donovan, has been invaluable.

I would like to extend my heartfelt thanks to my good friends, Sharon Ostrovsky and Kelly Johnston Solilo, who provided support as I wrote this book. Even from the farthest reaches of the world, your encouragement and enthusiasm kept me going even on the toughest days.

I would also like to express my appreciation to all my subscribers and supporters on YouTube, in particular these amazing Patreon supporters: Vincent Baker, Danni Bryant, Emily Burt, Bailey Quillin Cooper, Tina Frick, Jaime A. Heidel,

Ty Herzog, Shannon McKinnon, Ricardo Ponce, Marilyn Quilicot, Michael R. also known as Merlin Nitrous, Mint Faery, Katerina Richard, Susan Stepaniak, Peter Stocks, Earl Tower, Aleks Trubchik, Tiffany Tullos, Peg Tyree, and Katie Umble. Your belief in me and support of this novel, even before it was finished, has meant everything.

I would like to send a shout-out to my friends and colleagues at two sadly shuttered bookshops, Nicholas Hoare and Babar En Ville. I miss spending time with you, but at long last, I finally published it.

Finally, I would like to thank all the readers who gave this book a chance.

With love and gratitude,
Cecily

www.ingramcontent.com/pod-product-compliance
Lightning Source LLC
Chambersburg PA
CBHW021758190726
48290CB00005B/1307